THE FIRST JON AND TERESA ZACHERY STORY

ENSIGN LOCKER

THE FIRST JON AND TERESA ZACHERY STORY

ENSIGN LOCKER

A NOVEL BY
J. J. ZERR

Primix Publishing
11620 Wilshire Blvd
Suite 900, West Wilshire Center, Los Angeles, CA, 90025
www.primixpublishing.com
Phone: 1-800-538-5788

Published by Primix Publishing   08/12/2021

ISBN: 978-1-955177-39-9(sc)
ISBN: 978-1-955177-40-5(hc)
ISBN: 978-1-955177-41-2(e)

Library of Congress Control Number: 2021916556

CONTENTS

Author's note:

This is a work of fiction. Any similarity between the characters and any real person is coincidental and not intended by the author. Events are likewise fictitious. Ship names in the story are also contrived.

A list of acronyms and a list of US Navy ranks are provided in the end matter.

To: Those who served.

Officers assigned to USS *Manfred*

CDR Carstens	Commanding Officer	CO
CDR Peacock	Commanding Officer	CO
LCDR Messenger	Executive Officer	XO
LT Ralph Timmons	Deck/Weapons Department Head	Gun Boss
LT Paul Becker	Chief Engineer	CHENG
LT Allman	Operations Department Head	Ops O
LT Dave Davison (DD)	Operations Department Head	Ops O
LT(jg) Andrew Dunston	Engineering Division Officer	
LT(jg) Peter Feldman		
LT(jg) Tom Snyder	Communications Officer	
LT(jg) Fred Watson	Supply Officer	
LT(jg) Darrell Palmer	Navigator	
LT(jg) Don Minton	CIC Officer	
LT(jg) Ralph Timmons		
LT(jg) Charley Hansen		
ENS Carl Lehr (Almost)		
ENS Edgar Chalmers (Admiral Ensign)		
ENS Dennis Macklin (Cowboy)		
ENS William Stewart (Dormant)		
ENS Jon Zachery (Two Buckets)		
ENS Haywood (Tutu)		

PART I

US Navy Boot Camp instructor: "Listen up, Boots. If you remember one thing from this place, make this the thing you remember. Priorities. A sailor's priorities are these:

1. God

2. Country

3. US Navy

4. Family

5. Self

Period."

1

Brang, brang.

The rude, harsh noise woke US Navy Ensign Jon Zachery and set his heart pounding. He reached up to turn on his bunk light, couldn't find it, and panicked.

Brang, brang.

Then he remembered he wasn't onboard his ship, USS *Manfred*. He was in his apartment in Chula Vista, California. And his wife Teresa, he'd taken her to the hospital yesterday. She was two weeks overdue. Today they were going to induce her.

Brang, brang.

He fumbled for the bedside lamp and knocked it to the floor. The phone was on Teresa's side. He lunged across the bed and snatched up the phone.

"Mr. Zachery. Mr. Zachery. Are you awake, sir?"

"Sorry. Just a moment, please."

He turned on the lamp on Teresa's side of the bed and noted the time: 0507.

Teresa!

"What's wrong? Is there something wrong with Teresa?"

"Mr. Zachery, I'm a nurse at Balboa. The doctor wanted me to call you. We need you in at the hospital right away, please. We need you to sign a surgery release form."

"Surgery? What are you talking about? Teresa is having a baby. She isn't having surgery."

"I'm sorry, sir, but there isn't time to argue this. We're going to start prepping Mrs. Zachery for an emergency C-section very shortly. The doctor would like you to come in as quickly as you can get here and sign the surgery release form. So, will you please come to the hospital, sir?"

Getting dressed would have gone quicker if he had just stood still, but he tried to pull pants on as he moved toward the door. He put shoes on but didn't tie the laces. During the drive to the hospital, he kept the speed at ninety and, fortunately, attracted no flashing lights behind him. Cops shift change, maybe.

When he arrived at the hospital, he ran up and down a few hallways, trying to follow nurses' directions. Finally, he found her. She was by herself, on her right side on a wheeled gurney with no side-rails, and parked next to the wall in a hallway. Her eyes were closed. She moaned. An IV needle had been taped to the back of her left hand. White dried spittle coated her lips. Her face was almost as white as the pillow under her head, and her hair was a mess. It was darker than normal and in stringy tendrils, as if she had washed her hair and not dried it. A strange sweat smell rose from her. Teresa didn't sweat. That thought scared him to a new level of concern.

Holy Mary, Mother of God, please don't let the fact that I am a sinner—

"Teresa, can you hear me?"

She opened her eyes, looked up at him, and a smile flickered, and then it went out as she moaned again.

"Sorry," she said.

"Mr. Zachery, you need to sign this." A tall woman in a white uniform with lieutenant insignia on her shoulder boards held out a clipboard with a black government ballpoint pen under the clip. He hadn't heard her approach.

"It's a surgery release form. It says you agree that Mrs. Zachery should have a C-section. Mrs. Zachery could only put an 'X' on the form, and the doctor wants a signature."

He grabbed the clipboard, took the pen, and signed the form. A tear dropped onto the *Jon* of his signature. The fine line of black ink became blurry and jagged. The nurse took the clipboard, gave him a look, pulled a Kleenex out of a pocket, and blotted the wet spot. Then, she turned and started to walk away.

"Lieutenant, uh, Nurse, what's going on? What's going to happen to Teresa?"

"I have to get this to the doctor. Someone will be out shortly," she said over her shoulder.

The nurse disappeared through spring-loaded doors. Teresa moaned. He put his hand on her shoulder, but with all the fear coursing through him, he wondered if he was comforting her or not.

Then he wondered why the Sam Hill nobody came to help her. "I'm going to find somebody, Teresa. I'll be right back."

He started toward the doors through which the nurse had gone when the left of the double doors swung open, and two young men in white navy enlisted uniforms entered the hallway.

"Are you Mr. Zachery?" the second-class petty officer asked. Jon nodded. "Okay, sir. We have to take your wife to another building. They do all the surgeries there. You can ride with us in the ambulance."

The two petty officers acted as if nothing extraordinary was going on. How could a person get so used to something like this?

The sailors wheeled Teresa down a corridor, took her down an elevator, through more double doors, and loaded her into an ambulance. It was a short ride, a half city block at best, but there were bumps, and at each one, Teresa moaned and squeezed Jon's hand with a strength that was amazing. In a way, it pleased him that she hurt his hand. Maybe that would make up for him not being there with her through the night. They stopped in front of a new building, quite different from the old one they'd just left. That one had looked like it had been on duty since the Second World War. The two petty officers pulled the gurney out of the ambulance, and the wheels dropped and clicked into place, and they whisked Teresa inside.

Jon was left standing in a hallway looking at the double doors to surgery. He felt as if he had been watching a movie playing about ten times faster than normal speed. Now, the first reel had played out.

Then those double doors into surgery faded, and he saw himself driving to the hospital. He was scared to death for Teresa. His face, illuminated by light from the instrument panel, looked like it. At the hospital, he'd searched for Teresa and finally found her and the smell on her. In that smell of sweat, there had been a hint, and he knew what he perceived was only a hint of her ordeal last night. The ambulance ride, the bumps, her hand-crushing grip. It was like a roller coaster that didn't slow down at the end of the ride. It just stopped abruptly and dumped him in the surgery building. Those doors to surgery reformed, hiding what was going on in there.

A Naugahyde-covered bench fixed to the wall outside those double doors served as the surgery waiting room. Jon sat on the bench, checked his watch, stood up again, looked up and down the deserted hallway, and sat again. The ordeal Teresa had suffered alone as he slept dumped acid of guilt into his chest. He recalled dating Teresa when he'd been so smitten with her during senior year in high school. Other recollections tumbled out, one after another. The night he spoke to her about getting married and having children. Four of them. And although, he didn't say, "And live happily ever after." That thought had been there.

Have children. Such a peaceful non-threatening word: have. It should be all caps and underlined when coming before children. <u>HAVE</u> children. He'd thought of it as *them* having children. Like a together thing. It turned out though, he wanted her to <u>HAVE</u> their children, while he sat on the sidelines. Fat, dumb, and happy. Away from and above it all.

Women die in childbirth!

He prayed: Father God in heaven—

Then he chided himself for calling on the Supreme Being now that he needed Him, while before the need, God wasn't even in his thoughts.

Ask and you shall receive.

Jon latched onto that as his life preserver. And he prayed for Teresa, and their baby.

At the tail end of the prayer, he recalled how much Teresa had wanted to get pregnant, to bear a child, and how it devastated her that she had not been able to conceive during the first two years of their marriage. Then her doctor discovered a thyroid deficiency. She started taking thyroid pills, and thank you, Holy Mary, Mother of God; Teresa got pregnant and was overjoyed to be so. A baby pill, Jon had called those prescription tablets.

He would have gladly taken the child-bearing suffering onto himself, but of course, God didn't make man and woman for things to happen that way.

Thy will be done.

He thought about what he had suffered over the last month. Things had started going bad the day he checked aboard the destroyer, USS *Manfred*. On the quarterdeck, as the Petty Officer of the Watch entered his name in the deck log, and the time and date, 0619, 4 January 1966, Jon noticed the Officer of the Deck, a hulking chief petty officer looking down his nose at the ship's new ensign.

The Officer of the Deck had the messenger of the watch conduct Jon to his new boss, the Operations Officer. It turned out the Ops O was very much like Grandpa Zachery. Grandpa said if you sleep till the rooster wakes you, it's the same as denying God three times. The Ops O worshiped the same one-person god grandpa did: work. According to the Ops O, the only productive part of the day is 0430 to 0600.

Then, when he spent five minutes with the Executive Officer, the XO, just as Jon was leaving, the XO asked if he needed anything. Jon asked if he could take leave the last week in January. The ship was going to be at sea, but Teresa was due then. Jon had intended to ask the Ops O about it but hadn't had the chance since the Ops O was preaching the virtues of his god, work.

Jon's request earned him two lectures. One right then from the XO, on the chain of command, and two minutes later, from the Ops O on the ship's schedule. *Manfred* was slated to deploy to Vietnam and be in the combat zone in May. Prior to departing San Diego, every day at sea was a precious opportunity to train for combat. These opportunities were not to be squandered for frivolous things, like a wife having a baby. Ensign Jon Zachery would not be on leave when the ship went to sea.

To cap off that first day, just before leaving the ship for the evening, Jon almost got into a fight with one of the other ensigns aboard, Ensign Edgar Chalmers. Chalmers graduated from the Naval Academy and seemed to think Jon was his personal whipping boy.

Aboard *Manfred,* ensigns are roomed in a five-man broom closet called the Ensign Locker. Jon had been in the space when Edgar Chalmers entered.

"Zachery," Chalmers said, "You're the new guy. There isn't much room in here, so when one of us senior ensigns comes in, get up on your bunk to get out of our way."

"Senior ensign," Jon replied. "There's no such thing as rank among ensigns. We are all low life-forms to the rest of the officers."

"Listen you little—"

A six-footer, the biggest guy in the Ensign Locker, and five inches taller than Jon, Chalmers reached out a paw to grab Jon, but Jon slapped it aside and pushed him back against the bulkhead next to the door. "You listen, I will make room for you guys. As a courtesy, but I am not climbing up onto my bunk just because one of you walks in."

The look on Chalmers' face said he was surprised at the reaction, but then anger started burning behind his eyes. Jon said, "I'm leaving. The whole place is yours."

Jon left for home, knowing that he and the Academy grad had a pecking order issue between them that would have to be resolved.

At home, at the dinner table, Teresa wanted to know how his first day had gone.

"Fine," he'd said.

"Good." She smiled. "The Commanding Officer's wife called to welcome me to the wives' group."

"The CO's wife called you?"

"Yes. She knew I am pregnant and wanted to know if I needed anything. I told her I was fine at the moment and that you were going to ask for leave when the baby comes. She said, 'Don't count on that. The ship will be out at sea then, and your husband will have to be aboard.'"

Jon had dreaded telling her about not getting leave. He'd planned to tell her after they ate, but now he didn't have to. *Thank you, God.*

"My mother is coming out after the baby is born," Teresa told the CO's wife, and she offered to have the wives' group help until Mrs. Velmer arrived.

"So, Jon, you don't have to worry about the baby and me."

When Teresa said that, it reminded Jon of the priorities lecture he'd heard in boot camp. Soon-to-be-mother Teresa had her priority system as well, and baby occupied number one spot, or maybe number two, after God. Not worrying about her, though, was not going to be dismissed that easily.

All that thinking while sitting on the bench outside the OR, surely a significant chunk of time had passed. But Jon did not want to look at his watch. He was too afraid he'd find the minute hand had not moved much.

He rose, looked up and down the still empty corridor, stared at the closed double doors into surgery, sat back down again, and hunched forward to rest his elbows on his knees. A sigh gushed out.

Aboard the destroyer, Jon served as the Electronics Repair Division Officer. Chief Petty Officer Fargo was the division chief. At the end of his third day aboard, Jon called him aside. Chief Fargo, his subordinate, looked at Jon with a lack of respect clear on his face. That look was there every time Jon glanced at the man.

Jon said, "Chief, I don't care what you think of me. I don't care if you don't respect me. I do care when you openly disrespect me in front of the men in *MY* division. Knock it off."

A stare down followed, which Jon won.

A victory, Jon thought on his waiting room bench. *Too bad it was the only one this month.*

Manfred had gone to sea on the Monday before Teresa's Wednesday due date. The only thing that happened that day, though, the ship ran into a storm, and Jon got seasick. He'd gotten seasick, quite often, on his first ship when he'd been enlisted. His division chief, a man named Irons, considered him to be useless and called him a boar tit. Jon hoped he'd outgrown and gotten over seasickness. He hadn't, but what he did get was a nickname: Two Buckets.

During that at-sea period, Jon had also been embarrassed during Junior Officer of the Deck bridge watches. Twice. Both times, the CO wanted the ship maneuvered in a timely manner, but Jon had hesitated, trying to make sure he'd give the proper commands to the helmsman. Both times the CO had ordered Officer of the Deck to take control and, "Hop to it.".

It seemed to Jon the navy's way of teaching consisted of tying concrete blocks around a man's waist, tossing him into the deep end, and saying, "Swim, damn you."

But *Manfred* had come back into port on Saturday morning, and Jon would be there when Teresa delivered their baby.

Finally, out of the whole rotten month, something was going to work out. That's what he'd thought when he fell asleep last night.

But now, there were those double doors into surgery. What was going on in there? Why didn't someone come out and tell him not to worry? Double doors, he hated the darned things.

Jon thought about praying, but it seemed like everything he'd prayed for that month had turned out the other way. Maybe God had given him more blessings than he was entitled to have. Maybe it would be better if he didn't call God's attention to Teresa's situation. Maybe God wouldn't notice, and one more blessing could slip through.

Jon heard a bump at the double doors. A nurse backed out, pulling a small aluminum-wheeled cart behind her. A clear plastic basket sat atop the cart. A swaddled baby lay in the basket. Jon stood up as the nurse approached.

"Congratulations, Mr. Zachery," the redheaded nurse was smiling. "Would you like to say hello to your daughter?"

Jon jumped up and started toward her. "How's my wife?"

The manufactured smile blinked off. "They are finishing up after the delivery."

"But is she okay?"

"I'm sorry, sir. You have to wait for the doctor. I need to get your daughter in the ambulance and up to the other building." She started moving toward the door.

"Wait."

Jon looked at the tiny doll. She wore a little pink cap. Her eyes were closed. The lips seemed so distinctly and perfectly formed. *They are like Teresa's.* And then the nurse wheeled her away.

Through the glass doors, he saw the ambulance pull away.

Why wouldn't she tell me about Teresa? She acted funny when I asked.

He looked back at the double doors to surgery. *Teresa is dead. And I have a daughter. What do I do now? Teresa would know; I don't.*

He didn't remember going back to the bench, but that's where he was when the doctor came through the center of the double doors.

The doctor was a little taller than him, probably in his thirties. He had a fair complexion and reddish-tinged brown hair. His mask was down around his neck. Jon looked to see if there was blood on his scrubs.

"Mr. Zachery, your wife is okay. She has had a tough time of it, though. She went into labor last night, but she was too small to pass your nine-pound daughter. When we gave her the spinal—that's the preferred anesthesia—it didn't take with her, so we had to give her a general. She will be in recovery for a couple of hours. Then you'll be able to see her."

"Oh Lord, Doc."

2

Instead of going back to the apartment, Jon went out to the ship, which was anchored in San Diego harbor. He intended to ask the Ops O for leave again. Surely, after what happened to Teresa, leave would be granted. The Ops O was at his desk in his stateroom. Jon explained about the emergency surgery and asked for leave.

Of middle eastern descent, the Ops O's swarthy complexion reflected eons of his ancestors' exposure to desert sun baked into his genes. His black bore-right-into-you eyes, though, was what Jon first thought of when he thought of his boss.

"When are visiting hours?"

"Well, uh," Jon shifted weight from one foot to the other," two to four and seven to nine."

"Coupla' hours a day. When will she come home?"

"Monday, a week from tomorrow, sir."

"So, she isn't coming home from the hospital till after we get back in. What are you going to be able to do for her?"

Jon didn't know what to say to that.

"So pretty much nothing." The Ops O stood up. "We have this week at sea; then you're going to be gone for almost eight weeks of school. After you are done with school, you will only have two more weeks with us at sea before we deploy in May. Or, perhaps you already learned everything you need to know?"

Jon's sweat glands opened and exuded embarrassment as much as perspiration. He wasn't sure he'd learned anything about driving the ship or manning his battle station last week. What he had done was to expose how much he didn't know. He turned and grabbed the doorknob.

"Jon."

He stopped but didn't turn around.

"You can ask the XO if you want."

"There's stuff I have to do. I'll be back before taps."

"Wait," the Ops said.

Jon pulled the door shut. He had to get away from the man.

Jon returned to the empty apartment, showered, and changed clothes. Then he called Rose Herbert. Rose was a friend from Purdue. As Rose drove them to the hospital for afternoon visiting hours, Jon told her he had applied for leave, but his boss had turned him down.

"Jon Zachery, you're the nicest guy I know." She glanced at him quickly, then turned back to the road. "Not too dumb. Half ways good-looking. But you piss all that away when you whine." With Rose sometimes, looking out the window was better than conversation.

Rose's husband once told Jon she had had a *sympathectomy*.

They were on the flat stretch of I-5. National City and the Mile of Cars were off to the right.

Rose and Fred came from the coal country of West Virginia. Fred had had a troubled youth, and at age seventeen, a judge offered him the choice of military service or jail. Fred chose the navy. Rose started hitchhiking to follow Fred to San Diego, where he was going to Boot Camp. She got a ride all the way to Phoenix with a Mayflower van and thumbed the rest of the way. A Mexican gardener with a beat-up, twenty-year-old pick-up found her asleep on the sand next to a trash barrel on the Silver Strand Beach. The Mexican generally stopped and checked the trash barrels on his way back to Tijuana from Coronado. Rose stayed with the Mexicans for a week.

Rose was five feet, two inches, and 105 pounds, but you did not want to let her hear you call a Mexican a beaner, a greaser, or a wetback.

Rose got a letter to Fred when he was five weeks into the nine-week Boot Camp program. With the help of a chaplain, Fred got a credit union loan, and Rose was able to set herself up in a cheap apartment. After Fred completed Boot Camp, he married Rose. Fred had some navy schools to attend, and then at his first duty station, Rose had gone to a nursing school. She and Teresa met at the hospital in Lafayette, Indiana, while Jon and Fred attended Purdue. Soft, light, bright Teresa and hard, heavy, cloudy Rose became the best of friends.

Ahead of them, in the afternoon sun, Balboa hospital stood on the heights like a castle. A pink stucco castle. Who would paint a Navy hospital pink? Did they have guys from the brig paint it, and the brig guys decided to play a joke?

"What," Rose asked.

Jon thought about not saying anything but then went ahead. "I don't know whether to be angry at the hospital or grateful that they saved Teresa's life."

"Holy Mary, Mother of God, pray for our idiot, and please keep me from turning this into the hour of his death. Amen."

I should have thought some more.

"What the hell do you expect, Jon. It's a hospital. Everybody who works up there is just like you and me. Overworked, underpaid, and nobody appreciates a god damned thing we do. They have shitty bosses, and the most pleasant thing they do all day is empty a bedpan.

"Teresa went into labor sometime not too long after visiting hours last night. A Saturday. The nurses weren't going to call the doctor until she was dilated a certain amount. They got stuff to do besides watching Teresa. They had two other births during the night. So, finally, somebody goes to check on her, realizes what's going on, says Holy Shit, and then things start happening.

"That hospital you just snorted at may not have done everything perfectly. But they sure as hell did a lot better than *close enough for government work,* which is what the rest of the navy considers outstanding performance."

"I think they should have called me sooner."

Rose sighed. "Let's just hope your daughter inherited her mother's brains."

Even an ensign can be the senior guy sometimes. Jon was the senior man on the boat from Fleet Landing out to the ship, so he got to disembark first.

As he stepped onto the quarterdeck and saluted the OOD, the Petty Officer of the Watch pulled the microphone to the ship's announcing system, the 1MC, from the holder on the bulkhead just forward of the after gun-mount. "Taps, taps. Lights out. All hands turn into your bunks. The smoking lamp is out in all berthing spaces. Now taps."

"Mr. Z, got a minute?" Chief Petitte was the OOD, and he led Jon to the starboard side.

Once clear of the quarterdeck, the chief turned. "Understand your wife had a tough time of it this morning, Mr. Z. Is she okay?"

He sounded genuinely concerned. "Yeah, Chief. She did have a rough time. When I got to the hospital this morning, the way she looked, it scared the crap out of me."

Once Jon's mouth got going, it felt as if the mouth wanted to take off and do a massive verbal dump on the Chief. But that was the first civil word Jon had heard from Chief Petitte or any of the chiefs for that matter. Besides, a big confessional running off of the mouth, well, it just didn't seem like the right kind of thing to give in to.

"But, the doctors and nurses at Balboa, they got her taken care of. She is tired from the whole ordeal, but she was doing pretty well when I said goodbye to her at 2100. Sure glad we got back into port so I could see her with the baby."

"Glad it worked out, and congrats, Mr. Papa."

"Seems like you wait for it forever, but when it gets here, it still takes a while to get used to that notion, being a daddy, I mean."

"Glad Mrs. Z. is okay."

"Thanks, Chief. Thanks very much."

As Jon started up the port side, the boat that had brought him— he'd nearly stuck home into the thought—back to the ship, revved into a full-throated, bubbly grumble, pulled away from the side of the ship, and headed back toward Fleet Landing and the lights of San Diego.

Jon passed through the wardroom, the XO's closed door, and descended the ladder to the second deck. Inside the Ensign Locker, it was pitch black. He left the door open to let in a bit of illumination from the red light in the passageway and inched forward until he came to his bunk, where he turned on the bunk light.

Just inside the door, there was a two-bunk stack to either side. The two top bunks were occupied. Ensign Dennis Macklin, nicknamed Cowboy, lay in the bunk to starboard. Ensign William Stewart, called Dormant because he slept a lot, was in the top portside bunk. Dormant made the familiar *phwoo* exhale sound. Ensign Carl Lehr had the bunk under Dormant. Carl was the senior ensign and as such was called the Bull Ensign, but he also had a nickname: Almost, for almost normal. The other bottom bunk belonged to Edgar Chalmers. He wasn't back yet and didn't have to be until 0400.

Edgar Chalmers, Admiral Ensign, and the only US Naval Academy grad residing in the Ensign Locker. Even as a low-life ensign, he was obviously already bucking for admiral. His attitude proclaimed: *My dad retired as an admiral, and so will I.*

Just forward of Cowboy's and Edgar's stacked bunks sat a navy-grey aluminum set of drawers with a fold-down lid to form a desk. Just forward of that *piece of furniture* sat a row of five three-foot-high aluminum lockers. Jon's bunk sat atop the lockers.

There were two rules in the Ensign Locker: the junior guy doesn't use the fold-down desk, and everybody is in his bunk as much as possible to make room for people to move. Jon wasn't concerned with navy rules at the moment, and besides, everyone was asleep. He grabbed his stationery box from the angle iron next to his bunk and folded down the lid to make the desk.

Dearest Teresa,

When I first went into the navy, I wrote to you every night because it was a way to hang onto you. I was afraid I would lose you, that you wouldn't wait for me, that I'd get a *Dear John* letter like everybody else seemed to get. But tonight, I need to write to you. I NEED to, or I know I won't sleep, and tomorrow my heart will still be filled with all the stuff boiling around inside.

First, I am so glad you met Rose Herbert at Purdue and that she is such a good friend. She probably saved my life, or at least my sanity, today. And even though the XO's wife said that she and the whole *Manfred* wives' group were going to make sure you are taken care of, and even though your mother is flying out on Wednesday, Rose is the one making me feel like I can leave you and go to sea tomorrow.

Sitting here in the Ensign Locker, Cowboy and Almost sleeping quietly, Dormant making his *phwoo* sound, me at the desk in a little hole of light in the dark, and writing to you, it's like you and I are the only two people in the whole world who are awake.

Jon didn't like the *falling asleep* description. Sometimes, falling asleep, for him, was a sensation of falling. Then, just before deep sleep happened, he'd jerk back to wakefulness with the feeling if he hadn't awakened, he'd have fallen all the way to hell. During a day like that day, all kinds of anguished things got packed into his brain, or his soul maybe.

After he'd left the Ops O's room, it was as if he went on autopilot. He got the things done that needed doing, with Rose's help, but in a sense, he was just hanging on, too. Hanging on until he could sit down and write to her. With writing *Dearest Teresa,* it had started. It was like looking at a pile of sand ten feet high, and all that sand was anguish. Mixed-up thoughts roiled in his head and belly and left a sour taste in his mouth, like when he got seasick. But with *Dearest Teresa,* one grain of the sandpile turned into a grain of peace and calm. As words drained out of his ballpoint onto the page, neighboring grains became infused with the feeling that perhaps it would be okay. If he wrote enough words, it would be okay.

After they'd been married the summer before junior year at Purdue, he didn't write to her every day, as he had before. He did write her a poem on the first of each month, and on special occasions. She seemed to like the poems, so he started on one to include in the letter that would go out in the mail in the morning.

The strongest feeling lingering in his head was the fear he'd felt at finding Teresa in the hallway at the hospital, and later when he was sure she had died and that he had a baby daughter to raise by himself. Teresa, however, would want a poem about their baby. He wouldn't be able to write that kind of poem without getting the fear of life without her out of the way first. He wouldn't send the poem to her, but he had to write the *fear* poem first.

He looked around. They were all asleep. The drone of the ventilation blowers formed a backdrop to Dormant's *phwoo.*

He wrote about Teresa looking death in the eye and her death looking him in the eye. Lines of rhyme, one under another, marched down the page.

The door to the room pulled open. Edgar, Admiral Ensign, stood there. Jon couldn't see his face. Too dark.

Edgar rushed in and grabbed up the sheet of paper from the desk.

"Well, look here. Ensign Two Buckets. Our very own power-puking, pussy-whipped, pornographic poet."

Jon exploded off the chair and raised his left hand like he was going after the letter.

"Pissant—"

Jon hit him in the belly with a right. He bent over and backed against the bulkhead. His feet slid out from under him, and he sat on the floor, hard. He gasped for breath, then turned to the side and puked near the end of his bunk. A ferocious coughing fit seized him.

"Jees sus Chee rice tin hey yull." Even when he was excited, Cowboy never stampeded his words. Always, his words kind of loped out as if to the cadence of a peaceful campfire song.

Edgar continued to gasp and cough.

"Carl," Jon said, "get him up. He's drowning in his puke."

Jon had heard Teresa and Rose talk about drunken accident victims doing that.

There wasn't room in the Locker for Jon to help, but Carl managed to pull Edgar to his feet. Edgar seemed to be getting a bit of air, along with the other stuff, into his lungs. His coughing was just about to the level of having a cold.

The smell was awful. Jon's stomach lurched a couple of times. The vomit smell didn't make clear what Edgar had to eat, but he'd had whiskey to drink.

"God damned vulture ate a putrefied skunk and shat on our floor," Cowboy offered.

Carl said, "Go back to sleep, Cowboy. Two Buckets and I will take care of it."

"Cain't sleep in this stink. Dormant and me, we'll start here, y'all get Admiral Ensign squared away."

Cowboy rolled out of his bunk. "C'mon, Dormant, my man."

"Doesn't bother me." Dormant rolled onto his side facing the bulkhead and turned out his bunk light.

"*Aa yes hole*," Cowboy said as he followed us out the door to get some cleaning supplies from the locker across the passageway next to the head.

At 0155, Jon clicked off his bunk light. He lay on his back listening to the hum of the ventilation fans, Dormant's *phwoo,* and Admiral Ensign's slobbery snore. An unpleasant combination of puke and disinfectant smell hung in the air.

After the cleanup, Jon had tried to recapture the absence of anguish that he'd built before Admiral Ensign entered the room, and just then, Jon wished he'd punched Edgar in the face. He wished his own knuckles were scraped, cut, and bleeding.

He clicked his bunk light back on, plugged Chopin's Nocturnes into his cassette player, put on the earphones, and punched play. The low notes, and the rhythm they rode through space, moved in and took over. Jon ran his hand down the center of his belly, tracing a line, like Teresa's C-section scar. He clicked the light off again and reached out his hand, like Adam on the ceiling of the Sistine Chapel, reaching out a finger to God to get the spark of life. Jon, however, reached out to Teresa and their daughter, Jennifer. He wanted her little hand to close around his finger, just like she had that evening.

And then, he didn't want to hit anybody or anything, anymore.

PART II

NAM

But where's the foxhole deep enough
Where a sailor cares to park his duff?

3

Sunday, 29 May 1966. Last night in Subic Bay

Dearest Teresa,

I have a hole where my belly is supposed to be. It has been such a wonderful thing to be in port and get all your letters. Now we are looking at perhaps ten days before we get mail again, and that just crushes my heart.

Everybody else is kind of excited about us being in the combat zone just after midnight Tuesday, but I can't help it. I hate the thought of no letters from you, again, for a long time. I don't think I could get along without writing to you each night. It anchors me if I can use sailor terminology. When I go for a long time with no mail from you, I kind of feel like my own letters are just going into a black hole.

At least tonight, there is nothing scheduled, and I can just write to you. Every night this week, there has been something. Wetting down party, dinners at the O Club, division beach parties. I've had enough mandatory fun. Mail goes out at midnight, and tonight, I want to do nothing but write to you. I may even have to use two envelopes. Our postal clerk, PC3 Smeltzer, says I will save a lot of money on stamps when postage is free in the combat zone. So, that's something to look forward to.

What I really look forward to, though, is three and a half years from now. I will walk away from *Manfred* for the last time, and you and I and Jennifer will head off to a NORMAL life. Normal job, nice house, Jennifer will maybe have a brother or a sister, and I'll be able to reach out my hand each night and find your hip, not the angle iron next to my bunk.

When the press started talking about Camelot during the early part of the JFK regime, it about made me puke, partly, I guess, because I am not a democrat, but it was such trashy-flashy, shallow hype. Now, what I want for us does seem like Camelot to me, and I don't think we need a castle for it to be Cam—

The door to the Ensign Locker pulled open, and Lieutenant (jg) Peter Feldman came in.

"Two Buckets, chiefs challenged us to a softball game. Come on."

"I haven't played ball for years, Peter. I'll pass."

"C'mon. It'll be fun."

"I've had fun every night this week. I don't want to have any more fun."

Peter was six feet, five inches, and he walked around the ship hunched over all the time, and he always wore an apologetic look on his face from stepping on peoples' feet so often. He was responsible for the start of the ensign nickname tradition on *Manfred*. When Peter checked aboard as a new ensign, Andrew Dunston had been the Bull. After he saw Peter's huge shoes on the deck of the Ensign Locker, Andrew drew the ship's starboard whaleboat davit, except, in the drawing, there was no whaleboat in the davit. Instead, there was a shoe with a gun mount on the toe. And Peter became Gun Boats.

"Zachery, you little shit, climb down outa' that bunk, or I'll drag ya. You're playin' softball."

When Peter brings his 225 pounds into an erect posture, and when he scowls, he doesn't look like someone to take lightly, especially for a little guy, like a five-seven guy called Two Buckets.

Jon sighed, "Aw crap, Peter."

Peter pointed a finger. "*Unt, you vill haf fun. Ensigns who do not haf fun, vill be shot.*" He closed the door.

Jon dug sweat socks out of his laundry bag. They were still soggy. He'd run that afternoon.

Great!

The CO gave the chiefs the option of batting or taking the field first. Senior Chief Fire Control Technician Bechtold said they'd bat first. The chiefs thought they might not ever have to take the field. At least that's how Jon interpreted their smug looks.

The XO was umpiring from behind the pitcher's mound. Tom Snyder, the Communications Officer and the next most un-athletic officer after the XO, was pitching. Peter Feldman was the first baseman, assigned there on the rationale that first basemen are tall.

The first batter was Chief Petitte. He stood six feet, two inches, and weighed about 250 pounds of very solid beef. Each day, he spent a bit of time in the ventilation fan room, where the chiefs lifted weights. Jon served as catcher. With no protective gear, not even a mask, he stayed well behind home plate. Jon figured the CO assigned him that position because of all the officers, he was the most expendable.

The chiefs were all on their feet in front of their dugout along the third-base side, and they were making a lot of noise even before the first pitch. After Tom Snyder bounced the first two pitches well in front of home plate, the noise level ratcheted up several tens of decibels.

Jon looked over at them. The chiefs were hooting, and a couple of them were jumping around, like kids or monkeys.

Please, God, let the next pitch make it over the plate without bouncing first.

The prayer was not answered. The pitch bounced over again. Jon started forward to grab the ball when the chief cut loose with a mighty golf swing.

The ball dribbled just to the left of the pitcher's mound. Tom Snyder stood on the mound with his hand in his glove, and he seemed to be trying to decide if it was okay for him to leave his appointed place of duty. The chief started thundering toward first as the CO charged from his shortstop position, barehanded the ball, and fired underhanded to Peter Feldman. Peter was standing with both feet on top of first base, and caught the ball, mainly because the CO's throw hit his glove. Then Peter turned to face home, kind of hunched over like a linebacker in a pre-snap position.

Jon ran alongside the chief to back up the play. He glanced at the XO to see why he hadn't called him out. The XO was just staring at the scene playing out as if mesmerized by it.

Chief Petitte plowed into Peter, and it was very much like Charley Brown. Ball, cap, glove, and sunglasses went flying, and Peter wound up on his back, looking up at the sky, with his head and shoulders in fair territory, but his huge tennis shoes were well into foul.

Chief Petitte was swinging his right arm like a windmill, trying to get his considerable momentum vectored toward second. Jon got to the ball just before the right fielder, waved him off, grabbed the ball, and fired a strike to the Skipper's glove, which was about five inches above second base. Chief Petitte dropped into a slide. Jon winced because the chief wore cut-off blue jeans. The XO was looking at Peter Townsend. Chief Petitte stood up and started looking at the huge raspberry on his right leg.

"You were out. You agree, Chief?" the CO said.

"Out," Chief Petitte agreed as he started walking toward the dugout. He acted as if the raspberry wasn't even an inconvenience.

Hospital Corpsman Darby trotted down the first baseline with a little black bag in his hand. Carl Lehr, the second baseman, was helping Peter to his feet.

"Hang on there, Mr. Feldman. Stay down."

Carl started walking back toward home plate with Jon to get a Coke. There were enough people around Peter. The CO walked to the pitcher's mound and called Senior Chief Bechtold for a conference.

"So, Carl," Jon said. "All the heavies have talked about since I checked aboard is that everything we do has to be aimed at getting us ready for the combat zone. How is this helping?"

"Builds esprit," Carl said. "You know? All for one and one for all. Everybody knows that softball does exactly that."

Jon looked at Carl, and he laughed and went to get his Coke. Almost all the time, Carl was serious and didn't joke around. But he guessed even Carl could only be serious almost all the time.

HM1 Darby pronounced Peter Feldman okay. The Skipper said that Peter would sit out a couple of innings, and he also announced a new rule: no sliding if you are wearing short pants. Tom Snyder was moved to first base, the XO picked up pitcher duties, and Petty Officer Dawkins, from Jon's division, was shanghaied from the bleachers to be the umpire.

Chief Wicker batted second. The XO got his second pitch over the plate, all the way, without bouncing it. The chief bunted, on purpose, and started for first. This time, Tom Snyder charged the ball, barehanded it, wheeled, and threw to Carl Lehr, who was running to cover the base.

Carl tried to stop on the field side of the base—Jon was sure he remembered the collision—but he stepped on Tom's beer bottle propped on the field side of the bag. Carl's feet shot out from under him, and he landed on his back on top of first base. The ball had sailed over him and was rolling just outside the foul line.

Chief Wicker jumped over Carl, skidded to a stop, came back, placed a foot on his chest, and took off for second. The chief ran fast, and he saw that both Don Minton and Jon were still running for the ball as he neared second. He rounded the bag as Don got the ball, got himself oriented, and fired a rope to the third baseman, Lieutenant (jg) Charley Hanson. The ball bounced once; Charley caught it and tagged out the sliding and long blue jeans-clad Chief Wicker. ET2 Dawkins, a professional in all aspects of his life, watched the play closely; and he called the RDC out with an appropriate accompanying thumb gesture.

Petty Officer Darby helped Carl up. Carl took a couple of steps and gave Darby a thumbs up. Darby thumbs-up-ed the CO.

At the rate the game was going, Jon thought, it could take all night, and he'd never get his letter done.

Chief Fargo, from Jon's division, batted third. Not as beefy as some of the other iron-pumpers, but Jon knew he was all hard muscle.

Tom Snyder got his first pitch over the plate without it having to bounce to get there. The ball came over the plate a little high. Clearly a ball, Jon thought, but the chief cut loose with a mighty swing and popped the ball straight up, practically to the ionosphere. Jon tracked it up and back down, danced around a little to stay under it, and caught it. A one, two, three inning.

The chief petty officers took the field with mumbling, bitching, and belly-aching. "Lucky bastards;" "Damned pitcher, if he could just get the damned ball over the damned plate;" and "Just wait. Next inning!"

The first two officer batters grounded and flied out. The CO batted third. He smacked a drive between the left and center fielders. A double. The next batter grounded out.

The chiefs scored two runs.

The officers went down one, two, three.

The chiefs scored another run.

The CO had Jon bat ninth. He apparently didn't expect much from his ensign named Two Buckets. When it was his turn, Jon walked to the batter's box, wiped his sweaty hands on his jeans, bent down and grabbed some dust to dry his palms further, and stepped into the box. From the bleachers behind him came, "Ensign Boar Tit can't hit. Just pitch it in there. The boar tit'll strikeout."

The third baseman, Chief Bechtold, called time and ran toward the bleachers. The guy who'd shouted was Petty Officer First Class McGilfrey. He worked for Bechtold. Jon couldn't hear what Bechtold said to McGilfrey except, "—back to the ship."

Boar tit. When Jon had been a sailor, and on his first ship, he'd gotten seasick then, too, and his chief, Irons, had called him that name. Someone on *Manfred* must know Chief Irons, Jon thought. That would explain why the whole ship seemed to have a low opinion of him. Boar Tit, Two Buckets. Those kinds of things had a way of taking on a life of their own, and once established, they were impossible to root out.

The game waited while Chief Bechtold scolded his inebriated subordinate, but Jon felt as if more eyes were on him than on the drunk sailor. Jon sweated, and it wasn't due to the temperature and humidity.

Bechtold took his position. Jon rubbed more dirt on his hands and stepped into the box. A bit of cold fury sparked up his spine. He gritted his teeth together and gripped the bat handle. The first pitch was a little inside, but Jon swung and launched a mighty drive that curved to land in foul territory. A startled silence settled over the ballpark until the shortstop broke it, "He was lucky. He can't hit. Hey, batter, hey." The second pitch was outside. Jon stepped on home plate and sent a towering drive to right field, which landed well beyond the waist-high fence around the outfield.

The rest of the game settled into a decent sandlot game. The chief petty officers won nine to seven. The CO congratulated the victors and also announced, "I am officially changing Ensign Zachery's name from Two Buckets to Three Home Runs."

Right. Three Home Runs had a snowball's chance in hell of replacing Boar Tit and Two Buckets.

During the ride back to the ship, Jon listened to the easy banter of the riders in the passenger van, half officers, half chiefs, and he thought Almost had been right about the ball game building esprit. Both sides had acquitted themselves well. In the spirited banter, there was a kind of respect Jon didn't think had been there before. And no small part of that had been due to a boar tit Ensign called Two Buckets.

Sometimes, Lord, Jon thought as he sat scrunched against the side of the vehicle on the rear seat, *You do indeed work in mysterious ways.*

4

At 2215, Lieutenant Hank Allman knocked on the CO's door. The CO pulled it open and waved him in.

"You and Cowboy have a good time in Manila?" the CO asked.

The Ops O sat next to the XO on the fold-up bed sofa. "Yeah, Skipper. Nice hotel and we took in a good bit of the town between Saturday and today."

Skipper: a term of familiar respect awarded to a commanding officer rather than a formal, required acknowledgment of higher rank.

The Skipper nodded. "Okay. Tomorrow, the commodore shows up at 0500. So, XO, please have the stewards clean my room up for him, just like he was going to stay with us. I'll be out of here at 0400."

Commodore, commanding officer of a number of destroyers, nine or ten.

The XO made a note in his pocket-sized, green notebook, which the sailors called a wheel book.

"Navigation brief at 0430 so we can get that done before the

Commodore shows up. Then, once we are clear of the channel and at sea, I'll see if I can entertain him until we highline him back. That's set for 1030."

"I didn't know the Commodore was riding us out," the Ops O said.

"Commodore's Chief of Staff called me yesterday afternoon," the XO said.

"Do I need to do anything, like prepare briefs on our preps for gunfire support missions and for when we get to the Tonkin Gulf and operate from the North SAR station?"

North SAR station. North Search and Rescue station in Tonkin Gulf. *Manfred* and the Commodore's flagship would occupy that station for the next month and a half. Their purpose was to provide rescue support for US Navy aviators attacking targets inside North Vietnam. If a plane was hit by AAA, and if the pilot could get his damaged aircraft back out over the water before ejecting, a rescue helicopter could be sent to pick him up. Neither *Manfred* nor the other destroyer could land a helicopter, but *Manfred* could pass a refueling hose to a helo hovering alongside.

The Skipper shook his head. "No, Ops O. Commodore's Chief of Staff told the XO it was material readiness he was interested in looking at."

"Doesn't the Commodore know we spent the whole week getting the ship in shape? We chipped and painted from the top of the masts to the waterline, wrung out the weapons and electronic systems. Does he want to know about all the training we got done in port?"

The XO said, "According to the Chief of Staff, Commodore wants to make sure we don't use being in the combat zone as an excuse to let the material condition slide. He wants to look at deck and engineering divisions."

"Appearance and propulsion. Sometimes I wish my surface navy—" The Ops O hissed and shook his head.

The Skipper smiled. "Feel better, Hank."

A sheepish look washed over the Ops O's face.

"Skipper," the XO said, "just met with the Gun Boss and Cheng. Chief Engineer says he's one hundred percent ready, and so is the

Weapons Department. Fully ready to enter the combat zone and for the commodore, Cheng said. How about Operations, Hank?"

"We're 100%, too, XO. Last thing was the electronic warning receiver, and I just talked with Chief Fargo. The system is working thanks to some help he got from some techs from the base. Oh, and Fargo said the chiefs whipped the officers in softball this evening, but he said it was a hell of a game. Said the officer's team would have been embarrassed badly if Ensign Zachery hadn't been on the team. Zachery?"

The CO inclined his head and shrugged. "For a little shit, he's a regular hitting machine. He drove in six of our seven runs, and the last inning, we had a man on base when we made the last out. If Jon had come up again, I would have put my money on him."

The XO said, "More amazing to me, though, was the top of the last inning. Chief Petitte is on third, and the batter flies out to center. Andrew catches the ball and fires to Jon, who is catching. Jon stands there with Petitte bearing down on him like a locomotive with a full heada' steam. He grabs Andrew's throw just in time to put the tag on the Chief, then goes flying back, kind of tumbles asshole over teakettle, but winds up on his feet still holding the ball. Then he goes over to the Chief and asks him if he's okay. Chief thinks he's making fun of him, but Jon says, no, he was just hoping he hadn't hurt the Chief's skinned-up leg. Then Petitte reached out one of his big paws and tousled Jon's hair. I couldn't believe he got up at all after the Chief hit him."

"Jon Zachery, Ensign Two Buckets? I'm having a hard time picturing what you just told me."

"It happened, Ops O," the CO said. "I talked to him afterward. He said he got his strength working hay bales starting just after seventh grade. He said he played sandlot ball. He was his team's catcher, too. Said he learned to kind of give way when he was going to be hit by a big guy."

"Petitte was the third out, and as we walked back to the dugout," the XO said, "I asked Jon if he was okay. He looked at me and said, if I get to bat again, I will be. It's my turn to hit something."

A corner of the Skipper's mouth smiled. "One other thing happened when Jon batted the first time. Petty Officer McGilfrey was in the bleachers pounding down beers, and he called Jon Ensign Boar Tit. And he said it loud enough for everyone at the field to hear it. I think Jon got mad and focused all his anger at the ball. He smacked the hell out of that softball."

The XO looked down at his hands in his lap. "I never told you this, Skipper, but I found out right after Zachery checked aboard that Chief Petitte's brother-in-law was on Zachery's first ship. Petitte told Fargo that Zachery's chief used to call him a boar tit. So apparently, that story has gotten around the ship."

"I didn't know that," the Ops O said. "Chief Fargo, though, I do know he didn't have a high opinion of Jon at first. But lately, he says Jon is really turning into a good division officer. But the boar tit thing, you think it made him angry, and that's why he hit the ball so well?"

The CO shrugged. "It's one explanation."

The Ops O scooted forward on the seat a bit. "I've been trying to figure a way to get to him. He just seems like a Lone Ranger, like he doesn't want to really be a part of the wardroom."

The XO went *humph*. "Waste of time worrying about ensigns. You don't know what you have to work with until they become JGs."

"Ah, XO." The Skipper did his one-sided smile. "Problem is we are going to be in the combat zone in about forty-nine hours, and ensigns are going to be either in the gun director or driving the ship. They are going to be in key positions of our war fighting teams."

The XO was sitting next to the after bulkhead, and he reached out and patted the angle iron running parallel to the deck next to him. "Ready to go get in another war, old girl?" he asked.

Jon looked at his watch. 2344. *Crap.* He had wanted to include a poem with the letter, but with the stupid ball game, he hadn't had time. Now he needed to hustle before the postal clerk closed out mail.

A light tap on the door preceded the door being pulled open. The Messenger of the Watch from the quarterdeck stood in the doorway.

"Oh, hi, Mr. Z. Gotta' get Mr. Chalmers up for the mid-watch."

Edgar flicked on his bunk light, threw his covers back, turned, and put his feet on the deck. "I'm awake, Seaman Sheffield."

"Aye, sir." Sheffield closed the door.

Edgar stood, stretched, and yawned. Then, he saw Jon at the fold-down desk. He dropped his yawn, and then he dropped his arms.

Jon had forgotten Edgar had the mid-watch. He knew he shouldn't have used the desk. But his chest hurt from where Chief Petitte had clobbered him. It would hurt to write propped by elbows on his bunk.

Jon stood as Edgar reached to grab him.

Jon slapped the hand aside and smacked him hard on his sternum with an open hand. It stood him up. A sneer smeared across his face, and he reached out again. Jon grabbed the hand, twisted it, spun them around, and open-hand smacked him on the chest again. Edgar stumbled over the chair and went over backward and wound up on his back up against the forward bulkhead of the Locker, his legs on the over-turned chair.

Almost flicked on his bunk-light. "What the hell's going on, Two Buckets?"

"Nothing to worry about, Bull," Jon said. "Just building some mora' that esprit." Jon grabbed his letter-writing materials and went up to the wardroom to finish the letter.

5

On the bridge of a ship, the conning officer drives the vessel by giving orders to the helmsman and lee helm, the sailor who communicates with the engine room. It is *important* that these two sailors precisely follow the conning officer's orders. For certain evolutions, such as steaming close alongside an oiler to refuel, or negotiating a crowded, narrow channel to the sea when leaving port, it is *critical* that the helm and lee helm precisely follow the conning officer's orders. In those circumstances, the ship stationed a safety observer behind the helm and lee helm to ensure there were no mistakes. Jon Zachery served as safety observer on *Manfred*.

That morning, leaving the Philippine Islands, or the PI, as the sailors called them, felt different to Jon. He totted up the number of times he'd manned that position and came up with eleven times. *Maybe,* he thought, *I'm getting to be a salty sailor, getting the hang of this business.* Considering himself to be salty ran smack into the memory of being seasick that same number, eleven, days ago.

When the Boatswain Mate of the Watch blew the whistle, signaling the last line had been taken in, it made the hair stand up on the back of Jon's neck. The Ops O had the conn. He backed the ship away and clear of the pier, alternated the engines, port engine back two thirds, starboard ahead two thirds. *Manfred* pivoted until her bow pointed toward the sea.

The vibration of the propellors thrashing the sea pulsed up through Jon's shoes. He'd felt that vibration before, but he'd never been impressed with how much power was being spent to twist the ship around on a spot. Impressive came to mind.

Jon looked around the pilothouse to see if anyone else seemed to think it was different that morning. The quartermasters were doing their jobs, two of them on the bridge wings shooting bearings to navigation aids on shore, one of them plotting the bearings onto a chart. By the chart table, the Navigation Officer, Lieutenant (jg) Darrell Palmer, wore a sound-powered headset, with the earpiece on the right side behind his ear so that he could hear conversations in the pilothouse as well as the voices of his navigation team over the phone circuit. A low buzz of voices discussed primary and secondary navigation fixes. Someone called Fathometer readings. The signal bridge, one deck above, relayed the interpretation of the signal flags flying on the commodore's flagship, USS *Reilly*. She was standing out of port ahead of *Manfred*.

On the starboard side of the bridge, Lieutenant (jg) Andrew Dunston was the Junior Officer of the Deck (JOOD). He stood by the radar repeater near the Captain's swivel chair. The CO occupied that chair. He held the rank of commander, but on his ship, a commanding officer was called captain. In the US Navy, Jon thought, a guy could sure pack a lot of titles: CO, Skipper, Captain.

The XO stood next to the Captain's chair. The Captain nodded to the port side. The XO slipped behind Andrew, crossed in front of the binnacle, and stood next to the occupant of the chair on the starboard side. The Commodore. His rank was US Navy captain, but in his role as commander of a squadron of destroyers, one of them being *Manfred*, he was called commodore. The XO said something to Captain Brass that Jon couldn't hear. For a moment, he wondered whether it was the Commodore being aboard that he sensed? But he discounted that pretty quickly. Anything above the rank of full lieutenant, like his boss, LT Allman, Jon considered to be exalted territory. Up there, they were heavies, and heavies, for the most part, didn't seem to know or to care that Jon existed.

With the Commodore aboard, Jon was sure the CO wasn't aware of Ensign Zachery's presence. The CO sat with his elbow on the armrest of his chair, hunched forward a bit, his chin resting on the knuckles of his fist. His *The Thinker* pose. A little smile crinkled the bottom of Jon's face as he pictured the CO posing nude for Auguste Rodin.

A sudden sharp elbow gig in Jon's ribs erased the smile. He hadn't noticed the XO leave the Commodore's side. The XO scowled and nodded toward the binnacle.

It embarrassed Jon to be caught daydreaming like that, even though the ship really hadn't gotten an initial course to steer yet. But during the brief that morning, the XO had stressed, when they got underway, he expected them all to be focused on their jobs because they would be in the combat zone shortly. Their last opportunity for training was behind them. From now on, everything is for real. "From now on," he had said, "Consider yourselves engaged in combat operations. Your lives depend on it," he'd said.

Jon stood straighter.

"All engines ahead two-thirds. Steer course two-two-five." The Ops O's voice was clear, loud, and packed with authority.

That steering command sparked a realization in Jon. The combat zone was no longer a blurry concept well beyond his worry horizon. The PI was beginning to fall behind, and the combat zone was right in front of them. Teresa, their daughter Jennifer, Admiral Ensign, those things that had seemed to fill his head, well, they were going to have to move aside. Jon paid attention with most of his mind, but he also recalled the PT boat encounters of 1964, which seemed to have started the business in Vietnam. The American destroyers had not been damaged in those encounters. There'd been no encounters since then, at least none that Jon had seen in the papers. Maybe the string of luck would hold. *Please, God.*

Whatever Jon had been feeling now tingled the back of his neck, and it was as if ants shouldered their way through the hairs on his arms.

"Right ten degrees rudder. Steady on two-four-zero." The OOD's no non-sense voice sliced through the buzz of the navigation team.

The water of the bay was the color of grape juice with a bit of milk stirred in it. Not a breath of breeze riffled the polished, purplish-opaline surface until the Commodore's flagship sliced a wake into it. *Reilly,* ahead and leading them out of the harbor, seemed to be painted with duty and purpose as much as with hull-grey paint.

To starboard, the top half of the elevated terrain of Kalakran Ridge was bathed in the light of the rising sun such that the jungle foliage was light green on the top of the ridge, but where it was still in shadow, dark green at the base.

To port, an aircraft carrier was tied up at the pier adjacent to the Cubi Point Naval Air Station. Nothing was stirring on the airfield. About halfway up the high terrain behind the airfield, the Cubi Point Officer's Club stood out. It still surprised Jon that aviators and surface navy officers needed separate clubs. Separate clubs for chief petty officers and for the junior enlisted, well, that made sense in a way. But he wondered how many types of segregation did there need to be?

As the stern of the moored carrier started to slide past their beam, the CO sat up straight, cast a glance over at the Commodore, took a breath, and looked straight ahead for a moment; then he climbed down from his chair and passed in front of the binnacle.

"Commodore," the Captain said. "I'm happy to leave the bridge with the XO if you'd like to get started going around the ship. Or perhaps you'd like another cup of tea first?"

"No more tea. Let's get to it," the Commodore said as he slid out of his chair.

The CO was five feet, nine inches, and the Commodore was about an inch taller. But, while the CO was trim, the Commodore was kind of shaped like a football. His head and feet seemed small.

The shoulders were narrow, and his arms seemed to angle out to his sides, pushed out by the ample waist and unable to hang straight down. On his face, distinct lines emanated from the bridge of his nose and ran to the corners of his mouth. It looked like someone had hung an inverted V on his nose. The Commodore's mouth was also like an inverted V, but a sort of squashed V with the side legs pushed out a bit.

Jon had been staring at the Commodore, and he forced himself to look back at the compass. They were ¾ degree off heading, but the helmsman did not have a rudder correction in. He was staring at the Commodore, too. Not wanting to say anything out loud with the Commodore on the bridge, Jon gigged the helmsman in the ribs with his elbow, much like Teresa did to him—just like the XO had done to Jon. The helmsman looked down at the compass, muttered an expletive, and put in three degrees of rudder to correct back to the ordered heading.

"Commodore and Captain are off the bridge," the Boatswain Mate of the Watch announced.

Jon looked up and found the XO staring at him. He was standing next to the Captain's chair. The XO, Lieutenant Commander Messenger, was Jon's height, five feet, seven inches. He had red hair, and with his hat on, you couldn't tell that he was bald on top. A double chin and jowly cheeks give him a soft look. Since departing San Diego, he has been growing a mustache. His came out as a red Hitler type. Some of the guys in the Ensign Locker thought the XO looked funny with the mustache but Jon never saw anything funny when he looked at him. Jon saw his eyes, and his eyes were always hard and disapproving when they looked at him. The XO turned and looked out the bridge windows.

As the second hand topped at 0930, Jon knocked.

"Come," came instantly, slightly muffled, through the door.

The Operations Officer, Lieutenant Hank Allman, Jon's boss, sat at his desk, a lid that opened out of the grey sheet metal chassis that held both a file drawer for his papers and drawers for his clothes. He pointed at the fold-up bed sofa, and Jon sat and waited as the Ops O ran his finger down a list of items written on a lined yellow legal-sized pad of paper.

Jon looked around the room and, as always, marveled at the amount of space he had. Five lived in the Ensign Locker, a space not much bigger.

"So," the Ops O swiveled around on his seat, and his black eyes impaled Jon. Word had it that the Ops O was of Armenian descent, though he was born in the US. His grandfather had Americanized the family name. LT Allman had a swarthy complexion and a slightly hooked nose. When he looked at Jon as he had just done, his look said, in terms of total confidence, that he was the alpha male and that, if there was any doubt of that very hard fact, a demonstration could be cued up in very short order. Jon had yet to figure out what to do with his eyes when he was with his boss, like then. He didn't want to appear to be trying to stare him down, but also, he didn't want the Ops O to think he was total putty for him to squish any way he wanted.

"So," the Ops O said again, done for the moment with probing through Jon's eyes as if they were windows open to the clutter in Jon's head, "Captain says ensigns need a mid-year performance appraisal. You've only been aboard five months, but I wanted to do this before we got into the combat zone. So, Mr. Zachery, tell me how you think you've done."

Off-balance, already. It always amazed Jon how he could do that to him. He came in, sat down, waited for him to go down his list, and then, in an instant, the Ops O had him off-balance.

"Well, sir, um— I don't think it means anything, what I think, I mean. What you think is what goes on the paper."

"Jesus H. Christ, Zachery," the Ops O shook his head. "I don't expect to have to explain every little thing to you. Even an ensign ought to come equipped with a few of the fundamentals." The Ops O kind of scooted forward on his chair. "It does matter what you think, and it matters more than what I think, more even than what the XO and CO think. It matters. Now, we don't have time for one of these *pulling hen's teeth* discussions. We are going to set special sea detail in," he looked at his watch, "twenty-seven minutes to highline the Commodore back to *Reilly*. Now, tell me. How do you think you've done?"

Jon took a breath. "I think I have done pretty well as division officer. Chief and I have completed a development plan for each guy in the division, like the cross-training of the communications and radar electronics technicians. And not only the technicians, but we've done the same thing for the yeoman and personnel-men."

Besides the electronic technicians, the clerical types who manned the ship's office, were part of Jon's division.

"As for me, you told me on my first day that I should do correspondence courses. I have completed two. YN1 Gilpin told me that most of the ensigns gaff off the courses. He seemed impressed that I'd done two already. I haven't ordered a third one yet."

"I told the YN1 to order the Communication Officer course for you. That's the job we are thinking about for you when Tom Snyder leaves after the cruise—but that's assuming we get some things straightened out."

That surprised Jon. The Ops O was thinking about another job for him.

"Go on," Ops O said. "What else?"

"You told me to get myself up to speed on the functions of the other departments. I've done that. And, I think I'm picking things up on the bridge, the ship driving, I mean." He began to feel comfortable with his recitation, listing his accomplishments.

"That's it?" The Ops O glared.

What's he mad about?

"You're not even going to mention all the other crap?"

"Uh, Ops O, what oth—"

The Ops O moved forward another inch on his chair like he was getting ready to leap up and come at Jon. "You sent me a letter while you were still in OCS. That letter led me to expect a lot from you.

Then you checked in and had the worst first day aboard ship any ensign ever had, going back to 1775. The first time at sea, you get your nickname. Ensign Two Buckets, the seasick sailor. The whole four months we spent in training you never had your mind on your job. You had your mind on your wife and your baby. We, the XO and I, were hoping once we left the States, you might get with the program; but the dinner we had at the O Club Thursday night, same old Ensign Two Buckets crap."

Jon got angry, but it fizzled. There was truth in what the Ops O said.

The Ops O's voice buzzed on about the dinner at the O Club.

Jon thought about his first day aboard *Manfred*. He had stepped onto the quarterdeck, saluted the OOD, identified himself as reporting for duty. The Petty Officer of the watch spoke the words as he wrote them in the deck log: "Ensign Jon Zachery reported aboard the USS *Manfred*, 0606, 4 January 1966."

That morning, the Officer of the Deck was six-foot-two Chief Petty Officer Petitte. When Jon saw him that morning, the chief didn't look like he should be the OOD on a navy destroyer quarterdeck. He looked like he should be in a boxing ring, and the announcer should be saying, "In this corner, the heavyweight *champ-ee-yon* of the *woruld*, Chief Petty Officer Petitte."

The OOD said, "Understand you were a first-class petty officer before you got commissioned. That right, Mr. Zachery?"

Jon had explained that he had continued on active duty while he attended Purdue University. When he entered freshman year, he'd just made third class petty officer. And when he was eligible to do so, he took the rating advancement exams and had been promoted to second, and then to first class petty officer just before college graduation.

Chief Petitte dumped a look of pure disdain on Jon. Obviously, the chief thought Ensign Zachery had made first class petty officer in a less than manly way.

Then, of course, there had been the business of asking for leave, which had embarrassed Jon, but to characterize it as the worst first day any ensign had ever had in the history of the navy?

The Ops O continued to harp on Jon's sins. He mentioned pissing the CO off.

That had happened during the transit from Hawaii to the Philippines. *Manfred* was one of four destroyers in a screen in front of an ammo ship and an oiler. *Manfred* had been ordered to move to the waiting station for refueling behind the oiler. Jon had had the conn, and he had started the maneuver without getting a recommendation from Combat. It had been a very simple setup, and there didn't seem to be a point in asking Combat Information Center for a recommendation. But the CO had come out of his *Thinker* pose and stopped him and chewed him out forcefully and succinctly.

The CO said, "You always involve Combat when you are maneuvering the ship. When you are steaming in formation, and repositioning at night, you will need Combat to make sure you do it right and don't get us sliced in half by one of the big boys. Repositioning in good weather and broad daylight, every time you do it, is a golden opportunity to practice for the night, bad weather situation. Combat needs to be involved. Always involve Combat, no matter how simple the setup. Got it?"

Jon *had* gotten it. Back in the States, twice after being told to maneuver the ship, he'd taken time to make sure he'd convey the proper orders, and the CO had gotten upset. He'd wanted Jon to "hop to it." This time he'd hopped to it, but *this time* the CO wanted him to take it slow and easy. The public nature of the chewing out ensured he'd never forget it, either...

The Ops O was back on the dinner at the O Club, how Jon hadn't tried to fit in. He'd been required to be there, and so he was.

"Even Dormant works at fitting in," the Ops O snarled.

A new look settled over the Ops O's face. Jon frowned, wondering what that forecasted.

"Remember your first day aboard?" the Ops O said. "You asked the XO for leave? You should have asked me first. Then when Teresa had the emergency C-section, and you came and asked me for leave, I turned you down. But, I told you, you could go to the XO. You didn't go to him. If you had, he'd have given you leave."

Anger flashed white-hot. Jon stood and clenched his fists. Then he unclenched one of them to open the door.

6

Jon stood on the main deck, port side, outside officer's country. The ship was steaming at fifteen knots, probably. Ahead, ten degrees to port was the commodore's flagship.

His session with the Ops O pushed back into his head. The Ops O's main point had seemed to be about not fitting in. Fitting in was like a game you had to play; only the rules were secret, and you could only figure out the rules by getting a kick in the…in the gut. He'd almost thought *kick in the balls.* It took an effort not to slip into sailor talk. It took more effort to keep from thinking that way, even though, right now, a swear word seemed to hold the promise of some sort of release of the ugly stuff roiling in his belly and his brain.

Worst first day since 1775, he'd said. It had been a bad first day. Jon could agree with that, but it had ended well.

4 January, during his drive home, he'd been thinking about his day, not about Teresa's, and her first doctor visit since they'd arrived in California. When Jon walked into their apartment, and he saw

Teresa at the sink in the kitchen/dining/living room, he remembered the doctor. That spurred him to forget his troubles and to hope and pray, her eight-months-pregnant doctor visit had gone better than his day. Teresa had looked at him, grabbed a dishtowel from the counter, and started over to him, drying her hands as she walked.

"Close the door, silly," she'd said. Then she locked the door, hugged him, and told him she had a wonderful doctor, not like that dweeby God's gift to medicine she'd had when Jon was at Officer Candidate School. "And, the doctor said we could still make love. Carefully." Then she'd taken his hand and led him to the bedroom.

It had never occurred to Jon before, but now it did. She had known, just looking at him, how his day had gone. Jon felt the bottom of his face loosen. He'd been determined to keep her from seeing what a rotten day he'd had. But she'd seen.

Not too quick to see that, eh, Zachery? Took you four months.

Maybe he should go back to the Ops O and tell him to add, "Not too quick on the uptake," to his list of Ensign Two Buckets' faults. Instead, his mind went back to Teresa.

Just when I think I could not possibly love her more; I love her more.

The South China Sea went out of his eyes, and he saw Teresa on her side, her swollen belly up against him. She was and is a beautiful woman, and that day, she made him think of an angel, but the smell of lovemaking was in the air around them, and he had been thinking of telling her how angels and that lusty smell could coexist and wasn't that a marvel. Then the baby kicked Jon. He pushed back, but she pulled him close again.

"Zorro is just saying hello to his daddy," she said. Teresa was so sure she carried a little boy baby, but it was their Jennifer who had kicked Jon.

"Now set the special sea detail for highline," came over the 1MC.

"Damn 1MC," Cowboy had drawled once, "Cain't even have a decent wet dream without that damn thing buttin' in."

Sometimes, Jon thought, *my mind is quicker than I am, and it sticks those things in my head before I can stop them.*

When Jon got to the bridge, USS *Reilly* was to starboard, five hundred yards ahead. From his safety observer position, five hundred yards seemed close.

The CO was in his chair, and the commodore occupied the portside. The general bustle of watch change buzzed through the pilothouse as normal underway watch turned over responsibility to the Special Sea Detail bridge team. The Ops O arrived, stopped next to Jon, and looked at him for a moment; then he smiled and went forward to assume OOD duties.

That smirky little smile. Jon wondered what that meant. He'd been told he didn't hide his feelings well. Had the Ops O looked at him to see if he was angry? Well, he was. And the next question was, had the Ops O deliberately tried to make him angry? But Jon had a job to do, and anger, and Teresa, had to go in a box and shoved out of the center of his mind. And Jon did that.

After the Commodore was securely transferred via the body cage contraption suspended from a cable back to his flagship, it was as if *Manfred* heaved a sigh of relief. As he descended the ladders back down to the main deck, he thought about that feeling of relief. He'd felt it, but he felt the crew, the ship's relief as well. *There, Ops O, I fit in with that, didn't I?*

The way the Ops O treated him reminded Jon of his pop. Pop seemed to think Jon didn't have enough sense to tie his shoes in the morning without instruction to do so.

Jon passed through the wardroom, past the XO's office, and started down the ladder when he heard Cowboy's voice from inside the Ensign Locker. There was some indistinct mumbling but the words "Goddamned Commodore," came through loud and clear.

Jon opened the door and found Cowboy pacing between the tiers of bunks to either side of the door. The bottom bunk to the right was unoccupied. Almost was in the other bottom bunk, and Dormant, of course, was in his. Both of them had books open in front of their faces.

"Cowboy, hold your voice down," Almost said. "You can't be

bad-mouthing the Commodore like that with the XO's room and the wardroom just above us,"

"All right." Cowboy stopped pacing and looked at the bottom bunk. "But, damn." He started waving his arms about and resumed pacing. "I was with the Commodore and the Skipper for two hours as we went around the ship. The Commodore had this chalk, and he was circling all the things he said were going to cause rust. He was really focused on things like those extra cable brackets that are no longer used. We should have ground all those things off before we left the States, much less before we left the PI, he said. Why did he wait to tell us that until now?"

"He was probably saying that although we are going to be in the combat zone tomorrow, that we can't forget about the material condition of the ship." Almost didn't really speak fast. It just seemed that way next to Cowboy's drawl.

"Yeah, well." *Yeah* and *well* both came out with two syllables each. "The Skipper told us before we went into port that he wanted the ship in great shape before we left. He wanted us to make sure we did our painting properly, not just slathering face paint on an old whore. We did it right, and the Skipper was happy with what we did; he said he wanted to minimize the worry we put into the ship's appearance while we were in the combat zone. Then Commodore Big Butt comes over here and tells us just the opposite."

Cowboy stopped talking for a moment, giving one of them an opportunity to hurl a cup of conversational gasoline on the bonfire of his outrage, but no one took the bait. Jon squeezed past him.

"Well," Cowboy said, "I hope my application for flight training gets approved quickly. The ship's office said the CO approved it this mornin', and it will go off with the next mail," Cowboy said. "I'll bet aviators don't have to put up with this crap. Duke said the focus is on combat flying."

The Wednesday night of their week in port, *Manfred's* three newest Lieutenants (junior grade) had hosted a wetting down party. The party had been held on the covered second-floor open-walled area above the Subic Bay O Club. A number of people had crashed the party, including a marine A-4 pilot named Duke Savage. Cowboy had latched onto Duke and wound up spending a lot of time with him. Duke had gone on leave to Manila with Cowboy and the Ops O.

Jon kicked off his shoes and crawled up onto his bunk. When he had been enlisted, the destroyer he had served on had been on plane guard duty behind carriers at night several times. Each time, they had witnessed fatal accidents during the night carrier landings, and once, they had pulled two bodies from the water after an F-4 had had a carrier landing accident and gone into the water. After other accidents, the ship's boat had looked but hadn't found any bodies. Jon pretty much considered naval aviators to be suicidal after that, but he kept his mouth shut.

Cowboy was still standing between the tiers of bunks when Admiral Ensign entered the Locker.

"Admiral Ensign, I gotta deal for ya," Cowboy said. "Form over substance is more your cuppa' tea than mine. How 'bout if we go to the Gun Boss and see if he will let us swap jobs? I'll take care a the guns, and you can be admiral of the deck apes and keep the ship pretty for the Commodore. Great idea, don't cha'gree?"

"Screw you."

"I'm serious, Admiral Ensign. You don't care about the guns. And, man, the fifty-caliber mounts they welded on the 01 level last week! I sure hope I get the chance to look down the sight of a fifty into some gomer's eyes as I blow him to hell."

"You're a Neanderthal," Dormant said. "If you call a person a gomer, or a gook, or a hun, or a Jap, then it's okay to kill them, is that it? You probably feel the same way about redskins and Negroes."

Dormant rolled out of his bunk, and Cowboy allowed himself to be pushed forward into the space next to Jon's bunk. Dormant stepped into his shoes at the head of the tier of bunks and left the Locker.

Dormant had gotten his nickname about a week after he'd checked aboard. If he wasn't on watch or eating, he was sleeping. But unlike Cowboy, when he was awake, he didn't say much—normally.

Cowboy stared at the closed door for a moment, and then he said,

"Until last night, I thought Dormant was a little liberal, but man. He's a flaming red commie."

"This is just swell," Admiral Ensign said. "A Wyoming Neanderthal cowboy, a pacifist, and a power-puking, pussy-whipped poet to share the Locker with."

The first time Jon had met Admiral Ensign was close to the end of the day. No one was in the Locker, so he sat at the fold-down desk to work on a poem for Teresa. It always pleased her when he left her a poem. He had been there about five minutes when Admiral Ensign came into the room. He saw what Jon was working on, pushed him away from the desk, and now, he seemed to relish every chance he had to rag Jon about the poem.

"Yours had to be an arranged marriage," Cowboy said. "Your wife is too intelligent and too good-looking to have chosen to marry an asshole like you."

"Come on, children," Almost said. "It's lunchtime."

"Admiral Ensign," Cowboy said. "I was serious about the job swap. How about it?"

The others were stomping up the ladder. Almost had a foot inside the door. Jon went back to writing his letter.

"Come on, Two Buckets," Almost said. "You don't come to lunch; Ops O's sure to ask where you are."

Jon sighed, put the letter-writing materials back on the angle iron next to the bed, and crawled back down to the deck. As he stepped into his shoes, he wondered if being an ensign worked off any time in purgatory. He clicked the light off in the Locker and followed Almost up the ladder.

7

At lunch, Carl Lehr asked Jon to help him make *Manfred* history. That afternoon, with a bit of luck, he said, they would, for the first time, complete the takeoff checklist on the ship's DASH helicopter. Carl and his crew were going to do a ground turn-up of the remotely controlled helo, and he asked Jon to assist. Jon had gone to a six-week training course to learn how to fly the drone helo. He and Carl were the only two aboard qualified to operate DASH.

Manfred had been commissioned in 1945 and had joined World War II in the waters around Okinawa, but a number of things had been changed since then. Just before Jon reported aboard, the ship had completed a significant modernization. From the forward gun mount to the bow and from the after gun mount to the stern, she was the same ship she had been in World War II. Between the gun mounts, not much was the same. Additional fuel capacity had been added, all the electronics equipment had been replaced with up-to-date versions, and the ship's Anti-submarine Warfare (ASW) capability had been significantly enhanced. Drone Anti-submarine Helicopter (DASH) was one of the ASW improvements.

The QH-50 drone helicopter and shipboard monitoring and control equipment comprised the DASH system. The QH-50 had counter-rotating main-rotor blades, a radio to receive the telemetry control signals, a module to translate radio signals to flight control movements, the capability to carry two ASW torpedoes, and skids for landing gear.

Aft of amidships, the whole structure sitting on the main deck had been modified, mostly to accommodate DASH. Above after officer's country, a small helicopter deck had been added, and just forward of that, there was a hanger designed to accommodate the drone helo.

Carl was DASH crew division officer. During an actual mission, Carl would launch the helo and then pass control to Jon in Combat. Jon would steer the helo symbol on a tracking table over the symbol for an enemy sub, release a torpedo, then return the helo to the ship where Carl would land it. But today, they weren't doing a regular mission. They were going to do an engine turn-up with the drone helo firmly chained to the deck.

Across the fleet, the DASH system was notoriously unreliable. The system on *Manfred* had never been in an operable state since Jon had been aboard. Carl and his crew worked diligently to find and fix problems, but it always seemed that when the crew fixed one problem, they would discover two new problems as they checked the fix. But, after a long and frustrating effort, *Manfred's* helo had finally passed all its checks, and Carl was ready to do an engine turn up.

At 1256, Jon entered the DASH hanger through the forward door. The hanger was empty except for one of Carl's sailors sitting at a workbench on the forward starboard side of the space with a sound-powered phone set strapped around his neck, earphones in place. The sailor spoke into the mouthpiece. He had turned to see who was entering the hanger, and without interrupting his dialogue, he, Petty Officer Hansen, nodded to Jon; then he pointed aft toward the helo deck.

The roll-down door opening onto the helo deck was closed, so Jon used the personnel door to the left of the roll-down.

Whenever he was in the DASH hanger, Jon always wondered at the concept. The QH-50 was capable of carrying one or two ASW torpedoes out as far as the radio horizon. The problem was in detecting and targeting a sub that far away from the ship, which raised a question of the viability of the DASH concept.

But, who would care what Jon Zachery, the junior officer, the boar tit junior officer thought?

Jon found Carl on the helo deck with Petty Officer First Class (PO1) Banks. Banks was a Negro, thin and six feet tall, an engine mechanic, and the leading petty officer in the division. Both Carl and PO1 Banks wore flotation jackets and had goggle-equipped helmets in their hands. The drone was spotted in the center of the helo deck and secured in place with the same tie-down chains used on aircraft carriers. During engine starts, one of the DASH crewmen was stationed next to the helo with a CO_2 fire-fighting bottle in case of an emergecy. Normally, PO1 Banks assigned one of his junior sailors to the CO_2 bottle. Since this was the first engine turn-up in such a long time, Petty Officer Banks would man the bottle.

"Jon," Carl said, "I'm glad to have you here. With as much trouble as we've had, I just thought it would be good to have both of us here, just in case something else goes haywire. But even if everything works okay, we are not going to try to fly. I just want to make sure we can get a full set of ground checks accomplished satisfactorily. If everything goes well, we will complete the pre-flight checklist. If we manage to complete a good ground check, the crew and I will review the situation tonight, and decide if it looks good enough to try to fly it. So, we might fly tomorrow or the next day, depending on our operational commitments. Okay?"

The difficulty in keeping the DASH system operational was not unique to *Manfred*. Throughout the fleet, there were high failure rates of the complex and sensitive electronic systems both on the helo and with the shipboard portions of the drone control system. Many drones had been lost. Some failed to respond to turn signals intended to bring a helicopter back home. Others self-destructed when the counter-rotating blades, a design feature obviating the necessity for a tail rotor, contacted. When the 600-RPM counter-rotating blades contacted, it resulted in an impressive explosion of blade-parts shrapnel being flung over a wide area and a plummet to earth, or sea, of what was left. During Jon's training at the navy school on San Clemente Island, there had been three crashes.

Once, Jon had heard PO1 Banks say, "Only damn reason we haven't lost one of the damn things yet, is cause we can't get one of the damn things in good enough damn shape to fly it. And I damn well wish to hell we could get one of these damn things in the air and that the damn thing would never come back to this damn ship."

Jon had never heard Carl complain about the system. Carl was keenly sensitive to the notion that his sole purpose for assignment to *Manfred*, and the sole purpose for his crew, was to maintain the DASH System in an operable state. The DASH crew was diligent pursuing of its responsibilities, and despite the frustrations, never let up on the effort to get the system operable. And despite the occasional griping, PO1 Banks worked harder than any of them to try to correct problems. He was always there with his crew even if the work was on the electronic systems, for which he had no training and no expertise. He just wanted his troops to know that he cared for them and cared for how hard they worked on the problems.

Carl was at the control console, which consisted of a briefcase-like box about twenty-four inches by fifteen inches mounted on a pedestal. On the box was a joystick that controlled the pitch and roll of the helo rotor disk. There was a small wheel on the side of the box for controlling altitude. Other controls on the box were an engine start/shut-down switch and a button for disconnecting an electrical umbilical cable attached to the helo for start and ground checks prior to launch. There were small gauges to show engine temperature and RPM and another gauge for rotor RPM. There was also a switch for engaging and disengaging the rotors.

"Okay, Jon, we're ready to start. I'll be operating the controls, but if things start going haywire, don't be bashful about telling me what to do. And if it gets too hectic, and you can't tell me, and you think a switch should be thrown, just do it. Okay?"

"Well, all right, Carl. I'm not sure if I'll be able to do any good for you, but if you want me here, I'll offer what I can," Jon said as he put his goggles in place.

Jon didn't say it, but he was distinctly uneasy with the notion of flipping a switch when Carl was controlling the helo. Just like on a multi-crewed aircraft, or like on the bridge where only one person had the deck and one had the conn, only one person should be controlling the helicopter at a time.

PO1 Banks secured the chinstrap of his helmet, put his goggles in place, and took up the delivery horn of the firefighting bottle. Carl and Jon checked off the items on the Pre-start Checklist.

"PO1," Carl called. "Stand by for engine start."

PO1 Banks gave Carl a thumbs-up. Carl gave a turn-up engines signal by raising his right arm, with two fingers extended, and rotating the hand rapidly. He then pushed the engine start button.

There was a whine as the engine started rotating. Fuel was turned on in the helo automatically, and the engine exhaust gas temperature gauge started rising. The temperature gauge peaked at just below the over-temp limit, and then it dropped into the normal ground idle range. Carl gave a thumbs-up to Banks and signaled for him to exit from beside the helo. Banks pulled the wheeled fire bottle with him, entered the helo hanger, and closed the door.

Carl's flight helmet was equipped with a sound-powered phone. He spoke to his crew and verified that all diagnostic signals from the helo, which came through the umbilical, attached to the left rear side of the helo body, were in normal range.

Carl turned to Jon, and he pulled the ear cup up from my left ear. "Here we go, Jon. Everything looks good. I'm going to engage the rotors now."

Carl punched a button on the console. The rotor RPM gauge needle came off the peg as the two counter-rotating rotor blades started turning. Everything was progressing normally. The rotor RPM climbed slowly at first and then accelerated toward 600 RPM, or normal RPM for ground idle, takeoff, and flight. He was just beginning to think that it would go okay, but Jon had forgotten about the gust locks. At low rotor RPM, the gust locks prevented the rotors from moving in pitch or roll. At low rotor RPM, wind gusts could drive the counter-rotating blades to smash into each other. As close as they were to the helo, they were in real danger if that happened.

At 450 RPM, all hell broke loose. The little toy helicopter had been cranking normally, just the way it should, then the gust locks disengaged, and in an instant, it became a thing possessed. The rotor blades were moving rapidly and violently, spasmodically, in roll and pitch. Carl was standing at the console, trying to control the rampaging beast with the joystick and the altitude wheel. He flipped the engine shut down switch, but it had no effect. Nothing he was doing had any effect.

If Carl hadn't been there, if it had been just Jon, he knew he'd have dropped flat and started burrowing into the steel deck. But Carl stayed on his feet, so Jon did too. As he stood next to Carl and watched the berserk machine right in front of them, scenes from crashes he had seen during training flashed through Jon's mind. During one crash, the helo had been 200 feet above the runway when it started acting just like their DASH. Blades flailed and contacted. Chunks of shattered blades had been flung over a thousand yards. *Here we are,* Jon thought, *six yards from the tips of those blades.* The blades really looked like they were trying hard to smash together.

Carl continued to try the joystick and the various buttons on the console, and Jon stood beside him, despite thinking that very soon he would be dead with a chunk of rotor blade through his chest.

As Jon watched Carl work the controls and switches, he noticed that the one switch Carl did not try was the umbilical disconnect. Normally, the operator did not activate that switch until just before launch. This is a long way from normal, Jon thought. Bending down and reaching up under Carl's right arm to get to the button, Jon punched it. The umbilical popped off its mounting on the after part of the port side of the drone and fell to the deck. There were a few additional spastic gyrations of the rotors until Carl realized that the rotors were now responding to the joystick. He let go of the controls, and the blades started tracking level with the deck. Then, he tried a few small roll and pitch inputs, which the helo responded to perfectly. It was like the preceding moments of drone-helicopter-homicidal psychosis had never happened.

Carl did not take his eyes off the helo but turned slightly and shouted, "Okay, I am not going to try anything else. I am just going to shut this thing down—if it will let me."

He punched the rotor disengage button. Immediately, the rotors began to slow. The gust locks engaged at the proper speed, and the rotors coasted the rest of the way to a stop. Carl then shut the engine down. When the last engine whine ebbed into silence, Carl and Jon just stood and looked at the benign, innocent-looking helicopter for a moment.

Carl unstrapped his flight helmet and shook his head. "That, Ensign Zachery, was probably the most exciting three minutes I have ever experienced."

"I couldn't believe you just stood there," Jon said. "If I'd been on the controls, I'd have dived for the deck."

"Well, I couldn't do that," Carl said as he turned away and looked at the helo again. "Sure glad you were here, though, and glad you thought to punch the umbilical off. I never thought of it because I had no intention of flying the thing. I think we were just seconds before the machine ripped itself to pieces—along with two ensigns, probably."

They both turned as the door over the DASH hanger rattled up, and PO1 Banks and PO3 Hansen walked out onto the flight deck. Carl went to talk to them about what had happened. Jon walked across the helo deck, climbed down from the 01 level, trudged back to the fantail, and sat on one of the bitts on the port side. Jon stared at the wake. The choppy, wind-rumpled water swallowed it in fifty yards or so.

A peaceful day at sea, the sun shining brightly, a normal helo start process, and the next thing you know, the crap hits the fan. Carl had been incredibly brave. He stood there flipping switches, moving knobs, moving the joystick, trying to get the wild blade flailing under control. In contrast to Carl's bravery, Jon knew he would have hit the deck and tried to make himself as small a target as possible for the shrapnel of shattered blade pieces that was bound to happen very soon. Comparing himself to Carl, Jon did not feel he came off favorably facing down the mad helo.

Jon sat there on the bitt for a while, not thinking anymore, just looking at the wake, and seeing if some sort of calm could find its way into his belly and brain when he heard his name called.

At sea, there were three lookout posts manned as part of each watch. There were lookouts on each wing of the bridge and an after lookout on the helo deck. During DASH operations, the after-lookout position was not manned.

"Sir. Ensign Zachery," the after lookout called. "The bridge said there is a meeting in the wardroom right now. They'd like you there."

Jon turned around.

"Sir, there's a meeting in the wardroom right now, and they want you there," the lookout said again.

"Okay," Jon said. "Thanks. I'm on the way."

Jon still wore the flight deck flotation jacket. Beneath it, his khaki shirt was sodden with sweat. The breeze chilled him, and he shivered, only partly because of the breeze.

In the wardroom, the CO sat at the head of the table. The XO to his right, and the Gun Boss opposite the XO. Carl sat at mid-table on the XO side, and Edgar Chalmers was seated next to him. Jon stood opposite Carl and looked at the CO.

"Sit." Then, the CO said, "Okay, guys, I'd like to understand what happened with the DASH, and then I'd like to understand what we do next about this—system." Jon was sure the phrase "piece of junk" was just there on the tip of the tongue, but it stayed there. "So, Carl, tell us, first what happened, and then, do you know what the problem is this time?"

"Yes, sir," Carl said. "Well, the guys ran every ground check in the book last night. Then, they ran them again this morning, and everything looked good. I asked for Two…Ensign Zachery to be with me when we started the engine. If something went wrong, there'd be two brains working on how to solve the problem.

"Everything went well with the engine start. We checked all the signals from the helo on the ground station, and they were all reading properly. So, everything looked good for cranking up the rotors. That went okay, too, at first. The normal rotor RPM is 600. A set of gust locks keep the blades level and unable to flop around from gusts of the wind both when the rotors are speeding up and when slowing down. So everything was great until we got to 450 RPM. Then, as soon as the gust locks disengaged and were no longer able to hold the rotor blades level, things went totally to hell. The blades were flopping all over the place, and the helo did not respond to any control inputs. I tried every switch on the control console I could think of, but nothing had any effect. I tried shutting down the engine, but that didn't work, either. Then Jon reached up and punched the button that disconnects the umbilical, and the helo immediately began to respond normally to control inputs. So, Jon saved our bacon. I am sure we would have had the blades bashing into each other. Blade shrapnel would have been flying all over the place if he hadn't punched that button."

The eyes at the head of the table all shifted from Carl to Jon.

"Can I say something, sir?" Jon said.

The Skipper nodded.

"Sir, I'd just like to say that I think it was Carl who saved our bacon. When that thing started going crazy, I was sure the blades would crash together, and I was sure we were in big danger. I would have just gotten down on the deck, but Carl stood there like—like Stonewall Jackson. He flipped switches and moved the joystick, tried everything to get it under control. I just noticed that the one thing he didn't try was the umbilical disconnect. So despite what Carl said, he was the one who saved our bacon."

"Okay, Mr. Zachery, noted." The Skipper was staring at Jon, and it got unpleasantly quiet. Then he said, "So, both of you guys did good this morning. Across the fleet, we have lost about half the total buy of these things. We haven't lost one—yet, so we are still in the plus column in that regard. I know these things are a bear to maintain.

I know your guys work hard, Carl. That's not the issue. But, do you know what caused today's problem?"

"Yes, sir. It was in the umbilical. That cable and the umbilical fitting were the sources of a lot of our recent problems, so the guys looked there first. They found the problem right away. The umbilical cable has a lot of small wires in it that all plug into the umbilical disconnect fitting on the helo. This fitting is a large, heavy connector about as big as a football. When you disconnect it, which normally is done right before we take off, it falls to the deck, and quite frequently, one of those little wires breaks or comes loose. Anyhow, the guys had tried a sealant compound to hold all these wires together. As it turns out, the sealant conducts electricity. They had shorted three wires together, and that sent nothing garbled signals to the mechanism that controls the rotors. The shorts also prevented me from taking control. The system is wired such that signals from the umbilical have priority over control signals received by radio. Once Jon disconnected the umbilical, the spurious signals were removed, and the helo operated fine.

"And sir, our plan is to get some help from Mr. Zachery's ETs and rewire that umbilical. We're also sending a message reporting this particular problem and asking if additional diagnostic checks can be developed to identify a problem like this. So this is our recommended way forward."

"Okay, Carl," the Skipper said. "Mr. Zachery, anything to add?"

"We'll help anyway we can, sir."

Neither the Gun Boss nor the XO had anything to add.

"Okay," the CO said. "I'm okay with the way forward. But before you are ready to engage rotors again, I'd like the four of you to get together with the XO and me and review the bidding. And Mr. Zachery, brief the Ops O on this. Questions?"

There were none. The CO, the XO, and the Gun Boss filed out.

"Jeez, Almost," Jon said. "I couldn't believe you standing there like you did. Really did make me think of Stonewall: brave as all get out."

"Maybe stupid would be a better word," Almost said.

"No, it wouldn't. I'll have Chief Fargo plug in with Petty Officer Banks so they can get to work on that umbilical."

Carl left through the rear door of the wardroom; then the XO came out of the room with his coffee mug. After he filled it, he sat down across the table from Jon.

"You okay?"

"Oh, yes, sir." The XO was sitting with his hands cupped around his mug. "With your permission, I'll get the ETs to help with the DASH umbilical."

"In a minute. Something's bothering you. Care to tell me what it is?" The XO took a sip.

"Sir, it's…well, I was so scared back there on the helo deck. I was so sure the blades were going to bash together. If I'd been there by myself, I know I'd just have flopped down on the deck. Carl just stood up there and kept trying to find the thing that would save the situation. The only reason I stayed standing is because Carl did. So I was pretty much—I was a coward back there on the helo deck, sir."

The XO smiled. The XO smiled frequently in the wardroom, at social functions, and with the other officers and sailors. But ever since Jon's first day aboard, he never smiled when he talked with him. Jon had never seen it before, but now, his smile reminded him of his maternal grandfather. Both had saggy jowls, a bit of a double chin, and a few prominent blood vessels visible through the suntan on their cheeks. The XO did have a flaming red Hitler mustache, but just then, his eyes seemed to get warm when he smiled, just like his grandpa.

"Jon, if you hadn't been afraid back there, you'd be stupid. I will grant you that you can be stupid about some things, but not about what just happened to you and Carl." The XO's smile blinked off, he took a sip, and his business look occupied his face. Jon hadn't appreciated it before, but the XO had his look, too, like the Skipper's *Thinker.*

"What you did back there on the helo deck, you and Carl worked together to solve a problem that neither one of you would have handled if you'd been alone."

The XO sipped. "Do you have any idea what an aggravating ensign you are, Two Buckets?"

Jon had never imagined he could be as aggravating to the navy as it often was to him.

"Almost, Admiral Ensign, Cowboy, and Dormant, I've always known what to expect from them. You, Two Buckets, the seasick sailor, you just don't want to stay in any box I put you in.

"You start off with the worst day any ensign ever had since 1775…" Obviously, the Ops O and the XO had compared notes. "And you got seasick the first time at sea and again just before we hit the PI. I guess I kind of label ensigns. There's a box labeled 'useless, keep him out of the way.' That's where I had you, but then you do stuff as division officer that the Ops O characterized as pretty darned close to satisfactory. According to the CO, Ops O, and Andrew, you have a real intuitive feel for driving the ship. This morning on the bridge, you nudged the helmsman with your elbow rather than say something out loud and embarrass the ship in front of the Commodore. Just a bit ago, despite being scared shitless, you stayed standing next to Carl, and you figured out what to do.

"In the PI, Sunday night, the officer/chief's softball game, you were the star of the officer's team and really seemed to fit in with the rest of us. A couple of nights earlier, though, at the wardroom dinner in the O Club, as soon as the CO said we were dismissed, you stood up so abruptly that all of us thought you couldn't wait to get away from us.

"Since January when we started seriously training to come over here, the CO has been trying to get the wardroom to work together, to function just like you and Carl did this afternoon: work together, be stronger as a team than individuals would be. But the thing for me, Two Buckets, is I just don't know which one of you will show up tomorrow. Will it be the softball/DASH team player, or will it be the Lone Ranger?"

Jon watched the XO as he stood, went to the coffee pot, trickled coffee into his cup, and walked back around the table and into his room.

8

Dearest Teresa,   31 May 1966 0015, South China Sea

Just got off the 20 to 2400. That's eight to twelve p.m. for you landlubbers, for you beloved landlubber. We entered the combat zone at midnight. Doesn't really feel any different, though, especially writing to you.

Almost and Admiral Ensign have the mid-watch. Cowboy and Dormant are sleeping. I have my head in a bubble of light from my bunk light, and it feels like the rest of the world is asleep. And it feels like I can reach out around the world and touch you, just like Adam on the ceiling of the Sistine, reaching out his finger to God to get a life. It's just like that. And I can't help it. I like this analogy.

I will tell you I had an interesting day, and my head is so full of stuff. Laying here now, though, and writing to you, it's like all the jumbled pieces just might come together.

At 0100, Jon put away his letter-writing materials and turned out the light.

Gong, gong!

Jon's eyes opened onto pitch-blackness with his heart going *wham, wham, wham* faster than the gong that sounded in his ears. They had entered the combat zone off Vietnam at midnight. The gonging and the general quarters (GQ) alarm, this time it was for real and not a drill like all the others.

Jon's bunk light, plus two others, clicked on. "General quarters, general quarters. All hands man your battle stations," came over the 1MC, the ship's announcing system. As he grabbed his uniform hanging from the end of his bed, Jon glanced at the alarm clock on the angle iron next to his bed. 0307. The two guys in the bottom bunks had the mid-watch, or it would have been crowded.

More gonging, and another 1MC announcement: "This is not a drill. Condition Zebra will be set in three minutes." Jon pulled on socks and pants, stuffed his feet into shoes, tied the laces, grabbed his shirt, and headed out the door. Shirttails could be tucked as he hustled to his station, right on the heels of Cowboy. Dormant was the caboose of their little train.

Then, Jon was in a line of officers and sailors stomping up the ladders between the main deck and the 02 level, and it was as if they were marching in formation. They were in step as they banged up the ladder with practiced and efficient haste.

"Condition Zebra will be set in two minutes," the Boatswain Mate of the Watch announced. For Jon, the Bosun's announcement served two purposes. One was a message to the brain that he needed to get to his GQ station before condition Zebra was set. Condition Zebra involved closing watertight doors and hatches to contain fire, fumes, and flooding. The second message was to his glandular system, and it was to the effect that this was no time to save adrenaline for some later use.

Despite all the forces impelling Jon forward, the air in Combat always stopped him just inside the door. Intense, stale cigarette smoke stung his eyes and made him want to hold his breath.

"Keep movin', Mr. Z," Radarman Chief Petty Officer Wicker said from behind. "There's oxygen in the air. Just chew it a while." It was his standing joke. Nearly all the radar-men smoked, and most of those on watch had probably been smoking when GQ had sounded.

Jon's GQ station was in the forward, starboard corner of Combat. The electronics warning equipment, designated WLR-1, was located there. The WLR-1 picked up threat radar signals, sorted the signal characteristics so the operator could identify the threat, and determine the direction from which the threat signal emanated. An accordion curtain separated Jon's GQ-station corner from the rest of Combat.

Petty Officer Zambowski operated the WLR-1.

"Just about finished scanning all the frequency bands, Mr. Z," Zambowski said. He punched a button on the stack of equipment in front of him. "No threat signals. Only a couple of friendly radars."

The third member of the team was Seaman Honor. He served as a messenger from their cubicle to the CIC Officer, Lieutenant (junior grade) Don Minton. At GQ, Zambowski continuously scanned the entire threat frequency spectrum for indications of enemy ship-, sub-, shore-, or aircraft-based radars. If he detected a threat, either Zambowski or Jon would shout the information into Combat. Seaman Honor would fill out a message sheet with the threat parameters and time of intercept so that the action log could be kept up to date.

After they manned their GQ stations, Jon always waited until Zambowski completed his initial scan; then, he took the information to Don Minton. Don's station was next to the Evaluator position. Most of the time, the CO, Commander Carstens, manned the Evaluator seat at GQ, and he was there that morning.

"No threats on the electronic warning receiver, Don," Jon said. "What's going on?"

"We got a call from a marine patrol a couple of minutes ago. They sprang an ambush on some VC, but a number of the VC got away and ran back into the jungle. The marines don't want to chase them for fear of getting ambushed themselves. So we're going to be firing into the place the VC ran into."

Wham sounded from the forward gun mount, followed almost immediately by the more muted *wham* from the after mount.

Their Weapons Department head, Lieutenant Ralph Timmons, manned the gun director for GQ. The CO was talking to him on the phone.

"Okay, Gun Boss, after we do the twenty rounds of HE, cover the same area with ten rounds of anti-personnel." HE was a high explosive round, which detonated on ground impact. Anti-personnel rounds were fused to go off above the ground and cover an area with shrapnel.

Jon knew a bit about the guns and supporting the marines because the Operations Officer had sent him to school to learn how to be a Gunfire Liaison Officer (GLO) with the marines. He had gone to that school shortly after completing the one for the DASH helicopter.

Jon figured the CO was using the HE as much to blow away some of the jungle. Then the anti-personnel rounds would have a better chance of doing their job, killing VC.

As Jon walked back to the cubicle, the guns rapped out a steady big *wham*, little *wham* cadence, as if for a peg-legged pirate. He pulled the curtain closed and explained what was going on to Zambowski and Honor. No information flowed into the cubicle, so if they wanted to understand the situation the ship was facing, one of them had to go out into Combat to find out.

When he'd been first assigned to the cubicle for GQ, Jon was convinced the Ops O had stuck him there to get him out of the way. It was the same way he felt about the helm safety position. And, he had wondered the same things about the schools he had been sent to. Because of the schools, he had missed half of the at-sea training prior to the deployment. The Gunfire Liaison Officer job, it was

Jon's understanding that he'd probably never do that mission. The marines generally took care of that business themselves, as they were doing this morning.

It didn't matter too much. Jon intended to leave the navy as soon as he had served out his obligation for the college program they had given him. And it was clear that the Ops O didn't expect anything from him. Every time he had a session with his boss, he read nothing but disappointment on his face and in what he said. Still, he was trying to give the navy its money's worth. His pop said, "Make sure you give any employer you ever have his money's worth" Jon disagreed with his pop about a number of things, but that one felt right.

An ensign did not make a lot of money, but there was enough for a furnished apartment for Teresa and him and Jennifer, for the car payment, and there was a little leftover each month. It was the first time he'd ever felt like he, they, had enough money, and he felt grateful to the navy for that.

After he finished the update, Zambowski, Honor, and Jon reviewed signal parameters of the most likely threats they might encounter when they got up into the northern Tonkin Gulf. They would be assigned to the North SAR Station, roughly latitude twenty north and halfway between North Vietnam and Hainan Island. But first, they had to complete ten days of gunfire support missions along the coast of South Vietnam. Up north, they expected MiGs and PT boats to constitute the biggest threat. Watching for land-based radars was also important.

After the extra jolt of adrenaline from the first GQ in the combat zone, it quickly devolved into an evolution much like training back in the States, at least for the threesome in the electronics-warning cubicle. They were off the coast of South Vietnam, so there wouldn't be any threat radars to pick up, and in the cubicle, they weren't involved in firing the guns. They could have slept for all anyone cared, though getting caught sleeping at your GQ post would not be good. One of the correspondence courses Jon had taken was on the military justice system. Sleeping on watch or at a GQ post would be dereliction of duty. For Zambowski and Honor, they would go to Captain's Mast and get the maximum punishment. Jon, being an officer, would be court-martialed and thrown out of the navy. So, they stayed awake and did training.

As GQs go, this one was short. Jon was back in the Ensign Locker at 0339. Cowboy and Dormant were already there.

Cowboy, as usual, was speaking. "I tell you, Dormant, my man, the marines said they got four of the gomers in their ambush, but I bet we smoked a dozen more with the rounds we fired."

Dormant was five feet, five inches and weighed about 130 pounds. He had black hair that he never seemed to comb, his uniforms always had a lot of miles on them before he put them in the laundry, and he had brown eyes that Jon had never seen flash fire before.

"Neanderthal. They're not gomers. They're people, and we shouldn't be here. We sure as hell shouldn't be killing them." Dormant spewed his words on rapid fire.

Dormant was near the head of his bunk, and he pushed by Cowboy and Jon and entered the head.

"Commie pinko." Cowboy said as he checked his watch. "Jesus, gotta relieve the Gun Boss in the fire control director."

As soon as Cowboy rattled his way up the ladder to the main deck, the ladder rattled again. That would be Dormant on the way to take over the JOOD watch on the bridge.

It was 1 June, so Jon had known Dormant for about five months. In that time, he'd never heard him get fired up about any issue, except for the two times he'd called Cowboy a Neanderthal. He hardly spoke at all, but of course, everybody fought to get a word in edgewise with Cowboy in the room.

The sudden silence in the Ensign Locker had weight. It felt like being on the bottom of a ten-foot-deep swimming pool with the water pushing on him all over. Jon thought about going back to Teresa's letter, but Almost and Admiral Ensign would be coming down from watch in fifteen minutes. He climbed up into his bunk and went to sleep.

Andrew Dunston and Jon had the 0800 to 1200 bridge watch. During the turnover with Peter Feldman and Dormant, the marines called on the radio, which was broadcast over a speaker. They credited *Manfred* with three KIA from the early morning fire mission.

Jon looked at Dormant to see how he took the news. Dormant's face showed no sign of agitation or upset.

During the first ninety minutes of the bridge-watch, nothing much happened. The ship steamed back and forth seven miles off the coast at ten knots. There no calls for more gunfire support from the marines. The marine unit was still conducting its operation. *Manfred* was still on call.

On the bridge, Andrew let Jon have the conn most of the time, and he enjoyed driving the ship more than anything else he did aboard the ship. Maneuvering while they were in formation with other navy ships was what he really enjoyed. Independent steaming was kind of boring, although there was something to be said for the absence of adult supervision, like the commodore, other than what they have on the ship, of course.

At 0950, Jon had just reversed course to the southeast when, "*Manfred,* this is Hotel, fire mission, over," crackled from a speaker in the pilothouse. Hotel was the call sign of the marine patrol.

A shot of adrenaline pulsed into Jon's system, followed immediately by a heaping dose of disappointment. They'd be going to GQ for the mission, and Jon would be stuck in the cubicle again while the GQ team fired the guns. He stepped inside the pilothouse. Andrew had the phone to the Combat Evaluator, Lieutenant Ralph Timmons, the Gun Boss, to his ear. He hung that phone up, pulled out the adjacent phone, and gave the little buzzer lever a double tweak to ring the CO.

"Cap'n, OOD," Andrew said. "We just got a fire mission from the marine patrol. They chased four to six VC into a building on the edge of a village and are taking fire from the building. They want us to take the building under fire. I recommend going to GQ, sir."

Andrew listened to the CO for a moment, and then he hung up that phone and picked up the Evaluator phone and said, "Gun Boss,

CO says we are to fire this mission from our three-section watch. He will be up in a second."

Andrew hung up the phone.

Jon said, "We stay here on watch? On the bridge? While we shoot the guns?"

9

Stay on the bridge. While they fired the guns. That was a shot of GQ alarm juice directly to Jon's heart.

"Zachery," the OOD said. "Put us two miles off the beach. Flank speed."

"Engines ahead flank—uh, belay that," Jon said. "Phone talker, ask Combat for a course and speed recommendation to firing position."

Jon hurried over to the navigation table, checked the chart, and said, "Chart looks like good water and no obstacles to the south, do you agree, Quartermaster?"

"Looks good, sir," he said.

Jon walked back out onto the starboard bridge wing.

"Engines ahead flank, indicate turns for twenty-five knots." Orders to the helm and the engine order telegraph operator were always spoken loudly and clearly. "Right full rudder, steady on course one-eight-zero." Then, you always listened to ensure they repeated the orders back just the way you'd issued them.

"Combat recommends two-zero-zero at twenty-five knots," the phone talker called from in the pilothouse.

After he ordered the helmsman to take the new course, Jon looked inside the pilothouse and saw the CO standing behind the helmsman. The CO, *The Thinker.* Most often, he saw that in the CO when he sat in his chair. Now, even standing, he reminded Jon of the statue.

The ship heeled into the turn, and the deck thrummed with vibration from the energy of the propellers thrashing the sea. It would have been immature to smile, so Jon managed to clamp control over his face, but inside, his spirit danced a giddy jig.

The CO and Andrew stepped out onto the bridge wing, and Jon moved out of their way.

The CO said, "Andrew, I'm going to be in Combat during the firing mission. Send the messenger down and get the Ops O up. Tell him to come see me in Combat, please."

Andrew relayed the CO's order to the Boatswain Mate of the Watch, and then he said to the CO, "Gun Boss says our target is a two-story villa, the northernmost one in a row of five villas. The villas have red tile roofs, and they are just behind a wide stretch of beach." Andrew held his binoculars out to the CO. "You want to check it out, Skipper?"

"No," the CO said. "I'm going to Combat."

If Jon had been asleep when the ship accelerated, he knew the sound and vibration would have awakened him. He suspected most of the crew would have reacted the same way, especially when everyone knew they'd just entered the combat zone. The Ops O was different, though. On a good night, he got two hours of sleep. When he was awake, he never looked fatigued. But when he slept, only mummies slept more deeply. Half of the time, he slept through the GQ alarm. The sailors who stood messenger watches on the bridge were used to waking him, and generally, there was an unspoken contest between the Ops O and the messengers. Once, the Ops O had fallen into bed with his uniform still on. When the messenger awakened him, the Ops O got up, stuffed his feet into his shoes, tore out the door of his room ahead of the messenger, and he beat the messenger back up to the bridge. Now, the messengers were all determined to beat the Ops O to the bridge.

From inside the pilothouse, the phone talker called, "OOD, Combat recommends a firing course of one-two-zero, speed fifteen knots, in ten minutes."

Four minutes before it was time to turn and slow, the Ops O walked onto the starboard bridge wing. Andrew and I were both there looking at the target villa with binoculars.

"Andrew," the Ops O said, "the CO wants me out here to advise you. If you want advice, that is, but it is your show. You are the OOD. So do you have any questions, and are you comfortable with this situation?"

"I'm good with the situation, Ops O," Andrew said. "But, I'm glad to have you out here. Take my binoculars, and I'll get you on the target. See the row of five white, two-story villas with the red-tile roofs? Our target is the rightmost one. Four to six VC ran into the villa ahead of our patrol, and they are firing at the marines."

"Got 'em," the Ops O said. "Nice looking houses. Shame to have to blow even one of them up."

"The other thing, Ops O," Andrew said. "There is a village just behind the villas that we can't see. The marines don't want us to lob any rounds long."

As the Ops O and Andrew talked, the wind whistled past the bridge wing, and from the signal bridge above, signal flag halyards rattled against the aluminum forward mast making martial music. The day before, from inside Combat, Jon had thought they were like Yosemite Sam running in toward the beach, both gun mounts firing salvos. This wasn't like a cartoon at all. And despite Jon's first inclination to go directly to flank speed without first checking the chart for navigation hazards, *Manfred* wasn't charging into the beach based on some hair-triggered impulse. It was actually a proud, professional thing they were doing.

Jon thought, for an instant, of how it had been when he'd been enlisted. Then, he never knew what the ship was doing when they were at GQ. Now, not only did he know, but he and Andrew were in charge.

Zachery! Get your head out of your butt! That voice in his head sounded like Chief Irons. This time he was right to chastise.

"OOD," the phone talker called. "Combat recommends coming to firing course and speed."

"Do it, Jon," Andrew said.

"Engines ahead standard. Indicate turns for fifteen knots. Left five degrees rudder. Steady on one-two-zero." Jon was sure the excitement in his voice was clear to the Ops O and Andrew.

As the ship slowed, Jon increased the rudder. He was pleased with himself. He had managed the turn without causing much of a heel. The Ops O and Andrew exchanged a look that just might have been approval of how he had handled the rudder.

Probably wishful thinking.

The closer they got, the nicer the target villa looked. Not quite a Cliff Walk mansion, like those in Newport where he'd gone to Officer Candidate School, but a very nice house. Two stories and the red tile roof was a mansard style.

Jon agreed with the Ops O: It was a shame to have to blow the place up.

The phone talker called, "Combat says we will commence firing in thirty seconds, with bridge concurrence."

"Combat, bridge," Andrew said for the phone talker to relay to Combat, "we are visually clear to the target. Bridge concurs with commencing fire."

The after gun, mount 52, would be doing the firing. The CO wanted the after mount manned for three-section watches. In many situations, he believed, if you encountered a threat unexpectedly, the ship would turn and run at high speed away from the threat, and thus the forward mount would be masked.

Wham. The after mount fired one gun. Even though he was expecting it, it startled Jon. It was so much louder than the muffled sound that reached his GQ station cubicle. He watched the light orange-brown smoke from the gun carry in toward the beach on the morning on-shore breeze. Even with the wind, he still got a healthy dose of gunpowder smell on the bridge wing.

"Ah, the smell of cordite in the morning! Better than any cup of coffee I ever had," the Ops O said as he raised his binoculars and looked at the target villa, where a white plume of smoke from the phosphorus marking round rose from the beach in front of the villa.

"Nice shooting," came from the speaker in the pilothouse set on the radio frequency being used by Combat and the marines. "Add fifty, and fire two rounds of HE."

The first rounds had been on line with the target but fifty yards short. The marines now wanted two rounds of high explosive shells. Jon thought about the village behind the villa and said a silent prayer that they wouldn't fire long. With a *wham*, the two-gun salvo generated a smoke ring that rolled toward the beach expanding and then shredding and dissipating. Through the binoculars, he saw smoke and debris fly up from the roof of the villa. An urge to cheer welled up out of his belly, but he stifled it. But Lord, it felt good to be out there on the bridge wing and not stuck in Combat.

That gusher of excitement surprised Jon. But being on the bridge and seeing and hearing and feeling and smelling the guns fire, man! You could even taste it: the Ops O's cordite caffeine substitute. A small twinge of guilt finagled its way into Jon's head over deriving joy from destruction and maybe death.

"Ten rounds, HE, fire for effect," came over the radio.

At the next two-round salvo, a smoke ring formed again and started rolling toward the beach. The next salvo fired through the smoke ring. A clatter came from the fantail as the powder canisters were discarded out the rear of the gun mount onto the deck. After the last salvo, Jon looked at the target house through the binoculars again. Half the red tile roof was missing, as was a goodly section of the second story. Brown and white smoke rose from and obscured the structure. The last salvo struck and threw up a fresh cloud of debris and smoke.

"Cease fire, and nice shooting, *Manfred*," came over the bridge speaker. "You destroyed the target. But, we'd like you to hang close."

At the recommendation of Combat, Jon ordered a course reversal to keep *Manfred* close to the firing bearing they had used. Halfway through the turn, the Ops O, Andrew, and Jon trooped through the pilothouse to the other bridge wing. All three checked the target villa through binoculars.

Jon waited until the Ops O lowered his binoculars and then said, "Why didn't the Skipper want us to go to GQ to do this mission?"

The Ops O handed his binocs to the lookout and said, "This day started back in January. The Skipper has been training us for this ever since. Then, after we did the gunfire mission this morning, he told us he was going to have us do a mission from the three-section watch, but that he wanted a point target to do it."

"But wasn't he taking a risk? Firing into a village, I mean, where we want to avoid hitting the other buildings. Wouldn't it have been better to do this kind of thing when we were just firing out into the jungle, like on those first missions?"

"Well," the Ops O said, and Jon was surprised. He didn't see disappointment on his boss's face. "There is always some risk associated with firing in support of troops. In this case, the Skipper has the Gun Boss as the Evaluator in Combat, and Edgar Chalmers was in the gun director. Edgar got a lot of training to do the job while you were goofing off in your schools."

Was the Ops O joking with him?

Then he continued, "A lot of destroyer COs would have gone to GQ in this situation, but our Skipper believes, strongly, that all three sections need to be prepared to fight the ship. And, he, himself, is in Combat. He trained us, and he showed this part of the watch bill that it was ready and able to do the business at hand."

The Ops O turned and shouted, "Sigs," and immediately, a sailor appeared at the railing around the signal bridge above us.

"You guys see anything through your big binoculars?" the Ops O said.

"Can't see anything but smoke right now, sir. But, the gunners really blew the hell out that place."

The Ops O nodded and told Andrew he was going to Combat.

About two minutes later, the CO and the Ops O came back onto the bridge. The CO told Jon to pass the conn to Andrew and come with him to the other bridge wing. When he got there, the CO stood with his hands clasped behind him and he stared straight ahead as *Manfred* drove into a wind that had kicked up to about twelve knots, just strong enough to rip the tops off the small waves.

What did I do to warrant some personal attention from the CO?

The CO turned. "Just before I entered the bridge, I heard you say, 'Belay my last.' What did you belay?"

"Captain, Andrew had just told me to get us in to two miles, so I had ordered flank speed and started a turn toward the beach. I thought it might be important to get in there quickly to support the marines. But then I thought we wouldn't help anyone if we hit a reef or something. So I stopped, looked at the chart, got recommendations from the quartermaster as well as from Combat."

"Did you know I was on the bridge, and did that have any bearing on what you did?"

"I didn't know you were on the bridge until later, sir. But, I really don't think it would have made any difference. After my first thought, it occurred to me that Combat would have a good handle on where the target was, so it seemed like a good idea to get them involved in the business."

Jon had seen it happen before. The CO looked like he was going to smile, then he'd rub his hand over his mouth, and his poker-player-*Thinker* face would remain undisturbed.

"Are you happy with how you handled things, getting the ship in to two miles?"

"No, sir. I was pretty close to just responding to a situation without really thinking first. And, I don't think it took more than fifty-three seconds to check the chart and do it right."

"Fifty-three seconds?"

"Pretty close, sir."

This time the left corner of his mouth curled up into a hint of a smile. Then he walked back into the pilothouse. *I didn't get chewed out!* And, the CO had smiled, sort of. There were times when it seemed as if being a newbie involved trying to claw your way out of a deep hole in sandy soil. You scale the side of the pit a certain distance, then it gives way, and you tumble to the bottom again. Always before, when Jon talked with the CO, or the Ops O, the rim of the newbie-pit seemed unreachable. But now, after this little session with the CO, he felt as if he had gotten one leg over the rim of the newbie-pit. It was almost ensign hog heaven.

The rest of the watch ticked away with no more calls for fire. Just before Jon and Andrew were relieved on the bridge, the marines credited *Manfred* with five VC KIA.

When Andrew and Jon arrived in the wardroom, there were still ten officers there; only the five on watch were missing. The air around the table was decidedly upbeat. It was almost like back home when Jon was little, and the Cardinals had had a good season and might be going to the World Series. Then, the Cardinals were the talk of St. Ambrose in all the hangouts: the grocery stores, the post office, the grain mill where Jon's Pop worked, the American Legion Post where kids could put nickels in the jukebox, and Walter's Tavern backroom, where boys could play pool if the table weren't occupied by a beer drinker.

In the *Manfred* wardroom, the upbeat mood was from the morning fire mission and the five KIA, probably, but also from Cowboy. Cowboy had not been on watch during the fire mission, but he had watched much of it through the big binoculars on the signal bridge. Now he had the entire wardroom enthralled as he ambled out his description of the mission. Even the Skipper paid attention to him.

"You kin even see the shell leave the muzzle, if you're lookin' gist right." He looked around to see if he still had everyone's attention. "Not ever time, a'course. But sometimes you see that black hunka' commie death shootin' outa there…"

Jon looked at Andrew. He seemed to have slipped into the mood easily and naturally. Jon was bothered some. During the fire mission the day before, he had been in his GQ cubicle. He had had nothing to do with firing the guns. That's what he'd thought. But this morning, he and Andrew had the bridge watch. The two of them had been responsible for the ship and what it did.

Andrew and I had killed those five people.

Andrew didn't seem to be bothered by that thought, but Jon was. Now. When the action had been happening, he'd been so pleased to be out there on the bridge, to smell the gunpowder, and to see debris thrown up by our shells hitting the target. Jon didn't know what to do with the notion. It didn't seem like a sin that he had to confess. But it bothered him like one.

Jon had gotten a fair amount of practice at inhaling meals, and he was never the last one still eating. But that day, he was. After the others left, he sat for a moment over his plate, then pushed it away with the meal half-eaten—that was something he didn't do very often, either.

When Jon opened the door to the Locker, Dormant was at the fold-down desk, and Cowboy was in his bunk, a paperback book open in front of his face. Neither of them looked at him.

"Excuse me, Dormant. Can I scoot by you, please?"

Dormant flashed a hostile face up at him; then, he went back to what looked like a letter he was writing.

"You mad at me, Dormant?"

"You're just like all the rest. We kill five Vietnamese, when we have no business being here, much less killing innocent people, and you all act like we are at a high school football game. You're disgusting."

Dormant ripped the top sheet off the tablet, stood up, and slammed the desk lid closed. "The whole wardroom is a bunch of amoral troglodytes." Dormant pushed by Jon and slammed the door to the Locker closed behind him.

"You know what a troglodyte is, Two Buckets?" Cowboy drawled.

"I think there is a connotation of primitive beast, cave dweller maybe, associated with the word. Amoral and troglodyte might be redundant."

Cowboy still had his Louis L'Amour paperback open in front of him, and he spoke to it. "Redundant I kin handle, but if I gotta listen to any more'a his anti-American commie crap, I'm gonna need one a your puke buckets."

10

Dearest Teresa

2 June 1966. 0015. Off the coast of South Vietnam, steaming south, and en route to the Saigon River.

Quite a day, yesterday. I haven't quite settled into a routine here, yet, with three-section watches, I mean. Maybe being here in the combat zone, there isn't a routine. Don't know yet.

Anyhow, we entered the combat zone at midnight yesterday and had a gunfire mission to support some marines patrolling near the coast. The marines came under attack, and we were able to help them. But we were miles off the coast, so we didn't get shot at.

Before, Jon never felt like he had to think about what to write to Teresa. And there didn't seem to be that much that he should *not* write. There was the drinking and swearing and whoring that went on around him. Teresa didn't need to read about that. But the whole day, the whole of the first of June, was full of stuff that he needed to be careful with. If Cowboy were married, he wondered what he'd put in his letter about what they'd done yesterday.

He didn't want Teresa to worry, so he didn't mention the DASH trying to kill Carl and him. *We were able to help them,* he'd written. He felt like a politician, taking a grain of truth and wrapping it in layer after layer of balderdash. And here he was, wrapping a grain of truth in balderdash and evasion.

> 1620. My letters are going to be like this, I guess. Watch from eight to twelve, morning and evening. Actually, in the morning, we go on watch an hour early so the four to eight guys can get breakfast, and we relieve them for about thirty minutes in the evening so they can grab dinner. So, the good deal watch is four to eight, but eight to twelve is still better than the mid-watch. I've not had to stand that day after day before, but Andrew and I will get our turn. I do like to stand watches with Andrew. We work together pretty well, I think, and he lets me drive the ship all the time. That makes the watch go much quicker, and it is probably the thing I like second-most. Most, of course, is getting a letter from you and writing to you. Sigh. Still some days away from getting mail.

> In a couple of hours, we will be entering the Saigon River. Be down here for at least three days, maybe a little longer. We'll be in the river each night firing H&I; that's Harassment and Interdiction. We fire a number of rounds into the jungle throughout the night, just to keep the VC from using an area with impunity.

During the day, we leave the river and patrol along the coast, looking for the VC trying to smuggle arms and ammo into the country by boat. That's what the ship will be doing, and the watch schedule will drive my life.

The special sea detail was called away, and Jon assumed his safety observer position. Ahead, out through the bridge windows, Jon saw the mouth of the river sliced through tall jungle to both sides.

Compared to when they had left port in the PI, there was a lack of volume in the voices on the bridge. The CO sat in his chair. The XO stood by the chair to port.

Besides being at special sea detail, the ship was GQ plus some. The two fifty-caliber machine guns were manned on the 01 level amidships; both five-inch gun mounts were manned, and, on the 01 level, three-man teams armed with small arms had been stationed forward, amidships on the 01 level, and aft on the helo deck.

A tingle of dancing bug feet started up on the back of Jon's neck. The five-inch guns, the machine guns, and the small arms, all that together, did not seem like enough.

Then, they were in the river with the walls of the green jungle to both sides. Thick jungle. Capable of hiding hordes of Viet Cong. Jon had to continuously force himself to look at the compass to check on the helmsman, but he paid attention to his job better than Jon did to his responsibility.

When the anchor chain rattled out the hawse pipe, it seemed so loud. *The VC will hear!* Logically, worrying about a little noise at that point was wasted effort, but logic and illogical worry seemed to get along just fine in simultaneous occupation of Jon's brain since neither seemed to influence or bother the other at all.

The special sea and anchor detail stayed on station for a time to make sure the anchor wasn't dragging; then the three-section watch bill went into effect, with the machine guns and small-arms teams added.

It was almost dark when Andrew and Jon assumed the watch.

On the bridge, everyone spoke in hushed voices. There was no idle chitchat. Everyone probed the darkness with ears as well as eyes, though the ubiquitous drone of ventilation fans would mask everything—except gunfire.

The ship's mission was to provide H&I fire into the Rung Sat, an area southeast of Saigon that had been infested with both Viet Cong and North Vietnamese regulars until just after the first of the year. Since January, a number of operations comprised of strong, combined US and South Vietnamese ground, river-borne amphibious, and air forces had decimated the enemy strength in the Rung Sat. The H&I fire was just one of the ongoing operations intended to prevent the re-establishment of the Rung Sat as a VC sanctuary.

Manfred sat quietly in the dark channel with all external lights extinguished. In addition to the extra armament, Engineering was ready to get the ship underway quickly. The Deck Department was also prepared to haul in the anchor or, if urgency required, to sever the chain and leave the anchor.

Before the ship commenced H&I firing, a PBR—Patrol Boat, River—was supposed to deliver two officers from the boat unit to coordinate *Manfred* operations with one of theirs.

At 2135, the PBR glided out of the darkness and passed down the port side to the fantail. The boat engine whispered its grumble in idle, but it sounded like a stage whisper, or even a shout, in the heavy-dark stillness on the river. Boatswain mates were there on the fantail with fenders to cushion the side of the PBR, and they quickly hauled two passengers from the boat up onto the deck. The PBR then pulled away from the side and quickly disappeared into the darkness downriver.

"Those two guys who came aboard," Jon said to Andrew, "Do you know what they're doing here?"

"Yes. I was in Combat when the Ops O was briefing the Gun Boss during the CIC Evaluator watch turnover," Andrew said. "Ops O said we'd be getting a navy lieutenant and a warrant officer from the river boat unit that works this area. The SEALS are conducting an op, close to where we'll be firing. So, the PBR guys will be here monitoring things, and if we have to help the SEALS out, the lieutenant and the warrant will coordinate that effort. The PBR guys are briefing everybody not on watch in the wardroom. Then we start the H&I firing at 2200. That's what I know."

The riverbanks, which had seemed so threatening in the late afternoon, were out there somewhere, invisible in the impenetrable, moonless blackness. In the pilothouse, everyone spoke in whispers, as if trying to compensate for the noise the PBR had made. To Jon, the PBR noise had seemed like a shout: "Hey, Viet Cong, if you are looking for USS *Manfred*, here we are."

"OOD, Combat says standby for the first rounds in one minute," the phone talker called.

The *wham* from mount 51 was like the loudest sound in the world. The white flash lit up the bow and a patch of grayish-brownish river water. For an instant, the flash lay like a white oil slick on the lighted patch of water. There was a rattle as the empty powder canisters were discarded onto the deck behind the gun mount. There was a second salvo and flash, and, for an instant, the shore to the starboard was visible. The ensuing quiet hissed in Jon's ears, and yellow and white fire filled his eyes. It seemed to take forever for his vision to return. The ship was scheduled to fire ten rounds each hour, randomly spaced. Before the next rounds went out, they shielded their eyes. That didn't totally save night vision, but it helped.

After the mid-watch took over on the bridge, Jon went below, took a quick shower, climbed up into his bunk, and got out his letter-writing material.

Dearest Teresa, 3 June 0009

From the Saigon River. Almost a week since we left the PI, and it will be a couple of days before we get back up north around Da Nang. That will be the first time we can expect mail. Andrew Dunston told me that when we get up to North SAR, the mail service will be much better, but for now, it is going to be tough.

There wasn't much mail—

Wham. The forward gun mount was just a little forward of the Locker, and it was loud. Then the powder canisters rattled on the deck. With the *wham*, Jon's pen had made a tail on the L on *mail.* The guns fired again.

> I guess we are in the war now. The Skipper has been talking about this since January, but I'm not sure it felt real to me until we pulled into the mouth of the Saigon River this afternoon. Up north, when we did the gunfire support for the marines, that was real, but not like now. Now we are sitting at anchor and firing shells off into the jungle. But it is a distinctly uncomfortable feeling, knowing the jungle is so close on both sides of the ship and that a lot of enemy soldiers could be there, and we wouldn't know it until they started shooting at us. It's not like being two miles off the coast—

Jon stopped writing. *Not something I really want to send to Teresa.* The letter he'd written about killing the VC, he hadn't included gory details. He'd worried about the balderdash and evasion. No, he thought. He shouldn't have mailed that letter at all. It was in the post office and would go out at the first opportunity. Jon crumpled the sheet of stationery and started over again.

Dearest Teres…

Wham. That time he appended a tail on the S. He put his stationery back on the angle iron and picked up his book, *The Age of Louis XIV.*

Jon paged to the Dear Reader note in the front. "The pervading theme is the Great Debate between faith and reason." When he'd first started the volume, that sentence had stopped him. Now every time he picked up the book, before finding his bookmark, he reread the note. The authors, the Durants, seemed to be saying that faith was the enemy of reason. At Mass last Sunday in Subic, the priest, in his homily, seemed to say reason was the enemy of faith. Jon was pretty sure he had the ability to reason, and he was sure he had faith. The two shouldn't be enemies; it seemed to him. The two should be able to coexist. They had to be able to coexist, didn't they?

His bookmark was on page 553, in a section on English philosophy. He'd read the section before, dog-eared pages, and underlined passages. He started reading again, but he closed it, put on his uniform, and went up to the wardroom to get a cup of coffee.

A warrant officer, one of the PBR guys, sat at mid-table on the aft side, a coffee cup in front of him. He looked like a linebacker, and he was probably in his thirties. Brown predator eyes peered out from under thick eyebrows and followed Jon. He had dark-brown hair in a crew cut and a slab-sided face topping a thick neck and a hard-looking set of shoulders.

"Okay if I join you, uh, WO?" Jon said, almost addressing the question to "sir."

"Sure. But this is your wardroom," the WO said. "I'm just a guest here."

"I was on the bridge when you guys came aboard and didn't get to attend your brief." Jon started filling his cup as three more salvos were fired. "So, WO, is this a big operation?"

The warrant officer regarded Jon for an uncomfortably long time. The only sound was the trickle of coffee into his cup. And the ventilation blowers. They never shut up.

"So, what's your name, Ensign?"

"Well, si—. WO, I'm Jon Zachery." Jon pulled out the chair across from him. "On *Manfred*, I'm Two Buckets. It's a nickname, a thing we do on the ship."

"Okay, Ensign Two Buckets," the warrant officer said. "I'm George Parker, and no, it's not a big operation. We had a big op back in January. And we did well. Now, we're trying to get the South Viets to take over, and all we're doing tonight is to send in a SEAL team to grab some guys for our *Intel* pukes to interrogate. And we are out here, the LT and me, as backup. We hope the SEALs are covered by an army helo gunship, but the army only has a couple of guys who fly at night. So, if our SEALS run into trouble, we want to be able to get your ship's guns to help cover the extraction."

"It sounds like maybe you admire the VC more than you do the South Vietnamese," Jon said.

"The gomers are tough, ruthless, live on a handful of rice, get as much of their weaponry from us as they do from North Vietnam, and they all think they have already died for their country. I don't admire them, but I sure as hell respect them."

"Are you saying we can't beat them, WO?"

Parker looked at Jon for a moment. "Are you trying to pick a fight with me?"

"No, WO. That doesn't appeal to me at all. I'd just like to understand what's going on here."

Jon was sure the warrant was deciding whether to bother with Ensign Two Buckets.

After a moment, he said, "They are not unbeatable. We beat them in January. They are tough, but there's a lot we can do as long as we don't underestimate the problem they represent. The area we are working tonight, actually, was a real VC and North Vietnamese stronghold. In January, we destroyed their sanctuary, and now we're trying to keep them from turning it back into one. But we don't own the area. We really don't own much of South Vietnam outside our bases and the cities. I think it is pretty much that way from here clear up to the DMZ.

"The way it is right now, it's kind of like trying to hold back a big puddle of mercury with a broom. As soon as you stop sweeping, the mercury comes back. We do have a good connection with a village chief south and west of here a bit. The guy says his is one of a very few villages in the whole area where the people think they are safe. One of our big failures in this war, so far, is we haven't been able to protect the people in the villages. We go in and do search and destroy missions, we patrol the rivers and catch sampans with supplies and kill a few VC, but I think more supplies are getting through than we are catching. And the VC we kill, they make up for with local recruits and with North Vietnamese. In the villages, for the most part, we can go in and exert a little influence, but as soon as we go back to base, the VC come right back. The people are just really crapped on by both sides. If a village headman doesn't march to the VC tune, the VC mort him; then they put someone in who does toe the party line. When we go in and seize rice and other stuff we consider to be contraband, I wonder if we hurt the VC as much as we hurt the villagers."

"Get you a fresh cup of coffee, WO," Jon said as he stood and went back to the urn.

"I'm good."

Jon sat back down.

"So, WO, you said we could beat them, but you keep making it sound hopeless. Why are you here? Yours is a volunteer job, isn't it?"

"It's not hopeless," George said. "I'm saying there are some things we're not doing well right now, and we have to get better at them. As to why I'm here, I read a speech President Kennedy gave some five years ago. He talked about the cold war and said our way of life was under attack, although we were not in a declared war. He said that we are opposed by a strong, determined enemy who uses intimidation and terror instead of elections. Yeah, I volunteered because I thought it was the right thing to do. JFK really seems to have called exactly the situation we are facing.

"And I want to be here because of the village chief next to our base. He is a good guy. He talks about his province chief, and he says the province chief is a good guy. His province chief is a Catholic and left North Vietnam after 1954 and was able to get a position because President Diem was also Catholic. Our village chief and the province chief both think things are maximally screwed up right now with the Buddhists going berserk from Hue to Saigon. Some of the things that were starting in some positive directions have started going backwards now while the government fights the Buddhists. And there doesn't seem to be a leader anywhere in the south who can pull this thing together. But our village chief and the province chief, they have nowhere else to run to. So, I like these guys. They are worth fighting for."

The Warrant drained the last of his coffee. "So, Ensign Two Buckets, what's your story?"

"Well, uh, I really don't have a story. I owe the navy obligated service for the schooling they gave me. That's my story."

Warrant Officer Parker looked at Jon for a moment; then, he got up, put his coffee cup on the counter under the window to the galley, and walked out of the wardroom without looking back. He left Jon with something very much like shame working unpleasant things in his stomach.

Two more salvos were fired. Jon put his coffee cup next to the warrant officer's and walked out onto the port-side weatherdeck.. Off in the distance, streams of red tracers arced from the sky toward the ground. As the red tracers died out, green tracers arced up from the ground into the sky around where the red tracers had originated. Red tracers arced down. Green tracers arced up. Red down. Green up. Red down. Green up. Red down. Then, the eerily silent fireworks show ceased.

Back in the Ensign Locker, Dormant was sleeping on his back, and Cowboy was on his side with his pillow held over his ear with his arm. They would have to get up for the 0400 to 0700 watch in less than two hours.

Jon climbed onto his bunk and got a new start on a letter to Teresa. He couldn't go to sleep until he at least got a start on one he could send to her.

11

Sleep is overrated. Ops O says that all the time, and most of the time, Jon didn't disagree with it. But he spent a long time writing to Teresa after he left WO Parker, and that morning, he was dragging. But thinking about how the WO had looked at him made him sweat.

Jon stood at his special sea detail safety observer position. It was still dark out. The ship faced upstream. He walked out onto the starboard bridge wing and looked aft. The sun was yawning and stretching below the horizon.

Back inside the pilothouse, in the dim red night lights, Jon saw the Ops O by the CO, in his chair, now.

"Did you talk to the PBR officers before they left, Ops O?" the CO said.

"Yes, sir. They were happy. They got army helicopter cover for their operation, and apparently, they needed it."

The green and red tracer light show. So far, when they had fired their guns, no one had fired back at them. Jon wondered if that state of affairs would hold.

"We're supposed to get boats to sweep for mines ahead of as we leave the river. Any sign of them?" the CO asked.

"Yes, sir. Three boats are coming. Combat has been talking with the lead boat. They are sweeping as they come upriver. We can haul up the anchor as soon as the Gun Boss is ready. By the time we spin around, the boats should be up to us. Then they'll just turn and head back and sweep in front of us."

"Okay, Ops O. Thanks." In the dim red light, the CO was just a shadow. The shadow CO looked out the bridge window.

The bridge crew settled into the process of completing the items on the checklist for getting underway. As Jon listened to reports coming in from the other departments, it didn't seem right that everything sounded so normal, like they were getting underway from San Diego.

In short order, the anchor was hauled up, the ship spun about in the river, and followed the boats, one of them a minesweeper, downriver. Nobody shot at *Manfred*, the minesweeper didn't find anything in their path, and at 0655, they cleared the river mouth. Jon didn't know if anyone else breathed a little easier, but he did. The bosun announced, "Secure the special sea detail. Set the regular underway watch."

Jon and Andrew Dunston assumed the bridge watch with the ship steaming east-southeast at fifteen knots. The ship would patrol ten miles off the coast the rest of the day. Before dark, they'd be back in the river for more H&I. That was the plan.

At 0725, Jon had the conn. He stood in the center of the pilothouse looking out the forward bridge windows. There wasn't a wisp of cloud in the sky, but just above the horizon, the blue was watered down a bit with a light gray haze. His brain buzzed with fatigue, and it was filled with blurry stuff, sort of like that haze.

Chief Fargo, Jon's division chief petty officer, came around the engine order telegraph, stood next to him, and said, "Sir, I have to talk to you."

"Chief, I'll be off at noon. Can't it wait?"

"Sir, this'll just take a minute, but I gotta tell you something." The look on his face told Jon that, too.

Andrew bent over the navigation chart on the starboard side. Jon nodded toward the port bridge wing. Watch standers were supposed to have their attention on driving the ship and not doing administrative duties on the bridge. But, the chief looked upset.

As soon as he stepped onto the bridge wing, he said, "Sir, last night, about 0200, the Ops O was walking aft toward his stateroom, and he saw lights shining out from under the door of the Electronics Technician shop. So, he stopped to see what was going on. He wondered if some equipment was broken, and I guess he was just going to say hello to the troops. He opened the door, and he found three of the guys sitting there with soda and a bottle of Jim Beam. They are going to XO's inquiry this morning at 0900."

"A bottle of whiskey, aboard ship? Who was it? What the hell were they thinking?"

"Sir, it was Zambowski and the two seamen. One of the seamen, I think it was Honor, snuck the bottle aboard in Subic. But, I don't know for sure yet. I just found out this happened, and I wanted to let you know, and that XO's inquiry is going down at 0900."

"Judas Priest!" Jon said. "Zambowski! Can't believe he'd do something so utterly stupid."

Jon did not hear the Boatswain Mate announce that the CO had entered the bridge. The CO had been in CIC and had come out to the bridge to tell the OOD that he wanted the speed increased to twenty-five knots. He wanted the navigator called and a new course laid out. A Coast Guard Cutter had intercepted a large cargo vessel unloading supplies fifty-five miles to the southwest. The cutter had attempted to board the vessel to inspect the cargo, and the vessel had opened fire with small arms. The cutter returned fire, but the cargo vessel had run itself aground near the shore. As the cutter was approaching the grounded vessel, the cutter came under heavy fire from the beach. *Manfred* was ordered to the scene at the best possible speed.

Jon did not hear Andrew call his name. Andrew had called it

twice, he learned later. Jon did hear, "This is Mr. Dunston, I have the conn. All Engines ahead flank. Indicate turns for twenty-five knots."

Jon stepped inside the pilothouse. The CO was standing just behind the helmsman, and he saw his eyes move beside him, to where the chief was standing. A frown blinked onto the CO's face; then anger blinked on; then his lips compressed into a thin line.

"Mr. Zachery, what part of no administrative duties up here on the bridge do you not understand?" The CO's jaw muscles worked as if he were chewing some distasteful medicine. "Get the hell off my bridge. You are confined to quarters until further notice. Mr. Dunston, get Fred Watson up here to fill in on the watch bill."

Jon saluted the CO, and he said, "Just get the hell outta here." He turned away, walked over to his chair, and climbed up onto it.

In the passageway aft of the pilothouse Chief Fargo said, "Sir, I'm really sorry. I didn't want to get you in the crapper. I'll go to the Ops O and tell him it was my fault."

Jon had been worried about Zambowski, the two seamen, and the Chief. In an instant, he had become the one who was in trouble. The chief looked at Jon with pitiful eyes stuck in a face slathered with chagrin.

Jon shook his head. "Not your fault, Chief. It was my fault. I knew what the orders were, and I'm the one who disobeyed them. It won't do any good to go to the Ops O. The most important thing is, I have to figure out what being confined to quarters means. I'll stop by and talk to the XO on the way to the Ensign Locker; then I'll let you know. Maybe I can still go to his inquiry on Zambowski and the seamen."

Following the chief down the ladders, with each step, another dose of realization dumped ugly, seasickness-like stuff into the pit of Jon's stomach. Nothing that had happened to him on *Manfred* before today had been as bad as being on his first ship and under the thumb of his first chief, Chief Irons. Now Jon had a new benchmark for how bad things could be, and this time, there was only himself to blame.

The door to the XO's cabin was open, and he was on the phone. After he hung up, Jon knocked on the bulkhead next to the door.

The XO looked up at him and shook his head.

"Ensign Zachery," the XO said. "I don't know how you can walk. You have stepped in a bucket of crap with each one of your feet. Skipper just told me about what happened on the bridge, and I just told him about this message we got from his wife through the chaplain back in San Diego. Seems you wrote Teresa about the wetting down party and some details about Charley Hanson doing the backstroke in a puddle of booze. Teresa told some of the wives about it, and it got to Charley's wife. So, she's upset. Teresa apparently also said things like we are doing nothing out here but binge drinking. So, the wives' group is all stirred up. If the Skipper could have you shot, he'd do it. Hell, he'd probably do it himself."

The XO shook his head and made a *hiss* sound.

"Sometimes, there is a lag of ten days or so between mailing a letter to when they are received. What the hell else did you tell Teresa that is going to fling more turds into the fan?"

Jon stood there with his eyes on the corner of the XO's desk. It had been seven days since he'd mailed that letter. He thought Teresa should not have shared something he'd intended only for her.

"That was not a rhetorical question. What else have you written to Teresa that is going to blow up on us?"

"I…I, uh, I don't think I've written anything else like that. I have a letter mostly written now that I was planning to drop in the mail today. I'll get it so you can see what's in this one."

"God damn it all to hell. I don't want to read your mail. I can't watch everything you write. I can't listen in if you call her from the Philippines or Hong Kong, or wherever. What we need is for you to appreciate the need for some discretion here. It can tear a wardroom apart, this kind of crap."

The XO's face was scrunched into an angry frown, and his eyes spit fire at me.

"Oh Honey, I am here being a model of good Christian behavior. I go to church on Sunday. I don't swear. I don't drink. I don't chew. But you should see the other guys. What a bunch of drunken bums! And, Teresa will be bragging about her goody-two-shoes husband out here and rubbing the other wives' noses in it."

"Teresa wouldn't do it like that, sir, and I would expect when the mail catches up, she'll be mad at me for even being there when the thing was happening."

"Now I'm having even more trouble understanding this," the XO said. "You knew you would catch crap over writing about the wetting down party, but you told her anyway?"

"Well, yes, sir. I—uh, I'm just used to telling her everything."

"Goddammit." The XO slapped his desk. "This is really depressing. Last night, we were anchored in the Saigon River, firing guns in the middle of bad guy country. This morning, we are going to see if we can help out a Coast Guard Cutter that has come under fire, and you have the CO and me worried about this kind of crap! Jesus!

"We are shooting at people, and those people can and do shoot back. The only way this ship functions is if each and every member of the crew is totally focused on his responsibilities. Each of us needs to be able to totally count on everyone else aboard. Getting another officer's wife pissed off at him, that is just not helpful in this situation.

"Now, you are confined to the Ensign Locker until further notice. You can leave the Locker to go to the head, but that is all. I will have a steward bring you a tray at mealtime. You are no longer on the watch bill and relieved of all duties, including your GQ station. Chief Fargo will take over your duties as division officer. I want you to make sure there is nothing that will make this shit storm you've created worse in the letter you are writing. Also, if there are outgoing letters waiting in the ship's post office, and you are worried about them, tell me, and I will send the postal clerk to see you. If you are worried, ask the PC to get those letters back to you. Do not tell him I told you to do this; you tell him whatever reason, but it is your reason. Clear?"

"Yes, sir."

"So, do you need the PC?" the XO asked.

"Yes, sir. I think there are two letters there, and I think I should look at them. Can I ask a question, sir?"

The XO's eyes bored into Jon. The XO had started growing a mustache when the ship left Hawaii, and normally his flaming red

Hitler-like mustache looked a little funny. This morning it did not. The XO nodded.

"I'd like to apologize to Charley, sir, and also, I would like to come to your inquiry about my guys and the drinking-aboard-ship incident."

"Stay the hell away from Charley. Stay the hell away from everyone. You are confined to quarters. You can only leave to go to the head. You are relieved of all watches, including General Quarters. Chief Fargo will come to inquiry with *his* guys. He is the acting division officer. You don't talk to anyone unless I send him to talk to you. Now get the hell out of my face, and I'll send the PC to see you."

Jon entered the Ensign Locker. Dormant and Cowboy were asleep in their bunks. Admiral Ensign was standing and buttoning his khaki shirt, and Almost was sitting on his bunk, tying his shoes.

"Two Buckets, what are you doing here?" Almost asked.

Jon told them.

Admiral Ensign and Almost stopped what they were doing and just looked at him.

Almost stood up and put his hand on Jon's shoulder. "I don't know what to say. Sorry, man." Then, he sidled past and left.

Jon stood there, just inside the door, trying to understand what had happened to him. And his sailors. How could they have screwed up like this? Zambowski had so much potential. But at XO inquiry, the XO would send all of them to Captain's Mast, or he might even send them to a court-martial. Jon wanted to be able to at least speak up for his men—but then he remembered. The XO said they were the chief's men now. Jon thought about what he'd done. He'd disobeyed a direct order—one of the more serious articles in the Uniform Code of Military Justice.

Oh Jesus, Mary, and Joseph, what have I gotten myself into now?

Then, he remembered his letters to Teresa and that those letters had gotten Charley into trouble with his wife. He'd already called on Jesus, Mary, and Joseph. So, he asked God the Father and the Holy Spirit to please help Charley and Melanie Hanson get things worked out.

The escalated energy being expended to propel Manfred through the sea at twenty-five knots was dramatically manifested in vibration and the sound of water just outside the half-inch of steel separating the Ensign Locker from the South China Sea. Jon recalled when he'd climbed inside a boiler during one of his orientation sessions, and Chief Petitte had described how the boiler functioned. In the boilers, the fires would be turning the water to steam and then heating the steam. Insulated pipes conducted the steam to the high and low-speed turbines. The turbines drove reduction gears, which dropped the RPM to something the propellers could handle. In the fire rooms and the engine rooms, all the machinery would be whining and howling with the high speeds required for pumping the fuel, the lubrication oil, and the water to sustain twenty-five knots.

The ship was rushing to do a job that needed doing. People needed help, and when they got there, everyone aboard would pitch in to help, everyone but Ensign Two Buckets.

Jon regretted letting the Skipper down; he regretted not being able to speak on behalf of his—the chief's guys; he regretted the trouble he had caused Charley and his wife, and he regretted being stuck in the Locker when there were things happening that he could not be a part of anymore. This was much worse than being stuck in the electronics warning receiver cubicle during GQ.

The ship heeled to port. Jon knew that Andrew Dunston, or the Supply Officer, Fred Watson, had just ordered, "Right ten degrees rudder." *That's not what I would have ordered.* There was no need for more than five degrees of rudder at that speed. Five degrees would not have caused the ship to heel so much. Jon pictured himself on the starboard bridge wing, the wind in his face, as the ship turned smartly to the new course. But not today, and was the Skipper thinking *not ever?*

"I've heard that the attrition rate at OCS is only about 1%. Do you think that's true, Two Buckets?" Admiral Ensign said as he pushed him back against Dormant's bunk and left the Locker. Jon had forgotten he was still there.

Jon did not get angry over his insult. The attrition rate at the

Academy, especially the first year, was high, and he was saying Jon would never have made it through the Academy. But Jon had nothing inside with which to fuel any anger, even anger directed at Admiral Ensign.

Jon pulled the chair back from the lone desk and sat. When he'd left the bridge, he'd been numb. His feet and hands moved and did things, but it was as if he had watched them as limbs attached to someone else's body. As he sat, the numbness began to retreat somewhat, like when a dentist's Novocain begins to wear off. You know, though, that it will be a while before you can feel the drool that continues to leak out of your mouth.

Jon leaned against the chair back, tilted his head back, and closed his eyes. He thought about the last five months, about trying to feel like he belonged as an officer rather than an enlisted man, thinking about never seeing approval on the Ops O's face, and thinking about his battles with seasickness. Thinking about the last five months, it was much like contemplating a tornadic trail of destruction stretching across the calendar. Things had just started to get better, but now—

And I did it all before-he looked at his watch-*0817.*

Taking up his current letter to Teresa, he read through it. He had written about the talk with George Parker extensively, and as he read his words, he thought they were more appropriate to Dormant than to him. He tore the letter to shreds and threw the bits of paper into the rusted and battered gray trashcan next to the desk.

12

The postal clerk, PO3 Smeltzer, had been very reluctant to go into the outgoing mail and find the two letters that Jon had posted to Teresa, but he did. One of Jon's collateral duties was to perform the monthly audit of the postal clerk's books. PO3 Smeltzer and he had become acquainted through the process, and Jon considered Smeltzer to be conscientious and meticulous. Because of this relationship, Jon convinced him that the things he had written had hurt other people. PO3 Smeltzer agreed, grudgingly, but it was clear, Jon would never get another favor from him. Jon read no more than the first page of each letter and tore them up and confined them to the trashcan as well.

Later, he tried to start a new letter to Teresa. He got a paragraph written and knew it wasn't going to do anything to make things better. It would probably make them even worse. He couldn't accuse Teresa of betraying the confidences he had shared with her, but every time he restarted the letter, that accusation wound up in words. With ten days for the letter to get to her, and ten more for her answer to make the return trip, it just wouldn't do for this situation. When Jon tore up his last letter attempt, the trashcan had a couple of inches of torn bits of paper covering the bottom.

He got his book, but after a page, he couldn't remember a thing he had read. Going back to the top, he started over, but two sentences later, he gave up. He stood up, and it was as if that act had drained all the strength he had left in him. He had just enough left to climb up onto his bunk, but as soon as he turned his bunk light out, his eyes popped open. Sleep was not going to happen. What he wanted to do was to run. Wind sprints. He wanted to run as hard as he could as long as he could stand it, until he was gasping for breath and sweating through open floodgates instead of pores. But in the Ensign Locker, you can't even pace properly.

He got down on the deck and started doing pushups. At first, he counted them but dropped the count after twenty. When his arms burned and refused to lift him another time, he rolled over and did sit-ups. His skivvies kept bunching up, and he began to rub his butt raw, so he went back to pushups. On the second round, instead of sit-ups, he held his feet off the deck as long as he could. After working up a good sweat, he took a shower. After, he pulled on skivvies, climbed onto his bunk, and put on earphones. Chopin *Nocturnes* played. His high school Phys Ed teacher had told the class a good sweat flushed fatigue toxin out of their muscles. Jon thought the *Nocturnes* might wash toxic thoughts out of his mind as well. This Chopin tape had never failed to lead him to sleep. Jon clicked off the bunk light, closed his eyes, and listened.

His eyes blinked open. Not even Chopin was going to work.

Ah, Teresa. Bunk light on. He remembered his rosary. Teresa had made sure he brought it along, but he hadn't used it since they left San Diego. He and Teresa said one together at least once a week. They liked to pray it with Jennifer playing with her toys on the living room carpet while they sat together on the sofa.

Digging the beads out of his locker, he plopped onto the deck in the gloom shrouded forward corner of the compartment and started. Teresa didn't like to do all sorrowful, or all joyful, mysteries.

She preferred to mix them up. That's the way life is, she said. Her favorite arrangement is a Glorious mystery, followed by a Joyful, then a Sorrowful, another Joyful, and wrapping up with another Glorious. Jon decided to sandwich three Sorrowfuls, for himself which he deserved, and with two Gloriouses for God, which He more than deserved,

At 1100, a messenger knocked on the door and entered the Locker.

"I'm awake." Cowboy flicked on his bunk light and swung his feet over the edge of the bunk. "I'll get Mr. Stewart up."

"Thanks, Mr. Macklin." The messenger left to wake up the rest of the noon to 1600 watch.

Cowboy climbed down from his bunk, started humming *I'm an Old Cowhand,* and moved forward to his locker when he kicked Jon's foot.

"Jeezus Chee ricetin Hell!"

"Sorry, Cowboy. Didn't mean to startle you." Jon stood up.

"What in Hell you doin' there on the floor?" Cowboy seemed to take delight in using civilian terminology, and it always surprised Jon that it annoyed him when he said floor instead of deck.

He stopped. "What in Hell you doing here, period? You're supposed to be on the bridge."

Jon explained.

Cowboy looked at him for a moment; then, he shook his head and opened his locker. "Well, at least you're not missing much. Just lobbing shells off into the jungle all night. Not much of a war we got ourselves here, Buckets." He stripped, tied a towel around his skinny middle, headed for the door, and started humming again.

"You going to wake Dormant, Cowboy?"

"Hell no. Too early." He closed the door to the Locker.

Abruptly, the ship slowed to what Jon thought was probably ten knots. They'd been steaming at twenty-five knots since he left—got thrown off the bridge.

Jon climbed up onto his bunk as Cowboy reentered.

Cowboy said, "Forgot we started haulin' ass right after I climbed into the rack. Where were we goin' so fast? You know?"

Jon explained about the merchant ship and the Coast Guard cutter.

"Must be there since we slowed." Cowboy pulled his skivvies on.

Whump, whump, whump, whump sounded from the starboard side of the ship.

Cowboy said, "Wonder why we haven't gone to GQ," and shifted into get-dressed-fast mode. "Gonna' see what's goin' on," and he was out the door.

It was 1112. "Dormant, time to get up for watch."

"Shut up. I'm sleeping."

Jon thought he might get in trouble for not waking him up. Then he remembered. The XO had said, *Stay the hell away from everyone.* Okay, so it wasn't his problem.

He'd been on the second decade, seven Hail Mary's in when the messenger came in. He finished the decade and put the rosary on the angle iron. Writing to Teresa didn't work. Neither did reading. He didn't want to exercise anymore. He'd prayed himself out.

So, that was it. All that was left was to lay there and wallow in misery. Wallow in misery. Like it was a thing outside you, a mudhole that you could co-occupy with a pig or something. It wasn't outside at all. Misery was a total inside thing. And most of that misery was reminders of how badly he'd screwed up, reminders of how many people he'd messed up.

Of all these thoughts running through my head, Lord, why can't there be one that can help me fix what I've done, deal with what I've done?

Jon remembered Christmas from when he was five. Pop went to all the masses: Christmas Eve and Midnight Mass, then all the Christmas morning masses beginning with the six a.m. and ending with the noon service. Mama, Jon, and his younger brother went to Christmas Eve and the noon Masses.

Jon had asked his Mama why his Pop went to all the Masses. She said to ask him, and Jon did at dinner.

After the question, Pop stopped his fork on the way to his mouth, and he looked at Jon. Jon wished he hadn't asked. Pop didn't smile much. He talked even less.

"Everybody's got to have something to hang onto," he said. Then he held up his coffee cup, and Mom went to the stove and got the pot.

Mom had stopped putting Jon to bed a long time prior, but she came to his bedroom that night. What Pop had meant, she said, was that faith was a gift from God and Pop and her. The world would try to take my faith away from me, and I was going to have to hang onto it. That's what Pop meant, she said.

For three hundred sixty-four days a year, they worked to rob Pop of his faith. Pop attended Mass every Sunday and all the Holy Days, but that Christmas thing was an extra, and it sure seemed important to Pop. He credited attending all the Masses on Christmas with enabling him to hang onto his faith.

From time to time growing up, events brought Pop's message to mind, and it always seemed to be just what Mom had said it was.

The summer before he began to date Teresa came to mind. He'd started running with some older boys, a couple from town, and a couple from farms. The oldest was Delbert, a farm boy, and he was just out of high school. He could get a six-pack behind Walter's Tavern whenever he wanted. Delbert and the others liked to get a couple of six-packs and talk about girls, which girls would go all the way, which ones would let you feel on top but not the bottom. Every time he went with Delbert and his friends, the beer and girls burgeoned into bigger and bigger portions of Jon's total life ambition.

Then he asked Teresa out. And, after the first date, he knew that Delbert and his friends were trying to take his faith away from him, just the way Mom had said it.

It took only a couple of dates to see that Teresa's faith was as strong as Pop's. That no one would be able to take her faith away from her. And Jon had liked her from the *git-go*. The way he and the guys had talked about girls, and hands going where they shouldn't, with Teresa, Jon decided he'd rather stick his hands in a bed of live coals than put them on her in inappropriate places.

Thinking about it then, Jon saw what had happened. He wasn't doing anything to keep his faith from being taken away from him. He leaned on Teresa to do that for him. He remembered that Boot Camp lecture, the one about a sailor's priorities. With God first.

The rosary. He decided he'd do a decade each night, and each night, at the start of the decade, he'd say a Glorious, then a Sorrowful, and then a Joyful mystery because that's how life is.

Then Dormant flipped his sheet back, rolled out of his bunk, grabbed his trousers from the hook at the end of his bed, put his uniform on, jammed his feet in his shoes—he'd worn socks to bed and had his shoes already loosely tied so he could just slip them on—and he was one foot in the passageway when he stopped.

When he'd rolled out of bed, Jon watched his forty-seven-second getting dressed performance.

Dormant smiled. "Wish I'da figured out how to get put in hack." And he was gone.

At 1215, a steward's mate knocked on the door with a lunch tray. It was Seaman Alvey. Seaman Alvey was a slender black man about five feet, ten inches. Alvey pressed his dungarees and always looked squared away. Alvey was in Admiral Ensign's division, and he was working to be a gunner's mate. But he was not a petty officer, so he had to do a stint working as either a compartment cleaner or a cook's helper. Because he was considered to be extra *squared away,* he'd been assigned to the wardroom.

"BLT for lunch, Mr. Zachery."

"Seaman Alvey, thanks. I'm sorry to be the cause of extra work for you."

Alvey smiled. "Not a problem, Mr. Z. And, I'm sorry you got nailed like this. Word is you were talking with your chief about your guys who snuck the booze aboard. Word is you were worried about your guys."

He was surprised Alvey said anything. Alvey always seemed to have a big piece of himself off someplace, almost as if only his body was in the world with the rest of them while his spirit was in some other world.

Jon closed his book and climbed down from the bunk as Alvey placed the tray on the fold-down desk.

"What I did," Jon said, "was disobey a direct order from the Captain, and I sure didn't help my guys. As a matter of fact, now the whole division looks bad from me to the junior seaman. But, thanks, Alvey. I…I can't tell you how much I appreciate the thought."

"Not a problem. See you, Mr. Z," and Alvey left.

Jon picked at the salad and ate one of the triangular halves of the BLT. The sugar water bug juice tasted sickeningly sweet, and he dumped that in the sink in the head next to the Locker. At 1300, Alvey collected the tray, and just after he left, Andrew Dunston came in and gave him a copy of *The Rise and Fall of the Third Reich*. Chief Petitte had asked Andrew to bring the book to Jon.

"Thanks, Andrew. I'm really sorry I let you down. The Chief was… I'm sorry."

"It's okay, Buckets," Andrew said. "Your chief knew the Skipper's dictum about admin matters on the bridge, but he was obviously upset by what happened. I understand one of the guys just made second class. But man, drinking on board! Can't believe even the dumbest boatswain mate would try to get away with that. You'd think the electronics techs would be smarter. Anyhow, this'll pass."

"I'm not so sure," Jon said. "The CO and the XO were totally pissed off. The XO, especially, really lit into me."

"Two Buckets, hang in there. This'll blow over. But you do need to be careful what you say to Teresa in your letters. The wives' group can get pretty tight on a cruise. A lot of officers don't write much, and nobody writes as often as you do. They tend to share letters. It kind of helps them all to feel better connected. And you know, as I told you, there's a kind of WestPac code. The code says you don't write about another officer's behavior ashore, and you want to be real careful what you say about what an officer does at sea. An officer may choose not to tell his wife something for a specific reason like he doesn't want her to worry. Then, if you tell your wife, and she tells the others, then the wife not only worries but gets mad at her husband for not writing about it himself. And you know, I think we all expected more of you since you had been enlisted before."

"Well, I was enlisted, but—. Crap. I've got the message. I will be careful what I say from now on."

Jon paged through to the end of the paperback book Andrew brought. One thousand four hundred eighty-three pages before the end material began.

"Andrew, is it okay for me to ask what's going on?"

"Sure," Andrew said. "Early this morning, a Coast Guard cutter spotted a cargo ship unloading supplies by boat from about a half-mile offshore. The cutter approached the merchant to board and inspect, and the crew fired small arms at the cutter. The merchant then ran itself aground a couple of hundred yards off the beach. The cutter followed in fairly close, but then she started taking heavy mortar and machine-gun fire from the beach. The cutter stood off from the beach, fired at the ship and the shore batteries, and she called for help.

"We got down there and were about to start firing on the merchant when some air force fighters showed up. The Forward Air Controller had on-scene command, and he had us hold fire while he worked the fighters. They blew the bejeebers out of the ship. It was impressive. But the Skipper was torqued. He wanted to fire at the merchant in the worst way.

"Now we're standing by off the shore while FACs continue to check out the area. If they see anything, we'll get a fire mission. So we may not make it back to the river tonight."

"Thanks, Andrew, and, please, tell Chief Petitte thanks for the book."

Jon held *The Rise and Fall of the Third Reich*. Even as a paperback, it was a heavy book. And, it had come from Chief Petitte. That was a surprise.

One thing he had was plenty of books to read and plenty of time to read them; if only he could convince his mind it wanted to know what was in those books.

13

Jon had the Ensign Locker to himself. He sat at the fold-down desk with Chief Pettite's book.

Before he had started *The Age of Louis XIV,* he had not been in the habit of reading the front matter in books. But in the Durants' opening pages, he read the Dear Reader note. And in it: "pervading theme the Great Debate between faith and reason." The implication being that the two were enemies. When he'd first read that, it stopped him, made him think. And every subsequent time he read it, the same thing happened.

Sitting there in his pocket of light surrounded by gloom, he knew, from his reading of history, that those two entities had been mortal enemies at times. For himself, though, he needed both. With him, the two could not be enemies. His life could not exist without reason, and neither could it exist without faith.

Jon read the foreword to *The Rise and Fall of the Third Reich.* Mr. Shirer mentioned that it was remarkable that the diplomats and journalists, who were in Germany in the early years of the Reich, really didn't know what was going on behind the scenes. How could they not see, Jon wondered?

But World War I had been over for only twenty-plus years. Nobody was anxious to get into another world war. Maybe they did see but hoped they could get around it with patience, that surely, Hitler would see the error of his ways when those errors were so clear to others.

And in that, was there some sort of explanation for the country's involvement in Vietnam? The US did not want to go to war, but they could not tolerate letting more of the planet be taken over by Communism.

He turned the page and got into the book.

Nobody came into the Locker during the early afternoon, and after reading for three hours, he was stiff from bending over the desk. He leaned back and stretched and savored the respite he'd had. From misery, but just thinking about misery brought it back, and awareness of his current plight pushed into the front of his brain like a thick letter forced through the narrow mail slot in a front door.

It all began to parade through his mind: what the CO had said, what the XO had said, the trouble he had created between Charles Hanson and his wife, the trouble his sailors had gotten into, and of course, what he had done to himself. And, Teresa, he wasn't sure what he had done to her.

The door pulled open, and Admiral Ensign stood and stared at Jon seated at the desk. He held up one finger. *Rule one.* The way Edgar stared reminded Jon of a cat watching a quivering mouse, just waiting for the mouse to move. Jon sat and stared back.

A scowl crawled over Edgar's face, and he started toward Jon.

Jon jumped to his feet, and the chair fell over. Edgar reached out to grab his shirt with his left, and he had made a fist with his right. Jon grabbed the index finger of his left hand and bent it back. Edgar wound up on one knee, trying to push against the hand.

"Let go, you stupid bastard, or I'll beat the crap out of you."

"Edgar, I really don't want to break your finger, but I am not going to take any more of your ragging me." He bent the finger back farther. "It's your call. How do you want it to go?"

"You son-of-a-bitch." He tried to push against the hand and stand up, and there was a sound, like someone cracking a knuckle. "Aah."

Jon stepped back.

Edgar settled onto both knees. He cradled his left hand in his right. "Aah." He rocked his upper torso back and forth. "Aah."

Jon grabbed his right upper arm and started lifting.

"Stand up."

Jon pulled some more. "Ahh."

"Come on. I'm not carrying you."

Finally, he stood up, but he wouldn't look at Jon.

"Okay, Edgar. You have to let go of the hand and hold onto the chain. There isn't room for me on the ladder too."

When he got to the top of the ladder, Edgar took up his left hand in his right again, stood by the XO's open door.

"XO." The XO looked up from the paper he was reading. "Edgar hurt his finger. It got slammed in the door. Could be broken. Sorry, I left the Locker, but I thought I should help him up the ladder."

"Christ, what next? Sit down on the sofa, Edgar. You, you go back to the Locker."

As Jon went down the ladder, that's what he wondered. What next?

⸺∿⸺

Almost and Admiral Ensign came into the Locker at 1800 after they had eaten. Jon sat at the desk, working on his own dinner. Almost picked up the piece of paper Jon had placed on his pillow and read it.

"Rule One is modified by the Zachery amendment. What's that mean?"

"It means, Bull, that I'm going to use the desk to eat. When no one else is in here, I'm going to use the desk if I want. But, if any of you want to use the desk, even If I'm eating, I'll get out of your way."

Edgar walked in. "He's the junior ensign, and he's in hack. He doesn't get to make rules."

108

"Shut up, Edgar. The Zachery mod is approved. Observe it."

Edgar had a strip of aluminum, bent with a slight curve in it, taped to the index finger of his left hand. He glared at Almost as he untied his shoes with his right, and cradling his left hand in his right, he lay back on his pillow and turned on his bunk light.

Almost looked at the paper again. "The Zachery mod's okay for the time being. How'd it go down here today, Two Buckets?"

"Got a lot of reading done. Seaman Alvey brings me a tray at chow time."

Almost put his shoes at the foot of his bunk, crawled in his bunk, and turned on his light.

"I know it's my own fault," Jon said, "but the worst thing about being stuck down here is not even knowing what's going on."

"Bull shit," Admiral Ensign sneered. "The worst thing is what you've done to the Skipper's career. My dad told me I was lucky to be on *Manfred*. Dad told me the CO has a good rep and that he was probably going to make Admiral. Hell, after your letters, I bet he doesn't make Captain."

Jon was halfway finished with dinner, but after Admiral Ensign's kick in the stomach, he was all the way finished.

Admiral Ensign sat up and began putting his shoes back on. "I don't even want to be in here with you."

After he left, Jon stared at the closed door for a moment. "Did I really do that to the CO?"

Almost shrugged. "We got the message about your letters from the CruDesPac chaplain. The admiral must know."

CruDesPac. Cruiser Destroyer forces in the Pacific, headed by a three-star admiral.

"I never even thought about the Skipper. I thought about Charlie and Melanie Hanson. I thought about letting all of you down, letting the ship down. I thought about what I'd done to Teresa. The wives' group has been so supportive of her, from when we first checked aboard and after Jennifer was born, especially. I hope the wives don't excommunicate her or something. But, the Skipper—"

Almost was sitting on his bunk. He was pretty close to Jon's size, maybe five-eight, and 160 pounds. His round face wore a perpetual serious expression under his crew cut black stubble.

"Being a commanding officer," Almost said, "this kind of stuff goes with the territory."

"What can I do, Almost, to make it up to him, I mean?"

"You gotta build a thousand bridges."

"You mean, suck…commit one homosexual act, and even if you never commit another, and even though you build a thousand bridges, in the end, you are not a bridge builder, you are a homosexual?"

"I think, in your case if you build a thousand bridges, people will forget this homosexual act."

If the Skipper wouldn't let him out of hack, he'd never get to build even the first one.

"Almost, what did you think about that wetting down party? I thought it was a reasonable affair until somebody wanted the new JGs to drink a pitcher of beer to get at the JG bars. But then, it kind of went wild."

"I don't think it was all that wild. I've seen worse."

"It seemed wild to me. I never saw anything like that when I was enlisted; 'course, I think I only went to a bar with the guys once. They took me to a bar with girls. It was in San Juan. To pop my cherry, they said after we got there. They kept trying to line me up with bar girls. When I wouldn't go with any of them, the bar girls threw chicken feed at me. I left, and after that, I never went with the guys again.

"But when Peter Feldman said he wasn't making himself sick, and that he wasn't drinking the beer, and the guy grabbed the pitcher from Peter and threw it on his chest, that wasn't wild? Then Charlie Hanson said he didn't want to drink beer, he wanted a Subic Special, and he poured his pitcher of beer on himself, making a puddle of beer on the floor. Somebody said there was enough beer to swim in on the floor, and Charlie flops on the floor and acts like he is doing the backstroke, and he's in his white uniform. Then Don Minton takes the pitcher of Subic Specials and starts pouring it into Charlie's open mouth as he continues his backstroke. That wasn't wild?"

"It was rowdy; I'll grant you. But, Charlie and the whole wardroom were at work the next morning. Charlie, by the way, I have never seen him get really drunk. He spilled most of his drinks that night, and he gets happy and obviously has a great time. And there is a thing called the WestPac code. On cruise, some people get rowdy, rowdier than they would at home, and if they do, the code says we don't talk about it. In WestPac, there is a different morality."

Jon shook his head. "Different morality? You don't have a different morality, do you?"

"No, I don't. I don't think you do either. But, some of our shipmates seem to see things that way. They are still our shipmates, though."

"You don't drink at all, and you still cut them the room to act like they do?"

"I don't drink for two reasons: one, I don't like the loss of control that happens when I drink, and two, when I was in high school and had my first beer, I didn't like the taste. One of my buddies said it was an acquired taste. So it seemed to me, if I had to work at having fun that way, maybe it wasn't all that much fun to start with. And my dad told me that if I could stay away from booze altogether, my life would be easier and better."

"Your dad talked to you about that?"

Almost shrugged; then he got up and went to take a shower.

Jon's pop didn't drink, either, but he never talked to him about it. He really didn't talk to him much at all. There had been the hanging-on thing, but his Mom had orchestrated that. He probably thought he was saving his son's immortal soul. For that, he could work himself up to speak.

During the night and early morning, Jon woke when the messenger from the bridge came down to get the ensigns up for their watches. At 0237, he awoke again when he felt a thump reverberate through the hull. It took a moment to realize the after gun-mount was firing. It seemed like fifteen salvos, or so. There was no way to figure out what was going on, so he went back to sleep.

Cowboy told Jon what happened. It turned out that a FAC had continued to orbit over the area throughout the night, and around 0230, he had detected some movement near the spot where the VC had been unloading supplies from the beached merchant ship. The FAC had called *Manfred* for illumination and HE. There was no indication whether they had killed any VC or not.

The next two days passed with slow speed steaming off the coast during daylight hours. At night they were in the Saigon River firing H&I. Nighttime began for Jon with the anchor chain rattling out. When they hauled it up, that meant morning. Other than when Alvey showed up with meals, he read, did push-ups, pull-ups, and sit-ups until he couldn't do anymore, and he prayed the rosary. Twice each day, he started a letter to Teresa, but he never wrote a full page before quitting and tearing it up. He didn't know how to write to her while trying to be careful what he wrote.

Compared to how afraid he'd been when they had pulled into the Saigon River the first time, now, when the ship dropped anchor, he felt nothing. He could still picture the jungle along the riverbanks on both sides and hordes of VC hiding there, watching, waiting for an opportunity. But there was not one thing Jon could do about it. When the guns fired, Jon put his pillow over his ear; the way Cowboy did to muffle Dormant's *phwoo,* He managed to sleep reasonably well through the firing.

On their last night in the river, when the messenger came to get Cowboy and Dormant up for the mid-watch, Jon popped awake and rolled up on an elbow. The book he had been reading dropped to the deck with a *bang.*

"Bad dream, Two Buckets?" Cowboy said.

"None of my dreams are very good these days."

He had been dreaming that he had gone to Captain's Mast and that Admiral Ensign was the presiding official. Just before he awoke, Admiral Ensign had said, "Ensign Zachery, you are guilty of dereliction of duty, which is a violation of article 789654321 of the Uniform Code of Military Justice. You are no longer an officer and a gentleman, and you will never own a Corvette."

After OCS, Jon and Teresa spent two weeks' leave at home, alternating between her parents and his. They'd also attended a party where they met one of Jon's grade school classmates. Harold Harmody. In grade school, the kids had called him 'Harry high-pants,' because he wore his pants hiked up so high the waistband almost touched his shirt pocket.

Harry High-Pants was a skinny kid, wore glasses, and never played baseball or football with other boys. Harry had gotten an electrical engineering degree and gone to work for IBM. You would not picture Harry High-Pants in a red Corvette, but that's what he was driving when he arrived at the party. Jon had told Teresa he was going to get a Harry High-Pants Corvette. But only after they had a nice house to raise their children in.

Cowboy rolled out of his bunk. His feet splatted on the tiled deck.

"Come on, Dormant. Time to rise and shine, my man," Cowboy said.

"I hate people who wake up cheerful," Dormant said and rolled onto his side.

"Come on, Dormant. We got'ta relieve the watch."

"I'll make sure he gets up, Cowboy," Jon said.

"Okay, thanks," Cowboy said. "Holding up, okay?"

"'Okay' is a state reserved for people who haven't got both feet in a bucket of crap, I think. Allowing for that, I guess I'm coping."

"It'll pass. And, you've got Dormant, right?"

Cowboy was out the door three minutes after the messenger had left.

"Dormant?" There was no answer. Jon grabbed Dormant's arm and shook him.

"Touch me again, and I'll break your finger," Dormant said.

"What? Were you here?"

"No." Dormant rolled over onto his back. "But Seaman Alvey was cleaning the passageway outside the Locker. He heard it all. He told me."

"I don't know what it is about Admiral Ensign, but he seems to have it in for me. And, me, he opens his mouth, and I just get angry. I'm ashamed of myself, that I don't seem to be able to control it."

"I have always just ignored him. And, nobody is going to get Cowboy down. With you, he's found a way to set you off. And you seem to set something off in him that he can't control either." Dormant looked at his watch, which he'd worn to bed. "Move out of the way."

Jon stepped back. "You and Alvey seem pretty tight."

Dormant rolled out of his bed.

"Alvey is a good kid. I helped him apply for a GED. Now I'm helping him study for it. That's all."

Dormant got dressed and walked out.

Civil behavior from Dormant! Not as much of a surprise as it would have been coming from Admiral Ensign. Dormant probably thought the H&I rounds were only killing trees. Even Jesus had killed a fig tree.

14

8 June, midnight, Saigon River

Dearest Teresa,

I have lots to explain. First, I haven't written for a week, not since the first day out of port, and I am very sorry about that. Actually, I've written letters, but I tear them up. When I look at what I've written, it just feels so wrong. But I can't go on like this. I HAVE to write to you.

I need to explain to you that I am in hack. I violated one of the Captain's orders, and this is my punishment. There is nobody to blame but myself. Being in hack, I cannot go anywhere on the ship. I guess it's jail, except jail is the Ensign Locker. A steward brings me meals. And, all my duties are being covered by someone else.

Being incarcerated in the Ensign Locker and cut off from the things going on on the ship, well, I don't like that, but what is really bad is feeling like I am cut off from you. Before I did this to myself, to us, when I wrote to you, and I was here in the Locker, with the others asleep, it was really like I've told you before, like the Sistine painting of Adam reaching out his finger to God for the spark of life. I really felt like writing to you was like reaching out to touch you all the way around the world.

This hack business and being cut off from you has made me think about that morning of your C-section. Then, thinking of life without you was intolerable. Feeling so cut off from you now is not bearable, either. So, I can't NOT write to you. Not writing to you is a kind of death.

Probably, I'm supposed to be thinking about the error of my ways while I'm in hack. What I've really been thinking about is you. I've told you before about how I fell in love with you that day, just before the end of our junior year in high school. We were riding back to St. Ambrose, I rode with the Hollrah girl that year, and I saw you walking home from school, and the Cupid arrow got me. It took me into the summer before our senior year before I got the courage to ask you out, but it was that day when I saw you walking that I fell in love with you.

Being down here in the Ensign Locker and thinking about that, I guess I never appreciated all that happened to me that day. I fell in love with you, for sure, but something else happened to me, too. Seeing you that day, falling in love with you, well, it changed me. It changed me so much that picking me up and putting me on a different planet would not have been a bigger change.

Before that day, I always thought I'd never leave St. Ambrose. I never thought I'd go to college. Mom had told me Pop had only gone to school through fourth grade, that he'd put me through high school, and that I should be grateful for having so much more education than he did. Mom told me Pop was hurt that I didn't seem to be grateful. I guess I never knew I could hurt my Pop in any way. And there are other things with him.

But that day I saw you, and I decided to ask you out, it changed me. From the moment we got back to school in our senior year, I wanted to go to college. I wanted to get out of St. Ambrose and to have a house for you like the rich kid in town, James Grossman, lived in. I was sure that if I didn't get out of St. Ambrose, if I didn't go to college, if I couldn't promise you a house like James', I was sure you'd marry someone else, someone who could promise you those things.

It was a long letter, and Jon needed scotch tape to hold the flap of the envelope closed.

In the morning, the ship cleared the river and turned north. Jon could tell they'd turned left by the heel. In the afternoon, Almost turned up the DASH, and this time, the helo behaved itself. In the evening, Almost and Jon were in the Locker.

Normally, Almost wasn't talkative, but that evening, he seemed to want to talk. He spoke about completing the ground check, and then he asked what Jon's plans were for after the navy. Everybody in the Locker knew Jon had no intention of staying in, and that had been the case before hack. A better question was, would the navy let him stay? But Jon hadn't really thought about it that much. It was nearly three and a half years away.

Almost talked about how *Victory at Sea* had been his favorite TV show and how he had wanted to be in the navy since grade school. But, he also intended to leave the service after his four-year obligation, and he was going to get a master's degree and work in environmental protection. His story made Jon wish he had a plan.

The good thing, though, was he had written a long letter to Teresa. And he had Alvey drop it in the mail for him. Today, he decided, he'd bring up the subject of the future in his letter.

It felt so good to be able to write to her. He wondered if feeling good was a violation of the terms of being in hack.

The next morning, the ship took on ammunition while Jon wrote another long letter to Teresa and did exercises. Dormant came into the Locker after the ship pulled away from the ammo ship. Jon was at the desk reading.

"*The Rise and Fall of the Third Reich,*" Dormant said. "What do you think of it?"

"Well, I am about three-fourths of the way through the book. In retrospect, it seems amazing that the German people went along with Nazism. Though, I guess it is kind of hard to imagine what the Germans might have felt like coming out of World War I. And then, it seems there is a lesson on appeasement of people like Hitler."

"Everybody seems to talk about the appeasement thing and not enough about how the Germans just went along with Hitler,"

Dormant said. "My dad was a lieutenant colonel in the army, and we were stationed in Germany when I was in grade school. He took my brother and me to visit Dachau. One of the things that I will always remember is, from inside the compound at Dachau, you could see the roofs of normal houses very close by."

Dormant looked down at his shoes for a moment; then, he looked up at Jon. "You know what I thought about when I read that book, Two Buckets?"

"So, tell me."

"I think of America, not Germany."

"What?" Jon turned and looked at him. Most of the time, he thought Dormant looked troubled. At first, Jon thought it was because Dormant didn't fit in, either. He didn't care about fitting in, though, and now he had this calm look on his face. That look surprised Jon as much as what he'd said. "You think we have the same sorts of things going on in America? How can you even say that?"

"Blacks and Indians instead of Jews. Imperialism in place of *Lebensraum*. I could go on."

"Dormant, where do you get this stuff?"

"Two Buckets, how can you NOT get this stuff? That's my question to you. But, being from the Midwest, it's to be expected."

"What are you talking about?"

"You went to Purdue, right? Agriculture and engineering. No thinking, just get up and plow the field and plant the corn, or build a bridge. If you can read loads and stress tables, you can build a bridge. No thinking."

"So, let me—"

Jon didn't want to get into an argument over whether he came from a stupid section of the country or not, but he couldn't let things lay as they were. "I think Communism poses the same sort of threat to our country, and the world, as the Nazis did almost thirty years ago. Don't you think the Communists are a threat to our country?"

But Dormant was done talking, it seemed. He hung his clothes up on the front of his bunk.

"You went to Columbia. Eisenhower was president there. Not long ago, he said we should nuke the North Vietnamese. Is that the kind of thinking you go along with? Oh, I get it. Ike was a Midwesterner. He could not possibly do *your* thinking for you."

Jon shut up then, annoyed with himself. It was just that now he had two Admiral Ensigns to live with, one physical, one intellectual— intellectual wannabe, maybe.

The look on Dormant's face told Jon he'd scored. His troubled look was back in place, and Jon didn't feel good about putting it there. But then, Dormant climbed up onto his bunk, and very shortly, he was making his *phwoo* sound. Apparently, he had had no trouble dismissing what Jon had said, but Jon, himself, was agitated. Again.

When Cowboy came in, he was excited. Yesterday, the ship had taken a Swift Boat alongside. The CO gave them a gallon of ice cream, and Cowboy went aboard the boat and fondled their weapons. He had really wanted to fire them, but that wasn't in the cards. Still, it was enough for Cowboy to put his application in for Swift Boat duty.

During the wetting down party in the Philippines, Cowboy had befriended a marine A-4 pilot, Duke Savage. The day after the party, Duke showed Cowboy his airplane, and the two had gone on liberty together twice. Before they left the Philippines, Cowboy had applied for aviation training. Now, he was telling Jon that he was applying for Swift Boats and PBRs, too.

"Thing is, Buckets," his slow-motion voice out of sync with his hands waving around, "flight training is two years. XO says there is a waiting list for the boats, but it's just nine months. So, I could get at the gomers quicker on the boats. Bad thing is I didn't have the application signed until just now. It didn't go out with the mail this morning."

Cowboy was concerned with outgoing mail. Jon was concerned with incoming. For the first time, he dreaded receiving the letters Teresa had already written to him.

He had no idea what her letter, the one responding to his about the wetting down party, would say, but he expected it would be critical of him for even being there. But he couldn't just sit and do nothing until he got her letter.

He started another one and told Teresa about waiting for her letter and how much he depended on what she wrote. He assured her he was not just shrugging off what he'd done. He hurt a lot of people with what he'd written to her, and there was no way to make that go away. He wrote that God didn't want him dead. So, he was still alive and had to live some kind of life.

It felt good to write to her, even with the reservations and complications.

There was a knock, and the door was pulled open.

"Mr. Zachery, I'm Messenger of the Watch on the bridge. I'm supposed to tell you that the CO wants to see you in his cabin right away."

For days, no one wanted to see Jon or talk to him. Now, suddenly, he had to see the CO right away.

"Mr. Zachery, the Captain told me to tell you right away, sir." The messenger stood in the open doorway. "I'm supposed to escort you up, sir."

Shower shoes and blue jeans went off, and socks and a khaki uniform went on as quickly as Dormant got dressed. Jon double-checked his zipper and said, "let's go." with the belt left loose until the shirt was tucked in with military creases in the back.

Up three ladders following the messenger who ascended at I'm-going-to-my-GQ-station speed. He rapped on the captain's door.

The door pulled open.

"Messenger, thanks, and you can head back up to the bridge," the CO said as he sat back down at his desk.

The CO gestured for Jon to enter his cabin. Jon did and closed the door. And stood there. The CO was reading a message. After a moment, he looked up.

"Mr. Zachery, I will tell you that I have never been so pissed off at anyone ever before. First, I catch you on the bridge doing what I told you all to avoid doing: administrative duties while you are on the bridge. And then the XO tells me about your letters, which have gotten the wives' group all stirred up.

"A couple of days of you being in hack is not enough for me to get over this. I would have let you stew down there for a lot longer; hell, I might have left you there the rest of the cruise. But we have to put a Gunnery Liaison Officer ashore to support a marine operation today, and we may have to have both gun mounts manned, so I am running out of officers. You are the only one with GLO training, so I am sending you ashore."

It took a moment for it to register that Jon was no longer being chewed out, and a little bubble of elation started rising from somewhere deep inside his chest. However, smiling right then would not be a good idea, but he did stand a little straighter, a little taller.

"We'll be supporting a US Marine Special Landing Force. They have put a company ashore from an amphibious ship. This company is sweeping south toward another marine unit moving north out of Chu Lai.

So, we are way north.

"We just got in position to provide gunfire support. Any daytime fire missions we get, we'll be working with Forward Air Controllers. You'll be there in case there is a need for gunfire support at night. You might be ashore for three days. It shouldn't be more than that. As soon as you leave here, stop by CIC and get the details from the Ops O. He's there waiting for you. Then, see the Supply Officer, and he will issue you some fatigues and combat boots. A helo will be here to pick you up in fifteen minutes. Questions?"

"No, sir. Sir—"

"Just zip it," the CO said. "I've told you all I know. We have nothing else to talk about, so hop to it."

As Jon entered CIC, he tried to get his mind around what was happening. Two minutes ago, nothing moved. Everything was just stuck. Now everything was moving and at a gazillion miles an hour.

In Combat, the Supply Officer, Fred Watson, waited beside the Ops O. Fred handed Jon a folded set of fatigues with a pair of boots on top.

"Change while I brief you. There isn't much time." As the Ops O spoke, Jon shucked shoes and uniform and pulled on the other unfamiliar stuff.

The Ops O finished speaking and handed Jon a sheet of yellow paper. "There's a summary of what I told you. I know it would have been too much to remember. But some of this is classified, so as soon as you get ashore, destroy it."

The Bosun called for the helicopter team to assemble on the fantail.

The Ops O stared at Jon until he figured out what to do next. Jon tore out of Combat, leaving his uniform on the deck.

15

Back on the fantail, Carl Lehr and a four-man crew were there to receive the helo. Carl handed Jon a floatation coat, a helmet, and goggles.

A UH-1 was approaching from the port aft quarter, probably about thirty or forty feet in the air.

"Okay, Jon," Carl shouted against the noise from the Huey. "They will lower a horse collar. It's just a loop that goes across your back and under your arms. I'll get you in it. Then, clasp your arms together in front of you and don't let go until the marines have you inside the helo. They will tell you when to let go. Got it?"

Jon nodded. The helo came to a hover over the fantail. Carl took Jon by the arm and led him under the downwash, which threatened to rip his goggles off. In the calm eye of the windstorm, directly under the chopper, Carl ran the padded horse collar across Jon's back and under his arms. Jon's hands latched together, enthusiastically. Carl backed away from beneath the Huey.

The strap bit into Jon's back, his feet left the deck, and he began spinning slowly. Carl and his team wouldn't appreciate being puked on, especially being puked on out of a tornado. As he rose, the helo moved sideways over the water He closed his eyes, and rough hands grabbed him, spun him around, and jerked him backward and onto the deck of the helo.

"Let go, sir." Jon opened his eyes and saw a flight helmet, a set of goggles encasing two blue eyes, and a big grin. "You can let go now, sir." He reached down and pried Jon's fingers apart. Then the crewman got him onto a seat and strapped him in.

The helo tilted forward, and *Manfred* started sliding away behind them as the crewman slid the door closed. Suddenly, the helo banked to the left, and Jon felt a spike of panic. When that subsided, he noticed the constant jiggling. It seemed as if the helicopter was trying to shake itself to pieces. Looking forward, between the pilots and through the windscreen, he saw Vietnam getting big fast. A couple of days ago, the jungle-adorned banks of the Saigon River had seemed a threat and too close, but now, that same distance would have been a comfort.

The crewman placed his mouth near his left ear and shouted, "Just about there, sir. Stay seated until I unbuckle you."

The nose of the helo came up, and shuddering replaced the jiggling. Jon began to appreciate the DASH: a helicopter you couldn't ride in. A cloud of brown dust boiled up in front of the helo, and the chopper kind of danced on the skids for a moment before the load was taken off the rotor disk, and then they settled firmly on the ground.

The crewman released the straps holding Jon to the seat, shouted that he should leave on his helmet and float-coat, and then he opened the sliding door. Immediately, a cloud of brown dust swept inside. *Thank You, God, and the US Marine Corps, for goggles.*

Jon climbed out. As soon as his boots touched the ground, another marine grabbed Jon's arm and led him from under the rotor blades. He couldn't keep his eyes open. When the door had opened, he'd gotten some grit under the goggles.

The Huey engine revved up, and Jon's marine guide turned his back to it. Before Jon followed suit, sand stung his cheeks, and he thought he would suffocate in the dust he inhaled. The Huey took off, and the roaring brown tornado Jon had been standing in just quit.

Jon bent over, coughing, and tried to spit dust out of his dry mouth.

The marine corporal still had his arm. "Sir, excuse me for laughing, but I, for one, am glad as hell it is not the monsoon season when we are slogging in mud up to our gonads. Here's Lieutenant Stephenson. He'll take care of you from here."

The guide took Jon's helmet and flotation vest.

"Don't rub your eyes," the first lieutenant said. "You could scratch your eyeballs with the sand. Here, bend over and turn your head a bit."

The lieutenant poured some water from his canteen over Jon's eyes.

"Now, don't rub them," he said again. "Just blink a couple of times. It'll feel gritty for a while, but let it work itself out. I'm First Lieutenant Sanders Stephenson. Call me Sandy, and by the way, welcome to Company C."

Sandy proffered his hand, and Jon shook it. "Ensign Jon Zachery. Jon."

Then Sandy offered his canteen. Jon swished a mouthful and spat it out, then guzzled a long slug, with, "Thanks."

Sandy looked like a white Seaman Alvey, Jon's first impression. Tall and lean and, his fatigues were clean and pressed. But he was fair, blond, blue-eyed, and open and friendly. Alvey, however, did seem to hold more of himself in reserve.

Jon's second thought was that Sandy was someone to hang onto. Since the messenger had come to get him, he had been being swept down rapids while hanging onto a twig for salvation.

Sandy said, "Let's get you shifted into some shore duty gear. First, take another swig out of my canteen. No backflushing if you please." Sandy clapped him on the back. "Here, put this M-1955 body armor on—riff-raff would call it a flak jacket. And here's a helmet. We'll get the rest of your gear in a minute."

C Company was based on a US Navy amphibious vessel, a sort of helicopter aircraft carrier. They'd helo'd ashore up near Danang and had been patrolling Route 1 south toward Chu Lai. That afternoon, the unit continued heading south along a Vietnam highway called Route 1. Every once in a while, Jon caught a glimpse of *Manfred* a couple of miles offshore. Next to Route 1, waist-high brush covered the land. Jungle trees adorned the rising terrain to the right, to the west. And there were swathes of the jungle toward the coast as well.

Jon rode most of the afternoon in a truck with a dozen riflemen. Above and in front of them, an OV-1 spotter plane and a Huey constantly patrolling the sides and front of the marines' advance. Sandy, it turned out, had duties he had to attend to. He was not someone Jon could cling to. Sergeant Evans was his new babysitter.

The sergeant was probably five-eight or nine with short, blonde, curly hair on top of his head. Freckles bloomed through his tanned face, and veins bulged out on his weight-lifter arms protruding from his rolled-up sleeves. He accepted his babysitter role with mostly concealed displeasure. Jon didn't care what the man thought about his navy visitor; he just didn't want to let the sergeant out of his sight.

In midafternoon, the patrol halted. They'd been angling away from Route 1, plowing through the brush and away from the sea, and on a gently rising slope. Jon could see *Manfred* in profile a couple of miles offshore, inching along.

They had stopped because the UH-1 had spotted some bunkers. *Manfred* was called, and a fire mission was directed into the area. It was interesting, Jon thought, to feel the earth shake from the explosions of the shells. He decided he much preferred the vantage point of the bridge wing. After the firing ceased, the marines moved up and discovered bunkers and entrances to tunnels. Grenades and tear gas canisters were dropped into the holes, which elicited no enemy response. The marines then continued moving south for another hour. Then, they set up night defensive positions.

At dusk, Sandy Stephenson briefed Jon, Sergeant Evans, and a lance corporal on the OP, the observation post, they were going to establish. They'd climb the hill rising to the west until they had a good view of the terrain surrounding Company C's position. If the company was attacked, Jon would call in fire support from his destroyer. Sandy expected the VC to have their attention on the company, but they had to be alert to the possibility the gomers would put out a patrol looking for an OP. If they did encounter such a patrol, it should not be more than two men—four at the most.

Four at the most. With that comforting notion, Jon, with an M-14 across his back, humped up the hill behind Sandy, slipping through the brush. The hairs on the back of Jon's neck desperately tried to tell him that the VC were sneaking up behind them or hiding in front of them.

When Sandy decided they'd gotten themselves high enough, they set up the OP. The lance corporal had carted two radios on his back. He left those with the two officers, then followed Sergeant Evans some twenty or so yards to the southwest of the OP. Through the night, in the OP and the security position, one man would sleep and one would be on watch. There was to be no talking. Communication was to be by hand signals, and starlight provided by the moonless sky rendered that form of communication iffy. But it was what they had to deal with.

Jon pulled back the sleeve of his fatigues and checked his watch. The dial glowed 2333. Another hour and twenty-seven minutes before he could wake Sandy. He covered the watch glow.

The OP was located in a slight depression masquerading as a foxhole near the top of hill 136, 5.5 clicks inland from the South China Sea. Waist-high brush provided the only cover. Company C was below on the coastal plain, in the blackness, a little south of due east. If the VC attacked the company, Sandy and Jon would check map coordinates together; then, Jon would call *Manfred* for gunfire support. They'd gone over the charts and marked the company's position, and they'd marked the chart with how close they could bring fire if it were needed.

Jon held his helmet on and looked up at the zillions of stars. All the light in that part of the universe seemed to be up there, with none left for earth. Even though he couldn't see her, *Manfred* was out there to the east, but she was blacked out.

Sandy Stephenson was sleeping on his poncho next to the radio. He and Lance Corporal Talbot would take the next watch. Sergeant Evans shared this watch with Jon, and he was out there in the dark somewhere, with Talbot asleep in their shallow hole.

After checking that the safety on his M-14 was set—he did that about once a minute—Jon started crawling across the depression to check to the east and the north to see if there really was something out there to cause that troupe of tiny tap dancers to do their routine on the back of his neck. As he propelled himself with elbows and toes, his rifle gripped in front of him; he scooped sand into the waist of his trousers. *Sailors are meant to be on ships, and ships are meant to be at sea.* This was mostly a bachelor saying, generally trotted out after being in port for a while, and the bachelor sailors ran out of money. That night, though, it seemed like a fine statement of affairs. After how hot it had been during the day, now Jon was cold, and he felt dirtier than he'd ever been. Plus, the hair on the back of his neck was plumb scared.

Peering over the rim of the depression to the north, he looked, he listened, and he sniffed the air. Sergeant Evans had said that sometimes you smelled the VC before you saw them, but only the back of his neck sensed anything to warrant alarm.

The reason Jon was ashore with the marines and in that OP was because the Ops O had sent him to a school so that he could learn how to do the Gunfire Liaison Officer job. The regs required the ship to have one. Plus, he had done things that demanded punishment. Being there in that foxhole sure felt like punishment. And another thing. There were more than 300 people on his destroyer, and he, Jon Zachery, the junior ensign aboard, was the most expendable. The CO was a smart guy. He might have figured this was one of those two birds with one stone deals.

Jon figured it was about 2345. Out there on *Manfred,* the midwatch guys would have arrived on the bridge to start the turnover process. Lieutenant (jg) Darrell Palmer would be turning over the officer of the deck responsibilities to Peter Feldman. The off-going JOOD was Almost. The on-coming JOOD would be Dormant.

Suddenly, Sandy moved or twitched, and his poncho rustled under him. A gusher of adrenaline shot through Jon's system, and by the time he understood where the sound had come from, his heart was going *wham, wham, wham,* like the guns on the ship when they were firing as fast as the loaders could work.

A prayer started automatically. *Holy Mary, Mother of God, pray for us sinners, now and at the hour…* Jon had been looking for comfort, and that prayer wasn't taking him there. *Oh, Jesus.* He had flicked the safety off when Sandy had made the noise. After resetting the safety, he crawled back to the radio and checked his watch. At midnight, he had to do a comm check. Three minutes to go.

The radios were near Sandy's head. When the second hand passed through staright-up, Jon took the handset of the radio on the C Company command post frequency and gave a quick double click on the mike button, and he was glad he didn't have to talk. When he and Teresa had gotten married, and it was time for him to say, "I do," he had opened his mouth, but no sound came out for a long moment. He was sure the same thing would have happened then. But the plan was to not talk, just give a double push on the transmit button. He got an answering click and then picked up the handset of the other radio, the one set to the *Manfred* frequency.

"*Manfred,* this is Charlie, radio check, over." The C Company command post had just called the ship to ensure they had good communications connectivity.

"Charlie, this is *Manfred,* loud and clear, out."

They'd checked the transmit function of one radio and the receive function of the other without saying a word from the OP.

Sandy whispered, "Everything okay?

Jon almost told him they weren't supposed to speak but said, "Yes, sir."

"You don't have to call me sir, Jon."

"Yes, sir. I know."

Sandy made a little snorting sound and wiggled around on his poncho a bit. Jon crawled back to the north rim of the depression and looked, listened, and sniffed. The back of his neck hadn't stopped worrying. The question "What am I doing here?" flashed in his mind like the title frame of a movie. The school the Ops O sent him to, punishment, being expendable, these things did not totally answer the question. The answer came with a dose of anger like a log down a flume. He was there on that hill because Pop had shanghaied him into the navy.

It had happened on a Saturday morning in April 1959. He stocked shelves at Hollrah's grocery store and was due at work at 7:30. When Jon entered the kitchen at 6:55, Pop sat at their Formica topped table drinking coffee. Mom asked if he wanted eggs, but Jon was happy with cereal.

"You're not going to work this morning," Pop said.

Pop looked down at his coffee cup. His big, chapped hands with the knuckles swollen with arthritis circled the china cup sitting on the delicate saucer. The china looked like it belonged at one of Jon's sister's tea parties for her dolls, not in his crude hands.

"Uh, Pop, why…?"

"We're going to see the navy recruiter." He still wouldn't look at Jon.

In the car, as Pop drove, he'd said that the family had supported Jon long enough. It was time he was out on his own and let the younger ones get their share from the family-feeding trough. They were going to the navy recruiter, and he better start getting used to the idea. That was a lot of words for Pop to string together.

Whenever the shanghai memory popped into Jon's brain, anger flared and burned hot, but just then, it didn't last long. The back of Jon's neck was worried, and it wouldn't let him dwell on Pop.

As he moved around the OP, Jon never saw, heard, or smelled a threat. Still, the back of his neck never shut up. It kept scaring him with things it thought it sensed behind him.

At 0047, Jon started back across the OP toward the southeastern rim again when Teresa popped into his mind. He hadn't thought of her the whole time he had been on watch, occupied as he had been with smelling VC and not accidentally discharging his M-14. Whenever she suddenly appeared in his thoughts, a warm, glowing thing happened inside his chest and belly. He just melted. Jennifer, their little girl, was five and a half months old now. Teresa was so good with her. Jon recalled seeing her nurse Jennifer just after the two of them came home from the hospital. He liked to pull that picture out of his mind wallet now and then. It was such a tender thing, but a bit sad, too. There was something so exclusive, so excluding all others, going on there between mother and child. Jon didn't know what he was meant to be. Not a sailor nor a marine. But Teresa was meant to be a mother.

At the moment, though, there was the problem he had created with Teresa, and he would have to try to fix that back on the ship. But that was for later.

Then "Mr. Zachery" was whispered from the blackness off to his right, and it set his heart to whamming again. He clicked off the safety.

"I'm a good guy, for Christ's sake. Put your safety back on." Sergeant Evans crawled up over the rim of the depression.

"Jeez, Sarge, I thought you said you weren't much of an Indian. I didn't hear a thing from you." Jon's whisper seemed loud to himself.

"I said I'm not as good an Injun as the gomers. So that should be a lesson to you. It's 0059 and time to wake the LT. He and Talbot have the next two hours."

Sandy and Sergeant Evans hissed whispers at each other for a moment. Then the sergeant crept back out of the depression the way he had come, and Sandy told Jon to grab some shuteye on his poncho.

That last jolt of adrenaline hadn't gone out of Jon's system, and sleep didn't seem ready to visit yet.

Jon wiggled his butt and shoulder, digging little comfort holes in the sandy soil, and thought back to how the day had started. It had been the same as the preceding days since he'd been put in hack. The next thing Jon knew, Sandy told him it was 0300 and time to take the watch again.

The night snailed its way to sunrise. The OP crew descended the hill, mounted trucks, and ate K-rations breakfast in the back of their truck. During the day, there were frequent stops when patrols forayed toward the coast while others scaled the high terrain to the west.

16

Jon's second night ashore with the marines started off the same as the first. Sandy picked hill 55 for the OP. He said they should call it a bump since it wasn't high enough to be considered a proper hill. Still, it afforded an adequate view over the position occupied by Company C for the night.

The marine company position was again to the southeast of their OP. *Manfred* was visible as well as the LPH, the amphibious ship Company C had come from, farther out to sea. Like the night before, they marked the chart and reviewed the coordinates; then Sandy tore open a C-ration package and started on his dinner. He took a swig from his canteen.

"So, Jon, we've got another forty-five minutes before the sun goes down. Quiet talking is okay for now, but after dark, only business talk, same as last night. And always keep your eyes open and scanning the area for any glint, any motion, anything that looks funky to you.

If you see something or hear something, say so, and don't be afraid of crying wolf. Okay?"

Both last night and that night, they were on their bellies a lot. Jon began to appreciate all the practice he'd had in the Ensign Locker, being on his stomach in bed writing to Teresa.

"Right. Don't be afraid to cry wolf. You guys out here a lot, Sandy?"

"Not down here. Until now, we've operated just below the DMZ."

They'd been operating with ARVN, South Vietnamese Army, units. According to Sandy, they'd expended massive amounts of energy but had little to show for it. No real encounters with main units of either VC or North Vietnamese. "The VC always seem to get wind of the big operations and disappear before we get there."

Besides his whispering, he could hear Sandy's lips smacking. He thought Sandy was making an awful lot of noise, but Jon was just a goober sailor. What did he know?.

That afternoon, while riding in the truck, Jon had told Sandy about his talk with Warrant Officer George Parker from the PBRs, down on the Saigon River, and that George hadn't sounded very positive about how things were going down south.

"How do you think they are going up here?" Jon asked.

"Well, I'm just a one bar, and I'm pretty much a *the glass is half full* sort. That's what I've been told. That being said, we are doing some good stuff: our Special Landing Force on the amphibious ships and using helicopters for mobility advantage. The army air cavalry guys seem to be having some success with their helo ops as well in II and III Corps."

Like George Parker, Sandy said that one of the problems was protection of the villages. But in I Corps, the Marine Commanding General had begun assigning some fifteen-man squads full time to villages. The Marines didn't have enough people to do that in more than a couple of places, though, and there were a lot of vills. Sandy thought that if the ARVN would start doing that, it might make a difference. His perception, though, was that the ARVN liked to stick pretty close to their bases except for major ops. And major ops, well—

"But, there's plenty of guys with a *the glass is half empty* outlook, too," he'd said.

From the OP, Jon could still make out *Manfred's* silhouette. Light was fleeing earth fast. Sandy said they'd use the same watch rotation as last night, and he settled onto his poncho, and instantly, his slow, steady breathing said he was asleep.

Teresa did that. Her head hit the pillow, and she was zonked. Jennifer, needing to be fed and changed every handful of hours, day or night, made sleep a precious commodity. So many times over the last days and nights, he'd longed for sleep, but instead of it appearing immediately, it never appeared at all.

Sandy's soul, Jon thought, must be as free of sin and untroubled as Teresa's

Someday, Lord, please? If it be Thy will.

Jon was glad to be out of hack, out of the Locker, and doing something again. However, lying in a hole in the jungle, feeling so sweaty and dirty, he wasn't sure he'd ever feel clean again. There was no shower in sight for another day, at least. Things crawled over his skin. He finished his K-rats and wondered what Seaman Alvey would have brought on the tray that evening. The Ensign Locker, it seemed, did have some redeeming qualities, at least relatively.

The next day, the marines expected to link up with the unit patrolling north from Chu Lai. Maybe a shower tomorrow was in the offing.

Sergeant Evans appeared at the edge of the OP, just like he did the first night, and started Jon's heart to pounding. But that night, Jon put his finger on the safety but didn't move it.

Sergeant Evans whispered, "Mr. Z., heads up tonight. This is our last night in the bush. I hate last nights. More bad stuff happens on last nights. Just stay heads up."

Sandy stretched out on his poncho. "You take your malaria pill today, Jon?"

"I did."

Hate last nights! Heads up! Malaria pill. How the crap did those three things fit together?

After his question, Sandy dropped back into sleep, and Jon dropped back into crawling and peering and listening and sniffing. The hairs on the back of his neck must have heard the sergeant because they were more agitated than the night before.

As his watch wore on, he tried to keep focused on the job to hand, but Teresa insisted on a bit of attention. He worried that his letters might have gotten her excommunicated from the *Manfred* wives' group. After she had delivered Jennifer, the group had provided her with tremendous support. The wives' group had accepted her so readily, and he worried about her being cut off from that support. Jon also admitted he'd been jealous that she had been accepted so readily while he was getting the newbie treatment.

Heads up. Sergeant Evans' voice.

He moved around the edge of the OP. At a new position, he held his breath for as long as he could, thinking it would help him listen better. He was back at the southeast corner of the OP when he sensed something, a little to his right. He clicked off his safety and whispered, "Sergeant, you coming up?"

"Comin' up."

After he was beside Jon, he said, "How'd you know I was there?"

"I smelled you."

"Damn. I guess I'm going to have to start burying my dirty socks. You know, Mr. Two Buckets, you just might make a half-ways decent jarhead; that is if you give me your undivided attention for seventeen or eighteen years."

"A great recruiting line, Sarge. Course, I think it'll only work on seasick sailors."

"Wise-assed ensign," he hissed as he touched Sandy's shoulder.

17

Mid-watch sounds so normal. Yah, like Bonnie and Clyde, probably sounded before they became famous or infamous. Lieutenant (jg) Peter Feldman had to watch himself on the mid-watch. Sometimes he thought he was only thinking, and he'd say his thought out loud. He'd been embarrassed that way when he had been an ensign.

It was 0142, and there was a long way to go before the mid-watch was over. Already, his upper eyelids seemed to have been injected with lead. He groaned and walked out onto the starboard bridge wing. Dormant, his JOOD and the lookout were standing there, silent. The ship was heading southeast. Stars were above, and Vietnam was to starboard and, like the surface of the South China Sea, melted into blackness.

"Nothing on earth worse than a mid-watch, you agree, Dormant?" Peter said.

"Not really. All watches are pretty much the same to me."

After a minute, Peter tried, "Wonder how Two Buckets is holding up over there."

Dormant didn't respond to that conversational gambit, either.

"No thoughts to offer about that, Dormant?"

"Nope."

"I'm worried about you, Dormant." Peter raised his binoculars and peered at magnified blackness. "You talk so much, you could wear out your vocal cords."

Dormant shined his flashlight on his watch. "I'm going in to check our position on the chart. It's about time to reverse course."

After Dormant went inside the pilothouse, the bridge wing lookout said, "Mr. Feldman, it sounded like Mr. Stewart doesn't like Mr. Zachery."

"No, Seaman Randolph, that's not it. Mr. Stewart just has a few things bothering him at the moment, and I probably just made it worse trying to talk to him."

After the course reversal, Peter started cataloging his mid-watch miseries. His brain felt numb as if a deranged dentist had injected Novocain through his skull. But the dentist had missed a spot just behind his forehead. A persistent dull ache lived there. The scorched coffee he had been drinking left a disgusting taste in his mouth. There had been too much coffee, too, and his bladder was protesting. Sized to support his six-feet, five-inch frame, his big feet could contain more hurt than short guys' feet. Standing on the steel deck for hours at a stretch during the daytime didn't seem to be an issue for his feet, but during the mid-watch, they writhed in agony.

"Officer of the Deck," the port lookout called, "I've got tracers…"

Suddenly, the radio speaker mounted to the overhead at the rear, port side of the pilothouse crackled to life.

"*Manfred,* this is Zebra, immediate fire mission." Zebra was Jon Zachery's call sign. "Two rounds illumination, coordinates…"

Adrenaline obliterated the Novocain in Peter's brain, and he charged into the pilothouse, grabbed the phone to the CO's stateroom, and buzzed him. When he hung up the phone, he heard the Operations Officer, who was manning the Evaluator position in Combat, tell

Zebra that he would recommend to the CO that the ship go to General Quarters.

"This is Zebra, negative on the GQ. I need those illumination rounds now, over."

Peter heard the after mount slew around. *Wham* sounded, and a flash of white light lit up a patch of water. When the flash blinked out, it continued to fill Peter Feldman's eyes. He thought he could feel the heat on his retina.

"Shot," the Ops O called to let Zebra know rounds were on the way.

"Captain's on the bridge," called the Boatswain Mate of the Watch.

"Fill me in, Peter," the CO said as he headed to the port bridge wing.

Peter's vision was beginning to come back, but he still rammed into the chair on the port side of the pilothouse, trying to follow the CO out onto the bridge wing.

"Captain, we just fired two illumination rounds in response to a call from Ensign—Christ, look at the tracers!"

The illumination rounds popped like two little toy suns in another galaxy.

"*Manfred,* this is Zebra, two rounds high explosive—"

"I'm going to be in Combat, Peter," the CO said.

The guns fired and wiped out Peter's night vision again. He swore as "Shot" was called on the radio by the Ops O.

"Mr. Stewart," Peter called into the pilothouse.

There was no answer.

"He went out onto the starboard bridge wing, Mr. Feldman," the Boatswain Mate of the Watch said.

"Get him," Peter said and stuck one of his big feet in the pilothouse. "This is Mr. Feldman, I have the conn."

Before the personnel in the pilothouse could acknowledge the change of conning officer, the radio speaker blurted, "Add fifty, right fifty. Ten rounds HE. Fire for effect."

"Mr. Feldman has the conn, helmsman, aye, sir."

The engine order telegraph operator and the quartermaster also acknowledged the change in conning officer, but the guns drowned their words. The sound of powder canisters rattled onto the deck after each salvo from the after mount.

The Boatswain Mate stepped onto the bridge wing. "Mr. Feldman, Mr. Stewart—"

A *wham, rattle, rattle* stepped on the Bosun's words. He started talking fast to try to beat the next salvo, "He's just sitting on the deck on the starboard bridge wing, Mr. Feldman."

"What's his problem, Boats?"

"I don't know, sir. He just said he wasn't doing this."

"*Manfred*, this is Zebra. Right fifty. Four rounds of anti-personnel" came over the radio.

"Boats," Peter said, "you tell Ensign Stewart to get his butt out here next to me ASAP. If he won't come, drag him."

"*Manfred*, this is Zebra. Nice shooting. Just a little more work to do, though. Two rounds, illumination. New target…"

"Here's Mr. Stewart, sir," the Boatswain Mate said.

"Boats, take the lookout inside the pilothouse for a minute, please, and close the watertight door," Peter said.

The illumination rounds went out.

Peter waited until the dogging handle secured the door. "We are in the middle of some serious shit here, Dormant. I don't have time to discuss this. I need your help. Either you tell me you're going to do your part, or I swear to God, I'll throw you over the side."

Dormant didn't say anything, and Peter grabbed the front of Dormant's shirt.

"All right, all right. I'll do my part," Dormant said.

"*Manfred*, this is Zebra. Six rounds HE. Fire for effect" came over the radio.

Peter un-dogged the watertight door into the pilothouse and pulled it open.

"Boats, get the lookout back out here. Mr. Stewart, check with the quartermaster and Combat. See how long we can stay on this course," Peter said.

During the moment that the flash from the guns existed, Peter saw smoke rings rolling in toward the beach over what looked like a silvery oil slick on the water. He thought, God, I wonder what the CO would have done if he'd seen the business with Dormant.

Just as the last two powder canisters were being ejected from the gun mount, the radio came to life again. "*Manfred,* this is Zebra. Left 100, add fifty. Four rounds anti-personnel, over."

Dormant stepped out onto the bridge wing. "Peter, we're going to have to reverse course in a couple of minutes, according to Combat."

"Okay. I'd like you to take the conn back. Are you ready to do that?"

"Yes, sir."

"How would you reverse course?"

"I'll turn away from the beach, so I don't mask the after mount."

"All right. I don't know what the hell came over you earlier. We'll talk about it after we get off watch," Peter said.

Between the two salvos, the Boatswain Mate of the Watch announced, "Captain's on the bridge."

"*Manfred,* this is Zebra. Cease fire. Cease fire. The marines say they need a minute to take stock of the situation. But stand by, please. We may need some more help. I'll be back up in a minute."

"Okay, Peter," the CO said. "Reverse course and stay two miles off the beach." Peter passed the order to Ensign Stewart. "So, how'd things go out here, Peter? Any problems handling this from three sections instead of going to GQ?"

"Well, no, sir," Peter said. "Piece of cake, really. All the training we did from three-section watches, starting back in January…well, tonight, it seemed like all the training really came together."

"How'd Ensign Stewart do?"

"Uh, no problem, sir. Dormant, um, Ensign Stewart and I have been paired up for six months. We work pretty well together, I think."

The ship steadied on the new heading.

"Wonder where Mr. Zachery is? Seems like he's been gone a long time," Peter said.

"*Manfred,* this is Zebra," came over the radio. "Marines say you did a great job. Caught a fairly large unit in the open. You completely broke up the attack and drove them from the field. Battle Damage

Assessment will be provided in the morning. Marines told me to say thanks at least twice, and they also asked you to stay close because we may need you again before the night is over. And, uh, Zebra will be off the air for about fifteen minutes. I'll call to let you know I'm back up. Out."

"So, Skipper, Mr. Zachery sounded like he did pretty good tonight, wouldn't you say?"

"It sounded like it, but I'm sure we'll get something from the marines on that, Peter. Let's wait and see what they say. I'm going to check with the Ops O in Combat, and then I'm going back down to my room."

At 0404, Peter Feldman stood with William Stewart on the 01 level at the foot of the ladder from the starboard bridge wing. It was pitch-dark. Peter had used his red lens flashlight as he descended from the bridge wing.

"Dormant," Peter said. "Help me out here. What the hell was going on when we were doing the fire mission tonight? Why'd you disappear on me?"

Peter waited about two seconds, and then he clicked his flashlight on and shined it in Dormant's face. Dormant stood there with defiance and anger clear on his face in the red light.

"God damn it, Dormant, I don't have patience for your games. What you did was abandoning your post in a combat situation. It was dereliction of duty. It was cowardice in the face of the enemy. It…it was damned near treason. I told the Boatswain Mate of the Watch you were sick, kind of like when Two Buckets gets seasick. I've got it hanging out for you, Dormant. Now you talk to me."

"Peter, what we are doing here in Vietnam is wrong. I just can't do this anymore."

Peter turned off the flashlight, walked to the side of the ship, leaned on the railing, and muttered, "Jesus." Then, the only sound was a gentle swishing as the bow curved small waves back onto the surface. Peter hadn't even been aware of the sound until he'd walked to the rail.

Peter turned back toward Dormant. "Okay, you have to do

something first thing in the morning. You have to go to the XO and tell him. I can't have you on my watch team if I can't count on you. What you did this morning—what you just told me, you have to go to the XO. First thing, right? XO is up by 0530."

Dormant's voice was quiet. "I have already submitted a letter requesting conscientious objector status. The CO endorsed it with a recommendation to the Bureau to disapprove it. The XO said I had to do my duty until the Bureau told us otherwise. But, I can't do this anymore."

"I don't give a good God Damn about that. 0530. With the XO. And, Dormant, I'm going to be there to make sure you're there. I'm not going to cover for you again."

18

Jon jerked awake when the world blew up. He'd laid down on Sandy's poncho at 0103, rested his hand on his M-14, closed his eyes, and the world turned off. Then, a *whump* shook the ground. Close by, he heard *pop, pop, brrrrp.* He rolled over and saw Sandy firing to the south. There was another *whump* from just below the OP, and then it was like someone threw a scoop shovel of hail at the OP. Jon was showered with bits of brush. And Sandy lay on the ground next to him.

More popping and automatic weapon fire. From the south. Jon peeked over the brush. Sergeant Evans was off to his right. Dark forms hustled up the hill toward him. Fire erupted from the sergeant's position. The dark figures stopped. Six of them. They directed fire at the sergeant.

Jon fumbled, then found the safety. Aiming wasn't really possible, so he pointed his weapon and fired in semi-automatic, sweeping from side to side. Bullets *thwipped* past. He ducked to stick in a new magazine, moved sideways a couple of steps, stood, and resumed firing at the flashes below him. He spent that magazine and shoved in his last one. Down the hill, there were still two sets of muzzle flashes firing at the sergeant. Jon fired at one muzzle flash, shifted to the other, and fired. He expended that magazine in that way, alternating his target.

When he was out of ammo, he grabbed Sandy's carbine, stood up, and fired at the flashes again. Bullets *zipped* and *zicked* by him.

"Get down, you dumb-assed squid," boomed out of the darkness.

Jon fired two rounds, and then the carbine was empty. He ducked down and found a spare magazine on Sandy's belt. He stood again. Still two sets of flashes. He concentrated on one set and emptied his magazine at it. Then pulled another magazine from Sandy's belt.

That one stinking set of muzzle flashes was still there, and it traded fire with the sergeant. Jon again emptied his clip at the flash. John pulled his forty-five. That's what was left. The fire from before, for the moment, was silent.

"Sarge?" Jon half-whispered, half-shouted.

He coughed. "Check on Talbot, will you, sir?"

"You okay, Sarge?"

"Jesus Christ, Ensign. Check on Talbot. Now. Do it."

Jon stumbled through the brush to Talbot's position. He was slumped over onto his face. He rolled Talbot over and flicked his red-lens flashlight on, then quickly off. Talbot's face was a mess, and there was blood all over the front of him.

From down below the hill, from the company position, a fireworks show, like the finale, had just cut loose. But that was background noise. Jon focused on the area just below Private Talbot's position, where the muzzle flashes had come from.

He walked crouched over, screened by the brush. After a couple of steps, Jon heard moaning and fired three rounds at the sound. More moaning a bit to the left of the first. There was noise from the brush ahead of him, and Jon fired the rest of the clip. As he reloaded it hit him.

Company C. That's who they're after.

He flicked on his flashlight and hurried forward.

"Jesus, turn off the damned light."

Jon ignored the sergeant. There wasn't time. He had to make sure the wounded VC wouldn't stop him, and then he needed to call for support from *Manfred*.

He found two VC quickly. They looked like they were dead, but he put a round into the forehead of each. It took longer than he wanted, but he found four more and shot them too.

Jon hustled back to Sergeant Evans. "Sarge, we've got to get to the OP. The VC are attacking the Company. Can you walk?"

Sarge grunted. "Sorry, sir."

"Okay, I'm going to drag you. I don't have to tell you to hang onto your weapon, do I?"

"Wise-assed ensign."

Jon grabbed his flak jacket and started backing up to the OP. He was pretty winded when there got there. He used the flashlight again. Evans had been hit in the shoulder and the leg. Jon grabbed the rucksack next to the radios with the first aid stuff and tossed it to the sarge.

"Fix yourself up and watch for more bad guys."

"I got it, sir."

Jon pulled Sandy's forty-five from his holster, ratcheted the slide to make sure there was a round in the chamber, and placed the weapon next to the sergeant.

"Safety's on."

Then he sat on Sandy's poncho, placed the chart on a knee, shined the flashlight on it, and then he called *Manfred* for illumination rounds. The Ops O was the Evaluator in Combat, and he wanted to go to GQ. Jon wanted to scream at him. *No god damn time for no god damn GQ.* But he knew it was important to sound calm. He took a breath and let it out. He had to prod the Ops O once for the illumination, but, finally, the two shells popped. The light they threw off was a bit on the weird side, but it was effective. He got the binoculars.

"Oh, Jesus."

"What is it?" Sergeant Evans said.

"There's a pot load of them, Sarge."

Jon double-checked the coordinates and called the ship again for two rounds of HE. He prayed that he had figured it right and wouldn't hurt the marines.

Then he remembered Company C Command Post. He hadn't called them.

"Shot," the Ops O called. Hell, he couldn't talk to the CP and watch where the rounds fell. They were going to have to wait.

A blink of fire lit up the world in front of the marines' position, and the earth shook.

He grabbed the radio to the CP.

"Charlie, Zebra, looks like I should bring the rounds fifty yards closer to you, do you concur, over."

It was quiet for a moment; then, when the CP keyed the mike, Jon could hear the weapons firing both in the world and over the radio. "Charlie concurs, bring it in fifty yards."

The area below was crisscrossed with tracers, but he needed to stop looking at that. He rechecked the coordinates and made the call. Then, when he heard the "shot" call, he thought the flares were about to burn out, so he called for two more of those. The earth shook again. The two HE rounds were right where they needed to be. Jon called for more HE. The new illumination rounds popped; then, ten rounds of HE shook the earth like a 5.0 California earthquake. Next, he thought some anti-personnel rounds would serve pretty well.

Jon checked in with the CP. There wasn't much firing from their position, and he only saw an occasional burst from the direction of the VC. It probably meant the VC were disengaging. Almost certainly, they would move south and west, away from the coast. Jon ordered illumination rounds in that direction. He found some movement in the binoculars under the star shells, and *Manfred* dumped both HE and anti-personnel rounds on the area. Then he called a ceasefire.

Just as suddenly as the noise had started, it got quiet, and Jon slumped, totally wasted. *Jesus. Sergeant Evans.*

The bandage on his leg was soaked with blood, and blood had soaked through his shoulder bandage as well.

Jon grabbed the radio to the CP.

"Charlie, this is Zebra. I need a little help up here. I have two killed and one wounded, over."

It was quiet for a moment, then "Say again, Zebra." Jon recognized the the marine captain's voice.

Jon repeated the message and was told to hang on, that help was coming.

The radio handset was in his hand as he knelt in front of the boxy radio and prayed that it was over. Now that it had stopped, he didn't think he could start again.

But then an urgent and irresistible force drove him to his feet, and he hustled a few feet toward the eastern rim of the OP and puked till he thought his toenails had come out of his mouth too.

Jon grabbed his canteen, but it was empty. *The god damned gomers shot my canteen.*

"Damn, C-rats don't taste very good in that direction either, right, Mr. Zachery?"

"One thing I've learned. Marine sergeants are always right even when they're being wise-asses.."

Then he went to see if he could be of some help to Sergeant Wiseass. Hold his hand, maybe.

19

Winching back down to the deck of the *Manfred* wasn't any more fun than going up had been. He kept imagining his arms jerking up over his head and sliding out of the horse collar, so he hung on for dear life. Under the Marine Huey, downwash buffeted him, and he was spinning. It didn't feel like anything was under his control. That's what he disliked about the horse collar. When his feet hit the deck, he wasn't ready at all, and if Carl Lehr's sailors hadn't grabbed his arms, he'd have fallen.

"Jon, let go," Carl said.

Carl pried his fingers apart and slipped off the horse collar. As soon as he was clear, the winch operator in the Huey started retracting the cable. The Huey moved to port clear of the fantail, and he watched the nose dip as it started forward; then, it rolled to the left and headed back to the beach.

Carl was smiling as Jon took off his helmet. "Thought I might have to cut your fingers off to get you out of the rig. Twenty or thirty more rides, and you'll be a horse-collar pro."

Jon staggered a bit as he took a step. "Haven't got my sea-legs back yet, I guess. But it's right good being back aboard the US Navy warship *Manfred*. I'm so dirty. I'm heading right for the shower. We're not on water hours or anything, are we?"

"No, we're not on water hours, but the shower will have to wait. The CO wants to see you in his cabin right away."

"Oh, man. I'm such a mess. I'm going to call him and see if it's okay to clean up first."

Carl, Almost, laughed. "Two Buckets, you are a long way beyond a mess, but the CO said right away. He expects you to have some of Vietnam on you. You better hop to it, as the Skipper would say."

As Jon started along the port side of the main deck, he felt as if he had stepped onto some kind of sponge that sucked the strength out of him through his feet. Even on mid-watch, he'd never felt so wasted. His skull buzzed like a bumped hive.

When he got to the watertight door just aft of the wardroom, he rubbed his hand over his chin. Whiskers, a day and a half's worth. Under the mid-morning sun, his hands were dirty. His nails were caked with bloody dirt.

He took a breath, entered the door, and climbed the ladders to the CO's cabin. He knocked. The CO told him to enter. He was at his desk. The XO, the Ops O, and the Gun Boss were scrunched together on the fold-down sofa.

"Welcome back, Mr. Zachery," the CO said. "It looks like you had quite a night."

"Uh, well, sir, there wasn't any sleep last night after that VC attack, and today was pretty busy. Sorry, I'm such a mess. There was no time to get cleaned up."

The Skipper looked at Jon for a moment, and he saw what might be the beginnings of a smile and perhaps some kind of wise remark, but then he wiped his hand across his mouth and chin, and his *Thinker* look was back.

"First, Mr. Zachery, tell us about last night. Like to hear your side of it."

"Yes, sir." He stood in a relaxed parade rest, his hands clasped behind his back. "Both nights I was there, I was with three marines manning an OP. We split the night up into two-hour watches. Last night—" Then the world started spinning, and Jon grabbed onto the side of the CO's desk.

The CO stood, took Jon's arm, and placed him on his chair. "XO, get HM1 Darby up here."

"Wait, XO, uh, Skipper. I'm okay. I just didn't have anything to drink since late last night. I need some water, that's all."

The Skipper poured a glass of water from the carafe on his desk. Jon chugged it and two more. That emptied the carafe.

"Sorry, Skipper." Jon started to stand, but the CO held him in place.

"XO, please call the wardroom and have them bring up a folding chair and another jug of water—that is unless you want to countermand another order of mine, Mr. Zachery."

"No, sir." To Jon, his own voice sounded like Peter Feldman apologizing for stepping on someone's toes.

The Ops O stood up and gave the CO his place on the couch, and the CO asked Jon if he wanted to get some rest and report tomorrow.

"I'm okay, sir. Just needed some water. Thank you." Jon turned the chair and faced the couch. "So we had these two-hour watches. My watch was 2300 to 0100. Last night, sometime after I had gone to sleep at 0100 is when it started. I don't know exactly how many VC were there, but it looked like a lot of them when the first flares popped."

There was a knock on the door, and Seamen Benito and Alvey brought a folding chair and another carafe of water into the room.

"Jon," the CO said, "I wasn't on the bridge when your first call came. But you didn't want us to take the time to go to GQ, right? How come?"

"Well, sir, when the marines discovered the VC, they were already really close. I didn't want any delays from getting people shifted around in key watch stations. I thought a couple of minutes could be really important. And, I'd seen us handle things from three section, sir."

"If we'd gone to GQ, we could have been delivering illumination with one mount and HE with the other. Did you think of that?"

"I did think of that, Skipper, and Ops O mentioned that before I went ashore. But I was sure that time was a lot more important than both gun mounts. And actually, it worked out fine. All you have to do is keep track of how long the flares are burning and don't let them go out before calling for new ones."

Jon's lips were coated with dried spit, and he licked them. The Ops got up and poured another glass of water.

"Okay, Jon. I was in Combat for most of the firing. You mixed up HE and anti-personnel rounds. Any idea as to how that worked out?" the CO said.

"All I can tell you, sir, is that it seemed like a good idea to blanket the target area with shrapnel after dumping HE on them. From the school I went to, you get better area coverage with air bursts. That's why I called for them. The marines found twenty-seven bodies, and they estimated the VC drug several more off the battlefield. They showed me something that was sort of like a baling hook made from bamboo. The marines said that's what the VC use to drag bodies off the field.

"Before I left the marines, I talked to the company commander, and he said they were going to get out an after-action report tomorrow."

"We know the marines took casualties. Do you know how many?" the CO said.

"Yes, sir, they had four killed and nine wounded." Jon looked down at his hands, but what he saw was faces peering out of two body bags; then, the bags, one by one, were zipped shut over Sandy and Talbot.

Jon cleared his throat. Twice. And a third time to get the grapefruit-sized lump out of his throat. He took a sip of water. "Uh, Skipper." That dad-burned grapefruit tried to rise again. Jon clamped his jaw shut and rubbed his eyes. "That's really the story of last night—or this morning, I guess. Can I take you up on the offer to finish this tomorrow, please? How about if I write up what happened and get it to the Ops O this afternoon?"

"If we have to, I think we can wait a little longer than that. You look like you could use a little sleep. But take a shower first. And don't worry about running the ship out of water."

"Aye, sir. And thank you. And, sir, I'd just like to say I think, uh, you know if it means anything, coming from me, that *Manfred* did a great job for those marines this morning. I'm fairly certain they'd have had a lot more casualties if you hadn't delivered those rounds just where they needed to be. I remember back in January, you told us that every day we had to train was monumentally important to us. I think I know what you were talking about, sir. Now. And thanks for letting me go in there, sir, after *gooning* things up the way I did."

Then Jon was in the passageway outside the door to the CO's cabin. He leaned against the bulkhead. Water leaked out of his eyes. The grapefruit was back in his throat, and a sob was trying to shove the darned thing out of the way. But he clamped his jaws tight, and his throat hurt, but finally, the sob stopped trying to escape, and the grapefruit sank. He took a breath, and just before he gathered the strength to go below, he heard a murmur of voices from inside the CO's cabin, but he couldn't make out the words.

The CO moved back to his chair by the desk. "You heard from the marines this morning before you got off watch, Ops O, and they said Jon did a great job, that right?"

"Right, Skipper. The first report said we saved them a lot of casualties, and they indicated Jon was a key factor in getting the illumination and fire support they needed. Then I talked to the Company Commander. He said he almost wasn't going to take our offer of a Gunfire Liaison Officer, thinking we'd send them some snot-nosed, wet-behind-the-ears kid who'd just be underfoot. But, he said he was real glad to have Jon when the shooting started."

"I got the feeling there's something he didn't tell us," the CO said.

"And I still don't know what to make of him. He's been with the ship for almost six months. As a former enlisted man, maybe I expected too much from him. I don't know yet. But he's certainly had his share of ensign screw-ups. He gets seasick. But then so did I when I was a boot ensign. He's a good ship driver." The CO looked at the Ops O. "He's got a real feel for it, and as long as he doesn't get too cocky with it, he could be as good as you and Cheng."

The CO shook his head side to side. "When I got to Combat last night, he really sounded like he was in charge of the situation. There was no hesitancy. And the bit about managing the illumination— first time in a situation like that, night as black as sin, guns firing, marines taking casualties, and he's managing HE, anti-personnel, and illumination rounds like the pro from Dover."

"Skipper," the Ops O said, "when I told Jon I was going to recommend GQ, he was very insistent that we not do that, and then he said something like 'where's the illumination?' He wanted me worried about that and nothing else. There was no doubt in my mind that he was on top of the situation, and he was in charge. I have been pretty tough on him. But I was impressed last night, this morning. I'd go so far as a halfway close to satisfactory."

The XO piped in. "Back on the helo deck, with the DASH turn-up, if he hadn't been there, we could easily have had our own casualties back there. He talked about how brave Carl was, but he figured out the switch to push."

The Ops O said, "I think he may have turned the corner."

"What's the saying about 1000 bridges vs. one crudely phrased homosexual indiscretion? He's given us many more than a single indiscretion, and he's still short on bridges. I am still a long way from getting over those damn letters of his and his getting thrown off the bridge." The CO rubbed his fingers over his eyes. "With him and Dormant… Ensigns aren't the only ones who get character-building experiences, eh, XO?"

Jon was dirty, tired, and hungry, in that order, until he walked into the wardroom. The stewards were eating. They generally ate before serving meals to the officers, and they were grilling ham steaks. Hunger vaulted to the top of the list, and the cook was merciful. Seaman Benito brought Jon a ham steak as thick as the steel plate on the side of the ship along, with a salad and some bread.

Perhaps ecstasy was a bit much, but something to chew that did *not* come out of a K-rats container was close to it. It smelled wonderful. It tasted wonderful. Then it hit him. *Hack.* He should be eating in the Locker. He stopped in mid-chew just as the door on the after, port corner of the wardroom pulled open, and the XO entered.

He muscled the half-chewed mouthful down. "XO, I'm sorry, sir. I forgot. I'll go down to the Locker." He started to stand.

"Relax, Mr. Zachery. It's okay."

The XO sat down across from Jon at mid-table. "Go ahead and eat, Jon. You mind if we talk while you work on that?"

"No, sir."

The XO pointed to his plate. "You probably ate a lot better than that with the marines, eh?"

Jon was almost too tired to smile, but not quite. "We got a hot meal at noon yesterday, but K-rations were it the rest of the time, XO. We eat pretty well here on *Manfred*. It did make me glad Teresa was never interested in camping, though."

Jon looked up at the XO. "Uh, sir, did my letters wind up getting Teresa in Dutch with the wives' group?"

"That was something I was going to talk to you about. We got a message through the CRUDESPAC chaplain. The CO's wife talked with Teresa, and they went together and talked with Melanie Hanson. And Teresa talked to the wives' group all together at a coffee at the CO's house. The CO's wife said she was impressed with how Teresa stepped up to get the situation straightened out. All she needed was a little explanation of how the navy does things, it seems. Teresa is doing fine."

"I was worried about what I had done to her."

"She's fine. Tomorrow, we'll talk about getting you integrated back into things here. In the meantime, though, once you are done eating, you are still in hack. Tomorrow, after you get your write-up on your time with the marines to the Ops O, I'll come get you, and we'll talk about what needs to happen. Okay?"

"Yes, sir. Thanks."

The XO smiled, and it reminded Jon of his grandfather on his Mom's side. Grandpa Zachery never smiled. It wasn't hard to figure where his Dad got that tendency.

"XO, is it okay to ask what we, uh, what the ship is going to be doing now?"

"Sure. We're heading roughly north-northeast, twenty-two knots. We'll rendezvous with an oiler this evening and top off. Then we will join up with USS *Reilly* and relieve the North SAR ships at 0500. That relief will take place just south of nineteen-north. Then *Reilly* and *Manfred* continue to twenty-north to man the North SAR station for forty days. That's it."

"Thanks, XO."

"I'll talk to you in the morning, then."

When Jon opened the door to the Ensign Locker, both Dormant and Cowboy were on top of their bunks reading.

"Hey, Cowboy, Dormant, you guys really did good on the mid-watch last night. The marines really needed your help," Jon said.

Cowboy sat up, there was a grimace on his face, and he held his palm out to Jon, which he thought meant to stop. *Stop what?* Dormant rolled abruptly out of his bunk, grabbed his trousers, pulled them on, stuffed his feet in his shoes, grabbed his shirt, pushed roughly past Jon, and went into the head.

After Jon closed the door, Cowboy said, "Dormant has had a bad day. Early this morning, he saw the CO and XO for the second or third time about the conscientious objector business, but the CO says Dormant's only way out is with Bureau of Personnel approval. And the letter just went off to BUPERS. The CO told him if he didn't do his duty, he would be placed under arrest and court-martialed. Just after he left the CO, we got word about the 27 KIA. Dormant wanted to go back to the CO, but the XO wouldn't let him. XO told him the CO laid out how he had to perform. Word is the XO said, 'Your choice, Dormant. What's it going to be?' I heard that Dormant turned and tried to walk away, but the XO jumped up and grabbed him, and made him answer the question. Dormant didn't want a court martial. 'Then you know what you need to do,' the XO said, 'so do it, and stop bringing this BS to the CO.'"

"I wish I could feel some sympathy for him, but I can't," Jon said. "Four marines were killed and another nine wounded. If the ship hadn't responded the way it did, there would've been more."

"Bummer about the marine casualties, but we got twenty-seven gomers!" Then Cowboy called Dormant a Communist with several sailor-talk adjectival modifiers.

Someone, had to be Dormant, stomped up the ladder. He'd probably heard them. The walls of the Ensign Locker were just sheet metal.

But that was Dormant's problem. Jon took a shower that was as delicious as the ham steak had been; then, he put on clean skivvies, got between clean sheets, and took out his letter-writing materials.

Dearest Teresa

It is so massively tired out, but I love you from the depths of my soul, which is tired, too, but never too tired to love you.

Jon stopped writing and marveled how easy, how natural it had been to write those words. He counted them. Twenty-seven words, but he could have written 1027 words just as easily without mentioning where he'd been or what he'd done. It seemed like the first comforting thought he'd ever had in his entire life.

He put aside his letter-writing material, clicked off his bunk light, rolled onto his back, and told God he'd crank up the rosary tomorrow. Then he started a "Please, God, watch over" prayer. He listed Teresa and Jennifer before the world blinked off.

20

Gong! Gong! Gong!

Jon's eyes popped open. He didn't know where he was. *Marines don't go to GQ.*

"I hear you already, for Christ's sake," Cowboy shouted at the GQ alarm.

"General Quarters. General Quarters. All hands man your battle stations," the ship's announcing system blared. Then the gonging started again. It was 0517.

The ship heeled suddenly, and halfway out of his bunk, he had to hang onto the angle iron. You could feel the ship accelerating. First the GQ alarm, then the hard turn, then flank speed. All three were like separate full doses of adrenaline. Almost, then Admiral Ensign bolted out the door with Jon close behind. As Jon rattled up the ladder to the main deck, the ship heeled again, and he stopped climbing and clung to side rails. When *Manfred* steadied, he, and all the others, continued their race to their battle stations.

When Jon entered CIC, he noted the cigarette stench but didn't stop for it. The CO was at the Evaluator position, speaking into a phone. Next to him, Don Minton had a radio handset up to his face.

The other members of the electronics-warning receiver GQ team were in the cubicle. Newly demoted ETSN Zambowski had earphones on and was listening to a signal.

"Zambowski," Jon said, "what's up?"

"Sir, we picked up a North Vietnamese PT boat radar," Zambowski looked at his watch, "about seven minutes ago. The Commodore thought it was a friendly PT, but the Evaluator called the CO. I showed him the parameters, and he sent us to GQ. And I'm still receiving North Vietnamese PT boat radar on the WLR-1."

"Okay, Zambowski, thanks. Now do a general search through the high-frequency band. Make sure nothing else is irradiating us, like MiGs."

"Aye, sir."

Zambowski completed a scan through the entire high band and reported no other signals but the PT Boats. Jon scribbled a note to the effect there were no other electronic threats detected by the warning receiver. He directed, also recently demoted, Seaman Apprentice Honor to deliver the message to the CIC Officer.

Jon asked Zambowski to show him the basic parameters of the signal they had detected. Noting the frequency, pulse width, and pulse repetition frequency, Jon opened the reference book across his knees as he sat on his upside-down trashcan. The signal parameters corresponded to a P6 Torpedo Boat: Russian design and either Russian or Chinese manufacture. A P6 had 23mm guns and two 21-inch torpedo tubes and was capable of forty knots.

When the ship was at General Quarters, being in the electronics warning receiver cubicle was like confinement to the Ensign Locker. From inside the cubicle, you could feel turns and get a sense of the ship's speed. The rest of what was happening was a mystery. But at least at GQ, Jon could walk out into CIC and see what was happening. He started to leave the cubicle when it hit him. He was not supposed to be here. He was still in hack.

Too late now.

Jon left the cubicle and walked out into CIC to see what was going on. He looked over the shoulder of one of the radar operators. There were three closely spaced blips to the west at a range of about six miles. The CO was sitting at the Evaluator's desk in the center of the room. He had a radio handset pressed to the side of his head.

"Sherman, this is *Manfred*," the CO said into the handset. "I am requesting weapons free. Repeat, request weapons free."

"*Manfred*, this is Sherman. Negative. Weapons tight," came over the speaker mounted to the overhead above the CO.

Sherman was the call sign of Captain Brass, who was in *Reilly*, and in tactical command of the two destroyers. He controlled permission to fire for the formation.

"Sir, range to hostile contact alpha is now five and a half miles, and they are tracking at thirty-eight knots and closing," a radar operator called.

"Sherman, this is *Manfred*. I am urgently requesting weapons free. I have a clear hostile signal from the enemy boats, and I know all friendlies are clear of the firing bearing. Repeat, urgently request weapons free."

"Negative. Weapons tight. Out."

The CO muttered something, and he looked at the radio handset in his hand.

"*Manfred*, this is Sherman. Go to General Quarters."

The CO snatched up the handset. "This is *Manfred*. I have been at General Quarters for five minutes. Request weapons free, over."

"Negative! Negative! Negative! Weapons tight. Out."

The CO slammed the handset down onto the desk, and the earpiece shattered.

"God damn it all to hell. What are they thinking over there?" The CO sat looking at the pieces of broken radio handset on the desk in front of him. Then he turned to Don Minton. "Take over here. I'm going to send the Ops O in to man the Evaluator seat. I can't do anything in here. I'm going out on the bridge where I can see what's happening." He started to get up. "And, Don, call the Gun Boss and ask him if the sonar can pick up torpedo screw noise at this speed."

Jon got on the phone and called the ET shop and had them send a new radio handset up to CIC, and then he went back into the electronics-warning cubicle. "Well, guys, the three PT boats continue to close on us. They are probably about five miles away right now. The CO wants to open fire on them, but the Commodore on *Reilly* won't give him permission. The CO is really torqued-off. So all we can do is run at twenty-eight knots, but the PTs are doing thirty-eight."

The night before, as the ship crossed the latitude line running through the DMZ, the CO had ordered engineering to light off superheat in the two operating boilers. Many destroyer COs would not use superheat, especially in a three-section-watch condition. The superheat only afforded an extra two or three knots of speed at the cost of increased fuel consumption. Commander Carstens, however, had decided that in the northern Tonkin Gulf, a few more knots of speed were worth the price of the extra fuel. If he hadn't had super-heaters lit off, the ship's speed would have been limited to twenty-five knots, three knots less than they were currently making. At times like this, even a half-knot of extra speed seemed like a lot.

Jon left the cubicle again and stood behind the Ops O, who was now in the Evaluator chair. Seaman Apprentice Presley, the other newly demoted sailor from E Division, was screwing the connector on the end of the cord from a new radio handset into the console in front of the Ops O.

A phone talker reported, "Sir, bridge wing lookout reports aircraft are firing rockets at the PT boats." The phone talker paused for a moment listening. "Sir, the lookout says the planes hit one of the PTs, and it has stopped and is smoking. The other two are turning away."

A radarscope operator turned and called over his shoulder into the compartment, "Sir, I hold one of the targets from hostile contact Alpha dead in the water. The other two hostiles are in a port turn."

Hostile contact Alpha was the three PT boats. They had been in a "V" shaped formation.

The ship heeled as it began a turn to port, and Jon grabbed onto the back of the Evaluator chair, which was right in front of him. The Ops O was on the phone with the gun director. "No, Gun Boss, weapons are still tight. We do not have permission to fire."

The phone talker piped in again, "Sir, lookout just said, Holy Shit, one of the PTs just blew up. And he said the third one continues to haul ass back toward the shore."

"No, Gun Boss," the Ops O was shouting. "You cannot fire at the last boat.

Weapons tight. Weapons tight."

"Sir, lookout just said the flyboys got the last one," said the phone talker. He listened a moment. "It is stopped and burning."

Jon felt like he was watching a three-person tennis match on an equilateral triangular court. The phone talker was to his left, the Ops was right in front of him, and the radar operator with the surface picture was to his right.

Abruptly, the ship slowed to fifteen knots while continuing the port turn.

The phone talker again, "Sir, the signal bridge says they are looking at PT boat number 3 with the big binoculars. They see no sign of survivors. The boat is down at the stern and is burning and sinking. Sigs says PT number 1 is also sinking, and they counted a couple of guys jumping into the water."

Jon went back into the cubicle, closed the curtain behind him, and began to tell Zambowski what had happened when Don Minton opened the curtain and said, "Jon, CO wants to see you on the bridge."

As Jon entered the bridge, Andrew Dunston, who had the conn, ordered five knots. The CO was on the starboard bridge wing. USS *Reilly* was off the beam. Her dark destroyer silhouette—she showed no running lights—stark against the red glow of dawn.

"Mr. Zachery, we've got three survivors from a PT Boat in the water up ahead." I could make out white-capped, choppy wave action for a short distance ahead, but that's all I could see. The CO continued, "We're putting a boat in the water to pick these guys up. I want you to be boat officer. *Reilly's* launching a boat, too. So, get down to the starboard motor whaleboat. They'll have a forty-five for you there and a walkie-talkie. I'll be talking to you from this one." He pointed to a brown loaf of bread-sized radio on the deck beside him; then, he looked back at Jon.

"Mr. Zachery, these are enemy sailors. Be careful of them. If you have any concerns, just call on the walkie-talkie. Questions?"

"No, sir."

"Hop to it then."

It was getting lighter by the moment. Twelve knots of wind chopped the surface into shallow waves, which *Manfred* hardly felt. Their motor whaleboat, though, which entered the water before *Reilly* launched hers, bobbed and rolled like a demented beast. At first, it seemed to be something Jon had to fight, but it became clear that fighting the ocean was a useless expenditure of energy. After Jon decided to just hang on, it was almost as if the boat had been waiting for him to realize that. Then, all they had to worry about was, as they bobbed up and down next to the ship, would the hook and pulley from the davit hit one of them in the boat. The coxswain gunned the motor and steered clear of *Manfred*.

Besides Jon, three sailors were in the boat: The coxswain was in the stern steering and operating the engine controls; Seaman Alvey had a ten-gauge shotgun and was seated between the coxswain and Jon, and Seaman Sheffield had an M-16 in the bow. Next to Seaman Sheffield was a boathook, a long pole with a small blunt-nosed hook for seizing a line to aid in pulling the boat into a mooring. All of them in the boat wore battle helmets and Mae West life preservers.

Reilly's boat approached two of the PT boat survivors who were close together. Jon pointed to the third dark figure bobbing in the water between *Manfred* and *Reilly's* boat, and the coxswain started the boat toward him.

Jon picked up the walkie-talkie and held the awkward device up so he could talk into the mouthpiece. *Hope I don't drop the darned thing in the water.*

"*Manfred*, this is Whale Boat, radio check, over," Jon said.

"Loud and clear, Whale Boat," the Skipper said. "We don't see any other survivors. *Reilly*'s boat looks like they are getting two of them, and you are heading for the third. Just stay heads up."

"Whale Boat, roger."

Jon turned half-ways around and shouted over the growl of the motor. "Okay, coxswain, see if you can get the survivor in the lee of the bow."

Jon looked forward. "Seaman Sheffield, put the M-16 down and get the boat hook. Use that to try to get the guy in close. Alvey, put the shotgun down and be ready to help Sheffield."

"Be ready," the captain had said. Jon unsnapped the cover over the forty-five in his holster and drew the weapon. He ratcheted the slide to drive a round into the chamber and checked the safety. Then, he rested the weapon on his lap as he sat on the bench seat.

It looked like the situation was working out. The coxswain had maneuvered the boat, so the waves were coming against the port bow, and the survivor was just off the somewhat sheltered starboard side.

The survivor looked young, a kid, really. He'd just had his boat sunk, and he was in the water and helpless. He didn't seem like he could pose a real threat.

They were close now. Sheffield extended the boat hook to the survivor. Jon saw a look of pure hatred flash over the face of the North Vietnamese sailor. The North Viet grabbed the boat hook with his left hand. His right hand was underwater and not visible. Jon thought he might be wounded and that he might have been mistaken about the hatred.

Seaman Sheffield had pulled the North Vietnamese sailor in close to the side of the boat; then, holding the boat hook in his left hand, he reached out with his right hand to grab the black shirt of the survivor. Alvey leaned forward to help.

The man in the water lunged up and stabbed a knife into Sheffield's shoulder. Jon armed and raised the pistol, and the North Viet fell back in the water and went under. Sheffield was cussing, but Jon watched where the survivor had gone under. His head popped up, and he drew back his arm to hurl the knife, and Jon fired. The round hit him in the left shoulder and turned him, but he still held onto the knife, and

Jon had not been mistaken about seeing hate on the kid's face. The North Viet righted himself, facing the boat again, drew back his arm to hurl the knife again, and Jon shot him again. Striking the man in the chest, dead center. The North Viet went under again, and Jon fired a third round at the spot where he'd been.

"Mr. Z," the coxswain said, "Would you pass this first aid kit to Alvey?"

"First back us up twenty yards. That guy was hell-bent on taking one of us with him."

The boat grumbled but not loud enough to drown out the radio.

"Whale Boat, what the hell happened? Why'd you shoot that guy?"

Jon safed the pistol and laid it on his lap. Then he grabbed the first aid kit and handed it to Alvey. Then he picked up the radio.

"Skipper, the survivor stabbed Seaman Sheffield as we tried to haul him in the boat. The North Viet went back in the water, and he was ready to throw his knife when I shot him. I only wounded him. He tried to throw the knife again, and I shot him again. Now, I'm bringing the boat back. Would you call for the corpsman to meet us, please, sir? And, sir, would you have the lookout keep his binocs on the spot just forward of our boat? To see if that guy surfaces again."

To the coxswain, Jon said, "Let's go home."

Jon picked up the radio again. "Skipper, Whale Boat over."

When he responded, Jon suggested he call the *Reilly* and tell them to have their boat be careful with their survivors.

Alvey had placed some gauze pads over Sheffield's wound and wrapped it with bandage. The gauze and the bandage were soaked with blood.

"Bleeding's slowed down, Mr. Z," Sheffield said.

When they got alongside, Alvey attached the hoisting gear to the forward hookup point while the coxswain worked on the aft attachment.

Sheffield was staring over Jon's shoulder at the rear of the boat.

"How're you doing, Sheffield?"

He raised his eyes to meet Jon's. "We were trying to help him, Mr. Z."

"We were, and I'm sorry I didn't cover you properly. I should have had my weapon on him as you pulled him into the boat."

"Nothing for you to worry about, Mr. Z. He was just a treacherous little bastard. What the hell kind of people are they?"

Jon didn't have an answer for him. Sheffield was a good kid. Jon liked him from his first morning on the ship when he had been the messenger on the quarterdeck. Jon had stood quarterdeck and bridge watches with him several times. He was a quiet, competent young man, and Jon felt like he had let him down. Then he remembered what Warrant Officer George Parker had said about the Viet Cong. "They all think they have already died for their country."

When the boat was level with the main deck, the hoist stopped. Alvey climbed out of the boat, and HM1 Darby climbed in to take care of Sheffield. Darby was quickly satisfied that a move to sickbay was in order. Jon helped get the wounded sailor aboard, then he climbed out of the boat, too. Before he walked away, he thanked the coxswain and told him he'd done a great job.

Up ahead, *Reilly* was moving, throwing a wake, doing at least fifteen knots, and *Manfred* started moving, too, to fall in astern of her.

Home sweet home.

Crap! Another report to write. And I still owe the Ops O the report about yesterday. Or whenever I was with the marines.

21

"Secure from General Quarters" was passed over the ship's announcing system. 0750.

The CO came thundering down the ladder from the bridge, the 02 level, to the 01 level, where Jon stood with his hands on the lifeline railing. Jon stood at attention. He wore no hat, so he didn't salute.

"At ease. Jon, are you all right?"

"You're whiter than—"

"Than when I get seasick, sir?"

"Well, yeah. Like that. Again, how you bearing up? Looking a man right in the face and shooting him. I have no idea how I'd handle something like that."

"Sir, he wasn't a man. He was a kid. Like most of our sailors on *Manfred*. Uh, sorry, sir. I meant *your* sailors."

"No, you didn't, Two Buckets. And I'm glad you said *our* and even gladder that you meant it."

The Skipper had talked to the boat coxswain and Alvey. He recited the things they'd told him and asked Jon if he had anything to add. Jon told him about that look of pure hatred the North Vietnamese sailor had on his face.

The commodore, the Skipper said, wanted a report, so he had to get back to the bridge. After a hard look into Jon's eyes, the CO departed to call his boss.

Ahead, *Reilly* was off the starboard bow. Maybe a thousand yards. Maybe fifteen hundred. The two ships steamed smartly, probably twenty knots.

Jon watched how *Manfred's* bow wave pushed aside the small wind-driven waves as if to say, "Hot stuff coming through here. Stand aside."

Then the waves went away, and he was seeing the North Vietnamese sailor, just his head above water. His thick, short, black hair was water-plastered to his skull. There was a berserk rage and hate on his face. Looking into his black eyes was like the images Jon had seen on television of looking into the cone of an active volcano. There was the fire-red lava, some flowing out of the cone and some molten globs flying through the air, set against a black-as-hell backdrop of cinders. When he'd seen the image on TV, he thought he was looking into hell.

The image went from a still shot to a movie, and Jon watched as his first shot hit the sailor in the left shoulder with the tinge of red in the swirl of water as the bullet impact pushed his shoulder back. But that first shot only seemed to intensify the rage, the hate, and the fire in the boiler of the sailor's soul. The second shot hit him dead center and slammed him underwater. Then there was the third shot, at nothing but the water where his target had been.

"Mr. Zachery?" the CO said. "Should I tell Darby to give you a medicinal brandy?"

"No, but thank you, sir. There's been too many of us from Electronics Repair division drinking aboard ship."

"Huh. You're right. It's time to pick up the pieces and put *Manfred's* life back together again. If the North Viets let us. That's what you meant, right?"

"Uh, Skipper—"

"That's okay, Mr. Zachery. I know the answer to the question. But you might want to hustle down to the wardroom. The stewards are serving K-rations. You might want to get down there before the vultures devour it all."

The Skipper climbed the ladder again. It was out there around Jon. That last night with the marines, that morning in the boat and looking into the eyes of hell. Out there, and close enough to feel, but he hadn't let it in. He wouldn't let it in.

"Breakfast will be served on the mess decks at 0815," the 1MC blared.

Jon looked aft. The ship was now in a slight right turn, and he could see past the starboard motor whaleboat davit to where plastic garbage bags bobbed in the wake. Just moments ago, he had shot a man, and now the cooks were fixing breakfast, and the mess cooks were heaving garbage over the side.

When Jon walked into the wardroom, he noted the platter loaded with cold cuts, cheese slices, and bread in the middle of the table. He was hungry, but then, he didn't want to eat, either. He went down a level to the head, washed his hands, and came back to the wardroom and got a cup of coffee from the urn. He sat near the junior end of the table and sipped. It was scalding hot, and it burned his tongue.

The door to the wardroom opened.

"Jon," the Ops O said. "You okay? You look a little pale."

"Yes, sir," Jon said. "I'm okay."

The Ops O got a cup of coffee and sat across from Jon. "Well, I didn't see the encounter with the North Vietnamese survivors. I was in Combat, but the CO told me there was nothing else you could do."

"Sir, that stuff is really hot."

The Ops O blew across the top of the cup and took a cautious sip, winced, and nodded. "Just talked to the Skipper. We talked about the electronic warning system. Your suggestion about manning the cubicle during three-section watches paid off this morning."

Jon had made that suggestion back in April after an at-sea training period. When he'd checked aboard, they only manned the electronic warning cubicle during GQ. The Ops O never mentioned it, but when the ship arrived in the Tonkin Gulf, and the ship went to three-section watches, manning the cubicle was part of the watch bill.

Was that an attaboy? From the Ops O?

And why now, when it was such routine business compared to looking a kid in the eyes and shooting him?

"Skipper also said he's not quite sure what to do with you," the Ops O took another sip. "He's still PO'ed about your letters and having to throw you off the bridge. And then this morning, he said you wouldn't talk to him on the radio when you were boat officer. What happened?"

"Well, sir, you know the North Vietnamese we were trying to rescue cut one of the boat crew with a knife. So it got busy. The way it was, I could either do the business the Skipper sent me out there to do, or I could talk on the radio. I did the business."

The Ops O looked down at his coffee, blew across the top again, and took another sip. "Well, it may turn out you did the right thing. Still, after all our discussion about being a Lone Ranger..." The Ops O took a sip. "So, we'll talk about that later.

"Right now, I need some help with the after-action report, and I need two write-ups from you. First, cover the electronic warning receiver detection of the PT Boat radar. Cover the signal parameters, but also write about the training program you set up. Also, put in there that we added the electronic warning receiver to the three-section watch bill. Second, I need a write-up on your stint as commanding officer of the motor whaleboat. And take your time with the write-ups. Take say...twenty-seven-and-a-half minutes."

Jon got up from the table and took his coffee cup down to the Locker. Getting out a tablet of lined paper at the fold-down desk, he began to write. The pen started dropping words onto the paper as if it had a mind of its own.

Thirty minutes later, Jon knocked on the Ops O's door, entered when told to do so, and handed him three sheets of lined paper that contained a double-spaced, hand-written description of the warning receiver's part in the morning's activities. After scanning the pages, the Ops O nodded and held out his hand for the three additional sheets.

The second page contained the story of the whaleboat encounter with the North Vietnamese sailor. The Ops O was on the second page of the second report when his phone rang.

He jerked the phone out its holder on the bulkhead behind him. "Ops O, sir." After listening for just a moment, he said, "The Skipper wants to see you in his cabin."

"Did he say what for, sir?"

"He wanted to see you, is what he said. By the way, these reports are fairly close to satisfactory—considering the source. Now get on up to the Skipper before he calls again and has a piece of my butt for failure to follow orders."

As Jon went forward via the amidships passageway, he plowed over what he might have done that got him called back to the CO's room. He'd forgotten he'd still been in hack and went to his GQ station. Busting hack was probably worse than what he did to get put there in the first place.

The CO was at his desk, and the XO was sitting on the fold-down sofa. Both of them were wearing their own versions of the CO's *Thinker*/poker-player face.

"XO just brought me this message. It's a *personal for* to me from the marine colonel on the LPH who owns the company we supported the last couple of days. Sit down on the sofa there next to the XO and read this."

"You want me to sit down, sir?"

"It's not that complicated a maneuver, Mr. Zachery. See, even the XO figured out how to do it. Take a seat and read the message."

The message said that Jon had asked Company C commander not to mention the part he had played in the VC attack yesterday. Still, the Colonel felt he had to send this report to the CO. Sergeant Evans had told the Company Commander about what had happened at the OP, and then, the colonel's message said that he was putting Jon in for the Bronze Star. He requested his full name and service number. He also said that the guys in Company C had named the slight hill, where the OP had been, Zachery's zit since it was too low to be considered a proper hill.

Jon handed the message back to the CO. It was quiet for a long moment.

"Care to tell me why you didn't want them to mention what you did?" the CO said.

The XO was sitting kind of sideways on the sofa so he could look at Jon.

"Captain," Jon cleared my throat, "you know, those guys are out there slogging around in the mud all the time. They told me about booby traps, ambushes, pungi stakes, leeches, jungle rot, trench foot, all manner of nasty stuff they encounter every day. I show up out of the blue, am there for a couple of days, then back here with hot chow, hot shower, movie in the wardroom. Just didn't seem right that anything is made over what I did. I think Lieutenant Stephenson and Sergeant Evans got most of the VC. And, Lieutenant Stevenson and Private Talbot were killed. Sergeant Evans was wounded twice, but he kept right on functioning until we were done. Sergeant Evans could have bled to death, but he got the job done and didn't worry about himself. What I did, I was just lucky. When it was all over, I puked; and I was shaking so bad, I wasn't sure I was going to be able to get the sergeant bandaged up. And, uh…"

Jon thought he should just shut up at that point, but the CO made a "come on" gesture with his fingers.

The XO said, "You know, Mr. Zachery, having a conversation with you can be aggravating. Sometimes you grab onto an issue like a bulldog, and you won't let go of it to save your life. Other times it is like pulling hen's teeth to get you to say what you are thinking."

Jon opened his hands on his lap and looked down at them. He half expected to find blood on them. "The other thing was that I was on your crap list." He looked up at the CO. "And I figured I deserved to be there. If I get off that list, I wanted it to be because I earned my way off, not by some fluky one-time thing like this. It just didn't seem right to take advantage of that."

"Mr. Zachery, you are a real piece of work." The CO let out

a breath, and he shook his head. "The colonel's message said the sergeant gave you credit for three of the VC."

"Sir, it was pitch-black that night, and we were just firing at muzzle flashes. I don't know if I got any or not. I am certain, though, that Sandy, the lieutenant, got some, and I'm sure the sergeant did, too."

The CO moved his finger down the message. "According to C Company Commander, the fires you called in got there in the nick of time. The Illumination helped the marines fight off the sappers and scouts; then, the HE and anti-personnel rounds fell right in the middle of the attack force. I was in Combat during most of that evolution. I was…impressed, I guess, with how you managed the three kinds of ordnance. And you really seemed confident in what you were calling for. First time in a firefight, at night, then having to call in support… I'm not sure I'd be so calm about it."

"I wasn't calm about it, sir. I just knew it would be better if I sounded calm, so that's what I tried to do."

The CO looked at him for a moment. "I am going to send the info to the marines that they asked for. And, I think the wardroom and crew should know about this."

"Okay to speak, sir?" Jon asked.

The CO looked at him and shrugged. "Speak."

"Two things if I may, sir. So, first, if you have to respond to the marines, fine, but please don't say anything to anyone here on *Manfred*, and especially not the Ops O. Sir, I need to figure out how to fix things with Charles Hanson, and I need to show the Ops O I am not Marinas Trench whale manure, but it has to be done normally, without any of this." He pointed to the message.

"And, sir, second, can I go back on the watch bill?"

The CO's eyes flitted to the XO for just a second. "XO, will you take care of that, please? Okay, Jon, anything else?"

He got up and started to leave, stopped, and said, "Sir, I'm sorry I forgot about being in hack this morning at GQ. When the gong went off, I thought I was still with the marines. But, that didn't last too long; then I just went to my station. I didn't even think about hack until after I got to Combat. Do I still need to be confined to quarters?"

The CO nodded to the XO.

"Yes, Two Buckets, you are still confined to quarters," the XO said. "Because, quite regularly, you find new and innovative ways to piss us off. But, at 1537, you can leave the Ensign Locker and go up to the bridge to relieve the noon to 1600 watch. Your confinement to quarters will end at that time."

As Jon clumped down the ladder, he felt some relief over having told the CO and the XO what had happened—keeping quiet was sort of like carrying a load. Now, the load was a bit lighter.

After he got to the Ensign Locker and started taking his sweaty uniform off, Cowboy came in.

"Hey, Two Buckets, I saw what happened with the North Vietnamese from the gun mount." Cowboy sat on Admiral Ensign's bunk and pulled off his boots. "That North Vietnamese gomer was crazy. You had to shoot him."

Cowboy didn't hide his feelings any better than Jon did. You could see it on his face. He thought he should have been the one in that boat. Jon thought of his decision to keep his activities ashore quiet and found, in Cowboy's look, another reason to believe that had been the right thing to do.

"How's Seaman Sheffield, Cowboy?" The sailor who had been cut was in Cowboy's division.

"The corpsman said he is going to be okay, and he bandaged Sheffield up, but he wants a doctor to look at him. So the carrier is sending a helo to pick him up."

The door to the Locker opened again. Dormant stood just outside the room, and it was almost like looking into the eyes of the North Vietnamese sailor he had shot.

"You murdering bastard! How come you're not under arrest?"

"Whoa, there, Dormant." Cowboy stood up between the bunks. "Are you talking about what Two Buckets did? I mean, I saw the whole thing. He didn't have any other choice. That gomer had already stabbed one of my sailors."

"Yeah, I saw it, too, and I saw murder. Shooting a helpless guy in the water. And, of course, I wouldn't expect anything else of you,

Cowboy. Redskins, Negroes, gomers, they're all the same to you, aren't they?"

Jon backed all the way into the forward corner as Dormant shoved Cowboy farther into the room; then, he jerked down the door over the desk, grabbed an envelope from inside, left the Locker, and slammed the door.

Cowboy pulled out his handkerchief and wiped his cheeks. "Jesus! Spit was flying out of his mouth. God damned Communist! Hey, Two Buckets, you're not going to let him bother you, are you?"

"I thought I mostly got along with Dormant—"

There was shouting from the top of the ladder by the XO's room. Cowboy opened the door to the Locker, but the shouting had stopped. Still-in-hack Jon stood in the doorway as Cowboy climbed the ladder to find out what was going on.

Suddenly, the Boatswain Mate of the Watch announced over the 1MC, "Man overboard. Port side. Man overboard, port side."

The ship turned hard to port to swing the stern, and the propellers, away from the man. Jon heard nothing else from above.

Suddenly, the ship heeled in the other direction. Jon knew the conning officer had shifted the rudder from left full to right full. *Manfred* had been following *Reilly* at twenty knots heading for the North SAR station, but the ship had obviously pulled out of formation to contend with the man overboard situation. *Manfred* was executing a Williamson Turn, which was intended to put the ship on a reciprocal heading down the track the ship had been following and hopefully improve chances of finding and recovering someone who had fallen overboard.

Muster.

When "Man overboard" was called, everyone not on watch was required to muster. Sometimes, a lookout would spot garbage and think it was a person in the water. Taking muster identified the person, and it clarified if, in fact, someone was missing.

Jon walked up the ladder to the XO's room. No one was there. He used the XO's phone and called the Electronics Repair shop, mustered with ET2 Dawkins, and then returned to the Locker, as the ship reversed its propellors to come to a stop. The ship was probably lowering the boat.

Jon got his rosary and sat on the deck, his back against the forward bulkhead. It felt like the ship was dead in the water. Probably lowering the boat.

Jon thought about the *Manfred* sailor in the water and hoped he was okay, but he wasn't praying for him. He prayed that tomorrow he wouldn't have to kill anyone.

He finished the first Our Father and wondered if the North Vietnamese sailor had had a Teresa of his own before—when he was alive.

22

Almost told Jon that the man overboard had been Dormant and rescuing him had been a regular goat rope. He didn't want to be rescued. "Just shoot me like you did that Vietnamese sailor," he'd hollered. Seaman Alvey had to jump in the water and get his arms around Dormant to keep him from fighting off the rescue attempt, which finally succeeded.

Then Dormant was sedated, and along with Sheffield, helo-ed to the carrier for evaluation.

After the Dormant story, Almost took a shower.

Jon finished his prayer, climbed up onto his bunk, and pulled out his letter-writing material. He wasn't sure he'd be able to write to her, but he was.

Almost returned, pulled on a clean uniform, and departed.

Jon filled two pages. What he'd written, he'd mail to her. Then fatigue conquered him.

Upon waking suddenly, panic pounced. A hand shook him. A voice hissed, "Mr. Zachery, Mr. Zachery." Jon flailed, looking for his rifle.

"Mr. Zachery, I'm the messenger, sir. Time to get up for your watch. You awake, sir?"

Jon flicked on his bunk light, let out a breath, and said, "Did I hit you when I was flailing around?"

"Oh no, sir. There's a coupl'a you officers go kinda' ape-shit on us when we wake you up. We know to get out'a your way. You're awake, right, sir?"

He nodded, rolled over the side of the bunk, and started pulling on his clothes as the messenger left.

The 1600 to 2000 watch the night before, his first watch since getting out of hack, had been uneventful. Andrew let Jon drive, and he worked hard keeping as close to exactly on station as he could manage. North SAR station was a ten-mile box they steamed around at ten knots. So, the only real activity was a ninety-degree turn once every hour. They had been steaming counter-clockwise around the box, so the 190 degrees station from *Reilly* made the turns into *Manfred*. After the first turn they had executed, *Manfred* wound up a couple hundred yards too close to the guide. Jon had talked to the CIC watch officer, Don Minton, and they worked out how to execute the turn and wind up close to station without needing to alter *Manfred's* speed much at all.

That afternoon, the CO had been in his chair on the bridge for the last hour of Jon's watch. After he'd been relieved, the CO called Jon over to his chair and asked if he was happy to be back on the bridge.

"Yes, sir. There were a lot of things I didn't like about being in hack—which I guess is the point of it—but the worst of it was feeling like I wasn't contributing."

The CO had been quiet for a moment, and then he said, "I watched you execute that last ninety-degree turn. How'd you figure out how to do that?"

"Sir, Don Minton is CIC watch officer. I talked with him about how to do it. Worked out pretty well, and, uh, at least that's what I think, sir."

"Yes, it did. Did you talk with Don about how to work the turn if you were going around the box in the other direction, so the turn would be basically away from you, not into you?"

"Not with Don, sir, but Andrew and I spoke about it. Andrew worked up a maneuvering board solution. We'd cut through the wake—"

"Okay, Mr. Zachery. How do you think the Ops O would characterize your performance keeping station during your watch?"

"I think he'd say that I'd done a job that was fairly close to marginally satisfactory, sir."

"So, do you think you rate such high praise?"

"Well, sir, I don't think I rate any praise at all for that."

"Mr. Zachery, you did a very good job of maintaining station and working out how to avoid losing position through the turn; that was good. What did you do that wasn't good?"

"I don't know, sir."

"Mr. Zachery, don't give me that cop-out answer. Think."

For an uncomfortably long time, Jon's head seemed devoid of thought. Finally, and suddenly, the answer was there.

"Cap'n, I was so focused on the task of maintaining station that I was oblivious to the bigger stuff going on. Like, we are fifty, sixty miles from the North Vietnamese coast. More PT boats could come out after us. MiGs could attack us at 500 knots, and if they came at low altitude, we might not pick them up on air search radar. Is that what you were thinking, sir?"

Then, the CO had slid out of his chair and left the bridge. Jon stood beside the CO's chair for a moment, and first savored the absence of criticism; then he thought about the CO taking time to teach him something. Then he reminded himself that every time he let himself feel like he was crawling out of the newbie pit, he wound up on the bottom again.

The next morning, during Jon's 0400 to 0800 bridge watch, a helo arrived from one of the carriers on Yankee Station to the south. Chief Fargo and Seaman Sheffield, along with mail, were winched down to the fantail. A hose was then passed up to the helo to top off its fuel tanks. After delivering mail and parts to *Reilly,* the helo orbited near the two destroyers for the rest of the day. Every two hours, the chopper would hover over the fantail of USS *Manfred* to top off fuel tanks. The periodic refueling kept the helo prepared to rescue of an aviator whose plane was hit but had managed to make it out over the Tonkin Gulf before ejecting. During *Manfred's* first day on North SAR station, two aviators were shot down, but none of them had been in a place where a rescue could be attempted. The helo from the Yankee Station carrier arrived in the morning, orbited during the day, and returned to the carrier after the day's airstrikes were completed. That, apparently, was to be the routine for their time on North SAR.

At 0945, Jon sat across a booth table in the chief's mess from ETC Fargo. "Chief's mess coffee, nectar of the gods."

"So, Mr. Z, I wanted to tell you about Mr. Stewart. He was real quiet at first. They had him tranquilized pretty well. Poor guy. He looked like a whipped puppy. Right before we landed on the carrier, he told me to tell you he was sorry."

"Sorry for calling me a murderer?"

"I don't know about that, sir. He said he was sorry about when you were with the marines, he was hoping that if anyone was hurt, it would be you and the marines, not any Vietnamese. He said he was sorry about that. He didn't say anything about calling you a murderer."

Jon sipped. Admiral Ensign really did not like him, but he didn't want Jon dead. At least he didn't think so. He'd gotten along with Dormant right up until Dormant wanted him dead. That esprit the heavies wanted, Dormant sure didn't buy into it. Jon wondered what kind of sessions the heavies had with him.

Dormant thought the North Viets and the VC were the good guys and Americans were the bad guys. Jon remembered what the warrant from the PBR had told him about how the VC executed village chiefs who opposed them. Not good-guy behavior. And the boss communist said they would bury the US. No, Dormant was wrong. Jon shook his head.

"Okay, enough about Mr. Stewart, Chief. So, how about the troops? How about bringing me up to date on them. And, what about the drinking incident? I never understood what really happened there."

"Yes, sir. Well, the two seamen, Honor and Presley, smuggled the whiskey aboard in the PI, the day of the officer/chief softball game. They apparently had had drinks about 0200 a couple of times before. The morning the Ops O found them, Zambowski had gotten up because he couldn't sleep with the guns firing. He got to the ET shop and found the two guys drinking. He told them they had to finish their drink and then throw the rest of the booze away. That's when the Ops O walked in and found them."

"So Zambowski didn't really drink anything himself?"

"Both the seamen said that was the case, and Zambowski did, too. But he knows he should have done more. He figures he didn't act like a third-class petty officer."

"Let's see if we can come up with some way to help Zambowski get his crow back, okay, Chief? And next subject: the electronic warning cubicle. Great job training up a three-section watch. Ops O told me the CO was real pleased with how that turned out. I am going to talk to the Ops O and see if we can put you and the ET2 in for a Navy Achievement Medal."

"If anyone gets a NAM, sir, it should be you. The whole thing was your idea."

"Chief, first of all, I am so happy to be out of hack; I don't need a medal. Second, you know how it goes. You build a thousand bridges but commit one homosexual act, and you are a homosexual, not a bridge builder."

"Yeah, Mr. Zachery, I know how it goes. Still… All right, Mr. Z. I recognize that look on your face."

"Okay. Good. And, Chief, thanks for holding things together while I was in hack."

Chief Fargo's eyes shone with a bit of extra moisture that suddenly appeared. He cleared his throat. "Mr. Zachery, I really feel bad about that."

"Ah, Chief, I think we both, maybe, needed to learn a lesson from that business. I know you were concerned about the guys, and I was, too. And fact is, you were doing your job. I was not doing mine. So let's just put this thing behind us. Okay, Chief?"

"One other thing, Mr. Z." The Chief looked down at his hands around his mug. "I gotta tell you this. On your first ship, Chief Petitte had a brother-in-law who was there the same time as you, and he was friends with ETC Irons. Petitte's brother-in-law told him about Chief Iron's opinion of you." Chief Fargo cleared his throat again. "Petitte and me, we talked. We want you to know we were wrong about you."

"Like I said, Chief. Let's put this behind us."

When Jon got to the wardroom, there was mail in his slot. There were five letters, all from Teresa. Four of them were thick and postmarked on successive dates. The last had a three-day gap in postmark date.

This last one was thin, maybe a single page. A kind of spirit acid ate Jon's belly away and left just a hole. The letter chilled him.

Down in the Ensign Locker, he laid out the letters chronologically, by postmark, on top of his bunk. He considered opening the last letter first. If it was bad news, get it over with, but he wasn't sure if he really wanted to do that. Perhaps he should open the one postmarked just before the thin one. Perhaps—

Stupid. Jon knew, he just knew, what was in the thin letter. As certainly as he knew Teresa had had a girl baby in her tummy when she'd been pregnant, he knew what was in that letter. He knew it would hurt to read it. If he read it first, he wouldn't even care about the others.

He picked up the letter with the earliest postmark. Teresa's penmanship seemed so like her. She used a fine tip ballpoint pen, and her letters arranged themselves on the pages like a drill team, rows and ranks dressed perfectly. But there was a softness to the curves of her cursive that was so feminine. Just looking at the address on the envelope was almost like seeing Teresa at their dining room table across from him. At the table, that's where she would have written it. The back of the envelope had a SWAK: sealed with a kiss.

He tore the envelope open, being careful of the SWAK, and he devoured it and the next one. Teresa, and her days, and Jennifer, and shopping in the commissary, more shopping in the Marine Corps Recruit Depot exchange, lunch in Old Town with Rose Herbert, coffee with the *Manfred* officers' wives' group, and evenings writing to him, all of Teresa and everything she did were in the letters.

The fourth envelope had an imprint of Teresa's lips on the back. She had put a kiss on letters before, but on the inside, at the bottom of the last page, by her signature. This was the first time she had put a kiss on the envelope. It knocked the frantic out of him, and everything just slowed down. Inside the envelope were five pages of pink stationery, folded once. Reading as slowly as Cowboy spoke, Jon savored the paragraphs, the sentences, the phrases, the words, and the essence of the woman in her thoughts, in her words, and in her ink. On the last page, she crunched an extra line of tiny writing along the bottom of the page; then, the scrunched-up line continued up the right-hand margin. The scrunched lines said she didn't want to stop writing, but it was tiring her out, and Jennifer wants her breakfast early. Jon didn't want to stop reading, either. He touched his finger, like Adam on the Sistine ceiling, to the paper, to her. He put the letter back in the envelope and touched his finger to the imprint of her lips. This time, it felt like goodbye.

The back of the last envelope was barren. Inside, there was one sheet of paper, no salutation or heading, two paragraphs, and no signature.

She couldn't express how disappointed she was in Jon over the wetting down party. He hadn't mentioned what he'd had to drink, but with all that had gone on, and all the other drinking events he'd told her about before, she could only imagine.

She closed the first paragraph with, *It will be hard to trust you again.*

The second paragraph: *The worst thing is that in the month you've been gone, it sounds like you've lost your faith. I am afraid for your soul. I am afraid for our baby, and I am afraid for myself.*

Jon had been wrong. He thought he knew how tough the letter would be, but it was beyond that in the first paragraph, and he hadn't expected the second paragraph at all. After Mass on our last Sunday in Subic, he had written that he had been bothered by the priest's homily. The message in the homily seemed to be that we should trust faith only, and we should never let reason into our religious life. He had told Teresa that the homily made him wonder if there was a place just inside the door to the church where people should check their brains.

Jon's fingers put Teresa's letters away.

There was a large envelope on top of his bunk. It was the communication officer course. Jon's fingers opened the course.

Lesson One.

23

By lunch in the wardroom on the fifth day on North SAR, Jon thought he had become his father. Especially when company shared a meal at the Zachery table, Pop sat and ate kind of hunched over his plate. He never said a word, unless asked a direct question.

Jon, being the junior ensign, there was no reason for him to contribute to the conversation. The rest of the wardroom, generally, had things to smile and laugh about, but Jon didn't. None of them seemed to notice or care that he sat on the junior end of the table just like Pop would have: there physically but absent in spirit, attentive enough to catch a question directed to him.

Jon wondered if anyone else felt the absence of Dormant. He would have been in the place just across the table from Jon. Dormant also had sat at his place just like Pop. Dormant and Jon and Pop, peas in the same pod. There was a cheerful thought. Jon wondered if Pop, at a dinner table, had thoughts like he was having. That was as difficult to comprehend as what Mama and Pop had to do to create him.

"What time are we briefing for the unrep?" the CO asked.

Underway replenishment, or unrep, could refer to refueling, rearming, or taking on food or general stores. This evening, after the carrier strikes into North Vietnam, were finished for the day, the ship would steam south and take on fuel.

The Ops O said, "1830, Skipper. In the chart room, as usual."

The Skipper drank coffee while the others ate dessert. He let the dessert eaters finish, then pushed his chair back, and said, "Let's hop to it, gents."

After everyone else filed out of the wardroom, Jon went to the Locker and took out his correspondence course. But then he thought he really had become his father. Sleep, eat, work, eat, work, eat, work, sleep again. That had been his routine since he'd gotten Teresa's letter. No rosary, no exercise, just trying to move forward with one or two things.

He didn't want to be in the Locker anymore. Before he left, he picked up his rosary. Passing the XO's stateroom, the XO stopped him.

"I watched you at lunch. You just picked at your food, and normally, you practically lick your plate clean. You've got bags under your eyes. What gives?"

The XO was at his desk, and he was in the passageway just outside his room. "I'm okay, XO. Eating, well, you know, it's watch, sleep, eat. I don't want to get fat."

The XO just looked at him for a moment. Then, "The letter. You got the letter you mentioned the day you got put in hack. Teresa ripped you a new one. You want to come in and tell me about it?"

"No, sir. Not a big deal, really."

"It can help to talk about it."

Jon wanted to get outside the ship, and the XO stopping him started some sort of pressure building inside his brain. "Nothing to talk about, XO."

"How about confession? Confession's good for the soul, you know."

"Thought you had a thing about officers using shibboleths, XO."

The last full week in January, Jon's first time going to sea on *Manfred*, at lunch the first day, and just after the CO had said "seats," the Ops O had said *sailors are meant to be on ships, and ships are meant to be at sea.* An officer and a gentleman should be able to express himself without using shibboleths, the XO had said.

The XO snorted. "Okay, Two Buckets. You are dancing from one foot to the other like a schoolboy who has to pee but is afraid to ask about number one. I will tell you. It can be tough, trying to sort a difficult situation out by letter. You can get discombobulated. Glads and sads, mads and forgivenesses, they just get all out of sync with the delivery times of the mail. So, my door is open if you need to talk or to confess."

"Thanks, XO."

As Jon walked into the wardroom, the XO muttered, "Shibboleth, my ass. Damned ensigns." Jon came close to smiling. That had been for his benefit.

Jon walked back to the fantail and sat on a bitt, the same one he'd used after dealing with the berserk DASH, and took out his rosary. While he watched the wake, his fingers walked the beads. Afterward, he went back to the Locker, he wrote a note to Sergeant Evans and addressed it to his ship. Evans was probably at a hospital somewhere, maybe even the PI, but his unit would forward it.

Then he wrote a one-pager to Teresa. He told her he was sure she saw him as having a good time with the other officers while she was home alone with Jennifer. He acknowledged how she never felt safe being there without him beside her. The US Navy he said, asked more of her than it did from him, and he wished it wasn't that way. He wrote about saying a rosary while sitting on the fantail and how it reminded him of the poem they'd had to read in high school—*The Hound of Heaven*. Jon was sure The Holy Hound never had to pad along behind her because she never let God recede into the background of her life, but he had, he wrote. Saying that rosary, he woke up to the fact the Hound was right there behind him and had been all along.

He closed with:

> I am a better person when I keep the Lord before me
> and not behind me, and I am a better person when we

love each other with all our hearts and all our souls.
I'm sorry I'm such a klutz I need to be hit over the
head to remind me of these things, which like some
other truths, should be self-evident.

Jon put his letter-writing materials aside and turned out the bunk
light. It was 1325. He would have to get up in three hours for the 1600
to 2000. Then they were refueling, and after that, he and Andrew
were switching to the mid-watch. Getting to 0400 without any sleep
would be tough. His eyes didn't blink open. Good sign.

"Mr. Zachery, run the range scale out and give me the range to the
oiler, please," Andrew said.

The *Manfred* was tasked to be 500 yards astern of the oiler by
1930 and be alongside the oiler at 2000, ready to take on fuel.

"It's thirteen miles, Mr. Dunston."

They were steaming at fifteen knots, and they had an hour and
fifteen minutes prior to on-station time. No sweat.

At 1848, *Manfred* was five miles from station. *Reilly* had detached
them and had gone to take on ammo before refueling. The CO was
on the bridge.

The enlisted watch-stander with the sound-powered phone headset
connected to Combat was in the center of the pilothouse, aft. "Phone
talker" Jon said, "ask Combat for a new course recommendation to
800 yards astern of the oiler."

Of the two officers on the bridge, the one who did not have the
conn worked out maneuvers to reposition the ship when joining
or repositioning while in formation with other ships. Andrew had
worked out a two-four-six heading solution. Jon looked at the radar
repeater and noted the change in range and bearing since he'd last
looked.

"Sir, Combat recommends two-four-four at this speed," the phone
talker said.

"Very well. Helmsman, come left. Steer two-four-eight."

The CO stared out the window.

When Jon gave the new course to the helmsman, the phone talker had reported it to Combat. "Sir, Combat reports they concur with two-four-eight."

Jon maneuvered *Manfred* to 800 yards, dead astern of the oiler, and held the position for two minutes while he compared compass readings with the announced refueling heading. There was a one-degree difference with *Manfred's* compass reading one degree less than the three-four zero refueling heading. At 1928, Jon had *Manfred* in the waiting station at 500 yards astern and 100 feet to starboard of the oiler's wake. *Manfred* would refuel from the starboard side of the oiler. At 1930, the Boatswain Mate of the Watch called away the underway replenishment detail. Generally, most sailors were at their stations before the detail was called away, but there were some who were like Dormant had been. They would not move until the 1MC called them away.

The Ops O relieved Andrew as OOD, and then Andrew relieved Jon as JOOD and assumed the conn. Jon took his position as safety observer between the helmsman and lee helm.

Jon didn't understand what it was about being on the bridge, especially during an evolution like refueling, but the rituals, routines, and formalities, they were all comfortable and comforting. It was almost like church.

At 1956, the oiler signaled by flashing light that she was ready for *Manfred* to move up into the refueling position directly abeam the oiler at eighty feet. The CO and Andrew were on the bridge wing with the *Manfred* matching the oiler's speed of twelve knots. Andrew ordered seventeen knots and a course of three-three-eight-and-a-half. When *Manfred's* bow was even with the stern of the oiler, Andrew ordered twelve knots, and the ship coasted into position abeam the oiler.

One of the sailors on the oiler fired a line-throwing gun, which dragged a fine cord from the oiler to the *Manfred*. The light cord was used to haul over a heavier line, which, in turn, was used to bring the refueling rig and hose over to *Manfred*.

In addition to refueling every five to seven days, they took on food and general supplies such as mops and toilet paper on a weekly basis as well. These latter items were transferred via trolleys suspended on cables between a supply ship and *Manfred*. Ammunition was replenished in the same way on an as-needed basis.

The sailors engaged in the refueling operation on the oiler, and *Manfred* were all wearing Mae West life jackets and helmets. Under the red lights on the oiler and *Manfred,* which illuminated the pumping and receiving stations, features of individuals of the puff-chest sailors were not discernible. There was little talking between the sailors. Their tasks were well understood and familiar. And more than likely, at 2010, everyone involved in these tasks had been working well in excess of what would be a full day's work to most people in the world.

Jon recalled his conversation with the warrant officer from the PBR in the Saigon River and the marines in I Corps. They had indicated that the VC worked as peasants by day and were soldiers at night. On *Manfred,* it was the opposite, with the normal business of waging war in the day and then spending the night getting ready for war again in the morning.

On the bridge, there was just a muted buzz from business-related conversation. Combat reported a surface contact that would pass the refueling formation at three miles to the west, lookouts reported all-clear from their posts, and the helmsman and lee helmsman repeated orders and reported RPMs set and the course being steered.

Jon watched the helmsman and lee helmsman perform their functions flawlessly. He took an occasional glance at the red-light-bathed, robot-army sailors moving to their tasks like mimes. What he saw and the muffled voices he heard were indications that *Manfred's* business was well in hand and that everyone was doing his part.

The logistics effort to support the *Manfred,* a relatively small vessel, was not inconsequential, but when you included the carriers, cruisers, and other vessels of the flotilla operating off Vietnam, the logistics capability which supported it all, the effort was massive. A thing to marvel at. Oilers, food and general supply ships, and ammo ships were on a constant merry-go-round between Subic Bay, other ports, and the Tonkin Gulf. Fill up in the PI, steam to the Tonkin Gulf, resupply the warships on station there, then go back to Subic to fill up and start the cycle anew.

At 2145, Jon entered the wardroom and found three letters in his slot. He opened the letter from his youngest brother first. He never expected to get a letter from him, but he wrote to inform Jon that their dad had had to be hospitalized for three days. Their father had arthritis and was taking sixteen aspirins a day to combat his continual battle with pain and discomfort. The aspirin had caused a problem with his stomach, and there had been some internal bleeding. The doctors had also wanted to make sure all his medications were proper and in the right dosage for his condition. Pop was sixty-two and worked in a grain elevator in St. Ambrose.

Their dad was okay and back at work again, his brother wrote, but, in all, he'd been away from work for three weeks. That had been the hardest thing, for their dad to miss three weeks of work. He had never missed three weeks of work, and most years did not even take the two weeks of vacation to which he was entitled.

One of the other envelopes was from Teresa. It was postmarked from before she had gotten his letter about the wetting-down party. He read the first paragraph and felt a clutch at his throat, and a warm gush of feeling flow down through his chest. With the warmth were tenderness and communion of heart and soul from her words. The letter had been milling around in the navy mail system for a while, so it wasn't real. It wasn't reflective of how things were at the moment. Still, it was nice for this taste of how it had been.

The third letter was from his father, a source even more unexpected than his youngest brother. Pop's letter was a one-page, hand-written note along with several clippings from the *St. Louis Post Dispatch* newspaper.

The clippings were from the previous month, and Pop had arranged them chronologically. The first hinted at some massive overkill by thousands of US troops assaulting some jungle area in the Mekong Region to kill one Viet Cong. Then there was a series of articles reporting successful operations along the central coastal region of South Vietnam by US Army airborne cavalry units. In the northern region of South Vietnam, the US Marines were also reported as having completed some successful operations. The last article reported on Viet Cong attacks on US Marine, US and Vietnamese Army outposts, and South Vietnamese villages. The Viet Cong attacks were scattered throughout South Vietnam from the northern provinces all the way to the Mekong Delta.

In the letter, Pop wrote that he had been sick for a while and had been at home *"recooprating."* He would be going back to work the next day, but he had just wanted to write a note to let Jon know he was in their thoughts and prayers back there at home. Then, he wrote that over the last three weeks he had nothing much else to do but read the papers and watch TV, so he thought maybe Jon would like to see what the paper was saying about Vietnam. In part, the letter said:

> The month started off with the papers saying we were maybe killing more palm trees than Viet Cong. Then both the army and the marines started doing some good work. But it was like maybe the army and marines just stirred up the Viet Cong because it seemed like the whole country got attacked at once. Kinda hard to tell if you are winning your war or not. Like I been saying all along, Eisenhower messed this up a long time ago. He should have helped the French more in 1954, and if he wasn't going to do that, he should have kept us out of there. Let one Republican president in the White House, and he messes us up for years.

> Keep well. We're praying for you.

There was no signature.

Pop was convinced that Franklin Delano Roosevelt and, by association, all Democrats were anointed by God every bit as much as the Old Testament kings of Israel had been anointed. FDR had gotten them out of the Depression. FDR had won World War II. Truman had won Korea and fired that Republican, MacArthur. He must have been a Republican if he was arguing with an anointed president.

My war? Pop sure didn't think it was his war, but Dad never had a war. In response to the question, "Were you in the war?" he always answered that he had been too young for World War I and too old for World War II. He had been thirteen in 1917 and thirty-seven in 1941.

My war. Dormant probably thought it was my war, too.

24

Jon marked a calendar if something noteworthy happened. H&I Saig. Rvr. meant fired Harassment and Interdiction rounds while anchored in the Saigon River. However, since he'd marked "PT boats/Dormant ovrbrd," there hadn't much worth recording. Each day on North SAR was pretty much the same as the one before. He noted unreps once or twice a week, but mostly he just x'ed off the days.

Each day, in the morning, the helo came up from the carrier during the four to eight and dropped off mail and parts. During the next two watches, the ship refueled the helo every two hours. During the 1600 to 2000, the helo went home. Twelve hours airborne, that's what the helo pilots put in each day. Eight hours on the bridge didn't sound like so much compared to that.

All the bridge watchstanders rotated the watches every week, so one team wouldn't be stuck on the mid-watch, the twelve to four a.m. and p.m. Andrew and Jon had cycled through the mid-watch twice since they arrived. Both were glad to be rid of it for a couple of weeks.

194

One good thing about North SAR, mail service was great. The helo brought mail and parts almost every day. But Teresa wasn't writing every day, and neither was Jon. He received one letter from her where she expressed worry that he wasn't writing very often when he used to write each day.

He wanted to write to her and did try. But his words, when he looked at them on the page, were empty, devoid of feeling, of meaning. Her letter about the wetting down party had pulled a plug out of the bottom of his soul, and he was drained.

It was ironic. Before, he didn't fit in on the ship, and he didn't care because he and Teresa had each other. Now he fit in, mostly, but he didn't have her. Not like he had her before. He would jump at the chance to trade tons of "fitting in" for a couple of ounces of the way it had been with Teresa.

Each of them, Jon thought, was stuck at the bottom of their own newbie pits, and neither one of them could find the way to climb out.

One afternoon Jon and Cowboy had the Locker to themselves. Cowboy said, "Back in the PI, I asked Duke Savage what it's like to fly. He said, 'It's hours and hours and hours of boredom interspersed with moments of stark terror.'" Cowboy was on his bunk; a paperback book opened across his belly.

Jon replied, "I think that sounded suspiciously like a shibboleth, Cowboy."

Back in January, when the XO had chided the Ops O for saying *Sailors are meant to be on ships, and ships are meant to be at sea,* Cowboy had asked what the word meant. The XO made Cowboy look it up in the dictionary in the ship's office. Now, the word shibboleth had become a catchword of its own.

"Shibboleth my hairy-skinny butt," Cowboy said. "I was sure hoping the first morning up on North SAR was just an indicator of things to come. But since then, we've done nothing. Hell, you're the only one who has seen any action. First with the marines, then with that gomer from the PT boat. I talked to the Gun Boss when we encountered the PT boats, and he said he had his thumb just itching to mash the firing button that morning. But, the Commodore wouldn't let us shoot. Hell."

"Do you think maybe the Commodore wouldn't let us shoot because the planes were coming from the carrier? Wouldn't do if we shot our own guys down."

"We could have fired and not endangered the flyboys. Same as when we were way down south with that merchant ship, the day you got put in hack. We coordinated our gunfire with the flyboys. Some guys just can't seem to manage two things at once. Like the commodore. So we just sit with our thumbs up our butts."

"What, the poisonous sea snakes weren't enough excitement for you, Cowboy?"

Until that morning, the sea surface had never been what Cowboy had called baby-butt smooth. Before, there had always been enough wind to at least ripple the surface. That morning, however, when the sun came up, it illuminated a baby-butt-smooth Tonkin Gulf. Not a breath of air stirred to raise the tiniest ripple. Floating on the smooth surface was a coating of a yellow substance that looked like some sort of plant pollen. Then, one of the lookouts saw the first snake. After that, there were a number of sightings. The postal clerk, PC3 Smeltzer, brought an animal book he had up to the bridge, and he showed the captain an article describing the poisonous snakes indigenous to the area.

"Humph," Cowboy snorted. "I wonder if those things are there when the sea surface is choppy? We never saw them until it got so smooth. I wonder if Dormant would have jumped overboard if he knew so many of those things were there in the water?"

We both looked at Dormant's bunk, the stripped mattress folded in half.

"Never thought ah'd miss that *phwoo* noise he made." Cowboy picked up his book, and Jon went back to writing.

The XO sat on the fold-down bed/sofa in the CO's room. Bureau of Personnel had shot down their request for a replacement for Dormant.

"We've got the watch bill covered with the Supply Officer. No need to push it, XO."

"Last thing, Skipper. V'you been watching Zachery lately? He doesn't eat much, bags under his eyes. This afternoon, PC3 Smeltzer asked me if he was okay. Smeltzer said Jon isn't dropping any letters in the outgoing. Smeltzer said he had been putting in one a day until the wetting down fiasco."

"Seems to be doing fine on the bridge." The Skipper rubbed a hand on his chin. "Wouldn't have surprised me if he'd had some issues with what happened when he was with the marines and then shooting that North Vietnamese sailor. I watched him pretty closely for a couple of days after that. He seemed to handle *that* pretty well.

"My wife said Teresa really stepped up to try to fix the problem Jon's letter caused. But she did say it seemed as if Teresa made allowances for everybody but Jon. Apparently, she really has a thing against drinking. I don't remember talking to him at the wetting down. Do you know if he had a lot to drink there?"

"I talked to Almost. He said Jon had a scotch and water and didn't drink all of it. And Jon left with Almost and Peter Feldman when things started getting rowdy."

The Skipper shook his head. "Maybe I'll talk to him."

"I offered. Maybe you'll have better luck." The XO laughed. "I remember my first cruise after we were married. I don't remember what the issue was, but we were mad at each for half of the seven-month cruise."

At 2345, 11 July, on the bridge, Jon and Andrew were receiving the watch turnover brief from Peter Feldman. Peter moved and stepped on Jon's foot.

"Sorry."

"Actually," Jon said, "I hope my toes hurt for the next four hours. Maybe it'll help me stay awake,"

The ship was still in the same North SAR operating box, but Andrew liked to look at the chart to remind himself how close they were to the coast of North Vietnam. And to the east, Hainan Island boxed them on that side. Other than North Vietnamese Communists to the west and north and Chinese Communists to the east, everything was routine, and the brief was completed at 2352. Andrew Dunston assumed the deck, and Jon took the conn. The enlisted watchstanders completed turnovers, and they settled into their roles and places.

On the mid-watch, it was best to avoid looking at clocks and watches. Time moved slowly if you didn't look. If you looked, time stopped.

One way to tell time without checking a timepiece was by how his feet hurt. The deck was steel and covered with a thin rubber mat. The mat didn't help. On the mid-watch, the deck on the bridge was made of the hardest substance in the universe. Jon's feet hurt already, but he could still feel where Peter stepped on his right foot. About an hour into the watch, his feet would hurt up to his ankles, and his foot wouldn't remember it had been stomped on. By 0200, his feet would hurt up to his knees. Some forty days in a row, he'd spent two watches, a total of eight hours a day, there on the bridge standing on the godawful hard deck.

The Boatswain Mate of the Watch rotated his sailors at their stations every twenty minutes or so. That marked the passage of time also.

Jon's knees experienced foot pain. He checked their position relative to *Reilly*. On station.

Andrew was a shadow by the chair on the port side of the pilothouse. The quartermaster was hunched over the chart table marking the ship's position. Helmsman and lee helm stood at their posts like basalt statues in the dim red glow.

Jon walked back to the chart table. The ship was on the eastern edge of the box heading north. Walking behind the helmsman to the familiar safety observer position, he saw that the helmsman was exactly on course.

Jon stepped out onto the port bridge wing and looked up to the moonless sky. "How're you doing?" Jon said to the lookout.

"Good, sir." The lookout sounded disgustingly awake.

Above, the stars in their gazillions were glow-spot spattered across the black sky from rim to rim. Alongside the ship and aft, the bow wave and the ten-knot wake were luminescent, a faint glow delineating the path the ship was slicing through the dark water. The swooshing, splashing sound of the bow wave was irregular, indicating a bit of wave action.

"Sir," the port lookout said. "The stars shouldn't be moving, should they, sir?"

Jon looked at the gyrocompass. The ship was in a gentle turn to starboard. He put one foot inside the pilothouse.

"Helmsman, left ten degrees rudder." Jon's voice sounded like a shout to him.

Even in the dark, Jon saw the helmsman jerk from head hung down, chin on his chest, to erect. "Oh, Jesus," he said.

"Left ten degrees rudder," Jon said again. This time he moved the rudder.

"Mr. Zachery, what are you doing?" Andrew asked. He was at the rear of the pilothouse talking with the Boatswain Mate of the Watch.

Jon stepped inside the pilothouse and spoke just above a whisper. "The helmsman fell asleep, sir. We're fifteen degrees off course. Helmsman, steady on three-five-zero. Lee helm, indicate turns for twelve knots."

"Steady on three-five-zero, aye, sir. Sir, the rudder is left ten degrees, coming to three-five-zero."

"Very well," Jon said.

"Boatswain Mate of the Watch, starboard bridge wing," Andrew said.

Jon sighted through the alidade to take a bearing on the stern light of the *Reilly*. After slowing their speed a knot, he stepped onto the bridge wing with Andrew and the Bosun.

Andrew sent the lookout inside the pilothouse and levered the door handle closed. "Good catch, Mr. Zachery."

"It wasn't me, sir. It was the lookout."

"Jesus," Andrew turned and put his hands on the wood railing atop the bridge-wing bulwark and looked off into the darkness. After a moment, he turned and faced the Bosun and Jon. "Boats, do you know how lucky we are that we are here by ourselves and in such a simple formation? God, if this had happened during the transit when we were out in front of a bigger formation... Damn," Andrew said.

It was quiet in the darkness on the bridge wing for a moment.

"Okay, Seaman Randolph is a good guy, isn't he?" Andrew said. "Normally does a good job, doesn't he? Doesn't get in trouble? Have I got it right?"

"Yes, sir, you do," the Bosun said.

Jon couldn't see Andrew's face, but he could feel him moving pluses and minuses around in a sort of mental-moral arithmetic.

Andrew said, "The mid-watch is a bear, but that's no excuse. We cannot have people falling asleep out here. Christ, if the CO had wandered out here, all of us would be crapping through new assholes right now. I want you to make sure you get the fear of God into your whole watch. I need you to back us up, too, and keep an eye on the sailors. I will admit to you, Ensign Zachery and I were doping off, too. It was the lookout who caught it. I don't want to put Randolph on report. But, we need to make sure that this will not happen again. You understand what you have to do, Boats?"

"Yes, sir."

After the Bosun re-dogged the watertight door, Jon said, "Why aren't you putting him on report?"

"I told the Bosun how to handle it. I don't need to put him on report."

"Seems like this is just the kind of thing that does require Captain's Mast."

"The thing that most bothers me most is that I didn't catch it. The thing that bothers me second most is you didn't catch it, and you have the conn. How far off course would we have gotten if the lookout hadn't been paying attention? Would we have needed the guys on watch on Reilly to wake us up? Christ almighty! I will say, once the lookout told you, you did the right thing. But you and I need to be the most awake guys up here. Nothing can get by us. If something happens, it's not Randolph who fell asleep standing up who's at fault; it's me, and it's you. We have the deck and the conn. So, we need to take a mighty lesson from this."

Andrew turned and looked off into the dark again and spoke with his back to Jon. "There's another thing for you to think about. Putting him on report is not like you getting put in hack. There will be nothing in your record about that. But if Randolph is put on report, it will be in his record. He would almost certainly go to mast, and he would get busted in rank, lose money, and probably be restricted. When you got put in hack, you were the one who did wrong. In our case, you and I screwed up just as badly as he did. Do you understand that? And are you with me on this?"

"Yes, sir," Jon said, sounding like Peter Feldman at the toe-trod start to the watch.

"Good. Now get us squared away on station again." Andrew went back inside the pilothouse and spoke to the CIC watch officer on the phone.

It occurred to Jon, suddenly, that he had told Chief Fargo that they should try to figure out how to get Zambowski reinstated to petty officer, and he hadn't done anything about it.

25

Jon turned over the JOOD responsibilities at 0401 and walked aft to the fantail. He told the aft lookout he was going to sit on a bitt for a few minutes. He didn't want the sailor to think he was going to jump over. Like Dormant did. The sailors probably said something like, "Officers, what will those crazy bastards do next?"

He pulled his rosary from his pocket and sat.

Father, God of heaven and earth. You are my hope. You are my salvation.

For indeed, God was that for him. There was nothing else for him to cling to. There had been Teresa, but he'd driven a wedge between them. Then he had *Manfred* and his job, especially driving her. That night he'd let her down, just like he'd let Teresa down.

You are my salvation.

He started around the beads, and after the first decade, he began to sink into a puddle of release. Release from the grip of relentless anguish. The words of the prayers, so familiar. Didn't take a gram of thought for them to roll off the tongue of his soul or his body. But if you thought about what you were saying, the prayers were about as perfect an arrangement of words as there could be on earth. How would you make them better? Pack more meaning into them?

Jon had just prayed the third Glorious Mystery and said the Our Father and placed his finger on the next Hail Mary bead when he stopped. He had another thing he had to do. And it was an important thing.

He wished the after lookout a boring rest of his watch and went below to the Locker. There he got out his stationery.

12 July. North SAR Station.

Hail, Teresa, full of grace.

It was an extraordinary way to start a letter. It would be considered a sacrilege to some. Maybe Teresa would read it that way. He wrote that and told her he hoped she wouldn't see it that way. He told her about saying his rosary on the fantail. Beneath the ocean of stars above and the breeze wafting past him and the swishing of the waves as the ship sliced through the Tonkin Gulf, and how after decades of Hail Marys, it had occurred to him that Mary the Mother of God was a remarkable person, the second most remarkable person ever to walk the earth. And it had occurred to him that he, Jon Zachery, a sinner, was married to a remarkable person as well, married to a person who was indeed full of grace. And she, Teresa, had brought her grace into their relationship and blessed it and extra-sanctified their marriage sacrament.

In all, he wrote a three-pager, sealed it, dropped it in the slot in the post office, and slept through reveille.

The next night, during the mid-watch again, voices from the watchstanders were overly loud. Usually, mid-watch voices were muted, whispers almost, but apparently, the memory of last night and drifting off course gigged extra wakefulness into all of them. Jon kept himself moving, from one bridge wing to the other, stopping at the chart table, standing behind the helmsman for a moment, checking the radar scope, looking out the window at *Reilly*.

"OOD," called the CIC phone talker in a crank-extra-beats-out-of-your heart voice, "Combat reports they have detected a MiG radar on the electronic warning receiver. The MiG radar bears 280 true."

Manfred was heading 270. Andrew pulled a phone from its holder and buzzed the Gun Boss, who was the Evaluator. He spoke to him for a moment. Then he hung up the first phone and pulled the adjacent phone.

"Captain, OOD. Combat has picked up a MiG radar on the WLR-1. We have nothing on air search radar. Gun Boss says they got a couple of hits on the surface search radar, which they ran out to long range. Combat does consider the WLR-1 intercept to be good. Combat thinks there is a MiG and that it is at low altitude. We have reported this to *Reilly*. They haven't picked up anything and are not worried about it."

"OOD, Combat says they no longer hold the MiG radar," the phone talker said.

Andrew hung up the phone and said, "Phone talker, tell Combat the CO is on the way up."

Jon looked at his watch. It was 0112. The sleep monster would not be a problem that morning.

Reilly continued on the westerly, heading along the north edge of the operating box. Jon checked the navigation chart. Time to turn south in a few minutes.

"OOD, the Captain says to go to General Quarters," the phone talker fairly shouted.

"Bosun, sound General Quarters," Dunston said.

"OOD, the Captain says to be ready to douse the navigation lights, but to wait for his call."

"Quartermaster, standby the switches, please. Be ready to kill the running lights."

Jon had thought nothing adrenaline juiced the system like being jolted from a deep sleep by the GQ alarm. It juiced a man pretty effectively when you were awake, too.

A signal light flashed on *Reilly,* and the phone talker said, "OOD, signal bridge says *Reilly* signaled ninety-degree left turn."

Jon maneuvered the ship through the turn, and when they steadied on the southerly heading, Andrew relieved Jon as JOOD and conning officer. The Ops O had assumed the OOD watch.

In the electronic warning cubicle, ETSN Zambowski was sitting in front of the equipment. "Do you still have the MiG?"

"Not right now, Mr. Z. It comes and goes. The CO was in here earlier. He thinks there is a MiG at low altitude and orbiting right on the coast to the west of us. He said they had gotten intermittent hits with the surface search radar set at long range."

Zambowski was staring at one of his small cathode ray tubes and working the manual frequency control. Jon was sure he was focused on the MiG frequency.

"Zambowski, did you sweep the rest of the high band? Wouldn't want PT boats to sneak up on us while we're focused on the MiG."

"Yes, sir. I've been doing that."

"I was sure you would be. Sometimes we officers have to say stuff like that, so people think we are worth the exorbitant salary they pay us."

"Not a problem, Mr. Z."

"Okay. We were heading right for them, heading west along the top of our ops box. We just turned south. I'm going out to see what they have in Combat."

The CO and the XO were standing to either side of a radar-man operating a surface search radar display. The range scale was set at maximum.

"Captain, MiG radar bearing 100 relative," Zambowski called from the doorway of the electronic warning cubicle.

"There, see it, XO? We got him on three successive sweeps. Probably inland from the coast by a mile or so," the CO said.

"I saw it," the XO said.

"I saw it, too, sir," Jon said.

"Well, Mr. Zachery, when we got the WLR-1 indication coordinated with the surface search radar hit on the same bearing, I thought we were in for a low altitude attack. But the signal comes and goes, and this is the third time we've picked him up. What do you think?"

"Not sure, sir."

"Think, Mr. Zachery, think. What is that flying gomer doing?"

It was sort of like the night with the marines. Suddenly, Jon thought he knew. "He's not after us, sir. He has to be some sort of decoy, like the Indian that sucks the cavalry into an ambush. Are the carriers flying tonight, sir?"

"Just a Combat Air Patrol station about twenty-five miles south of us."

"So what do you think, XO? You think Mr. Zachery here has it figured out? Are they trying to suck the CAP into an ambush?" the CO said.

"Well, Skipper, it's as good a theory as I can come up with."

"So, Mr. Zachery, was I being overly cautious going to GQ?"

"Sir, um…"

"What is it, Mr. Zachery: Don't you have an opinion, or is it that you don't want to tell your CO what you think about what he did?"

"That MiG can do probably eight miles a minute. The surface search radar acts kind of funny at long range. Atmospherics, such as ducts, can cause the signal to skip and bounce. Probably wouldn't have even seen him without the WLR-1 hit. If he runs in at us, we may not be able to track him all the way on the surface search. But the WLR-1—"

"What if he's smart enough to turn his radar off and only turns it on for the last half of his attack?"

"An extra GQ is a small price to pay to minimize the chance of being caught with our pants down, sir. Uh, sorry, sir, two cents from an ensign."

"You just answered my question, Mr. Zachery. No need for the self-flagellation."

Three nights in a row, the ship had gone to GQ during the mid-watch. For the same low flying MiG. The third time, after the ship secured from battle stations, the CO invited the XO and Ops O to his room.

Yesterday, the CO had come up with an idea to try to dupe the MiG into coming out over the water and shooting it down with a guided-missile cruiser, but the commodore had scoffed at the idea.

"Yesterday," the CO said, "I talked to the commodore by secure radio about our idea to bag that MiG. Now, I want to send him an official US Navy message. Draft it up please, Ops O."

The next night, *Reilly* and *Manfred* would head south to refuel. After the unrep, *Manfred* and a guided missile cruiser would return to North SAR. The cruiser would keep her electronics silent so as not to divulge her presence to the North Vietnamese. Then, when they detected the MiG, they would vector the CAP—Combat Air Patrol aircraft, stationed a hundred miles from the carrier to protect it from attack—from their stations toward the MiG. Hopefully, the North Vietnamese would spring their trap and launch their fighters to shoot down the CAP. *Manfred* would tell the cruiser when to bring up her radar to shoot down the MiGs.

Jon thought it was a great plan. After the unrep, *Manfred* followed the cruiser back to North SAR, where the two ships entered their box and steamed around it. At midnight the CO ordered battle stations. As on the previous nights, just after 0100, the MiG appeared. The CAP aircraft were vectored toward the enemy fighter.

"A number of enemy aircraft just appeared feet wet," reported a radar operator in CIC. The CO picked up the radio and invited the cruiser to bring up its radar.

A minute later, the cruiser CO called to report that they'd detected a dozen enemy planes, but before they could establish a track on any of the targets, all the enemy planes turned, dove for the deck, and headed inland at high speed. "It was worth a shot, *Manfred*."

After the Skipper ordered, "Secure from battle stations,' he, the XO, and the Ops retired to the CO's cabin.

"Bummer, Skipper. I thought running the CAP in toward the beach would sucker them out. But they were watching for us to pull something," the Ops O said.

"It was a good try," the XO said. "The commodore is probably going to give us the *told you so* business."

The Skipper shrugged. "Guess we'll see on the nineteenth when we leave station, and he joins us to visit Hong Kong."

"Thought he was going to the PI with *Reilly* and wait for us there," the Ops O said.

"Guess he wants to go to Hong Kong twice. *Reilly* goes after our next period out here," the XO said.

"Okay, back to the MiG. Like to get an after-action message out prior to 0700. Can you handle that, Ops O?"

"Not a problem, Skipper. Jon was working up a draft while it was happening. I should be able to get it to you in about an hour."

"Did you ask him to do that?"

"No, Skipper. He said he had time, so he did it."

"You were going to talk to Jon this afternoon, Skipper." the XO said. "How'd that go?"

"Hah." The Skipper shook his head. "Not well. I talked to him for just a couple of minutes. Then Jon said that it sounded like I was saying he had his mind on work too much. And in my estimation, it went downhill from there. I really couldn't get him to talk about what is going on between him and Teresa. He wanted to know if I'd gotten the request to reinstate Zambowski. We talked about that a bit."

"Well, we'll be in Hong Kong in a week. Then we get another week in Subic, plus the trip to Zamboanga. So a lot of time out of the combat zone. Maybe that'll help," the XO said.

"What he really needs is to get on the phone with Teresa," the CO said. "I wonder if I'm going to have to order him to do it. Hell of a thing if you think about how June started."

26

The final day on North SAR, for a couple of weeks anyway.

Andrew and Jon had the 0400 to 0800 on the bridge. At 0545, Combat called the bridge to say two F-4s were going to do a flyby before heading back to the carrier.

Jon looked at Andrew. Andrew shrugged.

The port lookout hollered, "Aircraft, two seven zero degrees relative. Diving out of the sky and coming right at us."

"Holy shit!" from the starboard lookout. "I got one too. Uh, zero niner zero degrees, diving."

From the center of the pilothouse, Jon did not see any planes. Andrew ran for the port side. Jon took the starboard. Then he saw it. A fighter was leveling off from its dive and heading for the space between the bow of *Manfred* and the stern of *Reilly*, and really coming fast. They crossed *Reilly's* wake about fifty feet off the water. Then the jet engine sound hit. Both planes, they were F-4 Phantoms, pulled straight up and rocketed for the sky rolling and trailing corkscrew vapor trails.

Holy crap!

"How's that for reveille, Mr. Z?" The lookout was grinning and watching the jets.

Jon was busy watching as the planes became dots, then the dots disappeared.

The lookout had another question. "You ever want to fly one of those things, sir?"

"Nope. On my first destroyer—"

"When you were enlisted, right, sir?"

Everybody seemed to know that about him. "Yes. On that ship, we quite often pulled plane guard duty and were stationed about a half mile behind the carrier during night landings. Three times we pulled dead guys out of the water after carrier landing accidents. Carrier pilots, in my humble opinion, are suicidal maniacs."

"Still—" The lookout left that *still* hanging on the wistful look on his face.

Just before the watch ended, two other US Navy destroyers took over North SAR station, and *Reilly* led *Manfred* south.

The atmosphere in the wardroom at lunch bordered on giddy euphoria. The CO sat at his end of the table, watching his officers with a tiny smile on his face. A father whose normally rowdy children had somehow managed a day where they were all getting along with each other.

The ship had been underway for two months, and now, the ship's schedule included significant time in port a week over the next couple of weeks. There'd be three days in Subic Bay, in the Philippines, a week in Hong Kong, and then a trip to Zamboanga City on the southern tip of the island of Mindanao. All that in-port time sounded attractive to most of the officers. The Gun Boss, a former alcoholic, and Jon were probably the only two in the wardroom who didn't care too much about it. In the PI, Jon wanted to call Teresa, and he hoped there'd be a place to run. There was a lot of ugly stuff he wanted to sweat out. He hoped he could do that before he called her.

And the second day in port at Subic Bay, *Manfred* would have a change of command. Commander Carstens would be relieved as commanding officer. Jon hadn't really thought about it that much before. There hadn't been time with everything else he was trying to deal with, and he'd had the idea that one heavy was pretty much like another. But the more he learned about the commodore, Captain Brass, the more he came to appreciate his present CO and even admire and respect the man.

Hope our new CO is like Commander Carstens, not Captain Brass. Please, God.

At 1530, *Manfred* pulled alongside *Reilly* so that the Commodore could be transferred by highline. The Commodore would be officiating at the change of command after the ship arrived in the Philippines, and he would ride with *Manfred* during the visit to Zamboanga.

When they'd found out about all the time they'd spend with the Commodore, Cowboy treated the Ensign Locker to one of his arm-wavers. But Cowboy was not the Welcome Wagon Lady to greet the Commodore. The CO was. He stood by the spot on the 01 level where the high line transfer of his boss would end.

Manfred was close enough to the other ship such that the modified shotgun would not be needed to get a line across. A sailor on *Reilly* threw a heaving line with a monkey's fist on the end. This was tied to the secondary rope, which was used to pull a steel cable, which was attached to a fitting on *Manfred's* superstructure. Sailors on *Reilly* attached the Bosun's Chair, a man-sized cage with a seat in it, which rode on a pulley wheel on the steel cable. The Commodore, wearing a Mae West life jacket, was strapped into the cage, and on *Reilly*, a winch put the steel cable into tension and lifted the Commodore, in his cage, off the deck. Two sailors on *Manfred* then began to haul in on the line attached to the cage. About halfway between the two ships, there was a sudden slackening of tension in the steel cable, and the cage dipped toward the water.

Jon watched from the bridge wing. He gasped. He was sure everybody on *Manfred* wanted the Commodore's visit to begin without him getting wet. He bobbed there, about a couple of feet above the choppy water, for a moment. When the cage had dipped, it jerked the in-haul line suddenly, and although both *Manfred* sailors were wearing leather gloves, which protected their hands from rope burns, the sudden snap on the line had injured the wrist of one of the sailors. So, the Commodore dangled there for another moment while Cowboy, who was in charge of the sailors at the station on the 01 level, got two new sailors to man the in-haul line and to finish the process of pulling the Commodore over.

From the bridge wing, Jon saw chagrin etched onto the CO's face. Jon had seen the Skipper angry and even saw him smile once or twice, but he mostly wore a poker-player face. Chagrin, he thought, fit on newbie ensigns' faces, not destroyer commanding officers'.

When the Bosun's Chair settled onto the deck, the Commodore began to tear at the latch to the gate enclosing him. The CO went forward to help him undo the latch and get unstrapped from the apparatus. The Commodore, once released from all the constraints, pushed the CO out of the way as he exited the cage. Tearing at the straps of his Mae West, the Commodore glowered at the CO.

"Not a good piece of seamanship at all," the Commodore said. It carried clearly to the bridge wing. "About what I've come to expect from *Manfred*, though."

He had gotten the straps across the chest undone, but then, with the under-the-legs straps still tightened, he started taking the vest off by pulling it down, with the straps still clinging snuggly to his thighs, until finally, he had one leg free, then he tried to kick his other leg free, with the life jacket flopping off the end of his foot. He had to bend down and pull the clinging thing from his foot.

After he straightened, he growled, "Just get me to my room." The Commodore wouldn't look at the CO.

As the CO, poker-player face back in place, led the Commodore away, the Commodore's shoes squished. On *Manfred*, it had appeared as if the Commodore hadn't quite touched the water, but he must have caught a wave after all.

After the ship secured from the highline detail, *Manfred* shifted from three-section to five-section watches on the bridge for the rest of the trip to Subic Bay. The officers who had watch in CIC and the gun director during three-section watches were given priority to get some experience on the bridge. Charles Hanson, Don Minton, and Tom Snyder were assigned as OODs. Two ensigns were also assigned to stand OOD watches: Carl Lehr was one, and, to some people's surprise, Ensign Zachery was the other. Jon had been more surprised than anyone. Edgar Chalmers was JOOD for Carl Lehr, and Dennis Macklin was JOOD for Jon.

Cowboy arrived in the Ensign Locker last and started speaking as soon as he entered. "Holy crap! The Commodore was really steamed. His feet were wet when we got him over. The Skipper was helping get him out of the cage, and the commodore bit his head off. When we got his bag over, I took it to him in the Skipper's cabin. Commodore wanted to know if we had gotten his bag wet, too."

Admiral Ensign was in his bunk reading. "Well, dunking a Commodore in the water during a highline, hell yes, he'd be mad."

"Sure, but why'd he take it out on us?" Cowboy paced on the available postage stamp and waved his arms about. "It was *Reilly's* responsibility to keep the cable taut. I even had a guy on the inhaul line sprain a wrist when the cable suddenly slackened."

Almost piped up from his bunk. "I'd be willing to bet there is more to this than the highline. Remember when we had the encounter with the PT boats. The Skipper wanted to shoot at them, and the Commodore wouldn't give us permission? Remember how Two Buckets said that conversation over the radio went? It was over a tactical frequency, so at least the two ships we relieved heard the transmissions with our Skipper clearly pushing the Commodore for permission to shoot. Could have put the Commodore in a bad light in what amounts to at least a semi-public forum. And, it could be other stuff. Maybe the Skipper and the Commodore never got along. Sometimes, it seems, a ship has a reputation based on how she performs. Sometimes, it seems, it is the CO and how he does that determines the rep. The CO is the only man aboard who can all by himself determine a ship's rep, though."

"*Au contraire!*" Admiral Ensign said. "Why, we have Ensign Two Buckets here who has done the same thing. I bet it was his letters that got the Skipper on the Commodore's crap list. We know that CruDesPac sent a message to the ship about it. I bet the Commodore got a copy, so the CO and the Commodore would both have been put in an unfavorable light by those idiotic letters. And why the hell is the Skipper giving him Officer of the Deck watches after all that?"

There was so much truth in what he'd said. It didn't leave room for Jon to get angry. It felt like a punch in the stomach. There wasn't a thing Jon could say, so he climbed down from the bunk, slipped on his shoes, and squeezed by Cowboy. Cowboy stood by the fold-down desk. It looked like he wondered how the conversation had gotten out of his control.

As he was closing the door, Jon heard Almost say, "Admiral Ensign, I don't know how you do it, but each day you do seem to become a bigger horse's behind than you were the day before."

Jon went back onto the fantail, watched the wake for a while, and fingered beads for a while.

At 0355 the next morning, Jon relieved Thomas Snyder as OOD, and Dennis Macklin relieved Andrew Dunston as JOOD. It felt extremely strange to see Andrew on the bridge as a JOOD, and it felt strange those first moments after Tom and Andrew had gone below. Then Ensign Zachery was responsible for the ship. Jon was in charge while the rest of the crew slept. There was no question about what to do, what to check. That was all familiar. It was just the niggling discomfort over the absence of someone senior to ultimately bear the responsibility.

When Jon called the Captain the first time to report a ship contact, he did so with a bit of trepidation. Surface contact Delta, the fourth contact Combat had designated since midnight, would pass within 1.9 miles of *Manfred*. The Captain's night orders required the OOD to call the Captain and report contacts that would pass within two miles.

The second *bzzt, bzzt* phone call to the Captain seemed like the most normal thing imaginable. The call had gone to the XO's cabin, where the CO had temporary residence since the Commodore was in the Captain's room. The XO had moved in with the Gun Boss, who had a two-tiered bunk instead of the fold-up couch for just such occasions.

It was a black, overcast night. Jon looked at the compass repeater at the center of the pilothouse and on the bridge wings often, as there would be no moving stars to announce they were drifting off course.

But the watch passed uneventfully until 0530 when the CO came onto the bridge and climbed onto his chair. Jon talked with the CO briefly about how the morning had gone, and the Bosun brought him a cup of coffee.

"Commodore is on the bridge," the Boatswain Mate of the Watch announced at 0545.

"Mr. Zachery, have the Bosun call the wardroom and tell them to bring the Commodore his hot tea, please," the CO said.

In about three minutes, a steward mate showed up carrying a small silver tray with the tea paraphernalia on it. The steward held the tray while the Commodore fixed his tea. When the steward departed the bridge, the CO got up, walked over, saluted the Commodore, and said good morning. In the dim red light in the pilothouse, it did not look like the Commodore had returned the salute, and Jon hadn't heard the Commodore return the greeting.

"Mr. Zachery, come over here, please," the CO said. "Commodore, this is Ensign Zachery. He has the deck, for the first time, I might add. He has done a very good job picking up ship handling, and he has a good head on his shoulders, so I wanted to give him a chance to be OOD before I left."

"Good morning, sir." Jon saluted, but again, the Commodore did not return the salute.

"You were the one in *Manfred's* boat the morning we had the encounter with the PT boats." The Commodore spoke the sentence as a very clear declarative.

"Commodore, is there—" the Skipper began.

"So, Mr. Zachery," the Commodore's voice, in stepping on the Skipper's attempted intervention, was unseemly loud on the bridge. "That was six weeks ago now, but I'd be interested in hearing why you couldn't capture one survivor when *Reilly's* boat got two of them?"

"He was following my orders, Commodore," the CO said. "He had a walkie-talkie in the boat."

"Captain, I already have your report," the Commodore said. "Now, don't interrupt me again. I want to hear your ensign's story. So, Ensign Zachery, let's hear it."

"Captain," Jon said, "if the Commodore wants to talk about that, would you like to take the deck? Mr. Macklin has the conn."

"You impertinent little—" the Commodore stammered as he thrust his cup of tea at the CO, and the CO jumped back. Some tea had probably sloshed onto him.

The Commodore slid out of his chair and pushed past Jon. Jon couldn't see his eyes in the dim red light, but he could feel his anger like an electrostatic charge.

"Commodore is off the bridge," the Boatswain Mate of the Watch announced.

The CO took Jon by the arm and aimed him at the port bridge wing.

"Are we clear of contacts?" the CO asked of the port bridge wing lookout.

"Yessir," the lookout pronounced it as if it were a single word. "No contacts."

"Good," the CO said. "Step inside the pilothouse for a few minutes, please."

The CO made a noise that was kind of like a snort. "Holy Mother of God!" he said.

"What did I do, sir?"

"The Commodore was going to take that little opportunity to

humiliate me. But you, a snot-nosed ensign, told a full Captain that it was inappropriate to distract an Officer of the Deck with administrative matters during your bridge watch." It was dark on the bridge wing, with very little light spilling out of the small window in the watertight door. The CO was a shadow. "In the middle of the encounter with the PT Boats, I was way too obvious that I thought he should have given us permission to fire at the PT boats. It was a radio circuit that had a lot of other ships on it. So, in effect, I criticized him, my superior officer, in front of a lot of his contemporaries and some of his superiors. Plus, I don't think he liked our little scheme to try to bag the MiG."

The CO put his hands on the bulwark and looked off into the darkness to port. "So he was going to put me in my place on my bridge in front of some of my crew. You said about the only thing that was going to defuse that situation, but you have now gotten yourself on the Commodore's crap list, too. Now, I am not putting you in hack again, but I will tell the XO to take you off the watch bill. You can eat in the wardroom, but if the Commodore is there when you come in, turn around, leave, and sample the crew's mess. If you are seated when he comes in, ask permission to leave the mess. I do not want him to have any more ad hoc opportunities to work on you."

"Captain, I'm really sorry if I got you in trouble."

"You didn't get me in trouble," the CO said. "I did that all by myself. But I will tell you that if ever again you feel inclined to piss off a senior officer, aim that at me. I don't like it, but I have learned to anticipate it. You did fine this morning, Mr. Zachery. I will have a qualification letter for OOD, Independent Steaming, put in your record before I leave. Now you can finish up your watch but see if you can stay out of the Commodore's way for the next twenty-four hours. He will move to the BOQ when we get to the PI."

Through the rest of the day, the Commodore stayed in the CO's cabin, but everyone knew he was there. Word of how the Commodore had behaved and what he'd said of *Manfred's* reputation had spread through the chief's mess, the mess deck, and the wardroom. The crew was convinced that the Commodore was wrong about their ship. In the Ensign Locker, Cowboy had given a dissertation on how the crew was thinking. According to Cowboy, Seaman Apprentice Rodney, the junior sailor aboard and the one with the injured wrist from when the highline cable went slack, was especially upset. Rodney figured that he'd been injured trying to get the giant dwarf named Commodore Grumpy over to *Manfred*, and he should get a Purple Heart.

Rodney was a be-pimpled, skinny eighteen-year-old sporting a significant bandage over his right ear. His right ear lobe had become infected through an ear lobe piercing that had been done in the Boatswain's Locker, and then Rodney had kept the pierce-hole open with an insufficiently clean broom straw. Some of the sailors from the Bosun's Locker got on Rodney and told him he had injured himself more with his ear-piercing. You don't get a Purple Heart for a self-inflicted wound, they told him. But Rodney's characterization of the Commodore as a giant dwarf named Grumpy stuck and passed around the mess deck.

The chief's mess thought the Commodore was wrong about the ship, too, Cowboy said. The other three ensigns were in their bunks. When Cowboy was talking about the Commodore, he couldn't stay still. He paced, waved his arms about, and began to sputter as he tried to voice his own opinion of the Commodore.

The Commodore's opinion, however, was not something any of them could get at. He was a scratch, or one of Rodney's pimples, located square in the middle of the back, which neither the left hand nor the right could reach to itch or squeeze. But, life on *Manfred* went on. Her business could not stop because the Commodore thought ill of the ship, even if it was unfair.

27

The Ops O had conned the ship into port. After they were tied up, Andrew and the Ops O were talking out on the bridge wing. Jon filled out the Log for Andrew. As JOOD, it was Andrew's job, but Jon had time. The Ops O would sign it before he left the bridge.

The last part of the entry was "0703. 30 July 1966. Moored starboard side to pier 31, Subic Bay, Philippines. Officer of the Deck watch shifted from the bridge to the quarterdeck."

As soon as the brow was over, Jon left the ship and walked to the chapel on base. During eight o'clock Mass, he sat in the back. There were seven other people there. They were in front. Jon didn't go to communion. He couldn't. After the service concluded, the others filed out. He stayed.

As the priest devested, Jon could hear him whistling. It didn't bother him too much. He'd leave soon.

The priest exited the room to the side of the altar wearing whites, lieutenant stripes on his shoulders. A flicker of surprise bloomed on his face for an instant when he saw Jon sitting in the rear. When he got next to Jon, he said, "Anything I can do for you?"

It was the same priest who had had services two months ago, the one who had delivered the sermon on faith.

"No, Father. Thank you. Do you have to lock up?"

"No. The chapel is open during the day. Are you from one of the ships, or are you stationed here?"

"I'm from the *Manfred*, Father. We just came in this morning."

"Well, I am Father Masters, and I'm attached to Commodore Brass's staff. I've been visiting other ships in the squadron. If I remember right, I'm due to ride *Manfred* just before the end of August."

"Nice to meet you, Father, and it will be nice to have you aboard. Lay services, it's just not the same as the real thing." Jon was talking too much. He wanted the priest to leave, and he wouldn't if he didn't shut up. "Okay to sit here for a while?"

"Yes. There are no other services scheduled until confessions at 1600. Stay as long as you like." He put his hand on Jon's shoulder. "God's peace be upon you."

And he lost it. Tears and snot leaked out of Jon's face. In his head, the boxes holding things out of the way to be dealt with later just blew open and spilled over the inside of his brain. It wasn't just one thing. There were a lot of things, and he couldn't even say what they all were. And all of it together squeezed tears, snot, and sobs out of him.

Father Masters sat held out a pocket packet of Kleenex.

"You have on a short-sleeved shirt. Use the Kleenex."

Jon almost laughed but sobbed again instead. Then, he blew his nose several times, and when he was breathing normally, Father Masters was there with a battered, grey navy trashcan. *Is there a new trashcan anywhere in the navy?*

Father Masters waved him farther into the pew, set the trashcan on the floor, and sat.

"Again, I'm Father Masters. Would you care to tell me your name?"

He was probably two inches taller than Jon. He was fit, brown hair trimmed close, and mid-to-late-thirties maybe.

"Jon." He sucked in two sharp, closely spaced breaths. "Jon Zachery, Father."

"So, Jon. Take a deep breath and another. There. Now, perhaps you'd like to tell me what is bothering you."

"I don't even know what to confess, Father."

"No, no. Talk, just talk, shall we? Later, confess, if it suits. For now, just talk. All right?"

If the priest called him "my son," Jon would leave.

"You were on the way out, Father. I don't want to keep you."

"There is nowhere on earth that is more important for me to be."

Jon looked for evidence of manufactured concern but saw nothing on the man's face he could use as an excuse to leave.

Jon took in a big breath, huffed it out, and started. With the wetting down party two months ago. And it all spilled out of him, like an overturned witches cauldron of toil and trouble.

Those five KIA when he and Andrew had the bridge watch a few days after entering the Tonkin Gulf. The men he had killed while he'd been with Sergeant Evans. Being a coward during the DASH turn-up. The months of disappointment on the Ops O's face. His dad giving him to Heiny Schwartz for slave labor, the months of disappointment in the Ops O's face. Pop shanghaiing him into the navy. Admiral Ensign, seasickness, Chief Irons. The North Vietnamese sailor he'd shot three times. It was the third shot that bothered him and that he dreamed about.

And there was Teresa, and with Teresa, the tears and snot started again. Jon said as many words about her as he had about the entire litany of his troubles.

Father Masters listened until Jon was done talking.

"Why don't you join me for some lunch at the Club?" Father Masters asked.

Jon shook his head. "I can't, Father. I can't but thank you."

The priest left. Jon moved up to a first-row pew. It felt closer to God there. He put the kneeler down and knelt. After an Our Father, he sat again.

The silence had weight and comfort, like the layers of blankets and quilts on his bed in the winter in the unfinished attic where he'd slept growing up. Around him, light filtered in through exceedingly plain, stained-glass windows. In the silence, in the muted glow filling the church, there was no accusation, no ridicule, no guilt. He wallowed in the absence of those commodities. For a time, he then checked his watch. 0945. Ten-hour time difference to California. Morning here meant evening there. Best hop to it. He needed to call her, but he didn't want to wake her.

He had to return to the ship to get money for the call from the phone exchange. While aboard, he found two letters waiting for him. One from Rose. It was thin. And a thick one from Teresa.

On the back of Teresa's envelope, she'd printed WAML. With all my love. He tore the envelope open. The letter was addressed to Dearest Jon. She hadn't appended the superlative to the salutation since she'd received the wetting down letter. He was standing in the wardroom. No one else was there. He pulled out a chair, sat, placed Teresa's letter on the table, and opened Rose's.

Idiot,

Teresa isn't eating. She isn't sleeping. Get off the pot. Do something. Call. Write.

DO SOMETHING

Didn't take long to read a letter from Rose.
From Teresa, six pages. On those pages were pain and sorrow. A week after she'd gotten his letter about the rowdy party, she showed it to Rose. Rose read it and told Teresa, 'Jon didn't say what he'd had to drink. If I know Jon, he didn't drink much, and he certainly didn't get drunk. You need to climb down off your high horse and set this thing right.' Teresa wrote that she'd been mad at Rose for a week, then at confession, father told her she should not have gotten mad at her friend. Her friend was trying to help her. Maybe, the priest had said, you should accept her help.

And I did, Teresa wrote, and after that, I saw my own part in making the mess by sharing that letter of yours, along with my indignation, with the other wives.

Forgive me.

Jon bolted to his feet and almost tipped the chair over backward He grabbed Teresa's letter, hustled down to the Locker, took money from his clothing locker, and picked up his book. He'd probably have to wait a couple of hours at the phone exchange.

Read a book. It felt like forever since he'd read a book.

Then he hustled up to the main deck, aft to the quarterdeck, across the brow and down the pier and the two blocks to the phone exchange. He got his name on the waiting list and settled down with *The Rise and Fall of the Third Reich*. A pleasant subject to occupy him as he awaited his turn to talk on the phone to Dearest Teresa.

That night at the O Club, there was a going-away party for Commander Carstens. Prior to sitting down for dinner, the Skipper walked up to Jon.

"You called Teresa?"

"I did, sir."

"That silly grin says the call went pretty well."

"It was real close to satisfactory, sir."

The Skipper cracked a smile. "I'm happy for you and Teresa. And, Jon, I want you to know, it was an honor and a privilege to serve with you and see you grow into service to your country."

Crap. That day had been so chock full of emotion. He hadn't able to contain it all. Now the Skipper came real close to pushing him to where he'd lose it, again. Only a little moisture entered his eyes but didn't spill out, and there was no snot.

Jon cleared his throat. "Skipper, I learned a lot from you, and I would have learned a lot more and a lot quicker if I hadn't been such a blockhead. Thank you, sir, and may God go with you and Mrs. Carstens to your next place of duty."

The Skipper clapped Jon on the arm, reached into his pocket, pulled out a letter, and handed it to him.

It was Rose's letter.

"The XO found this on the wardroom table. It was lying there, outside the envelope, face up. The XO showed it to me and said I should read it. I didn't want to, but he said I had to, so I did. Forgive me for reading your mail; but I'm glad I did. I'd like to meet this Rose friend of yours. Now I better start glad-handing the rest of the goobers who ride *Manfred* with us."

Two Buckets, whoda ever thunk this could happen?

By the time dinner started, the needle on the Rowdy Party Meter had climbed to midscale. Was there a backstroke in a puddle of booze in the forecast? It didn't matter. Jon would leave as soon as he could escape. He had a letter to write. But also, he figured he owed it to the Skipper to be there.

When dinner was over, the Skipper left the table to make a head call. Jon followed him and waited outside for him to come out. When he did, Jon pushed off the bulkhead and said, "Skipper, can I ask a question, please?"

"Shoot."

"Tomorrow, Skipper, at change of command, can we keep you and send the commodore away?"

The Skipper shook his head. "It doesn't work that way. Besides, it's time for me to move on and for a new guy with new ideas to take over. Someday, when you're in my position, you'll understand."

The Skipper laughed. "I wish you could see the look on your face!" And he passed Jon to return to the party.

When you're in my position.

The most preposterous thing Jon Zachery had ever heard in his almost twenty-five years on earth? He'd just heard it. The Skipper was a US Navy commander, an O-5, a heavy. Jon was an O-1 and a junior one to boot. Jon didn't know how a man got selected to be a commanding officer, but he knew enough to know only the best O-5s got picked to be COs. To cross the gap between O-1 and -5 seemed to be like trying to pole vault across the Grand Canyon. The laws of

Physics forbade such a thing. Divine intervention, that was the only way Jon Zachery would be in the Skipper's position in—

Jon had no idea how long it took to make O-5. For that matter, he didn't know how long it took to make O-2. Two years maybe? It hadn't mattered.

And it really didn't matter then. What mattered was writing to Teresa.

His phone call with her that morning had been restorative, healing, joyful, and glorious. And he wanted, needed, to write to her again in that frame of mind, which through his own fault, had gotten lost to him. But now was found. *Now was found.* Like the hymn. Jon Zachery, standing in the passageway outside the head in the O Club in Subic Bay, PI, found grace and understood it for the first time in his life while surrounded by the sound of flushing urinals and unrestrained drunken revelry.

As he left the O Club, Jon was aware of the balmy tropical evening, the well-tended grass and bushes, the well-maintained buildings as he passed them. Then he started praying a rosary, using his fingers in place of beads, and his surroundings receded into a background so dim, it barely constituted a hint of where he was.

Back in the Ensign Locker, he got out his stationery, and before he lowered the lid to make the desk, he looked at the folded up mattress atop what had been Dormant's bunk.

Dormant, my man—Jon smiled at himself for sounding like Cowboy—*I wish I could tell you what grace is, and I hope you find some. Grace is the absence of having to fight something.*

Then he began to write and wrote about Teresa, the couple they were, Jennifer, and their family. He wrote a full side of a page about Commander Carstens. In the navy, Jon explained, there were a number of terms for a commanding officer. One of them was "the Old Man." A month ago, he wrote, he wouldn't have paid much attention to the change of commanding officers. It concerned the heavies, not the junior officer aboard. But lately, he had gotten to know his Skipper a bit, had come to appreciate him as an extraordinary man. He was going to miss him, and he wrote:

The Skipper said it was time for him to move on, but
I know he poured his heart and soul into *Manfred*.
He's going to miss HIS ship.

Jon wrote a couplet about the change of command scheduled for the next morning and used it to conclude the part of the letter about his commanding officer.

PART III

NEWBIE ALMIGHTY

The old man stops and takes a sec, just to pat the rail.

Back above, they tack a new name on the door with nails.

28

On the day after the change of command and following reveille, the Bosun announced the visit to Hong Kong had been cancelled and the ship would sail for Zamboanga the next day.

At 1250, the officers were assembled in the wardroom waiting for the new captain. The *Manfred* officers stood behind their chairs. In addition, a civilian in a light tan suit stood behind the XO's normal place. Across from him, a lieutenant commander, in whites. The new Captain entered through the port side aft door at 1300, precisely.

"Attention on deck," the XO called out.

The new Captain sidled his way along the aft side of the table, took his place at the head. Absent from the wardroom were Dormant, the Ops O, Cowboy, and the easy, comfortable air, which had prevailed with the previous CO. Yesterday, after the change of command, there had been a feeling of anger among the officers, which only Jon had had the temerity to express. But yesterday's anger, like a Fourth of July sparkler, had fizzed white hot for a few seconds, then blinked out. Now, uneasy neutrality prevailed. Like a mini-Cold-War. Circumstances forced antagonists to sit at the same table and act civilized while both parties knew each party had soldiers with fingers poised above buttons to launch nukes. Jon looked around the table. He wasn't sure he knew his fellow officers anymore. It was as if their personalities had been vacuumed out of them.

The moment Jon's bottom touched the seat of his chair, the XO said, "Gentlemen, let me introduce Mr. Hart and Lieutenant Commander Wesley from the embassy in Manila. They will both accompany us to Zamboanga, and they are here to give us a brief on the purpose of the visit from the State Department's perspective, and what we might expect to find there. Over to you, Mr. Hart."

"Thank you, XO. First of all, please call me Cecil. We will be together for the next five days, and your captain has graciously invited us, Jacob Wesley," Mr. Hart pointed to the officer across the table from him, "and myself, to consider ourselves a part of your wardroom. We are pleased and honored to do so.

"Now then, to the business at hand," Cecil Hart said. "Jacob, would you start us off with the military, or Defense Department, side of the business. Then I will wrap up with the State Department perspective, which of course, is the only one that matters."

Mr. Hart's attempt at a little humor dropped like a pebble into a still pool without making a splash and without generating the radiating concentric ripples the laws of physics, and polite social interchange, demanded. Mr. Hart looked across the table at Lieutenant Commander Wesley, who gave a little shrug.

Lieutenant Commander Jacob Wesley had thick, raven-black hair, a bit long on the sides and back for a military person. He said *Manfred's* would be the first visit of a U.S. warship to Zamboanga since World War II. Their visit was a goodwill visit, and their purpose was to do just that, to generate goodwill toward America in Zamboanga City, in the province, and, actually, in all of Mindinao. The media from the major cities on Mindinao would be at a press conference on Friday afternoon when they arrived.

Commander Wesley then covered the history of the Philippines from the turn of the century until the present. He told them almost 100 Congressional Medals of Honor had been awarded to US soldiers, sailors, and marines in the early 1900s. The US tried to help the Philippines establish a government, that could control the entire archipelago. World War II and the battle against the Huks were covered.

Jon recollected how he'd felt when he graduated from high school. He thought he knew history, not only of his country but of the world. What Cecil had just related told Jon he didn't even know the tip of the history iceberg.

Commander Wesley finished and nodded to Cecil.

Cecil made the point that many people considered the Filipinos to be a homogeneous people, but he emphasized the racial, cultural, and ethnic diversity present in the islands.

Cecil and Jacob continued to take turns with their presentation. Finally, Cecil wrapped up. He said that the Philippines were much like the rest of the world, where some of the natives like the U.S., some don't. There was a warning that they should be prudent, not get inebriated while on liberty, as that would compromise personal safety and their mission to generate goodwill. To underscore the safety point, he said that although there was no specific intelligence pointing to a threat, the Commodore and the Captain would have bodyguards and drivers.

"Now, then, are there questions?" Cecil asked.

Once you are used to seeing a lip with a mustache on it, even if it is goofy looking, or a scraggly and pathetic denigration of the whole male half of the species, for days and days after the mustache is shaved off, the exposed lip looks like something that should have fig leaves over it. The XO had shaved off his mustache, and Jon had been staring at his lip, trying to decide if the XO had the funkiest, just shaved upper lip he had ever seen. He almost missed Cecil's: "Any questions?" The XO started to thank the embassy people, but Jon cut in. "One question, if I might, sir."

Cecil looked down the table at Jon.

"Might I have your name, young man?" Cecil said.

"Yes, sir, I am Ensign Zachery."

"And did I not invite you to call me Cecil?"

"Sir, I am the junior ensign aboard, and the first name of everyone at that end of the table is sir."

"I see that we must be formal," Cecil said. "So then, Mr. Zachery, your question?"

"Sir, the efforts against the communists, the Huks, were effective here in the Philippines. I'm just wondering if you have thoughts about any lessons for what we are currently doing in Vietnam."

Cecil said, "I'll tell you what, Mr. Zachery, I will be with you all day Thursday riding down to Zamboanga. I'd be happy to share my humble thoughts and opinions with you then. Okay?"

"That," the XO said, his word and his look slammed the door on any more input from Jon, "is more than okay, Mr. Hart, Cecil. Captain, any remarks you want to make?"

"I just want to say thank you, Cecil, and Commander Wesley, for the enlightening briefing you've given us." The new Captain sounded normal, but he was glaring at Jon as he spoke. "We look forward to your company over the next week. And, I would like to assure you that we have taken your messages to heart. *Manfred* will acquit herself well on this mission of goodwill."

The Captain nodded to the XO, who called the wardroom to attention. As the Captain passed by Jon, he hissed, "Come with me."

After opening the door to his—the XO's —room, the Captain stepped back and pointed inside, and Jon walked in. The Captain followed, closed the door, stood with his head bent down for a moment, took a deep breath, and exhaled. When the Captain raised his head, their eyes met like a clash of swords. Jon took a small step back and bumped into the desk chair; then, he resumed the position of attention and raised his eyes back to the new Captain's.

"If you are slightly more stupid than I think you are, you will try to say something." The Captain's voice was flat, devoid of emotion, and surprisingly quiet. "Look down at the deck. I am not interested in some playground staredown here."

The green tile had a subtle black highlight in the surface Jon hadn't really noticed before.

"Now, then," the Captain said through clenched teeth, but then he took another deep breath, and after exhaling, continued in the flat, quiet voice, "you don't seem to be able to just follow orders like an ensign should. You can't keep your mouth shut the way an ensign should. You seem to need to question."

The Captain said that the Commodore thinks *Manfred* is the worst ship in his squadron. He thinks the last CO had no respect for higher authority. He saw evidence of that from the Ensign Locker. So it is only logical for him to assume the whole wardroom is a mutinous rabble. "The Commodore will ride with us to and from Zamboanga, and I intend to use the opportunity to convince him that the wardroom is not totally screwed up, and in fact is good, and with the right leadership, will even demonstrate its professionalism every day.

"And, so help me, God," the control slipped off his voice, "no goddamned Ensign Locker is going to prevent me from doing so."

As Jon had been looking down at the green tile ornamented with the subtle and irregular streaks of black, he half-listened to the new Captain, but a bit of understanding bubbled out of somewhere. He thought about his position: brand new Commanding Officer, a newbie, sort of, taking over a ship on which he knew not a soul and reporting to a senior officer who had developed a real aversion to the ship. Before, Jon had felt nothing but anger and animosity toward the new CO. Now, a little soap bubble of sympathy and empathy had formed. While Jon was thinking about perhaps trying to help the new Captain, he almost missed the end of his tirade.

"You, Mr. Zachery, are going to help me in this endeavor by keeping your damn mouth shut." Spittle droplets spattered on Jon's left cheek. "Now, get the hell out of here."

Jon pulled the door shut and leaned against the bulkhead. There had been times in the past when the Ops O had chewed him out, and afterward, he couldn't remember exactly what he was supposed to do differently. With the new CO, the message was clear: ensigns, if they have to be seen, must not be heard. That little soap bubble of sympathy did not survive very long.

Then, Admiral Ensign walked up to the CO's door. He didn't even look at Jon standing against the bulkhead. After staring at the door for a couple of seconds, he took a breath, rapped twice, and assumed a rigid attention posture.

The door was ripped open. Admiral Ensign stepped inside, and the door was closed. Then Jon heard the CO's voice. He didn't sound very happy with Admiral Ensign, either. *Wonder what he did?*

Almost was at the fold-down desk in the Locker when Jon entered.

Jon said, "Admiral Ensign just went in to see the new CO, you have any idea what that's about?"

"I got this from Peter Feldman. He said Admiral Ensign had talked to his father, a retired admiral, by phone, about the wetting down party and the ball game. He had described both as drunk fests. His father went to see CruDesPac about it.

"That is what the Captain was talking about when he said we have a problem with our reputation—aside from the part about the CO and the PT boats," Almost said.

"The ball game?" Jon asked. "That wasn't a drunk fest."

"Apparently, Admiral Ensign thought we were all drunk when we brought the chunk of ice from the game and stuck it in his bed."

Remembering that incident made Jon smile. Admiral Ensign hadn't been able to play ball because he had had duty that night. After the game, Peter Feldman brought a chunk of ice back from one of the tubs of beer and soda so that, as Peter had put it, Admiral Ensign could share in the fun we'd had at the game. The officers still talked about the yowl Admiral Ensign had made when the ice was shoved up into his crotch as he slept.

"So the new Captain was talking about what Admiral Ensign told his father, and it wasn't more fall out from my letters to Teresa?"

"Apparently not. As long as your letters don't wind up in the *San Diego Union*—"

The door to the Ensign Locker was pulled open, and Admiral Ensign stood in the doorway for a moment. Then he pushed past

Jon and Almost, got his wheel book out of his locker, and left again, slamming the door behind him.

"Well, so much for things being better between us," Jon said.

"Think about it. He gave you so much crap over your letters. We had pretty much gotten over your letters, and now his phone call blows it all open again. Another stink bomb out of the Ensign Locker."

Almost left the Locker, and Jon stood there in the quiet and in the puddle of light under the one bare bulb. A *scritch, scritch* sound came from above and forward. It sounded like dog claws scratching on the floor, which brought to mind *The Hound of Heaven*. Even though he knew the *scritch, scritch* was the boatswains mates on the forecastle getting the ship ready to go to sea, Jon thought it would be good if the Hound stayed close in the days ahead.

Manfred got underway at 1330 in a heavy, gusty, wind-driven downpour. The navigation team had trouble picking up their landmarks to use for bearings, and even the radar could not penetrate an especially heavy cell of rainfall sitting over the northern part of the bay. Lieutenant Paul Becker had the deck and the conn. Andrew Dunston was his JOOD and was using the radar repeater on the bridge to pick up the channel marking buoys. The Commodore was in the elevated swivel chair on the port side of the bridge, and the new Captain was standing next to him. Ahead and to port, you could see the carrier at the pier at Cubi Point, and you could see parts of the air station. To starboard, none of the shore was visible in the rain. A gust drove sheets of rain into the bridge windows, overwhelming the windshield wipers, and for a moment, you could not even see the Gun Boss and the sailors who were on the bow to let the anchor go in the event of an emergency.

"Navigator," the new Captain said, "how are we doing?"

"Sir, the bearing takers are not having an easy time of it, but I'm getting decent fixes and hold us in the channel."

"Well, Captain," the Commodore said, "it is nice to have decent weather for taking a ship out for the first time, but this should be a better indicator of what you have to work with."

"Yes, sir," the new Captain said. "Excuse me, sir. I am going to take a peek at the bridge radar repeater."

The Captain walked to the repeater near the center of the bridge, and Andrew stepped aside for him. Andrew had set the bearing cursor to the ship's heading.

"Mr. Dunston," the new Captain said, "why is the bearing cursor set two degrees off from our actual heading?"

"Captain, the ETs found this problem this afternoon just before we set the sea and anchor detail," Andrew said. "They wanted to go to work on it, but I told them to wait until we were at sea."

"Mr. Zachery," the new Captain said, "I was told last night and again this morning that we were ready, in all respects, to get underway. Don't you have a getting underway checklist in your division?"

"Navigation recommends new course two-eight-two," the Navigator said in a loud voice.

"Helmsman," Lieutenant Becker said, "come right, and steer new course two-eight-two."

"Come right. Steer new course two-eight-two, aye, sir," the helmsman said.

"Mr. Zachery," the new Captain said. "I asked you a question. Are you going to answer me sometime today?"

The helmsman was getting flustered, listening to the Captain and trying to listen to the conning officer. He was leaving his rudder inputs in too long.

"Helmsman, mind your rudder. The course is two-eight-two," Jon said.

The helmsman had overshot the heading by a half degree and had not put in rudder to stop the slight right turn.

"Mr. Zachery!" the new Captain's voice was elevated and tinged with anxiety. "Let the helmsman do his job. You do yours and answer me."

"Officer of the Deck, ship's heading is two-eight-three, but we are correcting back." Jon turned to the Captain. "Yes, sir, we do have a getting underway checklist, and it was completed satisfactorily yesterday."

"It was not completed satisfactorily if we have a problem this morning," the new Captain said. "As soon as we secure from sea and anchor detail, I want to see you, the acting Operations Officer, and the CIC Officer in my cabin. Is that clear?"

Everything Jon had learned about conduct on the bridge during an event like getting underway in bad weather told him they shouldn't be having a conversation about what was, relatively, a petty matter.

"Clear, Captain," Jon said.

The new Captain went to his chair on the starboard side.

Inside Subic Bay, the water was choppy, driven by the gusty winds; but *Manfred* moved with a stately, stable, and measured dignity out the channel until abeam the western end of Grande Island. Then, a hint of heavier seas just outside the harbor started the ship rolling and pitching slightly.

"Captain," Paul Becker said, "I recommend we secure the anchor detail and keep the navigational detail on station another fifteen minutes. It looks like it is going to be rough when we clear the harbor, and once we clear Grande Island on our port side now, we won't need them anymore. I think it is prudent to get those men in off the bow."

"Mr. Becker," the new Captain said, "it is the sea *and* anchor detail. We'll secure them together."

Lieutenant Becker walked over next to the Captain said something to him that Jon could not hear. The Captain looked at Paul Becker with a hard, angry look on his face, looking like he might be about ready to give Paul a dose of the same medicine he had administered to Jon the previous afternoon, but then the new Captain looked across the bridge at the Commodore.

"OOD," the new Captain said, "tell the crew on the bow to secure the anchor for sea, but to stay on station for the moment."

Just behind Jon's forehead, a headache had taken occupancy of the front half of his brain. The familiar acid taste, the immediate precursor to seasickness, soured his mouth. A bit of something like despair and hopeless, helpless resignation bubbled around inside him.

As soon as sea and anchor detail secured, Jon asked the Boatswain Mate of the Watch to call Mr. Snyder, the acting Operations Officer, and Mr. Minton for a meeting in the XO's cabin with the new Captain right away. Then, Jon hurried down to the head opposite the Ensign Locker and made it to the commode just in time. Pulling the flushing handle continuously while his stomach was still convulsing, he flushed away the vomit as it came up. After a moment, the heaving in his stomach subsided, just as the bow of the ship rose on a wave; then hung for an instant in near-zero gravity before plunging back down after the wave moved out from under the bow. Salt flushing water shot up out of the commode and splashed his face and soaked the front of his khaki shirt. Buoyant forces of the seawater arrested the bow's descent, then started it up again, and Jon felt a force well in excess of normal gravity try to pull his stomach out from between his legs.

Jon had to hold onto an angle iron to stand as the bow rose and fell and moved sideways as well, driven by waves and wind from the angry sea. He pulled back just in time to avoid a second jet of water from the commode.

Anger boiled up in Jon: anger at his weakness, anger at the forces of nature tossing the ship about like a cork, anger at the taste in his mouth, anger at toilet water on his face and shirt. Mostly, though, he was angry with the Captain. *How could he have been concerned with such a minor problem when we were navigating out of port in bad weather?* It was a known two-degree error on the bridge repeater, which everybody knew how to handle. It could have been repaired, but Andrew considered it a minor problem and sent the technicians away.

Jon rinsed his face and his mouth and dabbed at his wet shirt with a handful of paper towels. There was no time to change.

<h1 style="text-align:center">29</h1>

At 1915, Jon stopped at the ship's office and leaned in through the opened top half of the French door.

"Good evening, YN1," Jon said. "What's up?"

YN1 Gilpin returned the greeting, invited Jon in, and dismissed the other two petty officers in the office. After closing the door behind the two, he locked both the bottom and the top parts.

After he sat down at his desk, YN1 Gilpin handed Jon a sheet of paper. It was a statement saying that, ten years previously, Lieutenant Peter Peacock had crossed the equator.

"Sir, yesterday evening, the Captain called me to the XO's cabin, where he's staying since the Commodore is in his own room. He had hand-written this out, and he told me to type it up and get it into his service record. I don't know what to do with this. You were enlisted. What would you do?"

The ship's visit to Zamboanga would take *Manfred* to within seven degrees latitude of the equator. It would require a three-day delay of the scheduled port call to Da Nang, South Vietnam, to steam south from Zamboanga, cross the equator, and conduct the traditional ceremony to convert all slimy pollywogs to shellbacks. The decision to delay the port call to Da Nang resided with the Captain. If the CO requested the schedule adjustment, it would be approved; but the request had to be submitted prior to entering port in Zamboanga.

Shellbacks were sailors who had crossed the equator. Those who had not crossed were pollywogs, but the process of becoming a shellback involved more than just the equator crossing. To earn the right to be a shellback, pollywogs were required to endure hours of indignities at the hands of the shellbacks. Shellbacks, especially those junior in navy rank, took special delight in inflicting indignities, under the sanction of tradition, on their seniors.

"So, just to be clear here, YN1, the Captain is not a shellback, but he told you to type this up so that it would look like he is one, is that correct?"

"Yes, sir." Gilpin held up a service record with the Captain's name on it. "There's nothing in his record indicating he is a shellback."

"Do you have the hand-written paper from the Captain?"

YN1 Gilpin pulled his wheel book out of his shirt pocket, took a folded piece of paper out from between the pages, and handed it over.

Jon unfolded the paper. *I can nail him,* blinked on in his brain. For a tick, then it blinked out. The junior ensign taking down a US Navy commander and the ship's CO; that would be like a horny mouse crawling up an elephant's leg with rape on its mind. Jon shook his head. Sailors had an obscene saying for every eventuality.

This is not opportunity knocking.

But it was duty. "I'm going to take care of this, YN1. Give me a manila folder, please."

"Sir, uh, am I going to get in trouble over this? I mean, the Captain did give me an order to do this."

"What he told you to do is not ethical. It's wrong. If you had just gone along with it, you'd have done something wrong, too. No question, he can hurt a lot of us if he chooses to do so. All of us took oaths to obey the orders of the President and the officers appointed over us, but we are all still expected to do the right thing. You did the right thing telling me about this. I am just an ensign, but I will do everything I can to make sure nothing bad happens to you. Just don't say anything to anyone, okay?"

Jon stood in the passageway, the closed door to the ship's office behind him, and wished he was as sure about what to do with the letter as he had tried to sound in front of YN1 Gilpin. After that first moment, nailing the CO no longer seemed like a sure thing. If Lieutenant Allman were still there, he could take the letter to him, but this situation did not seem appropriate for an acting department head.

"Did you say 'crap,' sir?" Seaman Alvey was standing with a bag of laundry over his shoulder, looking at Jon.

"Yes, I guess I did, Seaman Alvey. Crap. There's another one."

"You okay, sir?"

"Yeah, I'm okay. Sometimes, being the junior ensign—" Then it occurred to him. Jon was about to complain to a junior Negro sailor about his personal problems. "Sorry, Seaman Alvey. I just have a couple of petty problems that I'm sure a JG could handle. Have a good night, okay?"

Jon went back to the ET shop and talked with ET2 Dawkins and ET3 Anderson until he was sure the movie in the wardroom was over. The XO, the Gun Boss, Tom Snyder, and Charles Hanson had been shanghaied by the Captain to watch the movie with the Commodore and himself and the embassy guys. Carl Lehr had agreed to run the movie projector for Jon.

When he got to the Gun Boss's room, Jon found the XO alone and working on some papers at the fold-down desk.

"XO, I just got this from YN1 Gilpin. He said the Captain had given him the hand-written note yesterday, and he told him to type it up and get it inserted in his record."

The XO read the paper in the folder, he shook his head side-to-side, and then his chin dropped onto his chest for a moment; then he raised his head and looked at Jon, "Do you have a least favorite gospel?"

The question felt like sacrilege. "No, sir. I—"

He was looking at the CO's note again. "My least favorite is John. One, I think he is arrogant. He seems to insist on calling himself 'the disciple Jesus loved,' and his is the only gospel that doesn't mention the agony in the garden. Father, let this cup pass from me, but Thy will, not mine, be done." He looked at me again. "That's a pretty handy prayer, don't you think?"

"Sir, I never looked at the gospels that way. I would have to agree that it is a handy prayer, but, sir, I am concerned about the Captain punishing the YN1. I'd like you to tell the Captain that I stopped by the ship's office to check on the guys, as just part of my division officer duties, and that's how I saw it. It would be better if he did not know the YN1 came to me over this."

"Jon, I will handle this," the XO said. "If even Jesus can say, 'Let this cup pass from me,' well, I guess a simple XO should be able to say it, too. But having said it, I will do what needs to be done, whether or not I like it. But you, you will not mention this to anyone. If the Captain asks you point blank, you will deny knowing anything about it. Is that clear?"

"But, XO—"

"Damn it, Jon, don't make me argue with you here. You were right to bring this to me, and now it is my responsibility to take care of this. Just remember what I said. If he asks, you will lie. Is that sufficiently clear?"

"Clear, sir. Should I get the hell out of here now? That seems to be the way most of my sessions wind up these days."

"Two Buckets." The XO smiled and shook his head. "I have little doubt that since 1775, there has never been a US Navy ensign with such an ability to both aggravate and provide comic relief in the span of two sentences. No, do not get the hell out of here just yet. There's one more thing.

"During sea and anchor detail, the Captain chewed you out, and later, in front of Tom Snyder, he said he was going to remove you from the safety observer position. I was on the bridge. I saw what you did. The helmsman got distracted by that discussion of bearing error, and by the Captain's tone of voice, I expect; and he overshot his heading. He would have overshot more if you hadn't caught it. You did well there. I have talked to the Captain. You will remain as safety observer for all the same situations as before. Understood?"

"Yes, sir."

"Good. Now get the hell out of here."

Jon popped to attention and clicked his heels together.

"Two Buckets, you son-of-a-bitch. I know you guys thought my mustache made me look like Hitler. You were going to give me a *heil*, weren't you?"

"Sir, the thought never entered my mind."

"BS, Two Buckets. Go practice your lying," the XO said.

4 August 1966, Thursday, en route to Zamboanga

Dearest Teresa,

These days, it was taking time to get beyond the salutation. Before, before the wetting down party the first time in the PI, Jon could just prop himself on his elbows on his bunk, and words would just pour onto a letter to Teresa. Now, he would write "Dearest Teresa," and then he'd pause. It was as if he had to turn off his navy self and turn on the person that belonged to Teresa. Unlike the Holy Trinity, being two people at once didn't feel holy. It didn't feel good, but it was how things were. After a moment, he'd get his Teresa person turned on, and a letter to her would start flowing. That night it took a little extra time for the Teresa person to emerge.

On Thursday, the sea presented morning as an angelic, innocent child with not one vestige of the demonic tantrum of the afternoon and night before. There was a blue, blue sky above a deep blue sea, the surface of which was mirror-smooth. Flying fish fled the shadow of the ship, diaphanous wings rippling the smooth water ahead of the bow wave as the fish skittered across the surface. Jon was on the signal bridge. Sometimes, you could almost feel alone up there greeting the morning. Behind him, the two signalmen on watch were in their shack, just in front of the forward mast. The murmur of their voices was like the noise of a ventilation fan, just background noise, and not really indicative of other human presence. There wasn't another ship visible.

Looking aft past the structure housing the helo hanger and the after mast, the ship was laying a wake about twice her width. They were going seventeen knots, two knots more than the most economical speed to make up for time lost during the storm. There was a sense of the power released from the fires in the boilers that generated steam to turn the turbines, which fed the reduction gears, and which in turn drove the propellers. That power felt impressive on this docile morning, in contrast to the previous day when it had felt more like *Manfred* had been a helpless cork.

To the east, nothing but sky and a low-slung sun dumping a stream of yellow-orange fire on the sea and that stream running from the horizon toward *Manfred*.

Teresa entered his mind, as did Jennifer. He closed his eyes and felt as if he could reach out and touch Teresa. Before that wetting down party, the first time in Subic Bay, he got that feeling almost every night when he wrote to Teresa.

He thought of Teresa bathing Jennifer in the sink of their apartment when Jennifer had been just two weeks old. Then, Teresa's hands had been gentle and supporting as she washed soapy water over the helpless, floppy little doll. Jon felt as if those hands were inside his chest now, holding his heart and giving just the gentlest little squeeze.

There was a buzz from the phone in the signal shack behind him. For a moment there, Jon's navy-self and his Teresa-self had been one. Looking back toward the bow, he took in the forward gun mount and the anchor chains running to the stockless anchors snugged up into the hawse pipes: war-fighting and sailor tools of the trade. Jon almost sighed. Teresa always teased him when he sighed. Then he did sigh.

That afternoon, Andrew, Carl, and Jon had a very interesting two hours with Cecil Hart, the embassy guy from Manila. Cecil has been with the State Department for twenty-eight years and spent most of World War II in China.

Jon had asked Cecil if there were any lessons to be learned from how the US had handled the Huks in the Philippines that could be applied to Vietnam. Cecil said that before talking about Vietnam, they needed to understand the real history of the US involvement in World War II in that part of the world. They couldn't start talking about Vietnam without understanding some of the history and some of his experiences.

Cecil spoke about his eight years in China from '38 to '46. He spoke about coming back to the US and supporting Mao vice Chiang Kai Shek. Chiang did not have the ear of the people, while Mao did. Neither would support the participative form of government the State Department seemed bent on forcing on the Chinese. So Mao seemed the better choice for the US to support. But then the hunt for Communist sympathizers in the State Department began, and Cecil's boss sent him to Europe, and a few years later on to the Philippines.

Cecil said that we in the US have a penchant for mental cookie cutters. We did not see Chinese in World War II. We saw Communists and non-Communists. In Korea, we saw it the same way. We analyze a situation, review our options, figure out what we would do in response to each option, and pick the most favorable one. But, we pick based on what we would do. We can't seem to grasp the notion that many peoples we share the planet with really do think differently. And, he thought some of that sort of thing was playing out in the way we are conducting ourselves in Vietnam.

In the Philippines, Cecil said that one of the most important things that had been done was a wide-reaching program of reform, attacking corruption, and providing some of what the Huks fought for. In Vietnam, he said, the government there was doing what Chiang did, just trying to hang onto power rather than to represent the people.

When two hours expired, Cecil said he'd talked himself dry, and unless someone had the makings for a gin and tonic, he was done. Jon wished he'd had a tape recorder. But that night, he wrote to Teresa about the things Cecil had told them. When he dropped his letter in the mail, he wished he'd used carbon paper with Teresa's letter and kept a copy for himself.

30

After *Manfred* entered the port of Zamboanga City and the sea and anchor detail was secured, Jon entered the wardroom on his way to the Locker, and as he always did, looked to see if there was mail in any of the officer's slots. There was a package in his slot.

Below, in the Ensign Locker and at the fold-down desk, Jon opened the package. It contained a copy of *Leaves of Grass*. And a letter from Cecil.

> Dear Mr. Zachery (I hope you appreciate the formality),
>
> I am not sure if you are a fan of poetry, and though we did not really have a chance to get to know each other, I do feel I know something of the kind of person you are, and I very much appreciated meeting you during our little voyage to Zamboanga. This book has meant a lot to me as I have grown from a young

man in college to the about-to-retire, old man I am now. In the *Leaves*, I think, is some of the real stuff of life. There is a joy and savoring of nature, a savoring of cities, a savoring of human interchange. There is loss and sorrow, for life is those things, too. And then, after the Civil War, Whitman seems to have encountered disillusionment. My wish for you, Jon, is that you can, as a young man, appreciate nature, appreciate the possibly special animal that we humans may be, appreciate the possibly special nation we may be, and carry some of those appreciations into old age without allowing the many things that will try to foist disillusionment on you, as the world managed to do to even such a soul as Whitman's. With all that, Whitman has a way with words that sort of help you calibrate your senses. With his calibration, I felt I could see, hear, smell, taste, and feel things that were always there but that I had not been able to sense fully without his help.

Very best wishes,

Sir Cecil

The door to the Locker pulled open. Seeing the package wrapping, Admiral Ensign asked, "Did we get mail here?"

"No, this was a gift from Cecil Hart."

Jon took the wrappings, put them on his bunk, picked up the book, and closed the desk.

"*Leaves of Grass,*" Admiral Ensign said. "Serious poultry. I didn't think you were *that* seriously into it."

"I wouldn't say that I am that seriously into it, either. Cecil just thought I might appreciate it."

Admiral Ensign took off his shoes, crawled into his bunk, and took a paperback book from the angle iron next to him.

Admiral Ensign's tone seemed less antagonistic than had been the norm; still, it was not a tone laden with an invitation to easy familiarity.

"What are you reading?" Jon asked, with as much neutrality as he could impose into his voice.

"*The Golden Ocean*, by Patrick O'Brian. It's a story about a British ship in the 1700s. A classmate of mine is really into sailing and sailing stories, and he gave it to me to read during the cruise."

"Along the lines of *Two Years Before the Mast?*" Jon asked.

The conversation ran into a box canyon pretty quickly. Admiral Ensign continued with his reading. Jon paged through *Leaves* and read a few of the short poems but wasn't absorbing what he read. Poetry, he thought, might be like the Hound of Heaven, not the poem, the Hound, Him, a thing to be found and experienced only in quiet. Jon left the Locker without saying anything. As far as he could tell, this détente established between Admiral Ensign and him was better served that way.

On Friday evening, the Commodore and the senior officers from *Manfred* attended a dinner at city hall. On Saturday, the ship hosted lunch in the wardroom for ten. Among the Saturday lunch guests were the manager of the Peace Corps effort on Mindinao and his wife. The woman created a stir among the sailors from the moment she extended a leg out of the car on the pier. Word of "a white woman" spread through the ship, and by the time that same right leg was placed on the brow to the quarterdeck, the port side of the helo deck, the 01 level amidships, and the signal bridge were crowded with sailors. The woman was tall and slender. She sported sunglasses with a white frame, and her blonde hair was caught up in a ponytail. She was wearing a short-sleeved, button-down-the-front, white dress, the bottom button of which was some four inches above the hem. When she had gotten out of the car, and when she walked, the dress would open below that bottom button, and two or three more inches of tan leg, occasionally a knee, were available for adulation.

Lieutenant Becker was on the quarterdeck to meet the guests, and he was smiling, with both sides of his face. Before, it always seemed to Jon that he only smiled with the blue-eyed side of his face. But today, the brown-eyed side was an enthusiastic participant in the business of smiling. In addition to Lieutenant Becker's brown eye and his blue eye, nearly two hundred other *Manfred* eyes locked onto the woman on the quarterdeck and followed her down the port side. When the overhanging structure outside the wardroom door closed off the adoring gazes, there was a collective, barely, but still clearly audible, *awww* of disappointment.

During lunch, the XO had the word spread to the crew that there better not be a repeat of the mortal sin of undressing the "white woman" with their eyes and ogling her when she left. Fear of God and the XO had been transmitted to the crew as effectively as any tent preacher's message. The XO's message was effective.

Following lunch, the Commodore and the Captain had another meeting with the press, and in the evening, there was, again, a dinner for the senior officers of the ship at a hotel in the city. With all the senior officers tied up with official obligations, the junior members of the crew were ashore performing their own form of a goodwill mission. Almost and Admiral Ensign had gone ashore for sightseeing, dinner, and to attend the cockfights. Jon appreciated the luxury of solitude and the opportunity to write a letter seated at the desk.

On Sunday morning, Jon went to the 8 o'clock Mass in the Cathedral. It looked like a real church from the outside, not like the just-get-the-damned-thing-built affair in Subic Bay. Inside, the air was heavy with solemnity and permanence, eternity even. The Latin prayers and form of the service were all familiar and comfortable. The homily was delivered in Tagalog. Jon paid attention to it, probably more so than he'd done to hundreds of them delivered in English. A choir sang five songs. All five were restrained, perfectly matched to the mood of the place. Nothing pulled at his thoughts to try to make him joyful or to be sorry for his sins.

When the Mass was over, and as he started walking out, he felt good, at ease, at peace. It had been the most passive Mass he'd ever attended. It demanded nothing of him, and he demanded nothing from it. *Passive. Sort of like lukewarm.* He recalled that God didn't care for lukewarm.

He stopped behind the last pew and faced the altar. He told God that he was sorry if his passivity, his lukewarmness, had offended Him. Then he walked out.

After walking two blocks, he caught a jitney back to the ship. There weren't many people about yet, so he got a seat in the vehicle. Jon had seen jitneys the day before with the insides crammed and young men standing on the running boards and hanging onto the outsides.

When he got to the wardroom, Carl Lehr and Andrew Dunston were sitting with cups of coffee.

"Jon," Andrew said, "Carl and I are just about to go get a taxi and do some sightseeing. Interested?"

Jon was surprised to be invited, even though he and Andrew had spent a third of every day together on the bridge for almost two months, that had just been the navy pushing them together, not a matter of choice.

"I don't have any money," he said.

"Not a problem. Quarterdeck, seven minutes." Andrew finished his coffee, set the cup back on the saucer, looked at his watch, and said, "Hop to it."

In the Philippines, jitneys were a common mode of transportation. A jitney was a combination of bus, taxicab, and streetcar without tracks. They came in various sizes, but all of them seemed to have been decorated by a direct descendant of the Canaanite who had designed coats for Jacob's favorite son. The jitney Andrew hired was one of the smallest of the breed. There was just room for Carl and Jon in the back seat and Andrew in front so that he could handle the communications. The driver did not speak English. That was clear. It was not clear whether Andrew's version of Spanish was working or not or whether the driver spoke Spanish of any version. But, somehow, the man seemed to get the idea that his taxi was wanted for the rest of the day.

"*Cuanto?*" Andrew said.

The man responded with a significant number of words, not one of which any of the three of them had understood. Andrew took a number of peso bills from his wallet, held them out to the driver. He extracted one bill and waved the rest away.

"He only took about five bucks," Andrew said. "I think he understood we wanted him for all day. I guess if we get twenty miles out in the boonies, and then he abandons us, we'll know I didn't give him enough."

Andrew had a map and showed the driver where he wanted to go. Driving away from the waterfront, they left the city, heading in a general westerly direction. They passed by flooded rice paddies, all but one of which were untended, with the Sunday sun reflecting off the dark, still water. Well away from the road, which was set atop a built-up levee, to the north, a toy man, knee-deep in water and mud, was trailing a toy water buffalo as it inched its way across the scene.

More untended rice paddies and palm trees paraded past the jitney. They had an occasional glimpse of the ocean. At 1130, Andrew was thinking of a hamburger stand. He was, perhaps, a bit over-confident in his burgeoning fluency in a communication methodology that was only vaguely related to established tongues. Still, he did manage to convey a certain necessity for finding mid-day sustenance. The driver turned the vehicle off the paved road and onto a somewhat graveled, somewhat dirt road. The road was about one and a half times the width of the jitney, and they began jostling and jouncing up a slight hill with palm trees crowding the narrow road and cutting off the sky with overhanging foliage.

Carl said, "They make these jitneys tough, but shock absorbers would be nice."

If the jiggling had been just a bit more cyclic, it would have been like riding in the Huey.

After fifteen minutes, the vehicle exited the palm tree forest and stopped in front of a building that appeared to be part of a clubhouse for a golf course.

The driver parked next to a bus and two jitneys, each of which could easily transport twelve people without anyone hanging onto the sides. Attached to the clubhouse, a large concrete patio was covered with a thatched roof and hosting a large number of picnic tables. A considerable crowd occupied the tables on the covered patio, but it had the appearance of a family gathering. It did not look like a restaurant open to the general public.

"This doesn't look right," Carl said.

Then, a man, tall for a Filipino, thin and straight as a fencepost, and in clerical garb, got up from a table near the center of the patio and walked over to them.

"You speak to him, Jon," Andrew said. "You're a Catholic."

"Well, I'm not going to be able to order lunch in Latin," Jon said.

"Gentlemen," the priest said, "you are Americans, yes?"

"Yes, we are, Father," Jon said. "And we did not intend to intrude on a private party. We were just sightseeing and looking for a place to have lunch, but I think we have made a mistake."

"No, no. Just a moment," the priest said.

The priest went back to the table he had just left, spoke for a moment, then came back and said, "You are invited to have lunch with us. The families here would be pleased and honored if you would join us. Come, come."

Three people got up from the table where the priest had been sitting and made a place for them.

"I am Father Cavallo. You are from the American ship in Zamboanga City, yes?"

Jon replied that they were and introduced Andrew and Carl. The priest interpreted for the people.

Father Cavallo then said, "Three families from my parish are here to celebrate the baptisms of their children. I was just about to say grace. Then, we can have lunch."

After Father Cavallo sat back down, Jon said, "Father, we do not have a gift for the children, the ones baptized, I mean. What if my friend took pictures, and then we send you copies? Would that be okay? Could that be our gift?"

Father Cavallo smiled and said something to those at the head of the table. The others at the table Jon took to be a grandfather, a grandmother holding a white lace-swaddled sleeping infant, a young man, and a young woman. The grandmother and the young woman conversed rapidly and earnestly for a moment. The grandmother then said something to the grandfather, who in turn spoke to the priest. Just into the conversation between grandfather and priest, the grandmother intervened and corrected the course of the grandfather's speech. He launched his dialogue again, only to be interrupted a second time. He held up one finger in the direction of the grandmother, and she became quiet. The grandfather then completed his statement to the priest.

"The family, the families, I should say, thank you for the offer of the pictures. They will be pleased to have pictures, but they do not want you to worry about gifts. They are pleased to have you as guests, and they thank you for sharing in the celebration of the baptisms of their young ones. And grandpa wants me to say that his father told him about the Spanish. He himself has seen Japanese and Huks and Americans. He said it seems in the Philippines, there will always be someone. And so, from what he has seen and learned, Americans are not so bad."

When the priest stopped talking, it was very quiet. Jon saw and felt every eye fastened on Carl, Andrew, and him.

Andrew said, "Father, we are touched by the warmth and hospitality here. Allowing us strangers and foreigners into the middle of your family celebrations—it is one of the nicest things that has happened to me." Andrew looked around at the crowd. "Thank you, all. *Gracias.*" He looked back at the priest. "And, Father, is it okay if

I take the first picture of grandfather? The first picture should be of him since he is a great diplomat."

After the priest interpreted, there was applause, and a flood of voices released the floodgate of the conversational dam, which had been closed pending how grandfather's foray into diplomacy turned out. From two tables over, a young man said something, and loud laughter erupted, and a grandmotherly woman at that table smacked the young man on the arm with her folded fan. Father Cavallo leaned over toward Jon and related that the young man had said his grandfather learned his diplomacy talking to the back end of his water buffalo each day.

Then, two women brought plates for the three of them from *Manfred* and the priest. People began moving to the food table, the centerpiece was a roast pig, and they began to help themselves. The women tended the young and old while a babble of happy voices spilled out from under the covered patio, making a little island of Sunday Filipino contentment on a grassy hill above a palm tree grove on Mindinao, a few miles west of the city of Zamboanga.

After ensuring with Father Cavallo that it would not be an insult, Andrew and Carl left the equivalent of five dollars in pesos for each of the baptized children. Also, they pressed money on the priest for his church as a fee for his interpreter duties. Following thanks, farewells, and handshakes with the heads of the three families, they boarded their jitney and descended the hill.

When they got back to the coastal highway, Andrew said, "Yesterday at lunch on the ship, two of the guests were a man and his wife. She was the blonde all the sailors were looking at. They are in charge of the Peace Corps effort on Mindinao. They invited any of us from the wardroom to drop in for a visit. So I talked to Father Cavallo about how to get there, and he told the driver. So that is next on the agenda today. Okay?"

Carl burped. "That was a yes in a little-known local dialect."

Jon forced a burp. "And that means heck yes."

Andrew grimaced and shook his head. "I should have gone sightseeing with grown-up JGs."

"Can't believe those people just let us crash their family party like that. Just amazing," Carl said.

"When I was enlisted, and on my first ship," Jon said, "we went up to the North Atlantic and participated in a NATO exercise—talk about rough seas, you guys would have called me Three Buckets—but anyway, after the exercise, we pulled into Cardiff, Wales. There too, we had been the first US warship to visit there since the end of World War II. And, man, the hospitality was something! A sailor would be walking down the street, someone would touch him on the back, he'd turn around, and there would be this old woman just grinning from ear to ear. Turns out that people used to do that during the war: touch the stars on the bib of an American sailor's blue uniform for luck. They wouldn't let you buy a beer in a pub, and there was a party every night. Anyhow, the Filipinos back there at the golf club reminded me of that time in Cardiff."

Twice, the driver asked for directions from people walking alongside the road, and thirty-five minutes after leaving the golf course clubhouse, they pulled into a dirt and grass area in front of a large frame house with a tin roof. Tall palm trees shaded the house. On the opposite side of the house from where they parked, a grassy expanse led to a sand and pebble beach.

31

Jon and Carl stayed beside the jitney as Andrew went up to the house and knocked on the screen door. From where they stood, beyond the side of the house, a well-manicured lawn, dotted with palms, led to the sea. They heard a muted and gentle *swoosh* as small waves caressed the pebbles and grains of sand on the beach. A slight breeze crinkled the sea surface, and the crinkles caught sunlight like slivers of clear crystal sitting on the blue surface.

John Johnson answered the door. Partial recognition but the inability to securely and firmly register Andrew Dunston flashed for a moment across his face. Then, Andrew explained the connection from lunch aboard *Manfred,* and he flashed a big smile. Then, he invited them to call him JJ. As the smile was burning itself out, Jon thought he might have picked up a nano-second of annoyance at the intrusion into a peaceful Sunday afternoon, but JJ seemed to push that aside and invited them inside.

He led them to a large living room with several cushioned rattan settees. There was a stack of folding chairs leaning up against one wall. So, JJ evidently accommodated large gatherings of the Peace Corps volunteers. That day, however, there was only one other person in the room: Cecil Hart.

"Cecil," Andrew said. "Fancy meeting you here."

"Oh, we embassy minions like to check up on our citizenry deployed to the hinterlands when we can. Jacob Wesley is babysitting the Commodore and the Captain, which gave me the opportunity to come down and see JJ. But, I say, I never expected to see you gentlemen here."

"We hired a jitney for the day, about five bucks, near as I can tell. Is that enough?" Andrew asked.

"If he agreed with the price, I would leave it at that, but you might just give him a few pesos tip at the end of the day," Cecil said.

Andrew related how they'd busted into a baptismal celebration and how they'd been welcomed. Jon tacked on his story about visiting Cardiff, Wales.

"Ah, yes, it seems that in remote and isolated spots where the natives haven't seen Americans for twenty years, we are still appreciated," Cecil said. "But there will be second and third visits. Then familiarity and contempt, those things, you know."

JJ said, "How about something to drink: beer, soda, tea, lemonade, wine? And Cecil and I were about to repair to the veranda in back. My wife, Stephanie—you may remember her, Andrew—is snorkeling with our other guest at the moment. They should be coming for something to drink shortly."

After JJ returned with drinks to the veranda, which looked out on the beach, Andrew said, "JJ, yesterday in the wardroom, you mentioned you and Stephanie managed the Peace Corps effort for the Philippines from here. We never got into how big an effort it is and how it's going. Can you comment on that?"

"Sure," JJ said. "We have volunteers scattered around a number of places on Mindinao and Luzon. Most of them are young, recent college grads with a real desire to help people. That has to be their motivation because we don't pay them. The government does have a training program that all the volunteers go through, and some travel, food, and lodging are paid for. But really, the people want to be here and don't mind forgoing, for a time, entering the workplace and making their millions. As far as how it is going, why don't I let Cecil talk to that?"

"I can do that," Cecil said. "But I like to put it in a longer-term sort of context. The Peace Corps is an effort that continues a series of positive things that the US has done here.

"For all of this century, we have been helping the Philippines establish a centralized government. It took some fighting, as Jacob mentioned on board your ship before we came down here. But in addition to the fighting, we have been providing assistance with industry, agriculture, and medical facilities.

"A key figure in our history with the Filipinos is Ed Lansdale—you remember I talked about him on Thursday?"

"The air force guy?" Andrew asked.

"He was an air force officer, and he wound up working for the government in a non-air force way. He and Ramon Magsaysay resettled some of the Huks here on Mindinao in a program called EdCor. In my mind, if they had not done that, there would have been other insurrections, maybe under another name.

"Right," Jon said, "you called it a nice variation on the theme *we beat you in the war, now go home and play nice, or we'll be back.*"

"Ah, Sir Two Buckets, you paid attention. And now, the Peace Corps is here providing assistance with agricultural improvements, education on hygiene, and some medical things. The Peace Corps has kept this string of positive contributions for two-thirds of a century intact, and it is, in part, why you were received warmly by the families at the golf course."

"Cecil," Carl said, "it sounds like there have been equal doses of military power and humanitarian assistance applied here."

"Well, I wouldn't be able to say whether they were equal or not, but I do agree that both were essential elements in getting us to where we are right now with the Filipino people."

They noticed the women walking up from the beach. Both women were wearing two-piece bathing suits. The tall blonde, she would be Stephanie, had a thin silky scarf-like piece of cloth tied around her waist. The other was shorter, darker, and had an athletic heft to her upper body and legs. They were having one of those timed-chess-game sort of female conversations, where it seemed that not one millisecond of silence existed before one or the other of them began speaking again. Noticing the three additional men on the veranda, Stephanie let her end of the conversation lag. Her companion picked up the slack and, as if now playing both black and white, single-handedly kept the millisecond of silence at bay.

As the two women approached the veranda, JJ stood, followed by the other four of us. At the edge of the veranda, the shorter woman stopped talking.

"Stephanie," JJ said. "You remember Andrew Dunston from lunch on the *Manfred* yesterday."

"Of course. Nice to see you again." She reached out and shook hands with Andrew.

"Steph, Valerie," JJ said, "this is Carl Lehr, and this is Jon Zachery. Gentlemen, my wife, Stephanie, and…an acquaintance, Valerie."

Stephanie shook hands with Carl and Jon. Valerie aimed a smile of forced politeness at them; then, she sat at an adjacent table with her side to them. JJ went inside to get glasses of white wine for the ladies.

"Are you with the Peace Corps, too, Valerie?" Andrew asked.

"No, I'm not," she said. "And you're soldiers." The last was firmly declarative and accusatory.

"Valerie," Stephanie said, "first of all, they are sailors, from a navy ship—"

"They're all the same: lackeys of our government's wars of imperialistic aggression."

"Valerie! I should not have to remind you that they are our guests, and so are you," Stephanie said.

"I am an American citizen. This is an American government establishment, and I am entitled to service."

Apparently, even an aggressive, imperialistic government was expected to provide certain services to obvious royalty.

"This," Stephanie said, "is my home. In it, I expect civil behavior on the part of my guests. Come with me and get your clothes. I am going to have our driver take you back to Zamboanga."

JJ managed to avoid Valerie as she stormed into the house without spilling wine in either glass. "Can't I leave you for a moment, Cecil, without you fomenting rebellion amongst the natives?"

"Quite frankly, JJ," Cecil said, "none of us had to say much of anything. Valerie got herself quite worked up without any help from any of us. Her behavior was rather imperial, wouldn't you say, Andrew?"

"I will stick my neck out and say she is not fond of the military," Andrew said. "But 'lackeys of the American government's wars of imperialistic aggression?' Is the Peace Corps a haven for Marxist, Leninist sedition, JJ?"

"Actually, Valerie is not in the Peace Corps. She was in our training program when she met a young man who wound up coming over here to serve on Luzon. But when she found out the Peace Corps would not assign her here with her boyfriend unless they were married, she quit the school. Then when her boyfriend came over here, she followed him. Until now, she has been a little help occasionally, but a fair amount of trouble regularly. Last week, we had to send her boyfriend back to the States because he apparently will be drafted. So the military is now the source of all the evil in the world. She apparently has never had to learn how to function without getting her own way all the time."

"It just seemed so out of the blue. They'd been swimming and were having a nice conversation, then she finds out we are military, and Blamo! A bomb goes off," Jon said.

Stephanie came back onto the veranda wearing yellow shorts and a white sleeveless blouse. "I'm sorry about that, gentlemen. Valerie, I'm sure, has been getting poor marks in *plays nicely with others* since kindergarten. She wasn't pleasant even before her boyfriend got drafted, but let's put her aside and talk about something else, shall we?"

Stephanie and JJ were cordial and pleased to talk about Peace

Corps efforts in the Philippines. Stephanie, an accountant and the financial mind behind the office, recounted with some pride that their budget was diminishing year by year as they transferred more and more work from salaried to volunteer workers. She said she thought there was probably not another branch of governmental service that got such a great amount done for such a small and decreasing budget.

An hour and a half and a second round of drinks passed pleasantly and quickly; then, the *Manfred* officers took their leave and rode back to Zamboanga.

During the trip, Carl remarked, "Funny, wasn't it, how the people at that baptism treated us so well, and then Valerie, a fellow American, treated us like we were *Ugly Americans*?"

"Oh, there was an Ugly American among us this afternoon," Andrew said. "But *it* wasn't male, and *it* wasn't blonde. Care to guess who it was?"

"Whom," Carl said.

Andrew: "What?"

Carl: "Not what. Whom."

"Whom's on first?" Jon said and laughed. And it felt good to do so. It dawned then what was missing: the ever-present atmosphere of malevolence radiating from the commodore and the new captain.

Following dinner in a restaurant near the waterfront, Andrew, Carl, and Jon returned to the ship. In the Ensign Locker, Carl wrote to his wife at the fold-down desk. Jon composed his letter from atop his bunk.

At 2200, over the 1MC came, "Taps. Taps. Lights out. All hands turn into your bunks. The smoking lamp is out in all berthing spaces. Taps."

"I, for one," Carl said, "am following orders. You want the desk, Buckets?"

Buckets did want the desk. He was not finished telling Teresa about the beautiful Sunday he'd spent and that the best part of it had been how close he felt to her. He wrote about how all navy matters had been put on hold for the day, and that had allowed him to be just Jon Zachery and not Ensign Jon Zachery for a whole, entire, complete day. He wrote about the Ugly American, Valerie. His pen was tempted to describe the *malevolent atmosphere* radiating off the heavies in command above him, but Jon would not do that. Those two were his burden to bear, not Teresa's. He concentrated on her, on their relationship, on how it took the effort to hold onto the good things she brought into his life. And as long as he kept her in his life, his life had good things in it.

When he was finished, he was pleased with his letter. He hoped Teresa would be, too. The postal clerk, however, would think the letter required extra postage.

32

On Monday, *Manfred* sailors pulled in the mooring lines at 0700.

"Underway. Shift colors," the Bosun announced.

Jon, in his safety observer position, pictured the flag being hauled down on the fantail as another was unfurled by the signalmen on the mainmast.

The commodore was not with them. On Sunday, he'd flown from Zamboanga to Manila and on Hong Kong, rejoining USS *Reilly*.

The new CO sat on his chair and stared straight ahead out the window. Jon cast frequent glances at him, but he never moved.

The Cheng, Chief Engineer, conned the ship out of port. The ship passed breakwater dikes to either side and left Zamboanga harbor for the open sea.

The new captain hopped down from his chair and left the bridge. He didn't tell the OOD where he was going. When the Skipper, Commander Carstens, left the bridge, he always said where he'd be.

When the new CO passed the helmsman, Jon caught a glimpse

of his face. Gone was the look of the hungry predatory bird. In its place, worry.

At least that air of threat, of edgy uneasiness, was gone. Maybe the commodore had been responsible for that.

When the special sea detail was secured, Jon went down to the ET shop. The chief was there, sitting on a stool at the workbench with a tech manual open in front of him. "Mr. Z.," he said. "Just discovered a problem with our IFF."

IFF. Identification Friend or Foe. Classified equipment which electronically queried ships and planes *Manfred* picked up on radar. If the radar target was friendly, it responded with an appropriate code.

"The system won't send out the query signal," the chief said.

"Do you know what the problem is?"

"I think so, sir." The chief pointed to a circuit diagram. "This bank of transformers generates the query code. We are sure that's the culprit."

"Do we carry the part?" Jon said.

"No, sir, but I spoke with the supply guys. They will get out a priority message this afternoon. With a little luck, the part will be there when we get to Danang."

"How many copies of the tech manual do you have, Chief?"

"Just this one, sir."

"Okay, chief, do you mind if I sit there and get myself up to speed on how this thing works?"

The chief relinquished the stool. "Hey, Mr. Z. Word is we are not ducking below the equator. That right?"

"That's right."

"I heard it was up to the new CO whether we went or not," the chief said. "I heard he said we were going south after leaving port. What happened?"

"I don't know, Chief. Maybe it was the extra days it was going to cost us. It'll take us four days to get there the way it is. If we did the equator, it would take seven days."

"This is a major bummer. I sure was looking forward to getting my hands on you slimy pollywogs. Sir."

At lunch, the officers stood behind their chairs and waited for the new CO to appear. When he sidled along the aft side of the table to his place, Jon saw the worried-looking new CO had been replaced with the other new CO, the one you had to worry about. Still, the salad was served and eaten with nothing to disturb the fragile peace.

The new CO ate what was placed in front of him. He didn't say anything. No one said anything, either, until the new captain took a bite of the main course. Then Andrew Dunston began telling Gun Boats about the trip to the Peace Corps headquarters. When that drew no lightning bolt of retribution, the other JGs chimed in with anecdotes of liberty escapades in Zamboanga. Only the center of the table conversed. The heavy end remained still. The ensign end was still, too, and the three most junior officers ate and watched and waited.

Jon didn't know if the others felt it, but he did. Something was coming, and when it did, it wouldn't be pleasant.

Main course plates were cleared, and the stewards served desserts. The new captain took a bite, and everyone dug in. The new captain sipped coffee, placed the cup back on the saucer, and invited Tom Snyder, the acting Ops O, to explain why a commanding officer would use CIC as his General Quarters station.

Tom was caught with a mouthful of cobbler, and he blushed bright red when all eyes turned toward him.

"Captain," the XO said, "I—"

"XO," the new captain said, "I asked Mr. Snyder. I asked him for a reason. So, Mr. Snyder, when you are quite ready."

Tom forced the remainder of his mouthful down, cleared his throat, and said, "Sorry, Captain. The Skipper thought—"

"Your former Skipper. That's who you are talking about, is that right?"

"Yes, sir," Tom said. "That's who I was talking about. Anyhow, the Skipper thought—"

"We need to be clear," the new captain said in a very normal tone of voice, "Mr. Snyder, I am *the* captain. I am *the* CO. I am *the* skipper. If you are going to be talking about the former Commanding Officer of USS *Manfred*, let's be clear. Call him *former* Commanding Officer, *former* Skipper. Are you clear on that?"

Tom Snyder was normally a passive sort. He was quiet, part of the backdrop rather than a main or even a supporting actor. His normal grey-tinged pallor had returned after the initial blush, but now, another subtle blossom of angry crimson rouged his cheekbones. He pushed his dessert plate away from him and looked up.

"That's clear, Captain," Tom said. "And just so I am *really clear*, what is the question again, please?"

"Tom," the XO said, "the question is, what is the rationale for a commanding officer being in combat for General Quarters."

The new captain seemed to contemplate saying something, but he didn't.

"Thank you, XO," Tom said. "The rationale is that CIC is the place on the ship where all information from our electronic sensors comes together. It is also where all communications from the chain of command come together. The rationale for a commanding officer to be on the bridge is that in close-in combat situations, when maneuvering the ship can be critical; the commanding officer should be there. On the other hand, there is some thinking that with the information available in CIC, if that information is processed rapidly and accurately, you can avoid those close-in situations where visual input and maneuvering the ship becomes critical. The other thing is that, on average, half of each day is dark, where visual cues are not available—"

The XO jumped in. "Right. I think that captures the essence of both arguments."

"And," the new captain locked eyes with the XO for a moment, and then he looked back at Tom Snyder, "your *former* CO supported the rationale for the commanding officer being in CIC for General Quarters, correct?"

"Captain," Tom said, "The Skipper, who was the Commanding

Officer of USS *Manfred* until seven days and about three hours ago, did support that rationale, and not only he—"

"That's enough. You've answered the question. And during the encounter with the PT boats, the *former* CO wound up moving out to the bridge at the last minute, and it was because exactly that type of close-in situation had developed. So, I want to make it clear that I do not support your former CO's or Mr. Snyder's rationale. My GQ station will be on the bridge, and the XO will be in Combat.

"One other thing that we will change is the policy on superheaters. Your previous CO had those lit off all the time in the Tonkin Gulf. That is wasteful of fuel. From now on, we will not light off superheaters unless I order them lit. So then, if there are no questions, we should get to work."

Carl Lehr gigged Jon on the arm with his elbow as the XO called the wardroom to attention.

As they were standing, Jon whispered to Carl, "I wasn't going to say anything."

"Mr. Zachery," the new captain said, "did you have a question?"

Jon was looking at the CO, but he felt the eyes of every other officer on him.

"Uh, no, sir," Jon said. "I just bumped Mr. Lehr as we were standing, and I said I was sorry."

"Sorry. Yes, well," the Captain said, "come see me in my cabin with your IFF circuit diagram." The CO dropped his napkin on the table. He was the only one at the table who hadn't put the napkin in a napkin ring. Jon saw that he didn't even have a napkin ring by his place.

Halfway to the door, the new CO said, "Right away."

Jon would not have been surprised if his qualification to stand OOD watch underway had been pulled, but the new CO let it stand. Jon had bridge watch once a day. His feet thought that was a very civilized way to conduct affairs. The watches were pleasant, with a lot of small boat traffic and occasional freighters and oilers of the larger vessel category. Weather, balmy, pleasant, calm seas. In addition to boats and ships, flying fish and seabirds shared the ocean with *Manfred*.

Four days after leaving Zamboanga, *Manfred* anchored in the harbor at Da Nang. A whaleboat was sent in to pick up crypto material, mail, parts, and two officers. The new operations officer and a new ensign, the replacement for Dennis Macklin, were waiting ashore for a ride to the ship. From what they'd heard in the Ensign Locker, the navy had not decided if a replacement for William Stewart, Dormant, would be assigned.

Carl Lehr and Jon were on the fantail when the motor whaleboat returned. Jon escorted the new operations officer to his cabin, and Carl took charge of the new ensign. The giant new ensign. He was well over six feet tall and had broad meaty shoulders. The normal-sized new Ops O had JG bars on his collar.

Jon carried the new Ops O's crammed-full, folded-in-half, hanging bag to his stateroom. He carried his other two bags.

"Here we are, sir," Jon said as he hoisted the bag onto the fold-up bed/sofa. "Home, sweet home."

"So, you're Jon Zachery, and your Ensign Locker nickname is Two Buckets, you said. I'm Dave Davison. Everybody calls me DD."

The new Ops O's tone of voice was friendly, open. He spoke to Jon as if they were equals. Jon wondered if the guy was setting him up, just waiting for Jon to become overly familiar before pouncing.

The new Ops O unsnapped the side-latches of his bag, laid it out full length on the fold-down couch, unzipped the inside closure, rooted around inside for a moment, and extracted a barracks cover hat. He placed his combination cover on the shelf above the fold-down couch. Zipping the bag closed and turning it over, he took a small box from one of the small pockets in the front of the bag; then he sat in front of the fold-down desk, took lieutenant insignia from the small box, and fixed it to his barracks cover.

"Just got promoted," DD said. "Didn't even get all my uniform items transitioned to my new exalted rank."

"Uh, sir," Jon began.

"I meant for you to call me DD."

"Okay, sir, DD. If you are ready, I know the XO wants to meet you."

DD laughed and shook his head. "Okay, Two Buckets, sir, we'll go, just as soon as I get bars on my shirt."

When DD and Jon got to the passageway outside the XO's cabin, Carl and the new ensign were talking to the XO through his open door. Ensign Gregory Haywood seemed to fill most of the space with his dark-towering bulk. Kong might be a good name for him, Jon thought. Greg Haywood appeared to be as tall as Peter Feldman, but he was considerably bulkier. He had a beefy upper torso and hairy arms that bulged with muscles. Under his close-cropped, thick-black hair, there was a narrow brow above his deep-set black eyes and potato nose. Jon shook his head. He'd just imagined a new Andrew Dunston drawing of Ensign Haywood hanging on the Empire State Building swatting at tiny airplanes.

The XO dismissed the new ensign, and Carl led the way forward and down to the Ensign Locker. The new ensign seemed to completely fill the hatch opening leading down to the second deck.

"XO," Jon said, "this is the new operations officer, Lt. Davison. Sir, this is the XO."

"Come in and have a seat, Lieutenant," the XO said. "Thanks, Jon."

Jon descended the ladder and met Carl coming out of the Locker.

"Gotta get back up to the bridge," Carl said. "We'll probably set the sea and anchor detail in a half hour for getting underway again. See you then."

Inside the Locker, Gregory Haywood seemed to have to stand sideways to fit between the tiers of bunks.

"Gregory Haywood," Jon stuck out his hand, "Jon Zachery."

Greg took the hand in his paw, and he seemed to be very conscious of his ability to transform the hand into a skin bag full of bone powder. He gave the hand the briefest and gentlest squeeze, which, coming from someone else, Jon would have considered effeminate. When you looked at Greg, however, *effeminate* was not a word that came to mind.

"Real nice to meet ya, and yeah, I'm Greg," he said, "or, rather, Newbie, according to the Bull. What's your name down here?"

"Nice to meet you, too, Newbie. I'm Two Buckets. I get seasick. You need anything…Newbie?"

"Yeah, how do I get laundry done here? I'm about out."

"Laundry was picked up today. Next time is four days from now. Long time on the road?"

"Yeah," Newbie said. "Hawaii, Guam, Clark Air Force Base, to Subic Bay, then I turned around and went back to Clark, then to Saigon, then Da Nang."

"How was Da Nang?"

"The best part of it was I was only there one night. Siren went off in the middle of the night. We all went into bunkers expecting rockets or artillery fire, but it was a false alarm. Then, I had put my sweaty tee-shirt over a chair in our hootch-BOQ room to hopefully dry it out a bit. I wanted to get another day out of it, but during the night, ants ate a lot of holes in it. Real glad to get to a ship."

"Tell you what, Newbie, why don't you and I go see if we can find the Supply Officer and see if he will approve a mercy laundry run for you?"

33

The next morning, Jon entered the pilothouse at 0607. The new captain sat on his chair, sipping at a cup of coffee. Jon walked over to him, saluted, and said, "Permission to speak, Captain?"

He nodded.

Jon forced extra amplitude into his voice. "Captain, here's the quarter I owe you. You were right, sir. The part we ordered did not fix the problem, but we do have the system running again. The ETs fixed it with a part we had in stock." Jon handed over a quarter. "So we have nothing on the electronics down equipment list, sir. Thought you might like to know that first thing. With your permission, I'll strike below, sir." Jon saluted again, the Captain nodded again, and Jon left the bridge.

When he walked into the wardroom, the XO stood up from his place at the table and motioned for Jon to follow him to his room. He closed the door behind Jon.

"I understand you just paid off a quarter bet to the CO, saying he was right about which part would fix the IFF," the XO said.

"Yes, sir, I did, but how did you hear about that so fast?"

"I have my ways. The problem here is that the Ops O told me late last night that the part you ordered did fix the problem. So we need to make sure the Ops O doesn't blow your lie for you," the XO said.

"I hadn't told him yet. I was going to right after breakfast. I guess I better do it right now, though," Jon said.

"I'll call him." The XO looked shook his head. "Two Buckets, I told you to lie if something came up about the shellback certificate. But lying is a messy business. Don't go there unless you have to." The XO reached for the phone. "Go eat your breakfast."

"Sorry, XO. You PO'ed at me?"

"You want to tell me what you were thinking?" The XO held the phone in his hand.

"The day we discovered the problem with the IFF and didn't have the part, the supply officer sent a priority message requesting it. The CO was miffed that a priority message went out without him knowing about it. He wanted to make sure we really had the problem nailed down and that we ordered the correct part. So he told me to bring a circuit diagram and show him why we thought we had the right part identified."

"The CO has a master's degree in Electrical Engineering," The XO said. "And he likes to remind me of that."

"Uh, well, I thought I was to meet him in his cabin, but he wanted to get up to the bridge. So, there, in front of the watch team, I showed him the circuit diagram and explained why all of us, the chief, my second class, and I thought we had the part identified. It's a sealed metal box full of small transformers. The CO looked at the circuit diagram and said that it couldn't possibly be the failed part. It had to be a vacuum tube or one of those new-fangled transistors. I told him our techs had checked that box of transformers with an ohmmeter and found one set of wires that had either burned through or broke. The CO wouldn't believe me and wanted to bet me five bucks I was wrong. I told him I couldn't afford five bucks and said I'll bet a quarter. He kind of sneered at me and told me I was dismissed.

"The other thing, XO, I found myself in a mode where, as soon as the new CO opened his mouth to speak, no matter what he said, I became angry with him. I didn't even stop to consider whether he was right or not. Whatever he said, I was automatically opposed to. I didn't think that was an acceptable way to relate to the CO, new or old. So I thought I needed to do something to support his program. The CO seems to think he needs to look like he is always right. So I thought I'd help him."

The XO put the phone back in its cradle and looked at it for a moment, and then he turned. "Get the hell out of here, Jon. Go eat your breakfast."

The wardroom stewards had eggs Benedict on the menu that morning. As Jon mopped up egg yolk and sauce with his toast, he thought: DD has not been aboard for twenty-four hours, and, already, it was natural to think of him as the Ops O. The captain, on the other hand, was still the new CO, a newbie. Good intentions, those were the things paving the road to hell, he reminded himself.

At 0705, Jon was sitting on the fold-down couch in the Ops Officer's Room. Even though it had felt natural to call DD the Ops O when he'd had been talking with the XO in the Ops O's room, it did seem strange. Sitting at the desk of the dark-haired, dark-complexioned, black-eyed previous resident of the room was his blond-haired, fair, blue-eyed replacement.

DD said, "Well, Jon, XO said we should talk at the first opportunity this morning. He explained why to a certain extent. So, give me your rundown on the situation we are facing here."

"Yes, sir," Jon said. "First off…"

"Hang on," DD said. "I asked you to call me DD. Would you please do that?"

The previous Ops O had never invited that kind of familiarity and informality. Presumably, Cowboy had been on familiar terms with him since they went on liberty together, but Jon never considered presuming that level of familiarity.

"Yes, sir," he said. "DD."

"I don't think you quite get the concept," DD said. "A proper response would be something like, 'Okay,DD.'"

"It just doesn't seem right, sir," Jon said. "I guess I spent the first six months here having it pounded into me what a useless fleck of pond scum I was..."

"Jon, we don't have time to debate this endlessly. I expect there to be a comfortable air between us. As a brand-new lieutenant with just about half the time you have on active duty, I want to be able to rely on your experience and for us to be partners in our efforts. And I want you to call me DD. So try it. Say, 'Okay, DD.'"

"Okay, DD," Jon said as he squirmed on the couch.

DD chuckled. "After a couple of times, you'll get used to it. This is important to me. After my junior officer tour, my CO had orders to the afloat staff out here in the Tonkin Gulf. He thought a few months on the staff with him would be a great experience for me, and I'd still make my slot in Destroyer School. So, he got me orders out here, too. I was just about to depart my staff job when your Ops O was killed, and I was ordered here.

"I really feel like I am at a disadvantage coming into this job without the school. My junior officer tour was spent in the Engineering Department. In Operations, I want to be able to rely on each of you division officers to hold up your end of the business, but also for you to help me with mine. I am not in a position to help you. Okay?"

"Okay, DD."

"Good. Even if our situation here weren't, shall I say, strange, I would want to do business like this. Oh, your Skipper reported in to the staff before I left. He kind of gave me a rundown on the situation out here, and he asked me to pass his regards. I presume you know that he is high on you. And, he will be a good addition to that staff, bringing a real combat orientation with him. Our Admiral, by the way, was real pleased with your ship's idea about going after that

MiG up near your North SAR station. That's why he asked for your Skipper to be assigned to the staff.

"Now then, what's the deal with the IFF equipment? I stopped by the ET shop late last night, found the ET2 there, and he told me you all had repaired the system with the part that came aboard the same time I did. XO said you told the Captain that part did not fix the problem. So what's what here?"

Jon ran over the whole story again, about the CO discussing the issue in front of the watch team on the bridge, that he had a master's degree in electrical engineering, while he only had a bachelor's, and about the bet.

"The XO has told me a bit about how you've become, or maybe made yourself, a lightning rod for the CO. We need to get you out of that mode." DD's eyes were light blue, very much like Cecil Hart's. He had his right arm across his chest, and his left arm supported his chin as he stared at Jon. But, he had no eye fingers reaching inside his brain, like the previous Ops O had.

"Lies," DD said. "We can't do business that way. I'm a simple-minded guy and not smart enough to remember even a straightforward set of lies. So, let's agree on a couple of things right off the bat. You are not to deal with the CO on your own if it is at all avoidable, and you will not deal from the basis of a lie unless we both agree. And the correct response is, Okay, DD."

"Okay, DD."

The day after the stop at Da Nang, *Manfred* steamed off the coast, just south of the Demilitarized Zone. The ship, back on a three section watch bill, was on call to provide gunfire support to U.S. Marines operating near the DMZ.

Andrew Dunston and Jon had the 1200 to 1600 bridge watch. At 1315, Lieutenant Timmons, the Gun Boss, who was the Evaluator in Combat, came onto the bridge. He said to Andrew, "We have an immediate execute order to join up with USS *Carmody* and proceed to about fifteen miles north of the DMZ. A Forward Air Controller found a large number of boats and barges pulled up on the beach. Our tasking is to destroy those boats. *Carmody* will be in tactical command until we get up there with the FAC. Radio Central is establishing a radio frequency for you to use when you need to talk bridge-to-bridge. I've told the Captain and the XO. Captain is on his way up. Take a course of three-three-zero and go to twenty-five knots. *Carmody* will be six miles in front of us on that heading. She will go to twenty-two knots so we can overtake her."

"Three-three-zero, twenty-five knots, Mr. Zachery," Andrew said.

After a small turn, the ship steadied on the new course. The power unleashed into the ship's twin propellers by opening the fuel control valves was transmitted through *Manfred's* metal body. Jon recalled being below, not on watch when the ship would suddenly accelerate, as they'd just done, and it juiced everyone. All they knew was something was going on, and they wondered if the GQ gong would sound next.

"Captain is on the bridge," the Boatswain announced.

"What are you doing, Mr. Dunston?" the Captain said.

"XO is on the bridge," the Boatswain called.

"Captain, *Carmody*..." Lieutenant (jg) Dunston looked at the radar repeater, adjusted the range bug, and read the range. "She is 5.5 miles ahead. We are coming up to twenty-five knots. She is doing twenty-two. We are assigned a station 1500 yards astern."

"Go to twenty-eight knots, Mr. Dunston," the Captain said.

"Captain," Dunston said, "we don't have the superheaters lit off. We can only do twenty-five."

"Well, light off the superheaters. I want to go twenty-eight knots," the Captain said.

"Sir, it will take an hour, and the Cheng will probably want to slow down to do that."

"Mr. Dunston, I do not want any discussion here." The Captain's voice had gotten shrill. "Pass the order to engineering. Light off superheaters." The Captain climbed up on his chair and added, "And, go to General Quarters."

"Wait a minute, Boats," the XO said. "Captain, we are an hour-and-a-half from being on station. We don't need to go to GQ for at least forty-five minutes yet."

"The next person who argues with me, or wants to have a discussion, is going to be court-martialed! That includes you, XO." The Captain turned in his chair and looked at the Boatswain Mate of the Watch, who was standing in the center of the pilothouse near the aft bulkhead. He shouted, "Now, Boatswain Mate, sound General Quarters. XO, go to your station in Combat."

The Captain's face looked okay until you saw his eyes. There was something strange about them. Those eyes reminded Jon of how he looked in the mirror when he was seasick.

Immediately after the General Quarters alarm had ceased bonging, the phone in front of the Captain's chair buzzed. It was soon evident that it was the Chief Engineer on the other end of the phone. While the Captain was shouting into the phone, then listening with an angry frown, then shouting again, DD relieved Andrew Dunston of the deck, and Andrew assumed the conn from Jon.

"Cheng," the Captain shouted into the phone. "I want superheaters lit off, and I do not want to slow down."

On more modern destroyers, superheaters were an integral part of the engineering plant design. In the World War II design, they were an adjunct feature tacked on and requiring an extra step to activate. Lighting off the superheaters was a delicate operation, as was starting up the engineering plant from a "cold iron" starting point. To light off the superheaters, steam from the boiler had to be cut into the superheater tubes at the right time and the right flow rate. It was crucial that the heat from the burners under the superheater tubes be absorbed by the steam in the tubes and not by the tubes themselves. If it was done wrong, the tubes could melt or explode. A safelight off was easier to accomplish if the ship's speed was below twenty knots, where the proper flow balances were not near the maximums. If the superheater light off was fouled up, a catastrophic failure could result, and there would be a significant danger to all the personnel in the boiler room.

Just before Jon left the bridge, he heard the CO say into the phone, "All right, Cheng. We will slow to twenty knots. But then you get those damned superheaters lit off and be damned quick about it." The Captain jammed the phone back into its holder. "Mr. Davison, slow to twenty knots, and tell Combat to tell *Carmody* we are slowing to twenty knots to light off superheaters."

As the ship slowed to twenty knots, the vibration energy in the hull diminished. That had happened a couple of times when Jon had been enlisted. The ship would suddenly speed up, and everyone would get excited. Then, the ship would slow down, and Jon always wondered what in blazes was going on. Did the officers know what in Sam Hill they were doing?

In Combat, Jon stopped behind the XO, manning the Evaluator position before going into the electronic warning cubicle. From a speaker in the overhead above the XO, I heard, "*Manfred,* this IS *Carmody.*" Even over the speaker, you could tell it was the Commanding Officer of *Carmody* speaking by the emphasis on the *is.*

"*Manfred,* this IS *Carmody,*" was repeated. "Do not light off superheaters. Repeat, do not light off superheaters. I need you to resume twenty-five knots immediately. Acknowledge, over."

The phone from the bridge on the Evaluator desk buzzed, and the XO ripped it out of its holder. He listened a moment.

"No. The Captain is not in here. Didn't he tell you where he was going?" the XO said.

The XO listened for a moment

"Okay, I'm calling Cheng to stop the light off," the XO said. "He'll call you when it's okay to go back to twenty-five knots. Call *Carmody* and acknowledge their message and say we'll go back to speed ASAP."

Jon was about to head into the electronic warning receiver cubicle when the XO called him back.

"Jon, something is going on with the Captain," the XO said. "I'm sending Don Minton to check his cabin, to see if he's there. I need you to fill in as the CIC officer until we get this sorted."

"XO, I'm really not qualified to stand the CIC Watch Officer position at GQ."

"Necessity, and I, say you are. Get yourself up to speed. I may have to leave you with the Evaluator position, too. Hop to it."

"Sir," the phone talker said, "the bridge says we are coming back up to twenty-five knots. They want us to tell *Carmody.*"

The XO handed Jon the radio handset and told him to make the call to *Carmody;* then, he grabbed Don Minton by the arm and walked him to the door, talking to him as they walked. After Don left, the XO came back and sat at the Evaluator position. For a long moment, he just stared at one of the grease boards in front of him.

"You okay, XO?" Jon said as he put the radio handset back in its holder.

"Ask me another question, Jon." He shook his head. "I don't know how this is going to turn out, but we are not getting off to a good start. So, just standby to help."

Don Minton came back and rushed to the XO.

"The Captain is in his cabin, XO," Don Minton said. "He is sitting at his desk reading. He asked me what I was doing there. I said we were worried about him and wanted to make sure he was okay. He said he was and that I should get back to my GQ station."

The XO turned to Chief Radar-man Wicker. "Give Ensign Zachery a run-down on the tactical situation. Mr. Minton and I need to go down to the Captain's cabin. I won't be gone for more than three minutes."

The XO rushed out, with Don Minton following.

Jon was feeling like that morning when Teresa had had the C-section. The world was moving faster, a lot faster, than he was.

34

Chief Radarman Wicker said, "Okay, sir, pretty simple picture, actually. This contact here is the Task Force flagship, a cruiser. They are doing gunfire support for the marines. That's why we never got a call today, I guess. The marines apparently like the bigger guns on the cruiser. And here is *Carmody*. And over here on the chart," the chief led Jon to the chart table, "about fifteen miles above the DMZ, this is where we are anticipating the boat targets. As far as threat is concerned, we are not expecting anything at all, except possibly shore-battery opposition when we start shooting at the boats. That speaker up there has the bridge-to-bridge circuit on it. So that's it, sir. Any questions?"

"*Carmody* is in tactical control, right?" Jon asked.

"Yes, sir," Chief Wicker said, and then he added in a mumble, "Thank God for that."

The XO entered Combat and sat in the Evaluator seat. "Okay,

Jon, I left Don Minton with the Captain for the moment. I need you to stay out here and fill the CIC Officer job."

"*Manfred,* this is *Carmody,* over," came over the CIC radio circuit.

The XO picked up a handset and rogered.

"*Manfred,* this is *Carmody,* we will go to General Quarters at 1445. We expect to commence firing at 1500. Our intention is that once we are in the target area, we will parallel the coast at a mile. We will use a speed of fifteen knots during the firing runs. The FAC says there are about thirty boats, barges, and junks right up on the beach. We will take the boats under fire from the north end. You target the ships at the south end of the group and start working north with your fire. Be prepared to shift from boats to counter-battery fire if either of us starts taking rounds from the shore. We expect your distance from us to still be more than two miles when we get to the target area. We don't intend to wait for you to close up to start engaging the boats. The CO will give you weapons free over the bridge-to-bridge when we are ready to commence firing. Acknowledge, over."

"*Manfred,* roger, out," the XO said.

"Jon, check the water depth on the chart a mile off the coast in the target area. Compare notes with the Gator, and make sure there are no navigation obstacles there. I'm going to brief DD on the bridge." The XO's voice reminded me of Commander Carsten's: calm but laced with an unmistakable undercurrent of energy.

A bit later, the XO left to check on the captain. He was gone for three minutes. When he got back to CIC, he sat at the Evaluator's chair and rubbed his hands over his face. The situation was obviously weighing on him, but it was nothing compared to how it weighed on Jon when the XO was gone.

"Jon," the XO said, "get with Chief Wicker and take a long-range surface look. Also, look at the air search radar and make sure we have nothing there. Just trying to check all bases before we get into blowing up the boats. Oh, and check with the electronic warning module. Make sure they are doing a thorough search for PT Boats and MiGs."

At 1458, the speaker in Combat set to the bridge-to-bridge radio came to life. "*Manfred*, this is *Carmody*, weapons free. Engage logistic boat targets arrayed along the beach. Acknowledge, over."

In Combat, they heard DD roger the message from the bridge.

"Sir," the phone talker in CIC said, "the bridge says they are coming right to parallel the coast and slowing to fifteen knots. Bridge recommends opening fire as soon as the director has a solution."

The XO passed a commence firing order to the gun director. The forward mount commenced firing ten seconds later. Jon imagined the light, ocher-colored smoke from the guns wash over the bridge windows and the powder canisters eject out onto the deck with a clatter.

Wham. The forward guns fired again, followed by the more muted refrain of the after mount.

Don Minton burst into Combat. "Captain is on the bridge, XO," he shouted from the doorway.

Later, Jon found out from Andrew what happened on the bridge.

Andrew turned and saw the CO standing behind the helmsman just after the Boatswain called, "Captain's on the bridge."

Andrew saw the Captain look out the bridge windows to port, and he saw what he described as a shocked look on the Captain's face. Andrew turned to see what the Captain was looking at. All that was there was the coast of North Vietnam, but it was fairly close.

"XO is on the bridge," the Boatswain called.

"This is the Captain. I have the conn. Right full rudder."

"Right full rudder, aye, sir," the helmsman said as he got ready to spin the wheel to comply with the order. But, Andrew said, the XO stepped forward and grabbed the helm.

"Belay that order," the XO said. "Steady as she goes. The Operations Officer has the conn."

The XO turned and grabbed the Captain by the arm. "Captain, you are coming with me."

"I saw shore battery fire," the Captain said, just before he and the XO walked out of the pilothouse door.

"It's okay, Captain," the XO said. "We're going back down to your room."

"Hey, good shooting, *Manfred*," came over the FAC frequency. "Your first salvo was right on. Fire for effect. Move each succeeding salvo fifty yards right to walk up the beach to the north."

"Officer of the Deck," the port bridge wing lookout called, "*Carmody* is taking fire from the beach. Shore battery is three-zero-zero relative."

"Phone talker," DD said. "Tell Combat that *Carmody* is taking fire from three-zero-zero relative. Tell them to switch to counter-battery and support *Carmody*."

"Officer of the Deck," the bridge phone talker said, "Combat says they are on it. They got coordinates from the FAC."

Andrew said that the guns had been firing steadily. Powder shell casings fairly covered the deck around the forward gun mount. The firing stopped for a few moments while targeting the battery firing at *Carmody*. In the lull, there was a sudden sound, like *zzzzswhoosh*, and a geyser of water erupted about 100 yards in front of *Manfred*.

"Sir," the bridge phone talker said, "after lookout reports a shore gun firing at us from relative bearing two-six-zero degrees."

"Phone talker," DD said. "Pass to combat. New counter-battery target bearing two-six-zero degrees relative."

"Mr. Dunston," DD said. "Flank speed, full rudder turn to northeast."

Andrew said that a second geyser shot up about seventy-five yards short of the bow.

"Great shooting, *Manfred*," came over the FAC radio circuit. "You got massive secondaries. That gun won't bother you again. Great shooting."

Andrew said that *Carmody* silenced the gun that had fired at her. DD then ordered *Manfred* back into a mile off the beach, and the ship resumed firing at the beached boats. After making one run on a northwesterly heading, both destroyers reversed course and completed another firing run heading southeast. The FAC declared the targets one hundred percent destroyed, and *Carmody* led the two ships back to the waiting station just south of the DMZ.

GQ secured at 1615.

After the ship secured from GQ, the XO made a watch bill of LT(jg)s. One of them would be with the CO until relieved by the next guy on the list.

Andrew Dunston and Jon assumed the bridge watch. The XO called the three lieutenant department heads to a meeting in his cabin.

As soon as Jon was relieved of the bridge watch, DD called him to his room. DD had roughed up a summary of the incident.

"Check what I've drafted against what you saw from CIC. Make sure I have the facts and the timeline right. Add things as you see fit. Then I want you to smooth up what I've written into a formal statement of what happened." A smirky little grin crinkled DD's face. "The XO said you helped my predecessor with some after-action reports. He said you write navy reports almost as well as you write letters to your wife."

Jon flushed. With embarrassment, and then flushed again with anger. The CO, the new CO, had come off the rails during an encounter with the enemy, and DD was cracking jokes?

"Anybody ever tell you, you wouldn't do well playing poker?" DD said.

Jon sat back.

"Look, Jon. This is as serious as a heart attack. I get that. It's just my way, though. In the middle of something like this, I want us both to back away from the heavy emotion of the thing and be as objective as we can be. Okay?"

Jon thought about it. His anger fizzled away. "Sure, DD. Our new CO runs amok, and our new Ops O does an Alfred E. Newman 'What, me worry!' What could be more okay-er than that?"

"Huh. More okay-er. So, Ensign Two Buckets, make my rough draft more okay-er. Hop to it." DD's smirky grin appeared again. "XO says your former CO used to say that all the time."

There was a lot in DD's draft that Jon hadn't known, hadn't seen. It was there with eyewitness statements from all the lieutenants, all the lieutenants (junior grade), and one ensign. It was a thoroughly believable story. The new CO had gone off the rails for sure.

Then DD's notes included what the XO had called: On the other hand, there were a number of circumstances that muddied the waters.

Jon's letters, Admiral Ensign's call to his father, the disagreements between Commander Carstens and Captain Brass, plus everyone on *Manfred* had thought highly of Commander Carstens. The crew's opinion of Commander Peacock, however, would be on the other side of the ledger. Especially after today. And one other thing, the captain claimed he saw fire coming from the shore just moments before the lookout reported it. Did he really see fire coming from the shore? If he did, why did he allow the XO to just lead him off the bridge?

Any formal complaint or request for a fitness for duty eval would go through Captain Brass. Snowball's chance in hell of that resulting in a favorable outcome. That's how the XO summarized things.

The XO concluded the meeting with instructions to write up two formal reports. One would be the after-action report and deal with *Manfred's* actions. This report would be forwarded as a navy message. The other report would deal with the captain's behavior. Three copies would be made of this document. The XO would keep one. The Ops O would keep one, and the third would be locked in the top-secret safe inside Radio Central, where the crypto materials were stored.

The XO had concluded the meeting with: "For the time being, we go on about our business. See what happened with the CO this evening and through the night. We reconvene in the morning and take stock of things in the light of the new day."

Jon finished typing the report on the captain's behavior twenty minutes before dinner. DD locked his copy in his safe and carried the XO's copy to him. Jon took the third copy, along with the carbon paper he'd used, to Radio Central and locked them in the crypto safe. Jon was the assistant crypto custodian. He'd gotten a top-secret clearance as an enlisted man because of some of the equipment he'd worked on, so, when he'd checked aboard with a TS (Top Secret) clearance, he was assigned the assistant custodian job.

After locking up the third report, Jon hustled down to the wardroom. Still, he'd be three minutes late. When he got there, all the officers, except for watchstanders, were seated.

And the new CO was at his place. Looking for all the world like he belonged there. Looking for all the world like not a single, even minor, thing was not as it should be.

There was no conversation, so Jon didn't have to wait for a lull. "Permission to join the mess, Captain?"

"Where were you, Mr. Zachery?"

"Sir," DD butt in, "He was with me writing up the after-action—"

The CO swung his gaze to his new Ops O. "The after-action message went out fifteen minutes ago." The new CO swung his accusing eyes back to Jon. "Where were you?"

"Sir. After I finished helping with that message, I went to check on the IFF equipment. I wanted to make sure it hadn't crapped out again. And it hasn't. Crapped out, I mean. Once we got the right part installed, it's worked like a champ."

"Yes. Well—"

Jon was sure the new CO was about to remind everyone that it was he who had identified the proper part to fix that equipment but then realized that Ensign Zachery had done that already for him.

"There is one other thing," the new CO said. "On *Manfred,* when I ask a junior officer a question, there is a tendency among you more senior officers to jump in and answer for the JO. I want this *tendency* to cease as of this moment. If the JO talks himself into trouble, well, he will benefit from the character-building experience, which is sure to follow.

"You may serve the salad, steward.

"Zachery, sit down."

35

Jon wasn't sure how the XO convinced the CO to helo over to the cruiser for the flagship's doctor to evaluate him, but the CO went. Maybe the threat of that document in the crypto safe?

After an evaluation by the doctor on the admiral's staff, CDR Carstens sent a message to the XO: The commander said that CDR Peacock told the doc that he had been concerned, very concerned with his officers, with their loyalty, and that he hadn't been sleeping. The cruiser doc hadn't found anything wrong other than signs of fatigue and stress. The admiral had queried Captain Brass, and the commodore replied that Peacock was right to be concerned with his officers. The admiral had also queried *Carmody* about *Manfred's* performance on the mission north of the DMZ. *Carmody* praised *Manfred* for their excellent response to fire from the North Vietnamese coast and excellent shooting at their target. The FAC had credited them with 100% target destruction. The doc on the cruiser wanted CDR Peacock to be evaluated by medical people ashore in Da

Nang. So the cruiser sent Peacock ashore. The medical people in Da Nang would issue their report on Commander Peacock's condition in the morning. In the meantime, *Manfred* was to remain where she was, steaming in a ten-mile box ten miles off-shore.

That night at dinner, the XO sat in his normal seat.

"XO, aren't you acting CO? Shouldn't you be sitting in the captain's chair?" Charles Hanson asked.

"No, I am the XO. The CO is the CO. He has a medical condition that has to be checked out. It should be sorted by mid-morning tomorrow. We will have dinner now."

At the other end of the table, Carl Lehr said, "Exciting first day aboard, eh, Newbie."

"Well, yeah, I guess," the hulking newbie replied. "I was supposed to be going to *Carmody,* but since she is going back home shortly, they thought you guys needed my extraordinary skills more."

"Well, it is nice to have a super-hero among the rest of us almost-normal guys in the Locker," Jon said.

Jon saw Admiral Ensign roll his eyes.

"I don't know, Two Buckets." Almost had a concerned look. "I think we should require Newbie to get a military hair cut on his arms, even if he is a super-hero. What do you think?"

"Not just his arms," Jon said. "I saw him in the head this morning. I think he needs to be sheared. We'd get enough wool to weave a nice rug for the Locker."

Newbie said, "Real funny. How about we go up on the 01 level, and each of us has a set of sheep shears. Let's see who winds up with a haircut."

Jon saw the XO look across the table at the Gun Boss and nod his head toward the ensign end of the table. DD was sitting next to him, and he followed the XO's and the Gun Boss's eyes.

"Ensigns." The XO shook his head and smiled. "God bless them all, each and every one."

At 0700 the next morning, *Manfred* steamed around her box five miles from the cruiser when the flagship vectored its helo toward the northwest. A US Marine A-4 had been shot down, and the helo was sent to rescue the pilot. A half-hour later, *Manfred* was ordered to refuel the rescue helo with an injured pilot aboard.

Andrew Dunston and Jon had the bridge watch. The XO occupied the chair on the port side of the pilothouse, not the CO's chair.

Jon turned the ship to put the wind twenty degrees off the bow. The helo approached and hovered off the port side of the fantail. Andrew Dunston, the XO, and Jon were all on the port wing and looking aft into the cockpit of the helo. Standing between the helo pilot and co-pilot was a lanky, light-haired young man with a grin that seemed to completely fill the space between the two pilots. There was no flight suit sleeve on his left arm, just a white bandage around the biceps with his arm in a makeshift sling. He gave a thumbs-up with his right.

"That," Andrew said, "is one guy who is happy to be alive. Just like the guy up on North SAR."

"Boatswain Mate," the XO said, "have the mess decks make up five dinners for the guys in the helo. They had steak today, right?"

While the XO was speaking with the Bosun, Jon said to Andrew, "I was wondering if it was going to be Duke Savage, but it's someone else."

"Okay, guys," the XO said. "Let's pay attention to the business at hand here and try not to run over anybody."

Jon left Andrew and the XO on the bridge wing, walked through the pilothouse, and visually checked to starboard; then, he stood in front of the helmsman and looked out the bridge windows straight ahead.

Being in the combat zone wasn't much different than being back home. At least it felt like it that morning. Vietnam was over there, to port. You could see it, but as far as their involvement, it felt far away, like it didn't involve them at all. It felt like it was someone else's war. And, it didn't feel right that things were going on and that *Manfred* could not be part of them. Because the Captain needed to be evaluated.

Manfred had been on deployment for over 100 days, but the days during which there had been real combat-related operations were just a handful. At best, Jon figured, there had been ten days of what he considered to be real contributions out of all the time deployed. Hank Allman had said once that their job was to own the oceans, and by his reckoning, probably every day contributed to that mission. Still, to Jon, the combat missions seemed much more important.

After topping off with fuel, the H-2 departed for Da Nang to return the A-4 pilot to the marines. At 1345, the XO received a message from Commander Carstens. Commander Peacock would remain ashore the rest of the day, and the doctors in Da Nang would issue their report the next morning. *Manfred* was to steam into and anchor in Da Nang harbor to await the medical findings.

At 0655 on Sunday morning, the XO let Jon conn *Manfred* to their anchorage in the bay north of Da Nang. Newbie manned the special sea detail safety observer position.

With the port anchor chain still rattling out the hawse pipe, the XO climbed down from his chair, walked to the other side of the pilothouse, and checked the navigation chart. Jon stood in front of the helm and used the centerline alidade, a telescope fixed with sights like on a rifle, to check the bearing to the navigation feature they used for the anchor bearing.

"Well, Jon," the XO said. "I think Hank Allman would have said that you might get the hang of this anchoring business with another thousand practices or so."

A wiseacre retort bubbled up from Jon's belly and sat on his tongue, ready to bounce off, but then, a smart-aleck comment just didn't seem … appropriate. He was right on the anchor bearing. Of course, there had been no wind and no current to contend with, so it should have turned out well.

Still, he pleased the XO, and he had allowed him to conn the ship. It would never have happened with the new CO aboard. Jon listened to the buzz of voices on the bridge. The voices were easy, relaxed. The sailors went about their business professionally, but occasionally someone would mention Subic Bay or a bar in Zamboanga. It felt … almost normal there on the bridge that Sunday morning.

The ship received a message from Don Minton, who had accompanied the CO to the cruiser and then to Da Nang. They should expect the medical report no later than 1400.

At 0930, a boat from the Da Nang base brought a Catholic chaplain to the ship, Lieutenant Masters, the Catholic chaplain assigned to Captain Brass's staff. He would ride with them for the next two days when they were scheduled to rendezvous with *Reilly*. Then, after the chaplain transferred to Captain Brass's flagship, the two ships would move north and do a second tour of duty on North SAR station. That was the current plan, but everyone knew that the medical situation with the Captain could alter things.

At 1030, the chaplain began Catholic mass on the helo deck. A folding table altar was set up in front of the hangar doors, and folding chairs were arranged in rows across the deck. At 1045, the priest had just completed the consecration, where, according to Catholic belief, bread and wine were changed into the body and blood of Christ, when a loud boom shattered the Sunday morning stillness, echoed off the hills to the north and west, and rolled across the water like a line of thunderstorms that couldn't stop grumbling.

"Jesus Christ!" A sailor in the back row of chairs was pointing to the north. "That LST is in a gunfight with a—" Then he stopped and said, "Sorry, Father."

Father Masters smiled at the sailor. "That's quite all—" Another loud boom stepped on Father Masters' sentence.

"I will end the mass here," Father Mathews said. "I bless you all in the name of the Father, the Son, and the Holy Spirit. Go in peace to love—"

This time it was the GQ alarm interrupting the chaplain.

"Go in peace to your General Quarters Stations," Father Masters finished when the gonging finished and just before the Bosun called away GQ.

Of the twenty-two who were at the service, seventeen disappeared in a moment through the helo hangar. Four lined up and filed down the ladder on the rear of the superstructure just forward of the after gun mount. Jon walked up to the chaplain.

"Padre," he said. "Can I help you wrap up shop?"

The priest drank off the mass wine, wiped out the chalice, looked at Jon, and said, "I don't want to keep you from your station."

"I've got ninety seconds to spare, Padre."

"All right. Then, would you get my mass case from inside the helo hangar, please?"

Jon returned with the black bag that looked somewhat like the boxy case airline pilots carted into the cockpit with them. The priest stowed the book, the chalice for wine, his stole, and the chalice with the consecrated hosts in the bag along with the altar cloths.

"There," the priest said, "five seconds to spare. I will just go down to the wardroom for GQ. That is a triage station on most destroyers, so I presume that is the case here?"

"Yes, it is, Padre. Good to see you again. I don't know if you remember—"

"Of course I remember, Jon Zachery."

Then Jon ran forward through the helo hangar and up the ladder to the port bridge wing.

The XO and DD were both on the wing, looking to the north through binoculars.

"Looks like that LST is getting underway, XO," DD said. "And I still have not seen anything that looks like fire coming from the shore."

"Bosun," the XO said. "Get in touch with the Gun Boss. Tell him to get a crew on the forecastle and prepare to haul in the anchor if we need to. DD, call the Cheng, tell them to let me know how long before we can get underway. Mr. Dunston, run down to the 01 level and make sure the guys manning the machine guns don't get itchy trigger fingers on us. Weapons are tight, and they are not to fire unless directed to do so by the bridge." The XO looked at Jon. "Mr.

Zachery, you're going to have to hold down Combat for the moment. Hop to it."

In Combat, Chief Radar-man Wicker said, "Mr. Zachery, just talked to the Combat Information Center on that LST that took fire. They said the gomers just fired two rounds and then boogied, apparently. The LST thought they saw where the rounds came from and fired a couple of three-inch shells into the jungle. They also said they were getting underway this afternoon anyway, but they'll just leave now. They never saw anything after the first two rounds landed about two hundred yards from them."

"Thanks, chief," Jon said.

There was no more excitement, and at 1115, with the day beginning to behave like a sleepy Sunday again, the XO secured the ship from General Quarters. At lunch, Jon made an appointment to speak with Father Masters that afternoon. Then, he and Andrew took the noon to 1600 bridge watch.

The bridge wing lookouts spent a considerable amount of time scanning the jungle on the hillside north of where they were anchored, but they found nothing to report. It was a sleepy Sunday with the bay mirror smooth and the tropical sun massive and yolk yellow in the blue sky. Four grey US Navy and a half dozen merchant ships were anchored in widely spaced spots around the bay. There had been jets and helicopters flying from and around the Da Nang airfield all morning, but, now, in the sun-baked afternoon, nothing was moving in the air except for one seagull.

As the watch progressed, Jon periodically rested binoculars on the wood rail atop the bulwark of the bridge wing, and he peered so intently at the dense jungle that he felt as if the binoculars were trying to suck the eyeballs out of his face. Imagined hordes of short, skinny, black-pajama-clad, evil-intentioned men, and perhaps women, were there with hatred smeared all over their faces as they scurried about, invisible, under the jungle canopy, just waiting for another opportunity to shoot at someone from ambush. Then, they would run away again. Jon hoped for some hint of movement. If there was something, they could bring the ship's guns to bear on those…those… gomers had been on the tip of his mental tongue.

He recalled the letter he'd had gotten from his pop. He'd written he couldn't, "— tell who was winning my war." *Was it my war?*

Nobody else seemed to want it.

In the jungle, nothing moved. Neither was anything moving on the water nor in the air, except for the lone seagull. And there was no sound, apart from the machinery hum of the ship and the periodic, grating squawk of the seagull.

At 1330, a phone buzzed, a jarring sound in the Sunday stillness on the bridge. It was the XO, and he told Andrew Dunston that the captain would be coming back to the ship via boat from Da Nang and would probably be there about 1400. The XO told Andrew to announce that the ship anticipated setting the sea and anchor detail at 1500 and getting underway at 1530.

Twenty-five minutes later, from the starboard bridge wing, Jon watched a launch with an enclosed cabin pull up to the accommodation ladder on the fantail. The captain climbed the ladder, saluted the ensign aft, and returned the XO's salute. Don Minton climbed halfway up the ladder; then he stopped as the Captain remained standing just at the top of the ladder.

The Captain and the XO talked for several moments. Jon saw the XO point to the north, toward where the LST had taken fire in the morning; then, the CO walked around the after gun mount, and the XO started forward on the starboard side of the main deck.

When the XO got to the bridge, he told Andrew, "Have the quartermaster put in the log that the CO returned to the ship with a clean bill of health from medical authorities in Da Nang. And, call away sea and anchor detail. The captain wants to get underway right away. He wants engineering to use emergency procedures to warm up the plant. That's for training."

At 1420, *Manfred* was moving toward the South China Sea. The bay, with its rim of rising hills to the west and north, dropped away behind. The anchor was clear of the water, and sailors used a fire hose to wash the mud from it before snugging it in the hawse pipe.

After being relieved on the bridge, Jon followed Ralph Timmons, the Gun Boss, down to his cabin. The Gun Boss got a copy of a classified operation order from his safe, and then he left the room to the chaplain and Jon.

"You can take that chair. Now, then, how may I be of service, Mr. Zachery?" Father Masters said.

Father Masters was probably in his late thirties, maybe forty. He was about 5 feet, ten inches with a slender build, sort of like the captain's.

"First of all, Father, I mean, I'm just an ensign, but I thought you were really cool back on the helo deck this morning."

"Oh, Mr. Zachery. Get thee behind me! You are an occasion of sin to me."

Father Masters was smiling, but then his smile blinked off.

"I'm just kidding. Just kidding. Have you heard the expression *praise God and pass the ammunition?* And do you know where it comes from?"

"I have heard it, but, no, I don't know where it comes from."

"Cruiser USS *New Orleans.* During the attack on Pearl Harbor. The chaplain was in a line of sailors passing ammo to the guns, and a sailor chastised the chaplain, a man of God, for being in the line. The chaplain responded with the line. I have always wanted to be able to respond with such grace to such a situation. This morning was well short of Pearl Harbor, but it did serve as a more than adequate temptation to pride." The chaplain shook his head. "So I had already wallowed in the deadly sin of pride. It really wasn't you, Mr. Zachery, who pushed me to sin."

His smile was back. "Now, then, Mr. Zachery, Jon, you didn't come here to hear about my sins, did you?"

Jon told him that he had come about forgiveness. In the PI, when Jon had confessed the third shot he had fired at Nguyen, the rounds he had fired into the six VC that morning with the marines, Father had given him absolution. The absolution of those sins had bothered him ever since.

"I don't want to be absolved. I'm afraid of what will happen to me, of what I will become if I just accept forgiveness. I mean, I may have to do something like that again."

Father Masters had been leaning forward a bit, with his hands on his knees. He sat back; then they spoke. They spoke about forgiveness, faith, and reason, about absolution, and retention of some elements of sins to change those things that lead to habitual repetition of particular sins.

After they had talked for almost an hour, he went back to his sin of pride, and he asked Jon to forgive him. At first, Jon wanted no part of forgiving a priest, but he insisted. He could be just as stubborn as Jon could, he said. So Jon did. He forgave him; then they went to dinner.

At dinner, the Captain sat erect and statue-still at his place at the head of the table. There was no wrinkle visible in his starched, short-sleeved khaki shirt. He looked healthy. His wavy, light-brown hair, not a strand awry, was combed back from a high forehead and the beginnings of a widow's peak. It looked like he had just shaved as his tanned cheeks sported a pinkish tinge. Dark brown eyes peered intently, never seeming to blink, and constantly flitted around the table. Jon thought of a hungry hawk gliding above a field, and he wouldn't have been surprised to hear the Captain make a *scree* call.

The chaplain, who was sitting across from the XO, had said grace. Then, with conversational silence reigning over the wardroom table, two stewards began to set salad plates in front of them, beginning with Newbie.

Bzzt, bzzt sounded, and the captain pulled the phone from its holder on the table leg to his left. He listened for a moment, said, "Very well," and then he hung up.

The previous Skipper would usually share with the table what the message had been: the OOD reporting a contact with a closest point of approach of 1.5 miles, or direction from the formation commander to alter course. All eyes at the table turned toward the captain. A little smirk curled up just the left corner of his lips, almost like the Cheng's half-lip smiles. As the captain, his salad was served last. When his plate was put before him, the chaplain passed him the bowl of salad dressing. Slowly, deliberately, he drizzled dressing from the spoon over his salad; then, he passed the dressing back to the chaplain.

Ensign Haywood, Newbie, was sitting next to Jon on the aft side of the table. He hunkered his mass over and whispered, "I know something you don't know," in a whispered falsetto playground voice.

"Mr. Haywood." The captain's hawk eyes were locked onto Greg, but his voice was controlled. "Do you have something to share with the rest of the wardroom?"

"No, sir," Greg Haywood said. "I, uh, I was just telling Ensign Zachery that his fly isn't zipped."

Jon reached down. His fly was zipped.

"XO," the captain said. "Have the bull ensign inspect the uniforms of the members of the Ensign Locker before every meal."

Everyone looked at the Captain. *Was he serious?* Jon was sure that's what everyone at the table was thinking.

"Uh, aye, Captain, I'll take care of that."

"And Mr. Haywood, I haven't had a chance to talk to you yet. XO, set that up for tomorrow morning. And, do we have a movie tonight?"

"Yes, sir, and we do have a movie, and it will be the premiere performance of Newbie as the projectionist."

36

The Captain didn't seem to be too interested in eating. When the steward picked up his salad plate, it had barely been touched. His eyes never rested, though, roving continuously and touching on each diner briefly. It would have seemed like a hummingbird flitting from flower to flower, except there was the hawk image. The eyes rested for periods of time only on the ensign end of the table. The captain's eyes seemed to be hungrier than he was. Of the main course, the Captain ate even less. Twice during dinner, Greg Haywood sat forward in his chair, and Jon could tell he was getting ready to say something. Both times he sat forward, Jon elbowed him, and he kept quiet.

The dinner meandered through dessert and coffee to a conclusion of sorts. With an unappetizing mood hovering over the table, ordinarily, most of the officers would have left the wardroom about three and a half minutes after dessert was served. On this night, however, every officer not on watch stayed for the movie. On *Manfred*, the junior ensign was responsible for running the movie projector.

Most ensigns came to the navy without ever having run a projector before, and Greg Haywood, Newbie, was true to this navy norm.

With Newbie hovering and hulking, Jon gave him instruction with the first reel. He demonstrated how to mount the projector firmly to the fold-out table in the passageway just aft of the door to the XO's cabin, pop the fold-down reel arms into position, fix the take-up reel on the after arm and to secure it with the little fold-down latch, fix the film reel on the front arm and secure it with the little fold-down latch, thread the film past the projection lamp; and incorporate just a finger-width of slack in the film before the toothed sprocket wheels that pulled the film past the projection lamp and fed the take-up reel.

After the first reel started flap, flap, flapping, Andrew Dunston stood up and turned on the lights in the wardroom. Newbie, as he had been instructed, unlatched the full take-up reel from the aft projector arm and placed it in the square film container on the deck. Then, he took the empty film reel from the forward projector arm, moved it to the after arm, and latched it in place. Taking the second reel from the film container on the deck, Newbie loaded it onto the forward arm, threaded the film past the projection lamp, and ensured he had just the right amount of slack in front of the toothed sprocket drives. His finger was thicker than Jon's, but he got the amount of slack just right, and then he got the film leader threaded into a slot in the take-up reel.

"Andrew," Newbie said, "would you get the lights again, please?"

The lights blinked off, and Newbie clicked the projector switch through the "drive motor on" to the "lamp on" position. Newbie, at this point, was the only one breathing in the wardroom. Since the lights had gone out, everyone else was holding his breath. The movie storyline picked up with a new scene to start the second reel. The actors, in black and white on the screen, spoke their lines, oblivious to imminent disaster. And just when some of the officers were about to give in and take a breath, it happened. The film reel fell off the forward projector arm. The film broke, and only white light showed on the screen. A community guffaw, propelled by eleven breaths held to the point of human endurance, filled the wardroom, then settled into a sustained belly laugh that had some of them gasping for breath. Newbie had done what almost all new projectionists did: forget to latch the film reel in place.

Jon looked at the captain. Even he had a smile on his face, but there was something else there, as well, something that seemed to take pleasure in the humiliation itself. It was not the way everyone else was laughing, half remembering the time when each of them had been the newbie running the projector. They had all had the same experience. Jon's had been in January, but he had made it to his second movie before he broke the film.

The Captain stopped smiling, but he did not stop staring at Newbie. Newbie and the Captain locked eyes, and Jon stepped between them, but Newbie easily saw over his head.

Jon grabbed Greg by the arm and turned him to the projector. "Okay, Newbie, all of us made this same mistake the first time we ran a movie. On reel two, we all forgot to flip down the little lock tab on the film reel. So, it's a little humiliating, but it's a mistake I don't think any of us ever repeated."

"Captain," the XO said, "do you want to continue with the movie?"

"No thanks, XO," the Captain said. "That was enough entertainment for me."

The new CO got up and walked out of the wardroom, and everyone else left except the XO, Newbie, and Jon.

When the wardroom door closed, the XO said, "Greg, I don't need you trying to take on the captain here. He thinks you came aboard with an attitude problem, and you need to understand that this is not just about you. It affects the whole wardroom. So, when you see him tomorrow, you eat whatever crap he dishes out. Got it?"

Greg Haywood stood still, his fists clenching and unclenching.

"Greg. This is not open for discussion, and there is no other way through our current situation. You cannot fight with the CO. Now, I want to hear you say it. Say aye, aye, XO. Say it."

Big Greg said it small. The XO looked at Newbie for a long moment, and then he went into his room.

"So, Two Buckets," Newbie said, "do I have it right? Nobody

really wanted to see this dumb movie? They just wanted to see me dork it up?"

"With all due respect to the actors, the director, the screenwriter, the musicians, the costume designers, etcetera, yes, that is exactly right. Everybody was here to see you roll the film across the deck. All of us did it when we were newbies ourselves."

"Seems awfully juvenile to me," Newbie said.

"Well, Newbie, coming from a voice of maturity such as yourself, I am hurt."

"Wiseass," Newbie said as he stashed the projector under the built-in seats on the port side of the wardroom.

"Newbie, I think I should warn you a bit about how the new CO looks at the Ensign Locker. A couple of us have done things to call unfavorable attention to the whole Locker, and I think he pretty much has it in for all of us. Just as a way of heads up for tomorrow, my advice is to just do what the XO said. Take whatever crap he dishes out, say the least you can get away with, and get out of there as soon as you can. Okay? On the brighter side, though, you may have given us the only thing we'll have to laugh about the rest of the cruise."

At 2345, Andrew Dunston and Jon started the turnover to assume the mid-watch. The ship was steaming back and forth in a ten-mile box, twenty miles off the coast of South Vietnam, some seventeen miles south of the DMZ. Part of the turnover briefing concerned orders for the ship. At first light the next day, they were tasked to begin searching, with their on-board sonar, for a Marine H-46 helicopter, which had been hit by anti-aircraft fire and crashed into the South China Sea. The H-46 was thought to be about a mile offshore. There was cryptographic radio equipment aboard, which navy authorities wanted to recover. One of the crewmen had not gotten out of the helo following the crash landing, and there was possibly a body inside, as well. *Manfred's* task was to precisely locate the sunken helo so that divers could descend and recover the classified equipment and the body. The ship planned to go to GQ when she arrived at a mile from shore.

The other significant item from the turnover was a tropical storm well to the east that was being watched closely to see if it would develop into a typhoon.

Manfred was steaming independently. There was no other ship traffic close enough to worry about, and by 2353, the turnover was complete. By 0012, the mid-watch had settled into one of those feet hurting, brain-numbing, eyelid drooping, head jerking up straddles of a line that separated deep sleep and wakefulness. The time between a tick and tock seemed long enough to get in a decade of the rosary. But it is hard to pray in Purgatory.

Two diversions helped the ticks and tocks march along. The first was when Jon was on the starboard bridge wing, and the lookout pointed out the luminescent glow in the wake under the black overcast. Then, at 0244, Jon was looking at the radar repeater in the pilothouse, and suddenly, a solid radar contact blip appeared on the port quarter aft, about a mile away. *Submarine periscope, PT boat?* But the blip looked too large to be a periscope, and a PT boat should have shown up sooner. It turned out that the radar-men had seen this phenomenon before, and they thought it might be a flock of sea birds skimming the surface. It had caused a spurt of adrenalin, though, and ticks and tocks move faster on that kind of juice.

Strange, though, Jon thought, how you never heard about things like poisonous sea snakes, luminescent wakes, sea birds generating false radar targets until you witnessed them.

Eventually, enough ticks and tocks accumulated, and Andrew and Jon were relieved. When he got to the Locker, it was quiet. Jon shucked off his clothes, and as soon as his head hit the pillow, his mattress started to turn itself into oblivion, when there was a rustling of bed cloths as Newbie rolled from his side to his back, followed shortly by a stertorous and rivet-rattling sound. Jon's eyes popped open. Thoughts of sleep were replaced by a concern for permanent hearing loss.

"Sweet Mother of God," Admiral Ensign said.

Newbie continued to rattle rivets. Admiral Ensign turned on his bunk light, got out of his bunk, took his pillow, and tried to swat Newbie with it, but he caught the corner of Newbie's bunk and ripped the pillow. In the dim light from the bunk light, Jon saw feathers fluttering to the deck. It looked like they were inside a snow globe.

Admiral Ensign grabbed Newbie, shook him awake, spit a feather out of his mouth, and said, "Dammit, Newbie, you were on your back and snoring so loud you blew up my pillow."

There was a mumble, a grunt, a snuffle, and a rustle of bed cloths.

Jon groaned. He was wide-awake, and GQ would probably sound in less than two hours. That, however, was his last conscious thought until the insistent clangor of the GQ alarm ripped him abruptly from a deep, dark, dreamless pit.

The gonging stopped, and the ship's 1MC announced, "General Quarters, General Quarters. All hands man your battle stations. Condition Zebra will be set in three minutes."

As the *gong, gong, gong* started again, Jon rolled out of his bed, grabbed his trousers from the hook on the end of his bunk, and had pulled one leg on when Newbie erupted from his bed and landed on the deck. His shoulder smashed into Jon knocking him to the deck and sliding on the feathers up against the forward bulkhead with one foot tangled in a trouser leg.

"Damn it, Newbie," Admiral Ensign said. "Move forward, so there is room for me to get out of bed."

Like a pet that had gotten the blue ribbon at obedience school, Newbie moved forward. Jon pulled on pants, grabbed a hat, shirt, shoes, and socks, pushed through the jam of bodies, went out into the passageway, and finished dressing there.

With perhaps thirty seconds to spare, Jon walked into Combat, and, as always, he was surprised by the intensity of the assault on his senses. Since 1945, the components of the noxious stew that passed for breathable air had been accumulating. Then, it had been Luckies and Camels. This morning, two minutes after the GQ alarm sounded, the last of the Cools and Marlboros had been stubbed out. His eyes, though smarting, registered that there were a lot of others in the room and that they were alive. So breathing, though not pleasant, was most likely not fatal, immediately.

PO3 Anderson was operating the equipment in the electronic warning cubicle. "Morning, sir," he said.

"Morning, Petty Officer Anderson," Jon said. "Let me know when you have completed a sweep through all the frequency bands. I'm going out to see what's going on."

Jon stood behind the XO at the Evaluator's position and looked up at the grease board where surface contacts were listed. *Carmody* was listed at fifteen miles north of us.

Jon walked over to one of the radarscopes set to the surface search radar, and the radar-man ran the bearing cursor up to the two blips to the northwest. "That's *Carmody*, sir," he said and then ran the range scale out farther. "This is the task force flagship, the cruiser."

The operator then brought the scope back to a fifteen-mile scale. The landmass of Vietnam was painted across almost half the scope. He ran the range bug to the coast. The range readout read 3.0. "Just like the Captain ordered," he said.

Jon started walking back toward the corner cubicle when the *ping*, long pause, *ping*, long pause, *ping* of the sonar sounded as it searched for the crashed helicopter.

In the electronic warning cubicle, "Find anything yet, Petty Officer Anderson?"

"Just friendly signals, sir. The strongest are US Navy air and surface search radars to the northwest."

"Okay," Jon said, "*Carmody* and a cruiser are out on that bearing. Nothing else really going on, so hopefully, we can find that helo with our sonar."

The ship steamed at seven knots back and forth along a track paralleling the coast at three miles. As the ship reversed course and was preparing to make a third transit of the same course, Jon walked out into Combat and stood behind the Evaluator seat.

"Captain," the XO said into the phone. "I recommend we move two miles from the beach and search there."

Jon heard the "no" of the Captain's response but heard no more of the reply.

The XO looked at the phone for a second: then, he put it down, and Jon saw his shoulders sag a bit. Then he straightened and turned to face the room. "Okay, team, we have been paralleling the coast. The Captain thinks we have searched thoroughly enough with that sort of orientation to the beach. He is going to run a series of approaches directly at the beach, thinking that the pings might have a better chance of finding the helo. But, we won't get closer than three miles to the coast."

The ship completed the next series of runs perpendicular to the coast with no targets found by the sonar. The Captain then had the ship make runs at a forty-five-degree angle to the coast, again staying outside three miles, and as before, there were no results. At 1100, the Captain called off the search, and the ship picked up a northeasterly heading at seventeen knots to make the rendezvous with the oiler.

"Secure from General Quarters. On deck, the 0800 to 1200 watch" passed over the ship's announcing system.

"Well, guys, another maximally exciting watch in the electronic warning broom closet. Thanks, guys," Jon said.

"Sir," PO3 Anderson said, "one of the high-frequency transmitters crapped out last night. I'm going to see if they got it fixed during GQ, in case you're interested."

The air in Radio Central was considerably closer to a breathable commodity than that in Combat. Radio Central, as many places were on a destroyer, was a tight place. On the forward bulkhead was an array of transmitter and receiver equipment in the deck to overhead racks. Along the aft bulkhead was a line of tables and desks where the radiomen typed, operated the speed key for sending Morse code messages, and where the XO sat writing on a pad of yellow lined paper. Jon could see "Personal For" across the top of the XO's pad of paper. Tom Snyder was standing next to the XO.

Tom said, "Yeah, Jon, your guys got us fixed during GQ. Your chief got permission to break Zebra to get a part out of a storeroom. Fixed us right up, so no down equipment in Radio."

Jon left Radio Central, went out on deck, sucked in a huge lungful of pure, clean air; then he walked aft along the main deck. The ocean raced by four feet below him. Astern, the green coast, fell away under a cloudless blue sky. The seventeen knots of wind blowing over him kept the heat and humidity at bay. He entered the superstructure through the watertight door just before after officer's country.

He knocked on the door to DD's room. The door jerked open, and DD stood there, glaring, obviously totally torqued off.

Then his face softened. "Ah! I'm not pissed at you, Jon. Come in."

DD closed the door. "Son-of-a-bitch! XO and I both tried to talk the captain into searching closer to shore. Son-of-a-bitch would not listen. Son-of-a—"

DD stopped talking. "Sorry." He flopped onto his chair by the desk. "What do you have?"

The outburst had surprised Jon; then, he was surprised more by its sudden cessation. "Sir, sorry, DD. Just wanted to tell you the ETs fixed the radio transmitter that crapped out last night. So, we have no down electronics equipment."

DD smiled, took a breath, nodded his head up and down, and said, "Thanks. I need to get up to Combat and take the Evaluator watch."

At 1130, the officers were standing at their places in the wardroom when the captain entered. He walked around to his place and sat. Normally he said, "Seats." But he said nothing. The XO sat; then the rest of them sat. Without an invitation to do so, the chaplain did not say grace. The XO nodded to the stewards, and they served the salad. Not a word was spoken until 1143 when Andrew Dunston asked permission to relieve the watch.

37

1450. *Manfred* was in the starboard waiting position behind the oiler. A hulking aircraft carrier steamed beside the oiler's port side taking on fuel. The oiler, longer and broader than a destroyer, was dwarfed by the gigantic flat top.

Jon was in his safety observer position, and Greg Heywood was observing. *Giant aircraft carrier, dwarf oiler. Giant Greg Heywood, dwarf Jon Zachery* passed through Jon's mind. He decided to tell Newbie about it after the refueling was completed.

Ahead of *Manfred*, another destroyer had completed fueling from the oiler's starboard side and had just passed the fuel hose back to the oiler. At flank speed, the destroyer cleared the starboard side of the oiler.

The Captain, Paul Becker, and DD were on the port bridge wing. Becker had the deck and the conn. DD was there to observe his first refueling aboard *Manfred*. He would be special sea detail Officer of the Deck from then on.

On the oiler, the red Bravo signal flag was raised partway on the starboard signal-flag yardarm to indicate a five-minute alert before they would be cleared alongside.

From the bridge wing, Paul said. "DD. We are opening just slightly on this course. See it?"

"Yes," DD said. "Half a degree left?"

"Half a degree would be okay, but I am going to put in a full degree. I want to see the effect before we start the approach. Probably have to take it out pretty quickly." Paul Becker turned toward the pilothouse and ordered the new course.

The helmsman acknowledged the order and put in the correction. Jon didn't say anything to Greg. That was not the time or place for non-essential voices, even whispers. So, he'd give Newbie a rundown after the refueling.

Jon glanced out the bridge windows. When he'd first been assigned safety observer, he could not detect a course change of one degree. Now, though, that degree seemed excessive, and the course correction would have to come out.

Paul ordered a half-degree right course correction.

On the oiler, the Bravo flag was raised to the yardarm, signaling that *Manfred* was cleared to move alongside for refueling.

A phone talker in the pilothouse called, "Signal bridge reports Bravo closed up to starboard on the oiler, sir."

"This is the Captain. I have the conn. Engines ahead full. Indicate turns for twenty-two knots."

As the lee helm acknowledged the order, Jon looked out at the Captain and wondered what the hell was going on. During the brief before manning refueling stations, a five knot overtake speed had briefed. On *Manfred*, they had always used a five-knot-overtake speed to move into position on an oiler or supply ship. But, the Captain had just ordered a ten-knot overtake speed. The Captain had not been at the brief, in contrast to Commander Carstens, who always attended the pre-refueling briefs.

Out on the bridge wing, Paul Becker turned and looked at the Captain, who was standing at the after part of the wing.

"Captain," he said, "what are you doing?"

A ten-knot overtake speed was used on some ships, with a backing of the engines to chop the speed. This could shave a couple of minutes from the approach, but the timing was critical. It was easy to overshoot position and easy to undershoot if you backed too late or too soon. And there was the danger that the two engines, in going from ahead full to back full, would reverse unevenly and turn either the bow or the stern into the oiler.

"Just step aside," the Captain said to Paul Becker.

Jon knew Paul understood the kind of approach the Captain was using. During Jon's orientation training, Paul had briefed him on it. But the faster approach had not been briefed to Engineering. They should respond to commands, regardless, but it was always better, always safer to fully brief all parties as to what would transpire in evolution like underway refueling. Paul stepped inside the pilothouse with his right leg.

"Lee helm," Becker said. "Engineering, Bridge, standby for a backing bell."

After the order had been relayed, Becker said, "Very well," as he stepped back out onto the bridge wing and positioned himself behind the Captain.

They passed the point where, in a five-knot overtake, the conning officer would have reduced speed, but they were still going twenty-two knots.

"We're closing the oiler," DD said.

Inside the pilothouse, Jon looked out the bridge window and could see that they were closing on the oiler. Unless a heading correction was ordered, it looked like *Manfred* would strike the oiler's bow.

"Jesus," the helmsman said. He was looking out the window.

Jon said, "Helmsman, pay attention to the compass. You steer the last course ordered."

On the bridge wing, Lieutenant Becker said, "Captain, we need to come right two degrees."

The Captain was staring straight ahead. Under their feet, the hull throbbed with an energy vibrato as the propellers thrashed the water, still vigorously seeking a new equilibrium state between propulsive force and water to hull friction resistance.

"Captain," Becker said again, and more insistently. "You need to come right."

"Dammit, Captain," Becker said. "Listen to me. You have to come right and do it now."

The Captain continued to stare straight ahead.

"The Captain has the deck," Becker said in a loud voice. "Quartermaster, write in the log that the Captain has the deck."

Paul walked into and out of the pilothouse through the after door.

"Engines back full," the Captain said from the bridge wing.

"Captain," DD said, "you need to come right, make it five degrees."

"Come right five degrees," the Captain said.

"Coming right five degrees, sir," said the helmsman.

"Zero-six-four," Jon said to the helmsman. "Say it. Coming to zero-six-four."

As the bow began to swing right, Jon was tempted to look to port at the grey side of the oiler, which seemed close enough to touch, but he forced himself to watch the compass.

When the ship accelerated, the power and energy transmitted through the hull seemed impressive. Now with a full backing bell on and decelerating from twenty-two knots, the energy juddering through the hull felt downright violent. It was like something was being destroyed. Jon always wondered how the reduction gears could handle all that energy, but despite how violent and destructive it felt, the ship was designed and periodically tested to handle backing down from even higher speeds.

On the bridge wing, DD was watching the bow swing through its correction and vector us away from the oiler.

DD said, "Why don't you let me take it from here, Captain. It will be good training."

The Captain said, "Mr. Davison has the conn."

"This is Mr. Davison. I have the deck and the conn. Come left. Steer new course zero-six-three. All engines stop."

The Captain entered the pilothouse, walked over to the starboard side, climbed up onto his chair, and looked away toward the forward starboard quarter, where there was nothing to look at but sea and sky.

The XO burst onto the bridge, with Lieutenant Becker so close behind he seemed to be pushing the XO.

The bow of *Manfred* cleared the stern of the oiler. The XO looked at the proximity of the side of the larger ship.

"Holy Mother of God," the XO said. "How close did it get?"

The oiler was beginning to pull ahead of *Manfred*.

"Engines ahead standard," DD said. "Indicate turns for seventeen knots."

"Uh, XO is on the bridge," the Boatswain announced belatedly.

The Captain turned in his chair, looked at the XO, and said, "Take it for a few minutes, XO. I'm going down to my cabin."

The XO and Paul Becker stood behind DD on the bridge wing as he maneuvered the ship back to a normal distance abeam and alongside. When the shot line came over from the oiler, the XO took Paul to the starboard bridge wing, sent the lookout inside, and closed the watertight door. They talked out there for a minute, then opened the door again, and the XO ordered the starboard lookout to resume his post.

Over the 1MC, the Bosun announced, "Taking on fuel. The smoking lamp is out throughout the ship."

The XO and Becker passed through the pilot house, squeezing past Newbie and out to the port bridge wing.

Jon caught the lee helm looking out at the discussion on port wing.

"Keep your mind on your job, Lee Helm," Jon said.

"Aye, sir. Sorry, sir."

"So you have the deck, DD, right?" the XO said.

"Yes, sir."

"So, keep it that way, and Paul, you stay here and be ready to assist. I've got to check on the captain."

About two minutes after the XO left the bridge, Tom Snyder entered. He looked over at the empty chair on the starboard side; then, he strode out onto the port bridge wing.

"DD," Tom Snyder began.

"DD has the deck," Paul said. "What's up?"

"Uh, well," Tom said. "I have three messages here. One is a 'personal for' to the XO. The other two, well, the XO wanted me to bring him all operations-related messages first. I looked in Combat, but the XO isn't there."

"Give me the Ops messages," Paul said, as Andrew ordered a half a degree correction to the left and added one RPM.

"This message is from *Carmody* to the Task Force Commander, info to us and the commodore," Becker said. "*Carmody* found the crashed helo. Some Underwater Demolition Technician divers were brought by helicopter to *Carmody* from Da Nang. The UDT guys retrieved the gear and a body, and then they blew up the wrecked helo. They found the wreck one thousand yards offshore."

"This one," Paul said, "orders the whole task force to take typhoon evasion measures." Jon couldn't stop himself from looking, for a moment, then forced himself back to his job.

Becker continued, "There's a bunch of stuff they want us to report immediately. Sometime later, we'll be assigned a formation to join."

The XO walked out onto the port bridge wing and said in a hushed voice that came across as a stage whisper, "the Captain's taking a shower."

That again drew Jon's eyes to the bridge wing. He saw wrinkles appear in Becker's low forehead, and his brown eye and blue eye seemed to meander in uncoordinated, independent motion through about half their range of scan for a second.

Nobody on the bridge wing spoke for a long moment, which was just as eye-attracting as the conversation had been. Jon forced his eyes to behave. He did glance behind to see what Greg Heywood was doing, which was staring at the bridge wing.

Jon decided not to say anything to Newbie then, but he'd talk to him later, after their time alongside the oiler was complete.

The XO laid out the priorities: finish refueling, get the message report out to the task force commander, and then the other matter.

The other matter, Jon was sure, was the new CO.

The rest of the refueling was accomplished with Paul Becker

as OOD and Jon as his JOOD. The XO had sent DD and Andrew Dunston to start working on the message report. The XO went down to check on the captain.

The refueling was completed without further incident.

After they were relieved by the regular underway watch, Jon followed Paul Becker out of the pilothouse. Paul stopped just before the ladders going down. "Just another day at the office, eh, Two Buckets?"

When they reached the main deck, Jon stayed in trail behind Becker to after officer's country. There, Jon knocked on DD's door and was invited, "Come."

Jon asked if DD needed any help with the message report.

The message had already gone out. Then he gave Jon a bit about the storm.

For several days, the fleet weather center had been keeping tabs on a tropical system that had formed in the waters east of Luzon. The system had progressed from tropical depression to tropical storm, and it had been following a general westerly track. Clearing the northern tip of Luzon, the storm seemed bore-sighted on Hainan Island. Typically, storms and typhoons that started on similar tracks would veer away to the north, but this one had persisted in its westerly track, grown in strength, and was now designated, Typhoon Mamie. All US Navy ships in the Tonkin Gulf had been ordered to evacuate the Gulf and evade the storm.

"Which means head south, right?" Jon said.

"It's the only option."

"DD," Jon said. "What's with the CO?"

DD took in a big breath and huffed it out. "The XO, as you might imagine, is pretty much tied in knots. He's been sending "personal for" messages. He has sworn the first-class radioman to secrecy, and the PO1 sends the messages and destroys all copies afterward. XO won't even let Tom Snyder see them. I'm sure the XO is trying to keep the rest of us from getting smeared with this. God bless our navy, but this could tar us all with, 'Oh, yeah, you were one of those disloyal *Manfred* guys who got your CO dumped.'"

"In the meantime?"

"In the meantime, Jon, keep on keeping on."

38

On the morning of 16 August, *Manfred* rendezvoused south-southeast of Hainan Island with the *Reilly*. After completing her port visit to Taiwan, *Reilly's* track kept her ahead of the effects of the storm. An hour later, the two destroyers from North SAR station also joined the formation. If it hadn't been for the typhoon, *Reilly* and *Manfred* would be relieving USS *Monacher* and USS *Spenthe* on North SAR. Now, once the typhoon was no longer a threat, *Monacher* and *Spenthe* would proceed to liberty ports, and *Reilly* and *Manfred* would take over North SAR.

The Commodore on *Reilly* was in command, and he ordered the ships into a diamond formation on a southerly course at ten knots. They were south of the track Mamie was following. Generally, such typhoons would not turn south, so the Commodore must have considered a ten-knot speed to be adequate, and if the typhoon, as was expected, veered north, they wouldn't be very far from returning to their mission area in the northern Tonkin Gulf.

Yesterday, after refueling had been completed, the XO had developed a four-section bridge and CIC watch plan, as the gun director no longer needed to be manned outside the combat zone. The Captain, however, had overruled the XO and had ordered a three-section watch bill. DD, Paul Becker, and Andrew Dunston were the OODs, and Peter Feldman, Don Minton, and Darryl Palmer were the JOODs. In Combat, Ralph Timmons, Charles Hanson, and Tom Snyder were the Evaluators. The XO had wanted to put the ensigns on watch in Combat, but the Captain refused.

At 1930, the four ensigns were in the Locker together. Admiral Ensign was at the fold-down desk; Jon was propped on his elbows in his bunk writing; Almost lay in his bunk reading; and Newbie stood between the bunks, took his newly laundered clothes from the laundry bag, folded them, and squeezed by Admiral Ensign to stash them in formerly Cowboy's, now his locker.

"Newbie." Admiral Ensign looked up from his letter. "For Christ's sake. Do you have to push past me with each pair of skivvies? Fold a whole stack of them, and I'll help. I'll pass them to you."

"Geez, Admiral Ensign." Newbie said as he stuck a finger up his nose, extracted it, and then examined the end of his finger intently. "Sure don't mean to bother you. But don't you just marvel at how God just makes everything fit, like my nose is just big enough to fit my big finger."

Admiral Ensign was wearing wash khaki trousers and a tee-shirt. Newbie wiped his finger on the sleeve of Admiral Ensign's tee shirt.

"You're a pig, Newbie," Admiral Ensign said as he examined his shirtsleeve as intently as Newbie had his finger. "Aahh!"

Admiral Ensign pushed back from the desk, bulled past Newbie, pushed the door open, and slammed it closed.

Jon looked at the door for what seemed like several mid-watch seconds, and like Cowboy, the silence got to be something he couldn't stand. "So, Bull, what do you think? Booger?"

Almost pondered the suggestion. "It certainly bears some thought. As a name, it has a poetic ring to it, certainly. But. *But,* I think it is overly evocative of just one facet of our multi-faceted Newbie. Let's give it a bit more time."

"I, for one," Jon said as he started writing again, "would like to go on record as opposing overly evocative characterizations centered on mere slivers out of a broad range of behaviors."

Admiral Ensign came back in the Locker without a tee-shirt. He pushed past Newbie, got a clean tee-shirt out of his locker, and pulled it over his head.

"You owe me a tee-shirt," Admiral Ensign said.

Newbie held out one of his, but Admiral Ensign just glared at him.

"You should have taken it," Jon said. "You could use it for a fart sack."

Fart sack was a term for mattress cover.

Almost said, "Now, now, children. Newbie, how was your interview with the Captain yesterday afternoon?"

"Blimey." Newbie said, "don't you blokes just marvel at the socially suave, debonair, and adept fashion in which the Bull Ensign changes the bloody subject?"

"So, how did it go?" Jon asked.

"Well, the XO said I should go at 1330. He thought the Captain would take about fifteen minutes, so there would be time for us to make it to the underway replenishment briefing at 1400. I got there at 1325, but he was in the shower, and his door was locked. I was about to leave at 1355 to catch the briefing when he opened the door and told me to come in.

"He sat at his desk. I stood. When I asked him about the briefing, he told me that I should stay the hell out of the way of those who knew what they were doing and not touch anything. That was my briefing for the UNREP, he said. Then, he said he was concerned with my attitude. He said the Ensign Locker was a problem on *Manfred*, and he said that if I wasn't careful, I could really mess myself up. He said I should be really careful about whom I listened to. I should listen to my Department Head, to the XO, and him, the Captain. If I had to listen to someone in the Locker, though, he said don't listen to anyone but Carl. I need to get my attitude straight right away. He said it didn't look like I took anything seriously. This is a warship, not a frat house, and I better learn that right away. That was it."

"Are you taking polished apples to the Captain, Almost?" Jon asked.

Almost snorted. "That just means I am not quite as high up on his crap list as some of the others from the Locker who can't seem to avoid attracting lightning strikes out of cloudless skies. That was it, Newbie?"

"Oh yeah. He held up a message," Newbie said. "He said it was from the Commodore and that the Commodore commended him for getting the ship turned around so quickly. He said the Commodore was pleased with the destruction of the North Vietnamese boats and how the Captain had thoroughly searched the area for the downed helo so that *Carmody* could go right to it.

"Then the Captain said that the Ensign Locker was one of the things that had been wrong with the *Manfred* until he took over the ship and that it was beginning to come around. He just wanted to make sure a new rotten apple wasn't going into the barrel now, and he wanted to know if I understood what he wanted from me. I said, 'Oh yes, sir, I most surely do.' He looked at me like he thought I was still a massive wise-ass, but then he told me to make sure I remembered what he told me. He said he was going to be watching me. He asked me if I had any questions. I said no, no questions, but I did congratulate him on the message from the Commodore. I said that was quite something to get an atta-boy like that since he was almost as much of a newbie as I was. Well, his face got red, but all he said was that I should get to work."

"Oh, Jesus, Newbie," Almost said, "we were just beginning to get Two Buckets out of the lightning rod mode and calling the Captain a newbie, not good. But, I guess the message from the Commodore was the biggest thing to the Captain. He was sure upbeat at dinner."

"Yeah, what a joke," Admiral Ensign said. "We didn't find the helicopter this morning and almost ram the oiler this afternoon, and then he is acting like we've had a great day."

Admiral Ensign was back at the desk working on his letter, and

Jon came close to popping off something derogatory about him agreeing with the rest of us for once.

"That sure sounds different from the message I heard the XO, Cheng, and DD talking about on the bridge," Jon said. "Cheng sort of said something like it was embarrassing to have *Carmody* go in and clean up after we couldn't get the job done. *Carmody* went in a lot closer than we did and found the helicopter right away."

"Do you know who the message was from?" Admiral Ensign asked.

"I think it was from *Carmody,*" Jon said.

"So what matters is what the Commodore thinks, not the Commanding Officer of another destroyer," Admiral Ensign said.

"Well, I think it just stinks," Jon said. "We get into something tense, and the XO, Cheng, and DD pull our bacon out of the fire, and the Captain goes and takes a shower. After the botched approach to the oiler today, the XO went to talk to the Captain, and that's what he was doing: taking a shower. How in hell can the Commodore commend the Captain when this kind of stuff happens? The navy is pretty screwed up."

Almost said. "The navy has its screwed-up moments, just like every other organization in the world. My dad is an English professor in Oregon. You should hear him bellyache about the tenured professors in his department. Dormant talked about his dad and the army. There are examples from all walks of life. I don't think what you mentioned means the whole navy is screwed up. Look at our previous Skipper. Look at the XO, the Department Heads, and JGs. All of them are good people who do a great job. Look at the *Carmody.* She's a good ship. And, when we were up on North SAR, the Task Force Commander took the Skipper's suggestion about trying to get that MiG. There are plenty of examples of good performance. It is easy to generalize when it's local and very personal."

"Well," Newbie said as he sidled forward to stow a stack of folded skivvies in his locker, "I'll tell you what is local and personal. That's when the Captain, every time he sets eyes on an ensign, immediately slips into the foul-tempered portion of his menstrual cycle."

Jon awoke in a panic to a lightless, weightless world. He seemed to be floating in pitch blackness, not connected to earth. Then, the bow of *Manfred* hit the bottom of a trough and started up the crest of the next wave, and g-forces pressed him into the mattress. As the bow started rising, there was a rattle and a clatter of things not tied down from spaces around the Ensign Locker.

"That was interesting," Newbie said in the darkness. "I guess there really is a typhoon out there. I thought it was just Communist propaganda."

"Shut up, Newbie," Admiral Ensign said. "Go back to sleep, but not on your back. If you get to snoring again, you'll weaken the rivets, and the whole bow could come off in these seas."

The ship rose on the next wave, hovered a moment as the crest moved aft from under the bow, then began the plummet, with the momentary lessening of g force in the forward section of the ship. At the bottom of the descent, the buoyant bow decelerated its downward motion, poised for just an instant in motionless stasis in the vertical axis, then accelerated up again.

"Oh please, please, Massa Admiral," Newbie said, "please don't be whuppin me wif yo pillow agin."

Jon remembered the incident. The Ensign Locker deck had been covered with feathers. Feathers filled shoes. Feathers stuck not only in the hair of Newbie's head but in the fur on his arms as well.

"And you know," Jon said, "if Admiral Ensign destroys another pillow, we will have to use seagull feathers to fill it again. I wonder if that would be bad luck, like killing an albatross."

"Will you dipwads just shut up," Admiral Ensign said and turned out his bunk light. "Go back to sleep." It sounded like there had been a smile in his voice. Perhaps it had to be dark for Admiral Ensign to behave like an ensign.

"Massa Two Buckets," Newbie said as the ship rose on another wave, "you ain't gonna be hurlin on us po workin fokes, is you?"

The bow bottomed, and as it rose again, there was an element of a roll to the motion. As the bow hovered over the next trough, it seemed to quiver with a bit of horizontal motion, as if the ship were shivering.

"Okay, Newbie," Almost said. "You have extracted the very last gram of humor out of that one. Put a sock in it, and let's get some sleep. All you children, go back to sleep."

Jon wedged his arms under the mattress, didn't try to fight the motion, and didn't exactly surrender to it as much as just let it be what it was. It occurred to him that he didn't have a headache. He hoped it wasn't bad luck to think that.

The next thing Jon knew, it was 0550. The bunk light was on in Almost's bunk, but he was not there. The ship seemed to buck and pitch and roll. There was no rhythm to the motion, just violent jerks in all axes. Carefully, Jon climbed out of his bunk as Newbie climbed out his. Admiral Ensign was still asleep. When Newbie's feet hit the deck, the ship buried the bow in a wave, like smacking into a brick wall. Newbie staggered forward and fell, knocking Jon to the deck and falling on top of his legs.

"Sorry, Two Buckets," Newbie said. "Did I hurt you?"

"I don't think anything is broken."

"Have you ever been inside a cement mixer?" Newbie asked.

"Nope, but I hope this is as close to that as I ever get."

Jon climbed back up onto his bunk, timing the move with one of the moments when the bow was not moving in pitch and left the deck space to Newbie. As he lay on his back and pulled on trousers, Newbie put on shower shoes; then walked bouncing off bunks, doorjambs, and bulkheads as he moved out of the Locker and into the passageway outside the head. Just after he closed the door to the Locker, the door opened again, and Newbie threw his shower shoes onto the deck in the Locker.

"Damn shower shoes tried to kill me," Newbie said. Then he went barefoot into the head.

Jon finished dressing and entered the head to use the urinal. Newbie banged against the wall of the shower stall as he sang "Anchors Aweigh" at the top of his lungs. The deck was awash from the geysers of saltwater that shot out of the commode as the bow rode up out of the water then plunged under again.

In the wardroom, the stewards had placed the rough weather plate and silverware-containing lattice on the table. As Jon considered the things to eat, nothing sounded appealing at first. He decided on a bacon sandwich. With the first bite, the salty bacon seemed to immediately satisfy some need in his body He took a drink of the coffee. It seemed almost as good as that served in the chief's mess.

"Good, eh, Two Buckets," the XO said. He was the only other officer in the wardroom, and he was looking into his cup almost reverently. "Nasty black stuff. Stomps across your tongue like Germans in hobnailed boots on the way to France. It says wake the hell up, heart."

"I was just thinking that it is almost as good as chief's mess coffee, XO, but your way of putting it sounds pretty good."

The XO looked down at the table. "How are you doing this morning?"

"So far, so good, sir, but I would caution you to avoid being caught in a confined space with Newbie. He is just bouncing between hard things this morning, and he flattens soft things that get between him and the hard things."

The XO chuckled. "So bodies were flying around in the Locker this morning?"

"Just Newbie, sir. And everything was okay until he and I tried to stand and get dressed at the same time. Then, he seemed to need all the space. So what's the latest on the storm, XO?"

"Well, you know the Commodore positioned us to the south of Hainan. These things normally don't turn south, but last night Mamie did, and she also strengthened to category five. It was as if Mamie knew where we were, and she headed right for us. This morning, she turned back to the west, though. According to the weather people, it should be making landfall on the southeastern part of Hainan Island this morning. Hopefully, when it hits land, it will burn itself out, and we may be able to turn back to the north sometime tomorrow."

Following breakfast, Jon walked aft to the ET shop. ET2 Dawkins was sitting on a stool tied to the workbench, and he was reading a paperback book as he hung onto the bench for support against all the movement.

"Good morning, ET2," Jon said. "How'd you guys fare in the berthing compartment last night?"

"Well, thank God we are not any farther forward than we are," ET2 Dawkins said. "Even so, the guys in the top bunks used the straps to tie themselves in. The Ensign Locker must have been fun, eh, sir?"

"Our new ensign said it was like being inside a cement mixer, and I think he was pretty close to right on," Jon said. "Everybody from the shop, okay?"

"Seaman Ferguson is feeling it, sir," Dawkins said. "He's sacked out on the deck back there behind you, between the test equipment racks."

Seaman Ferguson had joined the ship in the Philippines after having completed the Navy Electronic Technician School. Jon didn't have to go in back to see him. When he'd been enlisted, Jon had spent a fair amount of time on the deck in the ET shop, wishing he could just die.

"Well," Jon said, "I, for one, have sympathy for him. See if you can get him to drink some water throughout the day. It's easy to get dehydrated when you are seasick."

39

Jon then went up to the bridge and stood behind the helmsman, in his safety observer position. He stood with his feet apart and managed to compensate for the rolling and pitching to keep his balance. The Captain sat in his chair. He stared straight ahead and periodically sipped from a coffee mug. Darryl Palmer, the JOOD, was behind the Captain and looking through his binoculars out the starboard bridge door window. Darryl walked back toward Paul Becker, who was standing in front of the helm and binnacle.

"Never did see the *Monacher*," Darryl said. "And I only caught an occasional glimpse of *Reilly*. So visibility is reliably something on the order of three-quarters of a mile in fog and blowing spray."

Paul nodded. "Sure glad we topped off with fuel. The ride would be a lot worse if we were down to 50% of capacity or so."

Out the bridge windows, all Jon could see was an enraged ocean, waves overtaking them from astern, wave tops sliced off and hurled away as salty, horizontal rain. The water was grey and green, as was the sky. And the sky seemed to glow. It was like the skies back home in Missouri during times of tornado warnings. Jon had seen enough and went below to finish his morning business in the head.

Later that morning, Jon visited the ship's office to see how the rest of the division was coping with the heavy seas. At 1120, he finished with the yeomen and personnel men and closed the door to the ship's office. Carl Lehr was walking forward in the amidships passageway.

Jon fell in behind Carl. Carl opened the door to the mess decks and stopped abruptly, and Jon bumped into his back. He couldn't see what caused Carl to stop, not right away, but there was a lot of noise coming from inside.

Jon looked around Carl and saw a sailor fall and drop his tray at the drink station at the end of the serving line. Another sailor was on his hands and knees between rows of tables, one row to starboard from the serving line. The sailors in the serving line were hanging onto the counter as they tried to stand on a deck made very slippery with spilled food and drink.

Ensign Haywood, Newbie, was at the forward part of the mess decks. Standing with feet splayed, toes pointed out, kind of like a first-time skier ready to start snow-plowing down the bunny slope, he was holding a tray of food a little high on his chest with one hand, holding onto the back of a seat at one of the forward-most tables with the other hand. He was looking for a vacant seat. Spying one near the rear of the mess decks, he let go of the back of the seat. Just then, the bow of the ship rose on the crest of a wave. Newbie started sliding aft even though his feet were together, and he was standing straight and still. His mouth was open, but it was his eyes that shouted panic. His body started turning as he tried to keep his tray level. He held onto the cup of Kool-Aid in one corner compartment of the tray, and he kept his eyes fixed on the bulkhead aft. After 270 degrees of rotation, the cup of Kool-Aid flew off his tray and landed on a table where four sailors were seated. A few sailors were eating; most of them were watching the entertainment.

Newbie's cup shattered when it hit the table, and red Kool-Aid and broken glass splattered the four sailors at the table where the cup landed as well as those at the next table to starboard. There was something like a "Yeah" or the nondescript roar you hear at a sporting event. The entertainment was great.

Newbie continued to slide aft as he entered into a second rotation. He kept his eyes fixed on the aft bulkhead until he was looking over his left shoulder; then, he snapped his head around. It was very much like a ballerina, cutting a series of pirouettes across a stage in a straight line and spotting on some feature in the wings to maintain the line. Except instead of arms gracefully extended and floating at shoulder height, Newbie's arms held the tray at a sort of rigid high carry. Then, just after he completed a second turn, and just after his head snapped around from over the left shoulder, and just as he was facing straight aft, he slid into the back of a sailor seated at one of the aft-most tables on the mess decks. Like a dump trunk unloading a load of gravel on a roadway, he dumped the contents of his tray in the lap of ET3 Anderson.

A roar of laughter and cheers rose from the mess decks. The cooks serving food, a row of sailors hanging onto the counter at the serving line, and the sailors seated at tables all cheered and laughed. Some of the seated sailors applauded, and one of the sailors at a table in the starboard aft-most table shouted, "A ten. Ensign Haywood gets a ten."

Another cheer erupted, and there was more applause. There was more interest in extracting entertainment from lunch rather than nourishment.

Newbie was standing holding his empty tray, an appalled look on his face, as ET3 Anderson stood and began to scoop handfuls of chili, rice, and Brussels sprouts off his dungaree trousers and to slop the mess onto his tray.

"Man, I am so sorry," Greg said to ET3 Anderson.

Anderson looked up into the ensign's face, smiled, and started to extend his hand, then remembered the mess, kind of shrugged, and said, "not your fault, sir. It's not a problem."

Zambowski, who had been wiping a table with a towel nearby, had managed to get his laughter under control and handed Anderson the towel.

"Let me take your tray, sir," Zambowski said to Greg.

Jon followed Carl to the table where Greg was standing with Anderson. They both had to hang onto the bolted-to-the-deck chairs to be able to stand and move on the slippery deck.

Carl smirked. "You have a name, Newbie. After that performance, which I would characterize as a position two *glissade, avec pirouette chaine*, classically, gracefully, and beautifully executed, you are Tutu."

On the face of Greg, Newbie, now Tutu, it was as if stagehands carted off a backdrop depicting embarrassment and shame, while just behind came two more carrying a dark cloud scene. "Hey, wait a minute, Almost. You can't name me Tutu!"

That cinched it. Tutu objected to his name. Almost smiled at him. "While I was in college, my future wife tried out for the San Francisco Ballet Company. If she could have cut *pirouettes* like you just did, she'd have made it. Come on, Tutu. I'm not sure your adoring public can handle another prima ballerina performance immediately."

After lunch, the XO assembled the ensigns in the wardroom. The captain had found dead bugs in his underwear drawer. The XO sent Carl and Jon to the Captain's cabin to inspect it for bugs, dead or alive.

All the Captain's clothes on hangers had been brought down to the XO's cabin and laid on the bunk. All the Captain's skivvies and socks were in the laundry being rewashed.

Carl and Jon then pulled all the drawers out of the grey sheet metal racks, and they inspected in and under the empty rack for live bugs or any forensic signs of deceased or living bug presence. They used flashlights and looked under and in every accessible nook and cranny in the Captain's cabin, but they found no bugs, parts of bugs, or signs of bugs.

The door to the XO's cabin was open when Carl and Jon arrived. Fred Watson was in the room, standing, and the XO was sitting at his desk.

Fred Watson said, "XO, the guys that do the Captain's laundry are good kids. I picked them for the job because they are conscientious, and they are dependable. I personally supervised their instruction on how to do the Captain's laundry. And, since the Captain wants his laundry done every day, we have had some practice, you know. Once we understood what he wanted, there hasn't been a problem."

"Yes, yes," the XO said. "I know. I know."

The XO looked at Carl and Jon in the passageway. "Find anything?" he asked.

"No, sir," Carl said. "We looked into every corner of the place with flashlights and didn't see a sign of a bug."

"Okay, thanks, guys," the XO said. "You can go about your business."

"Yes, sir," Carl said. "We going to get back on the watch bill anytime soon?"

The XO said, "It's one of the things on my list. I'll let you know."

"Wow," Jon said. "XO is really nice to you, Carl. He always tells me to get the hell out of here."

During the afternoon, the seas began to abate, but the rough weather latticework was still in place on the table for the evening meal in the wardroom. After everyone assembled, the XO announced the CO would eat in his cabin that evening. Everyone sat, and as a steward placed a salad in front of the XO, the phone by the Captain's chair buzzed.

The XO walked around to the head of the table, pulled out the phone. "XO, sir," he said.

Everyone at the table heard the bellow, "Get up here!"

Fred Watson looked at the XO much like a steer in a slaughterhouse gazing up at a sweaty, burly Chicagoan with the sledge raised. "XO, you want me to go with you?" he asked.

"Stay here," the XO said. "Go ahead and eat."

Fred took his salad fork, started bringing a piece of lettuce to his mouth, but then he put the fork down on his plate; and if the latticework had not been in place, he would have pushed the salad plate away.

"Captain working you over on the laundry, Fred?" Don Minton

asked. "I understand you even had to keep people on board to do his laundry every day while we were in port in Zamboanga. That right?"

"Don, put a sock in it," DD said. "That is not something to discuss at the dinner table."

The aft door to the wardroom opened. The XO entered and closed the door as all eyes watched him stand still in front of the closed door, hands clenched into fists at his side. The storm boiling in him and flashing lightning through his eyes was not diminishing, as was the one outside. He took a breath, opened his fists, looked at his opened right hand in front of him, and in a quiet, calm voice said, "DD, Gun Boss, Fred. My cabin. Now."

The XO closed the door behind the four of them. Charles Hanson finished his salad and pointed the empty plate out to the steward, who began picking up the salad plates. When the steward was half-finished placing the dinner plates, the door to the XO's cabin opened. DD and the other two department heads returned to their places. The XO came out last, stood in the passageway outside his cabin, and said, "I want to see you four ensigns in the Ensign Locker. Now."

It was going to be crowded, so as soon as Jon entered, he kicked off his shoes and climbed up onto his bunk. Tutu squeezed past Admiral Ensign so that he would be next to the forward bulkhead. Almost stood next to the fold-down desk. The XO entered and closed the door behind him.

"Now," the XO said. "I don't have time or the inclination for niceties. I don't have time to be fair, either. So, we will just cut to the chase."

The XO opened his right hand, palm up, and said, "Do you all know what these are?"

Almost, Admiral Ensign, and Jon could see the XO's hand.

"Looks like bug legs, XO. Cockroach, maybe," Admiral Ensign said.

"Back up a bit, Almost," the XO said.

Almost pushed back against Admiral Ensign, who pressed back more tightly against the bulk of Tutu to enable the XO to pull down the fold-down desk. The XO took the three insect legs, all three close to right angles, and arranged them on the desk.

"So," said XO. "What does that look like?"

Admiral Ensign said, "Looks like an F and a V."

"It could be an F and a U, maybe," Tutu said.

The XO glared at Tutu for a moment. "I'm advising you to just shut up." Then he lowered his eyes to the desk. "The Captain found these legs on his pillow and showed these to me. They were arranged like I have them now. And in the ventilation duct just above the Captain's bed, a cockroach with the legs pulled off on one side. So the bug was scraping and frantically trying to climb up the pipe, but it just succeeded in making noise. The mesh of the screen over the end of the air duct was just fine enough to keep the cockroach from falling out."

The XO swept the cockroach legs off the desk into his hand and dropped them into the wastebasket. After the violence of the last few days, the rise and fall of the bow and the rolls seemed gentle. The ship noises, ventilation fans mainly, punctuated the silence in the Locker. Eight ensign eyes locked onto the XO, waiting.

"Since you ensigns obviously didn't do a good enough job inspecting the Captain's cabin, Fred and I will do it ourselves, starting in about five minutes. Then tomorrow, the Captain is doing a cleanliness inspection with the department heads of the entire ship, looking for insects, rodents—"

"Uh, XO," Tutu began.

"Shut. UP!" the XO said. "Say another word, and I swear to God, I will rip one of those hairy gorilla arms right out of your shoulder and beat the shit out of you with the bloody end."

The XO looked at his hands and then wiped them on his trousers.

"Fred has had enough trouble without these damned bugs. Myself, I would have preferred some other form of entertainment this evening rather than looking for bug body parts in the Captain's cabin."

The XO locked eyes with Tutu. Something like a billion-watt lightning bolt passed between the two of them. Then the XO turned, left the locker, and slammed the door shut. You could hear him stomping up the ladder to the main deck passageway forward of the wardroom.

"What the hell did you do, Tutu?" Admiral Ensign asked.

"Nothing," Tutu said.

Tutu pushed past Admiral Ensign and Almost and said, "I'm going to eat dinner…if they haven't thrown it out."

40

On *Manfred,* as the ship prepared for the inspection of the ship by the Captain and the department heads, the XO put the ensigns back on the watch bill. Andrew Dunston and Jon had the 0400 to 0800 bridge watch.

In the predawn light, the other three ships were visible. Ahead, Jon saw the grey structure of *Reilly* as a proud thing plowing through a field of white caps. Abeam was *Monacher.* Details of her silhouette were discernible: Air and surface search radar antennae on the forward mast were rotating; the single barrel 5-inch 54 caliber gun mounts were more modern, more automated than the manual, two-barrel, 5-inch 38 caliber guns on *Manfred;* port running light and the masthead and range lights were visible but washing out in the growing ambient light. On *Spenthe,* off the starboard quarter aft, the two white lights and a red were visible.

Scattered clouds, white with painted-on gray, were overhead. To the east, the clouds were pink, red, and orange pastels. The horizon was visible to the east but not in the other sectors.

Jon looked to the east just as the sun poked a fingernail clipping of yellow, red fire above the horizon as if cautiously peering over the top of a trench, ready to duck down again at the *thwup* of a passing sniper bullet.

Jon felt good being back on the bridge again, having the conn with the ship steaming in formation with other navy warships and responsible for some of the key *Manfred* functions. Being taken off the watch bill this time had been worse than when he'd been in hack. Then, he figured he deserved punishment. This time it wasn't that way at all.

Still, it was a great, glorious morning. *Sailors are meant to be on ships, and ships are meant to be at sea,* flitted through his mind, but that seemed to squirt a bit of guilt into his brain bucket. It didn't feel right to take joy in something that forced him to be apart from Teresa and couldn't really share with her.

"Officer of the Deck," the phone talker said, "Combat reports they have a failure in the air search radar. They have called the electronics techs."

The phone talker announcement brought Jon's brain out of reverie mode, but he was not about to pay any attention to the equipment problem while he was on watch. Andrew, as OOD, would worry about that.

While Andrew and Jon were in the process of turning over the watch to Darryl Palmer and Carl Lehr, the Commodore on *Reilly* sent a flashing light message saying that the formation would disperse at 1100.

DD was the off-going evaluator in Combat. He entered the bridge and briefed the on-coming OOD. The air search radar failure, and no repair part aboard, had been reported to the task force. The failure would prevent *Manfred* from going to North SAR station. *Carmody* would take *Manfred's* place on north SAR. *Manfred* would take over gunfire support for the marines near the DMZ.

After leaving the bridge and after breakfast, Jon went to the chief's mess to talk to ETC Fargo about the problem with air search radar.

"So, Mr. Z., the SPS-29 air search radar problem, pretty straightforward, sort of, sir."

"Straightforward, sort of?"

"Yes, sir. It is straightforward, actually, but there are two parts to it. The Klystron tube failed. It is in the cabinet above the signal bridge where the cooling water is piped in. The original failure, I am certain, was a valve in the saltwater piping for cooling. Before the over-temp circuitry could shut the system down, the Klystron tube fried itself. I woke up early this morning and was in the ET shop when the call came in. So I went up and found the Klystron, and you could see the insides were fried. When I checked the other circuitry and the cooling system, I found the saltwater valve that basically regulates the flow of cooling water failed in the closed position."

"You did the trouble-shooting?" Jon said.

The Chief had never before, as far as Jon knew, gone with the first response to a trouble call. He was on call if the junior technicians needed his experience and expertise.

ETC Fargo saw the look on Jon's face and said, "Uh, sir, I was up early. Couldn't sleep. So when the call came, I went up to take a look. I thought it might be something simple, you know, reset a circuit breaker, or something like that."

"So, Klystron and a valve, you said. We don't carry spares for those?"

"We do have a spare Klystron, sir, but there is no spare for the saltwater valve. And the Operations Officer already sent out a flashing light message to the other three ships with us. They don't carry it, either."

"Okay, so do you have the old parts in the ET shop, Chief?"

"Well no, sir, we don't. When I finished up there on the signal bridge, I was carrying the Klystron and the valve; and as I climbed down the ladder from the signal bridge, the ship rolled, and I dropped the tube and the valve overboard."

Chief Fargo was looking down at his coffee mug.

"Have we got the part on order?"

"Not yet, sir. I'll get that going right away."

"So, Chief, you said the Operations Officer was up this morning, too? Or did you wake him?"

"No, sir. I didn't wake him. I think the CIC watch officer did. And, I didn't want to bother you on the bridge and get you put in hack again."

"Okay, Chief, thanks," Jon said and started to turn away, stopped, and said, "Zambowski gets off mess cooking in a few days, right?"

"Yes, sir," Chief Fargo said. "I already turned in the statement from the cook to the ship's office as the last part of the program you worked out. It'll be good to get him back, and, sir, thanks again for trying to help him."

As Jon closed the door to the chief's mess, he looked forward and saw the Captain leaving the ship's office. Jon walked aft and knocked on DD's door. DD pulled it open.

"Jon. Come in. Sit down."

"Good morning, uh, DD, you look tired. Did you get any sleep last night?"

"Well, it has been a rough stretch." DD shrugged. "Watch, meetings with the XO—and I know I get circles that make me look like a raccoon. Anyhow, what's up?"

"Just wanted to make sure you had the latest on the air search radar. The ETC indicated you might already know, but two parts failed, and one is a cooling water valve that we don't carry on board. Just talked to the chief, and the message through supply requesting the part has not gone out yet. I asked him to get right on that."

"CIC called me when the radar failed. I got up and talked with the chief about it. I have also talked with Fred Watson. Everything is moving as it should. It turns out the Captain is going to be doing his vermin inspection with the Supply Department first. So, it could be a while before they can get to the message. And, that is okay."

"Sir, DD, I mean, a message asking for priority on a part, all we need to do is make sure we get them the right part number."

"Just let it alone, Jon. The Captain has set the priority for today.

The priority is cockroaches. This situation with the radar is under control. Let it alone. Now I need to take this," he indicated some papers he had been working on, "to the XO. Go back to the Locker. Read a book. Write a letter. Just lay low for a while."

Jon was trying to figure out what to say next, but nothing he thought of seemed to fit. He left after officer's country and walked forward, past the ET shop. The top part of the French door to the ship's office was open, and the YN1 was sitting at his desk reading some correspondence.

Jon rapped on the side of the door and said, "Hey, YN1, I saw the Captain leave here a few minutes ago. What did he want?"

YN1 Gilpin looked up. He took the reading glasses off the end of his nose and laid the glasses on his desk. He got up and walked to the door, opened the bottom part, and said, "Come on in, sir."

Jon entered, and the YN1 closed the bottom and top halves of the door and locked them.

"Sir, ever since the business with the shellback certificate, and every day since we left Zamboanga, the Captain comes in here, sometime between 0530 and 0800, and he wants to see every piece of correspondence from the day before. This morning, he found the documentation on getting Zambowski reinstated to third class, and he tore up all the paperwork and threw it in the trash can."

A number of things boiled in his brain. Jon was mortified that he wouldn't be able to deliver on his promise to Zambowski after he'd lived up to his end of the bargain. He was chagrined to discover that the Captain could wipe out the arrangement after he had worked on it for so long. When he thought about how he'd compromised his own integrity by lying to help the Captain look like he was right, Jon was ashamed. And now the CO was taking it out on Zambowski. More than anything else, Jon was just angry.

"Well, I have copies of everything," Jon said. "You said the Captain comes in here every morning?"

"Yes, sir, he does," YN1 Gilpin said. "Since I didn't do what he wanted, forge the shellback certificate for him; he thinks he has to keep his thumb on me."

"Holy, Mary, Mother of God," Jon said.

"Pray for us sinners, now, and at the hour of our death, Amen," Petty Officer Gilpin finished.

"Are you a Catholic, YN1?"

"Well, sir, I was baptized, but my wife and I go to Lutheran church now."

"Well, I am not sure I was praying or cursing. Guess praying is the better course with this business with the Captain." Jon looked at the YN1. "How're you holding up? You need some help with anything? Should I talk to the Operations Officer or the XO about all this?"

"Sir, the XO knows. I see him every day anyway, just on normal ship's business. He knows. So, no, you don't need to do anything."

Jon found the door to the XO's cabin open. The XO was at his desk, and he looked up when Jon knocked on the bulkhead beside the door.

"Good morning, Jon. What can I do for you?"

"Sir, I just stopped by the ship's office. YN1 says the Captain comes in there every morning to check on all the correspondence from the day before. But, I guess you know that, don't you?"

"I know."

"I'm worried about YN1. When that business over the Captain's shellback status came up, YN1 was a bit reluctant to go to you with it. I basically promised him I would do what I could to look out for him. I am not sure I can really live up to what I promised, you know, being a whale-poop ensign and all."

"In the first place, Jon, all of us have a moral and ethical obligation to do the right thing. You were right to bring the matter to me and to encourage him to talk to me. You know how in the Bible, Peter kind of takes it in the shorts for denying Christ three times? He had the courage to go, so to speak, to face the dragon in his den. Then, the dragon comes out, and Peter is there looking at the dragon as it opens its mouth. Down there inside, you can see a cigarette lighter flicking as the little gnome who lives in the dragon tries to get the pilot light lit on his fire-breathing apparatus. Peter's courage failed at that point. Perhaps if Peter had had someone like you to encourage him, he'd have stayed. YN1 did the right thing. He is really happier with himself than if he'd just done what the Captain wanted. And, I am trying to watch out for him. Okay?"

"Okay, sir. Thanks. But also this morning, the Captain found the paperwork on reinstating Zambowski. He tore it all up and trashed it. I do have copies of all of it. Before I do anything else with it, can I talk to you about it, sir?"

The after door to the wardroom opened. DD came through to the XO's doorway, and Jon stood aside to let DD in.

"Jon," the XO said as he pulled his wheel book from his pocket and wrote a note in it, "I will talk to DD about this, and we will get back to you. Just get your paperwork together and wait for DD to call you. Don't do anything until one of us talks to you. Now, he and I need to work on something that can't wait. Okay?"

"Get the hell out of here, right, XO?" Jon said.

XO waved his left hand in dismissal, and then he pushed the door shut.

Read a book the Ops O had said. Lay low for a while, he had said. It felt a bit like when he had been in hack. Something was going on that he was not part of.

Jon grabbed the chair out of the corner and pulled it up next to the fold-down desk.

Write a letter, the Ops O had said. That was one part of Jon's life that seemed to have come back together.

Dearest Teresa,

Going back to the letter I got from you when we refueled a couple of days ago, you talked about the tea that the XO's wife hosted for the new Captain's wife. You mentioned Charlie's wife, Melanie, dropping the teacup and how the XO's wife just sliced her apart. A couple of things from that. First of all, it just really seems funny that the XO's wife would be so hurtful over a broken teacup. Maybe I don't understand teacups. Out here, the XO is understanding, and he always seems to know just what to say to me, not when I was in trouble with the former Skipper, but when things started off bad with the new Captain. You and I have talked before about how strange some couples seem to be together, like what did he see in *her*. Why did she marry *him*? So when Melanie went out to her car crying, I wasn't surprised to hear that you went out to her, but it really sounded funny that the Captain's wife went, too. That is so different from the way the Captain is out here. Since he arrived, he has not shown one ounce of concern for anyone but himself. So, it's like the wives of the XO and the Captain are completely the opposite of what the Captain and XO show us.

Anyhow, the Captain's wife sounds like a nice person.

Jon filled up two pages of writing about Teresa and her life back in San Diego. Once a month, he liked to send Teresa a poem, and she liked to receive them. He always wrote a poem on the anniversary of their first date in high school. That was coming up in a couple of weeks. He had been working on a poem recounting their history, from that first date, the separation after he'd enlisted in the navy, finally getting married while he was in college, their inability to get Teresa pregnant at first, and a few other things. He was kind of pleased with himself at how he ended it. The last two lines were about underthings and angel wings.

Tutu entered the Locker and moved up to his locker. From his elevation, he could see Jon's tablet and see the form of the letter. "So, Two Buckets," Tutu said. "It looks like a poem about underthings. Care to share with another horny sailor?"

Jon blushed and perspired furiously. "Tutu, that's—" He stopped. Anything he said would only make the situation worse.

"Hey, Two Buckets, I was just kidding. Sorry." Tutu punched him on the thigh, and then a look of worry crossed his face. "I didn't hurt you, did I?"

"Tutu, you wouldn't hurt a fly. Cockroaches, on the other hand—"

"Cockroaches? Are you implying something, Two Buckets?"

Jon sat up and dangled his legs over the side of the bunk.

"No, not implying, saying. I think a lot of us know, probably even the Captain. The F U on the pillow was a bit much."

"If the Captain knows, then why is he making us tear the ship apart?"

"I don't know why the Captain does what he does. I do know he is not stupid. Too driven by what he thinks other people think of him, maybe."

"And you think the XO knows, Two Buckets?"

"He knows."

"Why hasn't he nailed me on it then?"

"The XO has a lot on his plate right now. I can't say why he hasn't nailed you on this, but I will say that if the XO thought nailing you would make our situation on *Manfred* better, your hairy hide would be nailed to the roll-up door on the helo hangar right now."

"Well, I am not going to stop fighting that bastard. Do you know what really set me off? I was helping Seaman Alvey with an application for taking the GED. The Captain found the application and tore it up. Petty Officer Gilpin in the ship's office would only tell me that the Captain disapproved the request. The YN3 later told me the Captain said that that Negro had gotten enough special attention from the Ensign Locker."

Tutu related that he had gotten to know him when Alvey helped shepherd Tutu's laundry through the process just after Tutu had arrived on the ship. Tutu thought Alvey was smart, exceptionally squared away, and thought Alvey ought to be striving for something other than steward. Tutu had spoken to Petty Officer Banks, Carl Lehr's leading petty officer, and one of the senior Negro petty officers aboard. Banks had said that Ensign Stewart had seemed to adopt Alvey as his personal salvation project. Banks thought Ensign Stewart was more interested in having some way to fight the navy establishment than he was in helping Alvey. It'd be best to just stop trying to do special things for Alvey, Banks said.

"So," Tutu said, "it just seemed like everybody was ganging up on Alvey. I decided helping him get a GED was something no one should be able to argue with. But, the newbie Captain did. Now I'm working on what to do next." Tutu's brow wrinkled in deep thought. "I wish we had a rat aboard."

"Tutu, listen to me. You can't go head-on after the Captain. You have to think about this. Be careful picking the time and place. For right now, let it alone. Let's work this thing together and see what we can come up with. So will you do it this way? Will you let me help with it?"

"Well, I'll think about it."

"Tutu, we are just about back in the combat zone again, and we need to be clear on what we are after here. Are we after the Captain, or are we trying to help Alvey? If it's Alvey, I think we really need to be careful and really think about what we do next. Promise me. Don't do anything until we have a chance to talk about things and really weigh the pluses and minuses. Promise?"

"You said 'we?'"

Jon nodded.

"Not to change the subject or anything, but we are firing the fifty-caliber machine guns right after lunch. Admiral Ensign said I could fire a couple of rounds. You want to come up?"

He had changed the subject rather abruptly, but Jon decided to drop the subject.

"Sure," Jon said. "I never fired a fifty before."

41

At 1330, two dozen sailors were on the 01 level amidships for the fifty-caliber machine gun firing practice. DD was the senior officer present. Edgar Chalmers and Jon were the other officers present. Two gunner's mates supervised the firing evolution for those who would stand watches on the machineguns. A few spectators observed from the bridge wings and the signal bridge. *Manfred* was steaming north, heading back to the combat zone, and still in a diamond formation with the three other ships. The port gun would be used so they could fire away from the formation.

The enlisted crews who stood watches on the guns would fire first. Petty Officer First Class McGilfrey was instructing the first crew on safety precautions, and Jon stood with Edgar to the side and rear of the group.

"I thought Greg Haywood was going to be here," Jon said to Edgar.

"The Captain is looking for cockroaches in the Bosun Locker right now," Edgar said. "So, he and the Gun Boss are there for that.

I'm sure Tutu will be up here before we are done firing. He is freakier over guns than Cowboy was."

Tat-tat-tat sounded from the machine gun.

"Good," GM1 McGilfrey said. "Short bursts. See where the rounds go. Adjust, then give 'em another three to five rounds."

Edgar inserted himself into the schedule as the fifth person to fire. After he fired twenty rounds, he went below to escort the Captain through his division spaces. After the rest of the enlisted men fired their training rounds, DD took a turn, and Jon would fire last. While DD was firing, Greg Haywood came stomping up the ladder on the starboard side, making more noise than the machine guns made.

"You got here just in time, Greg," Jon said. "I am the only one who hasn't fired. So, how did the cockroach inspection go?"

"He didn't find any roaches, but he did find a couple of silverfish and roly-polies," Greg said. "He looked at me like he thought I was guilty of something."

The smile of a mischievous imp played across the face of the large man. Jon didn't say anything, and Greg walked closer to the machine gun and watched DD complete firing his rounds.

Jon let Greg fire after DD completed his rounds. Then, Jon fired twenty rounds and went back to the Ensign Locker. At 1615, he was laying on his stomach on his bunk, writing, when the ship's announcing system came abruptly to life with "Flooding, flooding in the after crew's head."

That kind of announcement was rare, but things happened aboard ship. Old pipes or fittings burst. Sometimes a sailor made a mistake. Sometimes an announcement like that didn't even hint at how serious the problem was. Jon waited for a minute to see if there would be another announcement. When nothing further was said, he went back to his letter.

A few minutes later, Admiral Ensign burst through the door to the Locker. "Holy shit, holy shit! You won't believe what just happened. We almost shot the Captain with a fifty caliber!"

Jon rolled onto his side. Back in a deep corner of his brain, Tutu, followed by a question mark, suddenly appeared. It was like turning a corner on a trail and coming across a snake sunning.

"I'm not kidding," Admiral Ensign said. "We had just entered the armory, aft. The fifty-caliber firing had just completed, and the gunners brought the fifty down and had it on a table in the office area outside the armory. They were going to clean it and then take it back to the 01 level again when the inspection was over. The Captain walked right in front of the barrel and was getting ready to look into some of the angle irons along the bulkhead with his flashlight when the gun fired. Missed the Captain's butt by probably three inches."

"But that would mean they brought a loaded gun into the armory," Jon said. "I was the last to fire, and I saw two of the gunners, including the first class, look in the breech and confirm it was not loaded. So did somebody deliberately load it after the gun got back to the armory?"

There was a knock, and the door to the Locker opened. It was a third-class yeoman from the ship's office.

"Sirs," the YN3 said. "XO sent me to get both of you. He needs you in the wardroom to write up your statements regarding the fifty-caliber firing."

When they got to the wardroom, Lieutenant Timmons, the Gun Boss, was there with GM1 McGilfrey, who had supervised the fifty-caliber firing evolution.

"Yes, sir," McGilfrey said. "We did check the breech. Three of us, including me, looked to see if it was loaded before we broke it down and took it below. We were all looking for the same thing, though. We were looking for shiny brass, but when we looked, we all saw black in the breech. We thought the weapon was unloaded."

"God, we were lucky," the Gun Boss said, shaking his head. "I hate relying on luck."

The Gun Boss impaled McGilfrey with a stern accusatory look. "Sorry, Gun Boss," McGilfrey said and looked down like a chastised schoolboy.

There was a knock on the wardroom door, and Senior Chief Petty

Officer Fire Control Technician Berthold entered and stood near the ensign end of the table.

"Gun Boss, here's the culprit," Berthold said, holding up the base of a fifty-caliber cartridge. "The spent-round extractor ripped the base of the cartridge off the shell without extracting the unfired round. It must have happened on the last round, or there would have been a jam. So GM1, was there a jam on the last firing?"

"No, Senior Chief," GM1 McGilfrey said. "It was Ensign Zachery firing. I had been showing him how to fire in short bursts, correct, and fire again. It didn't jam."

Senior Chief Berthold said, "Gun Boss, here's a message we had in the fifty-caliber file in the armory. It warns of this type of failure happening every once in a while. The base of the shell is ripped off. Then the shell just sits there in the hot barrel until enough heat is absorbed by the brass shell casing to cook off the gunpowder, and the gun fires."

"Thanks, senior chief," the Gun Boss said. McGilfrey snuck a peek at the Gun Boss's face; then, he quickly looked away again. "Now, Edgar, Jon, GM1, I need you to sit down and write a statement saying what you saw and what you know about this. Don't leave until you give me your statement, and I read it and tell you that you are dismissed. Senior Chief, get all the others up there during the firing and the cook-off in the armory together on the 01 level. When you have them assembled, come back here, please, and get me. I want to talk to them and see if they have anything to add before we have all of them writing they didn't see anything. And, I am going to have to close out this report with some corrective action. I'd like your help with that, along with Ensign Chalmers, and you, too, McGilfrey. Okay?"

The Senior Chief pushed open the door, but before he could leave, Paul Becker charged in and blurted, "Seen the XO?"

"No," the Gun Boss said. "I spoke to him on the phone from the armory, right after the gun went off. He was in his cabin then."

"I'll brief him later, then," Paul said. "For your purposes, here's the Engineering input. The round penetrated the bulkhead between the armory and the after crew's head, then hit the saltwater flushing valve in one of the crappers, then hit a stainless steel washbasin on the other side of the head before coming to a stop against an angle iron in the after bulkhead. So the flooding was just saltwater flushing piping that had to be contained, not a big deal. But there was a kid sitting on the crapper next to the one that was hit. The kid said he had the most complete bowel movement he's ever had but that he wants a flak jacket to use the next time he goes in that head. And, he asked if he would get a Combat Action Medal for what happened. So no one was hurt, and that kid, he's really pretty cool about it."

The door to the wardroom opened again, and the XO entered, stopped, and looked at those sitting at the table and writing statements. The Gun Boss gave him a summary.

"Captain okay?" the Cheng asked.

"The Captain, well, I think the medical guys would say he's *okay*," the XO said. "But Cheng, see if you can find DD, then I'd like to see you, DD, and the Gun Boss in my cabin right away—uh, assuming all the immediate crises are under control."

For just an instant, the XO stood there, just inside the door to the wardroom, with all eyes on him. Then, he gave a barely perceptible shake of his head as if to cast off the mental, moral, and emotional demons besetting him for the moment, and then he walked to his cabin.

Jon watched the XO walk past the ensign end of the wardroom table. At least Tutu didn't have anything to do with the incident. He was sure that was definite…maybe.

42

Jon lay on his back on his bunk, his hands clasped under his head, *Leaves of Grass* open and resting on his belly, and stared up at the overhead. He had never had a book of poetry before. Reading a novel, he read until he had no more time to read. A book of short stories was the same. He read one story, and if he had reading time left over, he'd read another story. Poetry was different. He decided he'd only read a single poem and then do something else, pick up another book, history, fiction. It didn't matter. Write a letter.

Write a letter. He took out his stationery box and told Teresa about reading Whitman's *Song of the Open Road*.

> Poetry is different from prose. Prose is straightforward.
> The writer writes facts from the historical world, or
> in fiction, from the created world. The language in
> poems, however, is layered with shades of meaning
> covering fact. Not changing truth to something else

but covering truth with shades of meaning evocative of the truth. I don't know if this makes sense, but it is how I'm thinking about it now. So, I am going to make a pact with myself. I will never read more than one poem at a sitting. I will let it stew until I can try to sort those shades of meaning. Sometimes it isn't all that hard. I just read, "You have done such good to me I would do the same to you."

Thinking about it, that is what you are to me. Good. And you have done nothing but good to me since that day Cupid stuck his arrow in my gizzard. And I wish I could do the same to you, but I'm just a goober guy, and I screw things up.

Through those five years before we were married, I wanted nothing but to be married to you. And then we were, and I thought, Whoopie! The answer to all my dreams and all my prayers. But the problem was I didn't know how to be married to you. And I'd forgotten about the "for worse" part of our vows. So we've had some <u>for worse</u> stuff to contend with, and I hope and pray we have contended and that we can get back to doing and being good for each other.

And I pledge to you, Teresa Velmer Zachery, that I will strive each day to try to figure out how to be properly married to you.

Admiral Ensign walked in. "Just found out, *Reilly* is not going to North SAR, either. *Monacher* and *Spenthe* will go back up there. And we will reenter the combat zone at noon tomorrow, so three-section watches should start then."

"*Monacher* and *Spenthe*," Jon said. "They were supposed to be going off the line. I thought *Reilly* and *Carmody* were going to North SAR."

"That was the old plan. That's the way it goes sometimes. It happened to my dad a couple of times during the Korean War. We expected him home for Christmas once, and he never even made it by Easter."

"Rough on the guys who had liberty close enough to taste. What was wrong with Reilly and Carmody manning north SAR?"

"You know, Two Buckets, if the decisions of higher authority started making sense to ensigns, that would bode a pretty crappy future for the navy."

The door to the Ensign Locker pulled open. Tutu ducked his head and stepped inside.

"That's bull," Tutu said. "If higher authority on this tub made sense to this ensign," he thumped his chest like a silver-backed gorilla male, "our future would look a lot better. I guess the great cockroach-hunting safari is over for the moment. My guys had had all of the crap out of the paint locker for the inspection in the morning. We just got the word to put it all back in the paint locker. The inspection in the morning is off. Why couldn't they tell us before we unloaded the paint locker?"

Admiral Ensign said, "Tutu, if anyone is to blame for any part of the cockroach safari, as you put it, you should go in the head and look in the mirror. You'll see the guilty bastard."

"Oh, how you talk, Admiral Ensign," Tutu said. "I may have to sue you for slandering my good name if you persist in these false and baseless accusations."

Tutu was stripping off his sweaty, soiled wash khakis when his wheel book fell out of his shirt pocket, and a small metal tool clattered onto the deck.

Admiral Ensign picked up the tool. "This looks like a lock pick. Maybe my accusation isn't baseless."

Tutu bent over to look at the piece of metal in Admiral Ensign's hand and said, "You know, I think you're right. That could be a lock pick."

"Here," Admiral Ensign said, holding out the pick toward Tutu.

Tutu recoiled. "It's not mine, and I'm not getting my fingerprints on that thing. You might want to consider throwing that thing overboard. You wouldn't want to be caught with something like that on you."

Tutu wrapped a towel around himself and started for the shower.

"Real nice tutu, Tutu," Admiral Ensign said.

Tutu stopped and looked back into the room; then, he decided against saying anything further and left for the shower, his right hand holding the towel closed. The towel made a band of white between hairy, swarthy back and even hairier tree trunk legs.

The next day at 1145, when Andrew Dunston and Jon arrived on the bridge to take over the watch from Don Minton and Charlie Hanson. The XO was in the chair on the port side of the bridge. The Captain's chair was empty. No one had seen him since the fifty-caliber cook-off.

Andrew, Jon, and the two off-going officers were all on the starboard bridge wing.

"So here's the situation," Don Minton said. "The navy fleet weather center has concluded all threat from Mamie is over. As of now, we are reassembling the fleet in the Tonkin Gulf. Operations against North Vietnam will start again at noon tomorrow."

Don Minton pointed to the ships in formation. "Nothing new by way of formation. There's *Reilly* in front. *Monacher* is there abeam, and *Spenthe* is astern. We are heading northwest. At noon the formation breaks up. *Reilly* will head for the DMZ, the other two ships will set a course for North SAR station, and we will turn south and head for the mouth of the Saigon River. We have already sent a flashing light signal to *Spenthe* telling her our intentions, so the formation break-up should be a benign affair. Andrew, are you comfortable taking the watch now, or do you want us to keep it until after the formation breaks up?"

"No need for you guys to stay up here," Andrew said. "I'm ready to take it."

Andrew reported to the XO that he had relieved Don Minton of the deck and that Jon had the conn. Jon walked out onto the port bridge wing to ensure it would be safe to turn to the left in five minutes.

At 1200, the Bosun Mate struck eight bells, and the bridge tactical radio circuit came to life. The Commodore on *Reilly* dissolved the formation and told the three ships to proceed on duty assigned. Jon ordered a left standard rudder from the starboard bridge wing and watched the *Reilly* turn slightly to the left. *Monacher* and *Spenthe* held their present course, but they sped up to twenty-two knots. Just after *Manfred* steadied on the course to Vung Tau and the mouth of the Saigon River, the bridge phone talker said, "Officer of the Deck, signal bridge says they see a sailor on the signal bridge on *Spenthe* who is flipping us the bird."

From his chair inside the pilothouse, the XO said, "And well, he might. We just may have screwed them out of their chance to visit Hong Kong and probably got them extended an extra month before they can go home."

The XO climbed out of his chair, walked out onto the starboard bridge wing, and took a look at the three ships falling away to the north.

"Mr. Dunston," the XO said, "I'm going to be in my cabin. Make all calls to me, not the Captain, until further notice."

"Aye, sir," Andrew said.

"And Mr. Zachery," the XO turned toward me, "when you get off watch, stop by my cabin. I should be there."

"XO is off the bridge," the Boatswain Mate announced.

After Jon got off watch, he found the door to the XO's cabin open and the XO sitting at his desk. He knocked on the bulkhead next to the door.

"Come in," the XO said. "Have a seat on the couch there."

The XO handed Jon a sheet of paper. It was official correspondence from the Commanding Officer, USS *Manfred*, addressed to Seaman

Zambowski, reinstating him to third class petty officer, effective immediately. It was signed by the XO for the Captain.

"You look worried, Jon," the XO said.

"Sir, I… Well, sir, you've got an awful lot on your plate these days. You sure you want to go into this now?"

"I'm sure. Trying to take proper care of the crew is the only thing I feel good about right now. So, yes, tell me what you're worried about."

"Well, sir, you signed this for the Captain, but he goes into the ship's office each day, I presume, because he doesn't want anyone to slip something past him. I'm worried about the validity of this document. And will the Captain just tear it up and keep Zambowski a seaman when he goes in to check correspondence tomorrow? I don't want to get Zambowski's hopes up and then dash them."

"First of all, let me say how pleased I am that you are this concerned over one of your troops. Whether we are out here or back in port in San Diego, it is easy for the navy system to steamroller the troops. And, it's easy for the good ones to get overlooked by a system that is most comfortable looking at all of us as faceless, soulless bodies with service numbers. I just want you to know I appreciate what you're doing for Zambowski.

"But I'm wondering, did you have a path forward for reinstating your sailor?"

"Yes, sir, I did. What I thought was that the normal procedure, which would be to appeal the Captain's ruling to the next senior in the chain of command, had a snowball's chance in hell of coming to anything. The Commodore would just have disapproved it out of hand. So, my plan was to write a personal letter, from me to the head of the Bureau of Personnel, with copies to the Captain, the Commodore, and to CruDesPac, and a copy to you and DD of course."

The XO smiled, and kind of snorted a *humph* through his nose.

"Let me give you a couple of lines on what you were thinking about doing. You care about your troops, which, as I've said, I admire. Also, I think you are the kind of person who sees good or bad in terms of black or white. When you do that, you get into a mode that I've seen young officers use before. It's like you pull a pin out of a grenade, roll it across the floor, then say, 'Oh, look, a grenade;' and you hurl your body on the grenade, expecting your guts splattered all over the walls will be a dramatic statement that will make people see the rightness of the way you see an issue. That's probably what your letter directly to BUPERS would have done, stepping around the entire chain of command. Splattered your guts all over the wall, or bulkhead, if you want to be nautical about it. Do you see that?"

"Yes, sir. I pretty much knew that would probably be what happened to me, but I hoped the navy would know that I knew that and listen to the request for Zambowski."

"See. Grenade on the floor, but there would have been a pretty low probability that your guts on the bulkhead would have had your desired outcome. Do you see that?"

"Yes, sir, but I didn't see any other options. I also thought I'd be doing something very much like Dormant did. That was almost enough to make me not want to do it, but what other recourse does a whale-poop ensign have when you see something is really wrong with the way a CO is doing something?"

"There may be a time when you have to do the grenade thing," the XO said. "Your sense of right and wrong, and what is ethical, may drive you to do something like that. I'd just advise you to consider that carefully because the consequences to you are fatal, in a career sense. Even more importantly, you need to have a little faith in your navy. It's not the Captain or me doing this to Zambowski. It's the navy. And a third thing, you need to weigh the value of Zambowski to the navy versus your own value."

"I wasn't thinking about this in terms of value to the navy. I just saw the Captain using his position and power to screw over a junior enlisted man. And he was doing it because he has it in for me and the Ensign Locker. So, I can't help but think what he was doing to Zambowski was just to get at me."

"I understand how you were looking at it, but I'd like you to try to look at this from another perspective, from the navy perspective. As a nation, we were not prepared for World War I, we were not prepared for World War II, and then, five years later, we got into another war in Korea, and we weren't ready for that, either. Now we're in Vietnam, and I ask you. Does it look like we're ready to be here either?

"This is what I want you to think about. We can't do much to fix things that are wrong with the army, air force, marines, or coast guard, but each of us, as naval officers, can do a lot to support and improve our navy. So, I am proposing to you that as you consider right and wrong in situations like we are talking about, you need to see the value of a prepared military and a prepared navy to the future well-being of our nation."

"So, you're saying whether my country or my navy is right or wrong, I support the navy and screw Zambowski?"

The XO let out a sigh. He was sitting at the chair by his desk, his forearms resting on his thighs. He looked down at his opened hands. Then he clenched the hands into fists, looked up, and into Jon's eyes. His face, often soft-looking with his little saggy cheek jowls, looked hard. Abruptly, he stood up and crossed to where Jon was sitting. Jon leaned back, thinking for a moment that the XO was going to hit him. Instead, he grabbed Jon by the ears.

"If you are not going to use these things," he hissed, "I might just as well rip them off."

The XO let go. Jon wanted to put his hands up and check that his ears were still attached, but he didn't.

"I give you credit for some intellect," the XO said. "Don't disappoint me on that score."

He sat back down, resumed his posture, and leaned forward a bit with his hands on his knees.

"There are issues here," the XO's soft look was back, "that are bigger than you and me, bigger even than Zambowski. Think about this.

"Say we have a serious fire in a compartment, and you have to send Zambowski into the burning compartment. It is the only way to save the ship. There is a 90% chance he will be killed, and there is less than a fifty-fifty chance he will be able to save the ship, but you have to do it because it is the only chance you have. You might be in a position like that someday, and if you haven't thought about it beforehand, you will never pull a good decision out of your ass in the heat of the moment."

"I wouldn't send Zambowski or anyone into a situation like that. I'd go in myself," Jon said.

"Yeah, Jon." The softness was back in the XO's face. "I'm sure you would if we can't get another aspect into your thinking. Truth be told, I'd probably do the same thing. But right before he left, the Skipper talked to me about the officers aboard, and the Ensign Locker in particular, and he gave me the set up I just gave you: The ship is on fire, and you are in desperate straights. You could lose the ship unless you send a guy into a flaming compartment. Odds are 90% that the kid will die. Odds are 55% that you will still lose the ship. The Skipper asked me who, out of our Ensign Locker, would send the guy into the flaming compartment with no hesitation. We went over all of you, and he said you were the only one who'd send the guy in. And then he said you'd start worrying about what needed to be fixed next. The Skipper said, 'That's why I like that little son-of-a-bitch. Not because he can drive a ship or do a John Wayne with the marines, but because he will take a kid that he loves more than any other division officer loves one of his men, and he will send him into the compartment. He can be a cold-blooded bastard when he has to be."

It was quiet for a moment.

"Your mouth is hanging open, Jon."

"Yes, sir, and, uh, thanks for Zambowski. Thanks for talking with me as you have."

Jon reached up with his left hand and rubbed that ear.

The XO chuckled. "Both of them are still there. Anything else?"

"No, sir. And thanks again for Zambowski."

"You're welcome," the XO said. "Now, get the hell out of here."

43

Deck Log entry for 21 August: 1200 to 1600. Steaming south at 15 knots. 1300 passed abeam point Mui Ca Nu. 1400 altered course to 225. 1430 received Swift Boat number 236 alongside, Lieutenant (jg) Tom Lang, boat commander. LT (jg) Lang reported destroying a junk with weapons and medical supplies on the beach just north of Mui Ca Nu at 0430 this date. 1500 Swift Boat 236 cast off and headed northeast to return to base.

After Jon completed writing the log, Andrew, as OOD, signed it.

When he entered the Ensign Locker, Tutu was at the fold-down desk. He had a navy document open on the desk, and he was writing on a tablet of lined paper.

"That looks like official correspondence, Tutu," Jon said. "What're you doing?"

"Applying for duty on Swift Boats."

"What! Those guys let you fire grenades into the water, and you march right into the ship's office and apply for Swift Boats! Shouldn't you think about this a bit? Have you talked with the Gun Boss about it?"

When the Swift Boat had been alongside, Tutu had climbed aboard and fired some of the weapons the crew had.

"You're such a simpleminded dweeb, Two Buckets. I'm not applying because they let me fire the M-79 grenade launcher. I'm applying because they have ensigns and JGs as boat commanders. I'd be in charge of my own boat, and I wouldn't be just pond scum to a starched shirt coward who pees his pants when we get close to the beach."

"I don't think that's fair, Tutu. He peed his pants when the fifty went off and almost hit him."

"I can't believe you're sticking up for him. There were other guys in the armory when the round cooked off. Admiral Ensign said his gunner was as close to the barrel as the Captain was. None of the others left a puddle. Anyhow, I'm applying, and I can make my own decisions. I don't need input from the former alcoholic Gun Boss."

Jon squeezed past Tutu, untied his shoes, stepped out of them, and climbed up onto his bunk.

"You know, Tutu, Cowboy had looked into Swift Boats, and PBRs, too, for that matter. He found out they both have a pool of applicants. Lots of people are applying for both, it seems. There is a nine-month waiting list according to what Cowboy found out."

"Yeah, I know. I talked to the XO. He told me about the waiting list, and he said I should get the application to him ASAP. If I didn't know better, I'd think he's trying to get rid of me."

Tutu signed the document and looked at Jon.

"Haven't seen the CO for three days. Word is he's ill. You hear anything, Buckets?"

"Just that."

Tutu looked like he was going to say something else but thought better of it and left to get his application to the XO.

For the next two days, the deck log entries were the same.

> Anchored in Saigon River. Commanding officer is ill but not incapacitated. Firing H&I rounds into the Rung Sat district. Fired one-hundred-two rounds this watch.

The ship was firing a lot of rounds. The current in the river oriented the bow, sometimes upriver, sometimes down. At times the forward gun mount was used; other times, the after. On Jon's 0400 to 0800 watch, the forward mount fired with the mount swung around as far as it would go so that the barrels were pointed aft of abeam by some thirty degrees. When they fired, the concussive force could be felt on the bridge wing. The lookout on that side was brought into the pilothouse, and the door to the wing secured. During that watch, Jon also noted that the concussive force of the muzzle blast had knocked loose some of the metal straps binding cables to the mast. The cables connected all manner of electronics equipment to antennae. Jon pointed out the loose cables to Andrew.

Andrew said, "Yeah, the vibration from all the shooting is beating the crap out of a lot of engineering equipment, too. Pipes are springing leaks. Pumps are crapping out. I don't know if we are hurting the VC or not, but we are sure beating the snot out of ourselves."

"Tutu said he figured the odds at two percent that we were hurting the VC. He said we should change the name from H&I to WTFO."

Andrew looked at Jon with a question mark all over his face.

Jon said, "Wishful Thinking Firing Operation."

"You put WTFO in the log, Jon. You sign it. I won't."

Then Andrew called the evaluator, and firing ceased while the after gun mount was manned. Firing resumed from there. By the time Jon got off watch, his technicians were climbing the mast to wire the antennae cables snuggly in place.

Sailors were meant to be on ships, and ships were meant to be at sea.

At sea, not anchored in the Saigon River firing guns all day and all night. At sea, normal meant supporting the marines while steaming a couple of miles off the coast. Those couple of miles, Jon reflected, consisted of a huge *grunch* of safety.

Grunch. Jon had heard Zambowski use that word, or non-word, and asked him what it meant.

"It means a great big bunch, sir. You know, like a navy acronym or something."

Jon made up words, too, and Teresa chided him, "That isn't a word."

"Yeah, but it ought to be," he'd reply.

In the ship's present circumstance, grunch seemed like a good way to express how much safer Jon would feel if the ship were out in the Tonkin Gulf, *where she ought to be.*

One good thing was the ship would depart the river at noon the next day. *Manfred's* magazines were about empty, and she needed fuel. The parts to fix the radar were also on board the oiler. And Ensign Zachery needed a letter.

During the rest of the day, the ship used the after gun mount to avoid more damage to the cabling running up the forward mast.

When Jon got relieved on the bridge at 2000, he went below to the Ensign Locker, shucked his clothes, climbed onto his bunk, and slept the sleep of an innocent.

Until GQ sounded at 0107.

Paul Becker manned the evaluator position in combat. The XO was with the CO. Paul ordered Jon to report to LT Timmons on the fantail, with, "Hop to it."

On the fantail, Jon found the lieutenant with a half dozen sailors around him. They were all staring aft, at a clump of driftwood in midriver about a hundred yards from the stern. A spotlight from the signal bridge illuminated the clump.

Jon announced himself.

"Jon," Timmons said, "get to the starboard motor whaleboat davit. Guys there will have a rifle and a .45 for you. Go check out that driftwood. See if there's someone hiding in it. VC do that sometimes. Hide in driftwood and attach explosives to the hull of a ship. We're at slack water right now, but the tide will start going out in twenty minutes. The XO wants to know if someone is hiding in the brush. But don't try to capture the person or anything like that. If there is a person in the brush, shoot him. Otherwise, he could trigger the explosives and take out you, the crew, and the boat. Hop to it."

When he arrived at starboard davit, the whaleboat had been lowered to main deck level. In the dim red light, Jon saw Seaman Sheffield, who had been slashed by the North Vietnamese on North SAR station, sitting in the bow of the boat. Jon climbed aboard and took the middle seat. An M-1 leaned against the seat, and a .45 in holster and belt lay on it. As Jon strapped on the handgun, he said, "Seaman Sheffield, you up for another boat ride with me?"

"Ready to go, Mr. Zachery. But if it's okay with you, I'd rather leave the boathook behind this time."

"Good thinking." Jon signaled the davit operator to lower them to the water.

Once in the water and clear of the ship, Jon called for a radio check over the walkie-talkie.

The XO responded, "Loud and clear."

One good thing, the river was smooth. It was the only good thing about being out there.

They puttered past the stern of *Manfred*. The coxswain had them headed right for the floating brush. Jon ordered him to come left, to keep some distance from the clump of debris. Once abeam the driftwood, Jon flicked on a handheld spotlight, and he saw the man hiding behind a log. Dark hair, young face. That was what he could make out.

The other sailor in the boat was Seaman Randolph.

"Randolph, take the walkie-talkie. Tell the XO there is a man in the driftwood. We are going to take him under fire. And tell him we are going to be busy for the next couple of minutes."

When Randolph completed the transmission, Jon said, "Okay, guys, I don't think your shotguns will be much good from this distance. Randolph, be ready to shoot anyway. I'm going to try to nail him with the M-1. Sheffield, take the spotlight."

The man was clearly illuminated. The gunsights, however, were not. Jon fired and hit the log. The second round splashed on the other side of the target. The third round threw the man's head back, and he sank. They watched for a few minutes, but the man didn't resurface.

Jon picked up the walkie-talkie and reported what had happened.

"Whale Boat," the XO replied, "return to the ship."

After they pulled alongside and the davit had hoisted the boat to main deck level, Jon stepped out of the boat. The XO was there to meet him.

"The PBR outfit is sending a boat with an EOD (Explosive Ordnance Disposal) tech aboard," the XO said. "They don't want us to shoot those logs up with our fifty cals. If are explosives there, those could just sink to the bottom, and the VC could retrieve them. So, hustle up to Combat and write up what happened."

DD was the evaluator. As Jon finished his report, a speaker crackled, "*Manfred*, PBR dash one, one, over."

DD responded.

"This is PBR dash one-one. There was a packet of explosives tied to the log, which we've retrieved. Also, we recovered the body of a VC sapper also tied to the log. It was a teenaged girl. We're returning to base."

"Uh, Jon," DD began.

In the red light in Combat, Jon could not see concern on DD's face, but he heard it in his voice.

"Secure from General Quarters. On deck, the 0400 to 0800 watch" sounded over the 1MC.

The clock on the bulkhead said 0330.

"Jon," DD said, "I'll get someone else to take your bridge watch."

"No!"

A couple of the radarmen turned to look at Jon.

Jon clamped control onto his voice. "I'll stand my watch." He handed the pad of paper, on which he'd written his report, to DD and walked out of Combat. Before the door closed, he heard, "He shot a girl, and he's just going to stand his watch?"

Stand my watch. That was a thought inside Jon's head.

Shot a girl. That was a thought that wanted to enter, but Jon kept that one outside. He couldn't deal with it just then. So he didn't deal with it. Just then.

When Jon entered the bridge, the XO was also concerned over Jon standing his watch, but Jon said he wanted to stand it.

"You sure?" the XO said.

Jon considered saying, "I need to stand my watch, Sir," but he worried the XO might just overrule what he wanted, needed to do, so he said, simply, "Yes, Sir."

"Okay then, relieve the JOOD," the XO said.

Jon was in the process of doing that when Andrew arrived on the bridge, and the XO immediately took him out onto a bridge wing and whispered to him.

Jon smiled. He knew what the XO was saying, and wasn't it funny? Ensign Two Buckets knew for certain exactly what the XO was telling Andrew. "Jon just shot a girl. It was a VC girl who wanted to blow us up, but a girl. So, keep an eye on him. Make sure he's okay."

44

The ship resumed firing H&I rounds from the after mount at 0545. Twenty rounds were fired, then, after a halt of thirty minutes, Combat notified the bridge that another dozen rounds would be expended. The *wham* of a single salvo boomed out, and a muted echo returned. Followed by protracted silence.

Andrew walked to the center of the pilothouse and pulled the phone to Combat from its mounting bracket.

The bridge phone talker said, "Ceasefire. Combat says we have a cease-fire."

Andrew buzzed Combat and asked what was going on. He listened for a moment, then hung up and turned around. "Quartermaster. Enter in the deck log. 0547. Discovered a crack in the main deck around the after gun mount. Ceased firing."

Before Jon got off watch, Cheng (the Chief Engineer) had assessed the crack as major structural damage. No guns should be fired until repairs were effected. After reporting the damage to the Commodore and the task force commander, *Manfred* was ordered to the Philippines for repairs. "Proceed at best safe speed," the orders read. Bad weather, with high winds, was expected in three days, and the ship was in no condition to withstand a pounding rough sea states.

CHENG suggested eighteen knots to the XO, and he agreed. But the CHENG would monitor the vibration and recommend reducing speed if necessary. CHENG also had a welder tack on a strip of steel over the crack. It wouldn't hold the ship together, but it would keep moisture out of the ammo handling room below the gun mount.

Andrew and Jon were relieved by the special sea detail crew, and *Manfred* was underway at 0720.

Jon descended to the Ensign Locker and took his Dopp kit into the head to shave. With only half the lather scraped off, there was a knock on the door, and it was pulled open.

A sailor wearing his dixie cup hat stood with his hand on the knob. Wearing his hat meant he was on duty, probably the messenger from the bridge watch.

"Sir, the Captain wants to see you in his cabin."

"The Captain?" Jon couldn't remember how many days it had been since they'd seen him. More than a few, though.

"Yes, sir, and he said right away."

Jon hustled through shaving, cut himself, then back in the Locker, he pulled out a clean shirt and fixed his ensign bars to the color points and started up the ladder while buttoning.

The XO was at his desk, and Jon knocked as he tucked in his shirttail.

"Captain just sent for me, sir. You know what for?"

The XO shook his head. "I'm going with you."

The XO charged past Jon and through the wardroom and up the ladders to the CO's cabin. Jon hung on his heels.

The XO knocked on the CO's door and opened it.

The Captain looked up from his desk. "I don't need you here, XO. I don't want you here. Zachery, come in."

The XO got out of Jon's way, and Jon entered.

"Close the door, Zachery."

Jon did.

The CO sat and stared at Jon.

"I need to know, Zachery. Can I trust you?"

"Well, uh—"

"Can I trust you? Answer the damned question."

Only one answer to that one!

"Yes, sir. You can trust me."

The CO said he couldn't trust a single other officer on board, but he knew he could trust Jon. The Captain said he knew the XO had been sending out messages behind his back that undermined his authority. The CO had to recapture his authority. He had to resume being the commanding officer, which the XO had usurped, thereby committing mutiny. Tom Snyder, the communications officer, had conspired with the XO.

There was a knock on the door.

When told to do so, Jon opened it.

Tom Snyder stood there.

"Come in, Mr. Snyder," the CO said. "And no need to close the door. You are relieved and are no longer communications officer. Ensign Zachery is. Turn over your duties to him, and then you are confined to quarters."

The CO turned fierce eyes onto Jon. "As soon as you are done with the turnover, search the crypto safes for copies of messages the XO might have hidden there, and then come back and see me with what you've found. Go."

"Uh, Captain," Jon said, "It could take some time. A couple of hours probably."

"I want you back here in thirty minutes."

Tom Snyder led the way down one ladder and stopped outside Radio Central. "What in Sam Hell is going on, Jon?"

"Wish I could tell you, but we don't have much time. We need to get that special file you have locked up in the crypto safe. Then we need to get to the XO."

Tom led them through Radio Central to the back room, which was filled with racks of equipment, and it provided access to the crypto room. Tom dialed in the combination and opened the door to find his leading petty officer sitting at the desk and typing.

"What are you doing?" Tom asked.

"Sir, this is an *Eyes Only* message the CO told me to type up. On the ship, I am the only one allowed to see it."

"Shit," Tom said.

Jon pushed by the former communications officer and pulled the message form from the typewriter. The petty officer reached for the paper, but Jon knocked his hand away.

"Eyes Only for Commodore Brass," Jon said. "My executive officer has fomented mutiny," Jon read.

"Fomented?" Tom said.

Jon continued reading. "He has turned the entire wardroom against me except for one ensign. It is my intention to steam north at flank speed toward your location. I request a half dozen responsible officers be helo-ed to *Manfred* as soon as we are in range. That should be enough to help me run the ship in the short term. Further, I request a board of inquiry be convened to examine the charge of mutiny, and if warranted to convene courts-martial for all who violated their oaths."

"Were you going to show that to the Captain, or were you to send it right away?" Tom asked.

"He wanted me to send it from his hand-written page, but it's hard to read his scribbles. So, I typed it. I was about to send it as soon as I had it encrypted."

"I'm the new communications officer," Jon said. "Wait here, and don't talk to anyone, including the CO. Understand?"

"PO1," Jon said, "You are not the only one who is in a position he doesn't want to be in. But I've given you an order. It is my opinion that the Captain is sick, that he is suffering from a nervous breakdown.

We need to get a handle on this situation. Stay right here in this room with the door locked. Do not talk to anyone, including the Captain."

Jon picked up the phone and dialed the XO. He picked up.

"XO. Tom and I have something we need to show you. We're coming right down." Jon hung up, opened the door, and pushed Tom through it. Then he hustled out of Radio Central and down the ladder to the main deck and into the passageway just aft of the wardroom, where he ran into, literally ran into, Tutu.

"Whoa up there. What's the big hurry."

"The CO," Tom said. "It's hit the fan."

"Tell you later," Jon said and hustled through the wardroom and into the XO's room and closed the door behind Tom. He explained about being called to the CO's cabin. He explained about Tom being fired, and he handed over the message the PO1 had typed.

"Shit, shit, shit."

"XO.," Jon said. "The CO expects me to report back to him in seventeen minutes. If I don't show up on time, I think things are going to get worse."

"Why me, God?" the XO said. "What, Zachery, even Jesus asked that of His Father. Me, I'm just a simple, sinful XO."

Then he shook his head, picked up the phone, and dialed.

He ordered the Gun Boss to have sailors bring twenty handguns and holsters to his cabin. Then, every officer was to assemble in the wardroom ASAP. Also, the Boss should check in the chief's mess. Every chief there should assemble in the wardroom.

Next, the XO called the Cheng and ordered him to wait fifteen minutes, then increase speed to twenty-two knots. That could get them to the PI ten hours sooner, he said. Put someone on the crack. Monitor it round the clock. "I'll call the bridge and tell them to crank on the extra knots. And Paul, I need you in the wardroom as quickly as you can get there."

The phone from the bridge rang, and the XO answered. At the same time, the 1MC blared, "Medical emergency in the CO's cabin. Medical emergency in the CO's cabin."

"What the hell's going on?" the XO said to the phone.

Peter Feldman, the OOD, said, "XO, the CO just tried to shoot himself. Tutu was walking by the CO's cabin and heard a gunshot. The door wasn't locked, so he went in and found the CO lying on his bunk. He'd apparently tried to shoot himself but missed. Tutu also found an empty vodka bottle on the deck. Tutu restrained the Captain and called the bridge."

Dec log USS *Manfred*: Commanding Officer suffered a nervous breakdown. Tried to commit suicide. LCDR Messenger assumed duty as acting Commanding Officer. Increased speed to twenty-two knots. After one hour, no adverse effect on crack in the main deck behind after gun mount. Speed increased to twenty-five knots. Expect to arrive at Subic Bay, PI, in thirty-six hours.

45

Dearest Teresa,

Lots to tell. The big news is we are coming home early! Our damage can't be repaired over here, so we need to come back to the States for repairs. I will call when we get to the PI, and I will see if I can figure out the right time to call, so I don't catch you in the middle of the night.

And even more news. Tom Snyder is going to be leaving when we get back to the PI. He is going to an Admiral's staff, the same staff where the Skipper, Commander Carstens, is now. And I am going to be the Communications Officer. ETC Fargo will take over the division officer duties for the electronics techs, and Don Minton will catch division officer duties for the yeomen and the corpsman. I spent the afternoon with Tom Snyder as he tried to pass on enough for me to get by in my new comm duties. Normally, I would have gone to school before getting this job. But, we are a long ways from normal on *Manfred* these days.

Also, Tutu and Admiral Ensign will leave us in the PI. Tutu is going to the same staff as Tom Snyder while he awaits orders to Swift Boats. Admiral Ensign is coming back to start flight training. So we are going to be down to twelve officers for the trip back. I guess they think that is okay for the transit.

But, all that news aside, it is so nice to be able to think about coming back home. Of course, that is still a month away. We have one or two weeks to spend in Subic for the repairs we need.

Jon didn't write much. It was too sleepy out.

Jon was at his safety observer position when *Manfred* moored port side to at Subic Bay. The Bosun announced, "Moored. Shift colors. The Officer of the Deck is shifting his watch from the bridge to the quarterdeck." Jon walked out onto the port bridge wing and descended the ladder to the 01 level. About thirty sailors had assembled there.

On the pier, two three-man groups waited for the brow to be put over. One group, a navy lieutenant commander, and two sailors carrying a folded-up stretcher, while a navy captain and two commanders comprised the other.

As a crane lowered the brow into place, Jon heard someone stomping down the ladder from the port bridge wing. The XO. In a hurry.

"Make a hole there," Jon shouted. "Clear away from the rail. Let the XO get by."

The clump of sailors peeled back, the XO hustled past them and down the ladder to the main deck, and the clump swept back to the rail.

Back on the fantail, as soon as the crew there had lashed the brow into place, the stretcher threesome filed aboard, and the XO led them down the port side. The sailors all watched them move forward, purposely, below them. Jon looked aft. The captain and commanders filed aboard. The Gun Boss met them and led them to the starboard side of the ship. They would take over the wardroom. They were the board of inquiry.

On the port side, the XO led the medical team inside at the door into the superstructure just aft of the wardroom.

From the messages that had gone out the day before, Greg Haywood and Tom Snyder would be the first two the inquiry board would question. Greg and Tom both had orders to the Tonkin Gulf Task Force commander's staff. They had US Air Force transportation to Saigon scheduled for that afternoon. The inquiry board had agreed to that as long as nothing came out of the interview requiring further investigation.

Please, God, help Tutu figure out what to say. And Tom, too, please.

The door onto the port side weather deck opened. A sailor backed out and guided one end of the stretcher. The second sailor followed. The former CO—the XO was now acting CO, again and made official by message yesterday—was strapped to the wheeled stretcher with his arms bound to his side.

The Captain was in pajamas. His hair was a mess, and he struggled against the straps. "Let me off this thing. They tried to kill me." He kept struggling against the straps during the entire trip from just aft of the wardroom to the quarterdeck, but the straps held him firmly in place. On the pier, the Ops O got in the ambulance with the medical personnel.

The ambulance drove down the pier.

Several of the sailors near Jon looked at each other. He didn't know what they were thinking. Jon, however, was pondering the oath he took to *Obey the orders of the officers appointed over me.*

Just after the ambulance drove up the pier, a gray passenger van stopped near the brow. Six men got out and walked across the brow. The CHENG met them. They had to be a crew from the Subic Bay shipyard to assess the crack in the fantail.

The sailors began to trickle away from their 01-level vantage point. Jon went to Radio Central. The only way to the Ensign Locker was through the wardroom, and that belonged to the board of inquiry for as long as they needed it. One of Jon's new duties included burning outdated crypto material and other classified documents. He set to work with two of his radiomen, inventorying and bagging up the documents to be destroyed. Classified material in general, but particularly classified crypto material, required meticulous record keeping. After Jon had stuffed six bags with crumpled-up documents, Tutu called Radio Central. He and Tom Snyder had completed their interviews and were departing. They were on the quarterdeck and wanted to say goodbye to Jon.

Jon left Radio, hustled aft, and found them on the starboard side of the fantail with bags and suitcases on the deck next to them.

Tutu's face busted into a grin. "Buckets! I'm glad you came back. I wanted to tell you not to worry about being interviewed by those inquiry guys. Tom and me, we got them all softened up."

"Softened up! You probably told them it was all my fault."

Tutu reached out and knocked Jon's barracks cover off. "He sure figured us out quick, didn't he, Tom?"

"Tom," Jon said, "how about dropping me a note when you get to the staff. The gorilla here can't write. And tell the Skipper, Commander Carstens, hello for me, please?"

"Will do. See ya, Jon,"

"And good luck, Tutu."

"Another good thing about getting off this tub. I'll leave that stupid name behind."

"Tom, you're not going to let that happen, are you?" Jon said.

Tom stuck out his hand to Jon. They shook and "Good Luck"-ed each other.

Tutu grabbed Two Buckets and hugged him, lifting Jon's feet off the deck.

Tutu put Jon down, slung his seabag strap over his shoulder, and lifted his hanging bag, and walked to the OOD, saluted, requested permission to go ashore, and walked over the brow and up the pier. He didn't look back. Tom followed him to a navy van that would take them to Clark Air Force Base, an hour's ride north.

Jon watched until the van turned off the end of the pier. He wondered what the future held for the two of them.

For that matter, I wonder what the future holds for Ensign Jon Two Buckets Zachery.

He shook his head and went back to bagging classified material to take to the incinerator on base the next day.

At lunch, the junior officers ate on the mess decks. The XO and department heads ate with the chiefs.

At 1530, the board called Jon to the wardroom.

The navy captain sat on the aft side of the table with the commanders beside him. Jon was invited to sit opposite the captain.

"Ensign Zachery," the captain said, "Just after you left the Saigon River, your former CO relieved the communications officer of his duties and appointed you to take his place."

The commander to Jon's left said, "Why did he do that?'

The one to the right said, "He didn't tell you why, did he?"

"No, sir. He did not tell me specifically why. He asked me if he could trust me. At that point, I don't think he trusted any of us, but he needed someone, and especially he needed a comm officer he could trust."

"So why would he trust you, a very junior officer?" Left Commander said.

Jon explained about the bet between CDR Peacock and himself over the repair of the IFF. "My opinion, sir, is the former CO was big on appearance. I also think he behaved much like a schoolyard bully. If he didn't get his way, he took it out on whoever was around. So, even though he lost the bet, I publicly said he was right, and I was wrong over the proper way to repair the IFF. I thought it would be better for every one of us aboard if I propped up his image. Rather than giving him something to get even for."

"Did you talk about this with any of the other officers?" from the captain.

"I did not, sir."

"You figured this all out on your own?" from Right Commander.

"Yes, sir."

Left Commander: "Your letters to your wife put CDR Carstens in a bad light with his superiors. Why would CDR Peacock trust someone who did that?'

"Sir, my letters put CDR Carstens in a bad light. Just like you said. Anyone who put his predecessor in a bad light was doing a good thing for CDR Peacock."

The three inquisitors looked at each other for a moment. Then the captain said, "You can go, Ensign Zachery."

The board of inquiry departed *Manfred* at 1700. At 1705, the XO called all the officers to the wardroom.

The Acting CO sat in his XO position. "The inquiry board gave me a dump on their findings: CDR Peacock had a severe anxiety disorder. He did not want the navy to know, so he went to a civilian doctor and had meds prescribed to treat his condition. He also abused alcohol. We found a half dozen bottles of vodka in his room in addition to his meds. He apparently stopped taking his meds, and his behavior deteriorated.

"When Ensign Haywood walked past the CO's cabin and heard the gunshot, he went inside and found CDR Peacock on his back in bed with a forty-five in his hand trying to aim the thing at his head. There was a bullet hole in the pillow next to his head. The ensign took the pistol away. An empty vodka bottle lay on the deck next to the bed. CDR Peacock struggled to get the gun back, and Ensign Haywood wound up with scratches on one arm from the fingernails clawing at him. Haywood then rolled the CO over onto his stomach, leaned on him to hold him in place, and called the bridge. Before the corpsman got there, CDR Peacock vomited. He had next to no food in his stomach. He'd puked up a lot of vodka, though. And then he passed out."

It was quiet for a long moment.

Then Charles Hanson said, "I stayed with the … with CDR Peacock the next morning. He claimed Greg Haywood tried to shoot him and made him drink the vodka."

"He made that claim to others," the Acting CO said. "The inquiry board looked into that claim but found no evidence it had happened and discredited it."

Jon was pretty sure that if there had been any question about Greg's role in what had happened, he would not have been permitted to depart the ship. But it was good to hear he'd been cleared.

"Any other questions?" the Acting CO said, and gave the table a couple of seconds, then, "Dinner goes down at 1730." And he stood up.

At 1730, with the officers standing behind their chairs, the Acting CO entered the wardroom from the XO's stateroom. "LT Becher. What are you doing? You're in my place."

"Oh, no, sir. I'm not." He pointed to the CO chair. "That's where you sit."

As one voice, the wardroom said, "Good evening, Skipper."

The Acting CO stopped, sniffed, and said, "You sons of bitches make me cry, and you're all in hack for the duration of our stay. And, and when we get back to the States, I'll put you in hack again."

"I didn't make you cry, Cap'n," Paul Becker said.

"Me either," from the Gun Boss.

"I didn't do it," DD added.

And it cascaded down the table, in seniority order, till one was left, and all eyes were on him.

Ensign Jon Two Buckets Zachery sighed. "At least I know some stuff about being in hack."

Then the officers had a fine, a mighty fine, meatloaf dinner aboard their ship and in their wardroom.

Jon had planned to spend forty dollars on a phone call to Teresa. He spent sixty.

The word had been *Manfred* might spend two weeks in Subic undergoing repairs. She spent five. The shipyard workers labored around the clock to get her ready to sail with three other destroyers assigned to escort the aircraft carrier USS *Sandia* back home. *Sandia* had suffered a major fire while on the line in the Tonkin Gulf. The navy wanted the carrier repaired and back in the war quickly and approved a transit speed of twenty-two knots.

The news made Jon uneasy. It seemed like there was too much good news of late.

But nothing dashed the exalted hopes inspired by the string of favorable news.

Manfred departed the PI five days after arriving and joined the destroyer screen preceding the carrier. *Sandia* and her escorts raced across the Pacific, slowing down twice to refuel, then resumed the high-speed transit. Halfway home, the carrier brought the formation to a stop and conducted a burial at sea service for four sailors who perished in the fire. The ceremony took thirty minutes, then the race for home resumed.

PART IV

HOME

No X for today, today's the day that's circled.

46

Jon stood in the safety observer position entering San Diego. When the Bosun called, "Moored, the Officer of the Deck is shifting his watch from the bridge to the quarterdeck," Jon hustled out to the bridge wing and saw Teresa right away. But the baby she held was like a Tutu-sized baby. How could their little Jennifer have grown so much, so fast?

Jon waved. Teresa saw him, and her face lit up, and his heart felt like it melted a hole through his chest, through his belly, and just plopped onto the deck.

He had just fallen in love with his wife of three and a half years and with his steady girlfriend of eight years, and it was all so fresh, so new, and so much better than the first time he fell in love with her.

That day, half the officers and crew departed on leave.

For the crew who did not go on leave, there was plenty of work to keep them busy. The deck crew on a US Navy ship was never without rust and corrosion to chip and grind away and paint over.

The engineers had plenty of pumps, pipes, boilers, and machines of all types of equipment in need of preventive and corrective maintenance. After two weeks, Jon was able to go on leave.

In mid-October, *Manfred* was scheduled for repairs in the shipyard at Long Beach, California. For Jon and his radiomen, they had to remove the ship's classified crypto equipment and store it in San Diego. The shipyard workers would need access to the crypto space, and most of them did not possess even a low-level clearance.

The workdays, though, were not overlong. Jon arrived at work at 0700 and left the ship at 1700. A nice, civilized ten hours. At the end of which, after the drive home. of course, was the welcome home from the two most important women in the universe. On their first honeymoon, there had been no baby with them. On this, the second one, it would not have been a real honeymoon without Jennifer there, too. She called Jon Da Da.

During the second week in port, Carl Lehr's promotion to JG came in, which made Jon the Bull Ensign and the Only Ensign. Jon also got a letter from Tutu. The waiting list for Swift Boats was longer than a year now, which was a major bummer. Tutu hoped Two Buckets wasn't too bummed having to handle being the junior ensign for a second time. Jon hadn't thought of that. Bull, Only, and Junior Ensign. A three-for.

It was Wednesday of the second week home. Teresa had worn honeymoon negligées to bed the first couple of days Jon was home. Then she shifted to regular nighties. On Wednesday night of his second week, she wore a new negligée.

They lay facing each other in bed.

"That looks nice on you," Jon said.

Jon began kissing her as he started undoing the little pearly buttons on her bodice. He finished those, but then he found a row of hook and eye fasteners. He pulled back. She pulled him back into the kiss, which was a nice one. He enjoyed it as he undid the hooks from the eyes, but beneath that, Jon found a set of snaps, still keeping him from the treasure he sought. That's when Teresa laughed in his mouth.

The deadly sin of wrath shoved aside his brother lust in Jon's head, but Teresa didn't let wrath hang around long. After she made it up to him for the joke, she confessed she and Rose had been shopping that day and found the nightie. Teresa hadn't wanted to spend the money on it, so Rose bought it for her.

"You have scarred me emotionally. For life," Jon said.

It got quiet in the bedroom. Jon had meant it to be funny. Maybe she was thinking about some emotional scarring of her own. But then she rolled onto her side facing him and said, "You'll get over it."

She was right about that, and later, as she slept, with her head on his arm, Jon smiled. It was pretty funny, actually, except, of course, for the emotional scars.

When it was his turn, Jon didn't take leave. He and Teresa planned to take two weeks over Christmas to take Jennifer back home to Missouri to meet the grandparents, uncles, and aunts. He did take off at noon on Friday. Teresa's Uncle Theodore and Aunt Penelope had invited them up for the weekend.

The Prescotts lived in a sprawling ranch-style house overlooking the San Fernando Valley and the 101 Freeway. Teresa really liked Aunt Penelope, and Penelope seemed to really like Jennifer. Jon wanted to talk to Uncle Theodore about job prospects after he served out his time.

They'd visited the Prescotts three times before Jon had left on cruise, and Teresa had driven up once while he was gone. Jon first met Uncle Theodore at their wedding reception. Uncle Theodore worked for an airline, and he had picked up their wedding gift, the cassette player/ AM-FM radio, which he had had on the angle iron next to his bunk during the cruise.

As Jon drove them north, Jennifer was in her infant seat between them. She alternated between gumming and shaking the plastic toy tied with a ribbon to the rail in front of her seat.

Teresa knitted.

"Teresa."

"Umm," she said as her knitting needles clickety-clacked almost furiously.

"I really appreciated having the Prescotts' wedding gift to us on cruise, being able to play cassettes, I mean. It helped a lot. I am going to tell Uncle Theodore, but I wanted to tell you thanks, too, for letting me take it."

"Umm," she said to her knitting needles.

The motor hummed. The tires whispered little staccato thumps as they slapped the seams between slabs of concrete on I-5.

"It was… It was nice, going out to dinner with Rose Wednesday." Jon said. "It was, I don't know, maybe light is the way to describe it. There had been so many heavy things to deal with on the ship. Do you know what I mean?"

"Umm," she said.

Usually, it was Teresa trying to prime his conversational pump. He couldn't ever remember being on the other side of that situation.

"You don't keep any secrets from Rose, do you?"

"Umm," Teresa said, and the clicking stopped. "Not many;" then the clickety clacking cranked up again.

Jon wanted to tell Teresa about the marines, about Nguyen, about the VC girl, but now, apparently, was not the time.

They passed the turn-off for the US Marine Corps base at Camp Pendleton. Jon saluted the marines in general and his fellow OP-mates from Hill 55 in particular.

Teresa clickety clacked. Jennifer rattled her toy.

Aunt Penelope was the younger sister of Teresa's father. Her husband, Theodore Prescott, had been a P-38 photoreconnaissance pilot in World War II. After the war, he had gotten flying jobs, first in Chicago and then in Los Angeles. Uncle Theodore was no longer an active pilot. Now, he was the vice president of operations for a cargo airline.

Jon had enjoyed their visits with the Prescotts before he'd gone on cruise. Uncle Theodore seemed to enjoy hobnobbing with a military person. Uncle Theodore would want to know about the cruise. Jon decided he'd have to be careful. He didn't want to tell Teresa's uncle things he hadn't shared with her.

"Jon."

"Umm," he said as he negotiated the turn-off from The 101. He thought Los Angeles people sure seemed to love their freeways. They never said take 101. Rather it was take The 101, The 405, The I-10.

It registered that it was quiet in the car. Jennifer was asleep in her seat between them, and Teresa had stopped knitting. At the stoplight at the bottom of the off-ramp, Jon looked at her.

"Are you going to drink at Aunt Penelope's?"

They had ridden all the way up practically in silence. Then she popped out with the drinking business. The light turned green, but he took another glance at her.

"I wish you wouldn't."

When Teresa started on the drinking, it always made Jon resentful. He always asked himself, like he wanted to ask her: *Why can't you appreciate how carefully I watch what I drink?* And, always, the next thing he told himself: *I wouldn't dream of asking you to change something of yourself. I love you as you are.* Jon knew they should talk the issue out, but their opportunity to do so was back there, in the rearview mirror. They had arrived.

The Prescotts' house was a sprawling stucco ranch with a red-tile roof. The backyard was entirely taken up by a pool and patio. From the front of the house, you did not get a feel for the size of the place. Inside, a large formal living room, a large formal dining room, and a den with a bar and a sliding glass door led out onto the patio. To Teresa and Jon, Uncle Theodore and Aunt Penelope were rich. Theodore and Penelope carried themselves as if they knew they were rich, as if they were entitled to be, but they had had humble beginnings that they were not ashamed of. It seemed as if the role of self-made-millionaire was just made for them. But, they both seemed to genuinely enjoy the Zachery's company.

Jon figured Uncle Theodore probably considered him to be a sort of project. He seemed to think that Jon had the potential to really make something of himself but that he was still too much of a country bumpkin and too content to just be a plodder. On the last two visits, Jon wound up in the den with Uncle Theodore. During those times, the talk generally got to, in a not very graceful way, how Jon might build a career for himself, preferably in aviation; how he should not waste time after he left the navy; and how Uncle Theodore could help him get started in the right way.

They arrived at the Prescotts an hour before Uncle Theodore got home from work. Aunt Penelope came out of the front door as they parked in the driveway. Words bubbled out of her as she hugged Teresa and then came around the car to hug Jon. When she got back to Teresa's side of the car, it didn't seem as if she had taken a breath since they arrived. Jon thought Jennifer would shy away from that effusive babble, but when Penelope held out her hands, Jennifer leaned forward and went to her.

Penelope led them into the house and used most of the hour to coo and fuss over Jennifer. Jennifer, like the little princess she must have thought she was, took it all in as if it were her due.

When Uncle Theodore got home, he and Jon went out to the patio where he grilled porterhouse steaks on his hibachi pot. Without asking, Theodore gave him a drink that he considered a Scotch and Scotch and not the Scotch and water he had asked for on previous visits. Theodore had a martini, and he used an eyedropper to add one drop of vermouth. Jon was pretty sure that's how he had put the water in his drink.

Theodore asked about the cruise. Jon told him a bit about being a newbie, about the encounter with the PT boats, which had been in the papers, about the months of boring routine, and the visit to Zamboanga. When they brought the steaks in, Penelope and Teresa were at the table, and Jennifer was in her highchair, which was a fold-up affair that they'd brought along in the back seat. Jennifer behaved throughout dinner, but she did start to fuss when Theodore served Jon a cup of espresso.

"Nighty-night time, Jennifer," Teresa said as she started pushing back from the table.

They all looked toward the entryway when they heard the front door open. A voice called, "Mom, Dad, I'm home. Whose car is in the driveway?"

"We're in the dining room, Christine-honey," Penelope said.

Penelope often called their only daughter "Christine-honey." Penelope was a little fond of hyphens. Sort of British, those hyphens, you know. It seemed to her that the British, of the hyphenated-name kind of British, represented a certain level of social status worth keeping in her sights.

There was a *toot* of farewell from Christine's ride as the car drove off down the street and the sound of a bag dropped on the floor of the foyer.

"Christine-honey, come in and say hello. Teresa and Jon are here," Penelope said. Then to Teresa, "We weren't expecting her home this weekend."

Christine appeared in the doorway to the dining room. A smile, whose only intention was to wound rather than warm, appeared below her slender nose.

"How very nice to see you, cousin," she said to Teresa.

Then she snapped her green eyes to Jon.

"And how many babies did you kill while you were in Vietnam?"

In the silence that followed, Jon felt himself flush, and sweat popped out on his upper lip.

Christine spun on her heel and said over her shoulder, "I'm going to Charlotte's."

Theodore stood up abruptly, his chair crashed over behind him, and he hurried after his daughter. The front door slammed, then it opened, and after a moment, it closed again more gently.

"Oh, I am just so sorry." Penelope shook her head. "That… that was just so…so ill-bred."

"Aunt Penny, I'm sorry to be the cause of this friction in your family." Jon stood up. "Come on, Teresa, we have to go."

"Oh, no. No," Penelope said. "You are staying the night. Theodore and I both looked forward to your visit. Please don't let Chrissie spoil this."

"Aunt Penny," Jon said, "you have always been so gracious to us, and it's always a pleasure to see you and Uncle Theodore. But, I just don't want to be the cause of any trouble between you and your daughter."

There was the sound of the front door opening, then closing.

Theodore walked into the dining room and around to his place at the end of the table. "She was running." He frowned down at his chair. "No way old tub of guts was going to catch her." He righted his chair, sat, and looked at Jon.

"Sit down, please," Theodore said as he forced his voice to a softness that was not natural to him. "Please."

Jon looked at Teresa. She nodded, and he sat.

"I am very sorry this happened to you in our house, and I am speaking to the two of you," Theodore said. "She's only been at Berkeley for a month, but she began spouting anti-war stuff from the moment she got there. But I never expected her to behave this way to any guest of ours, much less to family. I ask you to forgive us, and it seemed when I walked in that you might be getting ready to leave. I'm asking you to stay, please. Penny and I both really enjoy seeing you whenever we can get together. Please stay the night, as we had all planned."

Teresa said, "It's up to you, dear."

Jon said, "Teresa would like to stay, and so would I. But, we can't if my being here causes trouble between you and your daughter."

Jon looked at his hands, which were clasped together on top of the table in front of him, for a moment; then, he looked back up at Theodore.

"Do you think you could get Christine to talk to me for two minutes, Uncle Theodore? I will go to where she is, or I can talk to her on the phone. Or if she will come here—"

"Ted, dear," Penelope said. "I'll call Charlotte's house. It might be better if I make the call."

Penelope left. Jennifer had stopped fussing when Christine

came in, and the excitement had started. She was quietly observing everything that was going on. Teresa got Jennifer out of her highchair and took her back to the guest bedroom. There was just a little bit of wine left in the bottle, and Theodore divided it between the two of them.

"So, Uncle Theodore," Jon said. "This anti-war and anti-draft business, if Christine is that fired up about it, it must be quite a movement up at Berkeley. When we saw you and Christine before I left on cruise, when Christine was still a high school senior, I thought I got along fairly well with her."

"It's in the papers more frequently these days," Theodore said. "Berkeley does tend a bit toward the radical in their politics, but it's not just there. There have been demonstrations and sit-ins on the east coast, as well. By our phone calls, I knew Christine was getting caught up in it. I hoped she'd grow up, grow out of it once she saw what these hippies were all about."

"After you are on cruise for five months, you almost feel like you were off the world for a while because you are so cut off from all the news that is so much a part of life back here."

"Well, I knew how Chrissie felt about the war, but I sure never expected her to behave as she did," Theodore said. "And I have no idea where she has gotten her ideas from or why those feelings should run so hot."

"She'll be here in about five minutes," Penelope said when she came back into the room and sat down. She took a sip of wine. "Chrissie said they had been talking about Vietnam the whole way down from the Bay area. She had gotten a ride with the Fender boy and two others, and I guess they had gotten themselves worked up quite a bit. Then, she gets out of the car, walks in, and finds you here. I think she feels bad for how she acted, but of course, she could not admit that to me."

47

They were still at the table when Christine came and stood in the doorway to the dining room. For a moment, it was as if there were a rotating discothèque ball in the room with the facets reflecting remorse, then defiance, shame, then anger, affection, then independence onto Christine's face.

"Christine," Jon said. "Thanks so much for coming back. Will you let me talk to you, for two minutes, on the patio, please?"

She immediately headed for the patio. Jon followed and pulled a canvas deck chair around to face her. The look on her face told Jon that she had already judged what he was going to say before he had opened my mouth. It was exactly like it had been with Dormant.

"Christine, the last time we were here was last spring, and we had the big discussion about our country's support for Israel versus the Arabs. You and your friends believed one thing. I believed another, but we were able to discuss the situation, and I think we both gave each other some things to think about, even if neither of us changed the other's opinion. Now, I see what is almost hate in your eyes when you look at me."

Christine looked down at her hands in her lap.

"You called me a baby killer. If you really believe that is what I am, then I am going to take Teresa and Jennifer, and we are going to leave. I will tell you I am not a baby killer." Jon thought for a moment about the girl in the Saigon River, but he plowed on. "Basically, I am the same person you saw in your house last spring. I hope I am a little more grown-up, but the navy did not turn me into a monster. I have a conscience. I have a sense of what is right and wrong. The navy expects me to bring that into the service with me, and they expect those things to guide me into ethical behavior."

Jon spoke to her for six minutes. *Getting wordy in my old age*, he thought. But, he was glad he had poured most of his pre-dinner Scotch into Aunt Penelope's Birds of Paradise next to the patio door. During the whole six minutes, Christine never said a word. She just listened. Suddenly, she put a hand up to her mouth, and then she stood up, came over to Jon, bent over, and gave him a hug.

After she straightened up, Christine said, "Really, Jon, it is not supposed to be personal. I was wrong to make it that way. It's the establishment we are against." Then she left through the back gate.

Teresa was just walking back into the dining room when Jon came in.

Theodore said, "I didn't hear any shouting."

"Christine took the back gate to go back to Charlotte's," Jon said. "She said she'd be home by midnight. And, she is going to make me an egg-white vegetarian omelet for breakfast, which I will just love."

Jon sat and took a sip of his wine.

Theodore said, "Well? What else?"

"I just thanked her for her protest. I told her that if there had been a Fraulein Christine Prescott in Germany in the '30s, maybe we'd have avoided World War II. I told her I thought it was important for people like her to question what our national leaders get us involved in, but we need to discuss things from the point of view that all of us are trying to do the right thing. Then, I told her that I really liked and respected her mother and father and that you wanted us to stay, but that I wasn't going to stay in her house unless she said it was okay. That's it."

Teresa and Penelope went into the kitchen to take care of the dishes. Theodore tried to push a cognac on Jon, but he declined. He'd had enough to drink. Uncle T. poured himself a dollop into a snifter, got a cigar, and led him out onto the patio. They talked for almost an hour; then Penelope slid the patio door open.

"Ted, dear, you are going in to work in the morning, remember?"

When they got in bed, Jon reached out for Teresa's hand, and he started telling her what Uncle Theodore had said about job possibilities after he left the navy. They both whispered so as to not awaken Jennifer.

"I am looking forward to having you home every night. All the time you were gone, I felt like I had to sleep with one eye open, worrying about someone breaking into our place and harming Jennifer and me. A little part of me, though, will miss associating with the women, like the *Manfred* wives' group. They are just a wonderful group of ladies."

"Well, we do still have another three years. Lots can happen in that time."

They were quiet for a moment, and he rolled onto his side, leaned over, and kissed her.

"You taste like wine," Teresa said. "And, I smell it on you."

Later, Jon figured he should have shut up then, but he had been thinking about Christine and Valerie at the Peace Corps place in Zamboanga, and Dormant, and he wanted to talk to Teresa about it. He didn't know what to say about the wine.

"Teresa, remember the letter I wrote on the way home from the PI, where I was writing about the ship having a soul when Commander Carstens was our Skipper? I said that when Commander Peacock took over, it was like *Manfred* no longer had a soul. I was just wondering about the US. Does the country have a soul? I've always considered our government to be the best the human race has come up with, given that it does have its faults. Anyhow, I never thought about it in terms of a soul until I got to thinking about *Manfred.* And this protest business, it just makes me wonder if that is the soul of our country, or are they trying to rip the soul out of it?"

"Jon, I can really smell the wine on you." Teresa disengaged her hand and rolled away from him onto her other side. "You go all talkative when you drink, do you know that?"

In a session Jon had had with the XO on the way home, the XO told him he thought a man who didn't swear was better than one who did. Still, he had said, sometimes there's nothing that will do for a man other than a good goddamn.

Goddamn!

"Jon, Jon, wake up. Someone's outside. I think they are trying to steal our car."

That got Jon's heart going every bit as effectively as a GQ alarm. Then, he heard a noise, too. He flipped the covers off, went to the window, and peeked through the blinds. From the streetlights, he saw a car parked on the street just behind their car in the Prescott's driveway. A shadow figure moved toward their car.

Jon pulled on trousers, slipped out of the bedroom, crossed the living room, and stopped just inside the front door. He heard whispered voices, eased the door open, and stepped out onto the front porch.

Three shadow figures were huddled around the open back door of the Zachery's four-door Chevelle. They were doing something in the back seat. There was a sidewalk from the front door to the driveway, and Jon made it just a couple of steps away from the front door when one of them saw him.

There was a shouted, "Run."

Jon started after them. The one who had been leaning into the back seat was the last to start running toward the car parked in the street. After a couple of strides, he went down hard. He had gotten his feet tangled in a garden hose. He was the smallest of the three, about Jon's height, but he was lighter, maybe 130 pounds. Jon grabbed the collar of his shirt and hauled him to his feet. He started flailing fists. Jon grabbed his wrist and landed a big roundhouse on the side of the guy's jaw. The guy went down hard.

In the next instant, lights exploded in Jon's head, and he was sitting on the driveway in a puddle from the hose, and his mouth hurt. He had a tooth missing. His mouth was full of blood. He spat out a tooth and blood.

A big guy was helping up the little guy Jon had decked. Jon jumped to his feet. The big guy saw him and let the little guy back onto the driveway. Jon spat again. The big guy started toward Jon. There was enough light from the streetlight on the corner to see the big guy clench his fists. Jon waited for him. When he launched a right-hand punch, Jon ducked and kicked his right knee. He went down and wound up rolling back and forth on the wetness from the garden hose that was still watering the driveway, and he was moaning.

The first guy he had hit was on his feet.

The guy in the car hollered, "Come on," and he revved the motor.

The guy started running toward the car, but Jon ran after him and drove his shoulder into the guy's back and, and they went down. Jon lost some skin from his left forearm as they skidded along the driveway.

The car peeled out.

Jon thought it was a yellow Camaro. It skidded through a left turn at the end of the block. The big guy was down on the driveway holding his knee and moaning. The little guy sat near the end of the driveway and cradled his left arm, and cried. Broken bone, maybe.

"Jon!"

It was Uncle Edgar on the front porch in PJs.

Jon took off running after the Camaro. At the end of the block, he heard a garage door and ran toward the sound. The closing sound had come from about halfway down the block. When he got to where he thought the sound had come from, he stopped. The house in front of him was dark and quiet, as was the one he had just passed. In the next house down the street, a light blinked off, so Jon went up to the front door of that house and rang the bell. The *ding, dong* sounded through the house. He knocked on the door and rang the bell again. Jon listened for a sound from inside and knocked and rang the bell a third time.

"It's 2:30 in the morning. What the hell's going on?" asked an irritated voice from inside.

"My car was just trashed, and I just chased somebody in here," Jon said.

"Nobody just came into my house. We have all been asleep here since 11:30. Now you get the hell away from my door, or I'm calling the police."

"Do you have a yellow Camaro?" Jon asked.

It was quiet on the other side of the door. Jon repeated the question.

"I'm calling the police," the voice said again.

The layout of the house was almost like Uncle Theodore's, with a sidewalk curving away from the drive and up to the front door. Jon crossed the drive and went to see if there was a window on the far side of the garage. There wasn't. He continued around and found a four-foot-high chain-link fence around the backyard. After looking and listening for a dog and not hearing one, he vaulted over the fence and went to see if he could see inside the windowed back door into the garage. It was dark inside, and the door was locked.

Then Jon heard a siren, and it was close. He re-crossed the fence, went back around to the front of the house, and sat in the middle of the driveway just before the two police cars screeched to a halt in the street, and two officers boiled out of their cars and drew their weapons. Jon had his hands up.

Two officers approached Jon with their weapons in two-handed grips. The one from the second car holstered his weapon, cuffed his right arm first, and lowered it. Then he lowered the other arm and cuffed it to its mate behind Jon's back. The officer from the first car went up to the house and rang the bell. Jon heard the officer and a man talking for a bit. The officer asked some questions of the man; then the officer came back and stood in front of Jon.

"So what's your story?" the officer asked Jon.

Jon told him but had to stop periodically to spit blood. He was missing an upper front tooth, and his upper lip felt about five times its normal size. After Jon finished the story, the officer from the first car pulled Jon to his feet, led him to his car, and stuck him in the back seat. The other officer went back and talked to the man in the house.

Jon's police officer drove them to the Prescott's house. Theodore and Penelope were in the driveway wearing robes over their pajamas. Theodore was talking to the big recumbent guy who was in a lot of pain from his knee. Penelope had an arm around the shoulder of the little guy as he continued to cradle his left arm.

Both officers got out of the car and left Jon in the back seat. One of the officers talked to the big guy, and the other took the little one. Uncle Theodore went around the side of the garage and turned off the water to the hose. Another police car pulled up and stopped in front of the driveway.

Jon looked up and down the street. The flashing lights from cop cars weren't the only lights on in the neighborhood. Most houses had lights on. At a couple of places, people stood on front porches in robes over PJs and stared.

One of the officers from the second car stayed at the end of the drive, where he could keep all the players in front of him, Jon thought. His partner walked up to the Zachery car and shined his flashlight in the back seat. He held up a bent coat hanger, showing it to the other cops. Then he picked up a garbage bag, looked inside, and wrinkled his nose. He said, "Looks like they were scattering dog—" The officer looked at Aunt Penelope. "They were scattering dog poop around the inside of the car then running the hose over it. It's a mess."

The front door of Jon's police car was open, so he could hear what everyone was saying. One of the officers spoke with Uncle Theodore for a moment and wrote in his notebook.

"So, Mr. Prescott, would you and the Mrs. please step back there, on your front porch."

Then Jon saw Teresa on the front porch. Christine was next to her, holding Jennifer. He wondered how long Teresa had been there.

Two officers went back to the big and little guys and spoke with them again. Both officers wrote in their notebooks.

From what Jon heard, the guy with the yellow Camaro was Martin Fender, and he had driven Christine and the little guy home that afternoon. The little guy was Harold Tucker. Martin and Harold were sophomores at Berkely. The big guy was Nathan Runner, a senior and a football star at the high school Christine had attended. One of the officers told another that Nathan had football scholarship offers from a number of colleges, but with that knee—, his voice had tailed off to silence.

The little guy, Harold, had told the officers that Christine had called Martin shortly after Martin got home and told him about Jon being there and that he had just come back from Vietnam. Martin then called Harold and Nathan, and they had come up with the scheme as to how to trash their car. Nathan worked at the SPCA shelter about a mile away from the Prescotts' house. The shelter had plenty of dog poop.

From down the street, two ambulances headed toward the Prescott house. Their lights were going, but the sirens were off. While the ambulance personnel attended to the big guy and the little guy, one of the officers opened the rear door next to Jon. He had more questions. Then one of the ambulance medics approached, and the cop got out of his way. The ambulance attendant had a flashlight, and he had Jon open his mouth.

"You're going to have trouble with corn on the cob," he said. "But, you should take the watermelon-seed spitting contest."

The attendant straightened up and said to the officer, "He going to jail?"

The officer was looking at him, and Jon could hear a cell door clang shut. Then, he shook his head, no. Jon tried to be cool like he knew they weren't going to lock him up, but he couldn't pull it off. His shoulders sank in relief. From the moment he heard the siren, he figured there was a seventy-five percent chance he'd wind up in jail. Now, though, he worried about what Teresa would think.

The officer grabbed Jon by the arm, shielded his head with the other hand, and pulled him out of the car. Jon looked up and saw Teresa in the driveway. She was holding Jennifer, and Jennifer was her inquisitive little self, taking in the flashing lights and all the other exciting things going on. Teresa, though, had a horrified look on her face. At first, Jon thought it must be for how he looked. But then she looked at the ambulances, and when she looked back at Jon, he knew she was more horrified at what he had done than at how he'd looked. He'd crippled two kids.

"A piece of advice, Mr. Zachery," the officer said. "Next time you see three guys breaking into your car, you might consider calling the police as your first action."

"Yesh, shir," it came out.

The officer snorted as he unlocked the handcuffs. Teresa turned and walked back into the house.

Goddamn, Jon thought. Just goddamn.

48

On Monday morning, when Jon crossed the brow onto the quarterdeck, Chief Petitte was the OOD.

"Jesus, Mr. Z. You must have had some kind of weekend liberty!" the chief said.

By way of answer, Jon opened his mouth.

"How does the other guy look?"

"It was three of them, Chief, but it's a real long story."

"Sorry, Mr. Z."

Chief Petitte was in the engineering department. Like most sailors assigned there, you could go weeks without seeing them when you were underway. They lived in the engine and fire rooms, and they only came out to eat and sleep. They worked in hot, sweaty conditions, and they put in more hours than most other ratings. There were a lot of things that could go wrong in the engineering spaces, and Jon was impressed with how diligently they drilled to be ready to handle the extensive set of possible, suddenly arising problems that could cascade into a catastrophe if the crew didn't respond promptly with the precise antidote.

Ever since the officer/chief softball game in the PI, Chief Petitte and he had gotten along well. He razzed Jon some over his lip and the tooth, absent from its place of duty. Jon flashed a big open mouth grin for the chief, and then he started down the port side to show himself to DD.

As Jon walked forward along the main deck on the port side, he was surprised to find a feeling of comfort, a feeling of familiarity, a feeling almost of being home, bubbling around inside. During the homeward trip, all the way across the Pacific, he had been so anxious to get back to Teresa and Jennifer and to get off the ship. Now, Teresa was still angry with him, and he felt comfort at being back aboard the ship. *Damn, just goddamn.*

DD wasn't in his room, so Jon headed forward for the Ensign Locker. When he got to the XO's room, he found Ralph Timmons, the Gun Boss, sitting at the XO's desk. The desk was piled with folders and documents, and pieces of lined paper were scattered across the entire surface of the desk.

"Uh, Gun Boss, where's the X—uh, Acting CO?"

"Jesus. What happened to you?"

Jon gave him the Reader's Digest condensed version and then handed over a copy of the statement he'd given the police.

He read through it quickly and handed it back.

After taking a deep breath, he let it out as if expelling an evil spirit. "Okay, Jon, first thing, you need to get over to dental and have them take a look at you. Second, I'm going to call the Legal Office on the base. You need to talk to someone there as well."

"I also need to get to the credit union, Gun Boss. I need a loan to pay back my wife's uncle. He loaned me the money to buy a new car, so I'm not going to be worth much on my first day back."

"Not a problem, Jon. Get yourself taken care of."

"Uh, Gun Boss, the XO?

"Yeah, well, the biggest thing was the XO and DD both resigned Friday afternoon."

"Resigned? Why did they resign?"

"I don't know. But the XO did leave a letter for you. Oh, and the Bureau of Personnel has a new CO on the way to us, and they are looking for a new XO and a new Ops O."

The Gun Boss rummaged around through the mess on the desk and pulled an envelope out of the pile. It said "personal for Ensign Jon Zachery" on the front. Jon started turning away, then stopped and turned back.

"So you're acting CO, right?"

The Gun Boss shrugged.

Next, he checked his mail slot in the wardroom. There was a letter from Cecil and one from Edgar Chalmers. In the Ensign Locker, he grabbed *Leaves of Grass*. He expected to do some waiting in the dental clinic.

As he drove out of the parking lot behind the chapel, he yawned big and split his lip open again. It had been a heck of a weekend. After Teresa had awakened him early Saturday, he never got to sleep again that morning. When the police finally finished with him, he came into the bedroom and found Teresa in bed on her side. Jennifer was in her playpen and looked to be asleep.

"You awake, Teresa?" he whispered.

She rolled over and said, "You attacked those boys because you were drunk."

Teresa rolled back onto her side, and Jon walked out into the Prescotts' living room and sat in one of the chairs. He sat there, not thinking, not feeling, just waiting.

At 0630, Jon heard noises in the kitchen, and shortly, there was a smell of coffee. He stopped by the bathroom and combed his hair. The rest of how he looked wasn't going to get fixed by anything he could do except heal. His upper lip was huge, reddish-purple, and split right where his upper front tooth used to be. As long as he didn't smile, he was just short of gruesome looking. The other thing he had was the gauze dressing on the massive raspberry on his left forearm.

To drink Aunt Penelope's coffee, he had to put an ice cube in it and take it a teaspoonful at a time. While Uncle Theodore ate his scrambled eggs, he related what he had learned from Christine. After running out of the house, she called Martin Fender and told him about Jon just coming back from Vietnam. Christine knew that Martin was going to do something, but she didn't know what. After Christine had talked to Jon, and nothing had happened by that time, she had thought that Martin probably was just mouthing off and acting big.

Uncle Theodore and Penelope had talked, and they agreed that Christine was not going back to Berkeley. Christine didn't know that yet, but she would when she woke up. Theodore had to go in to work that morning, but he said he would be home by 1 p.m. In the meantime, Penelope would take Jon to the police station to give them his written statement; then, she took Jon to the Prescott's dentist. Theodore had called him at 0600 and told him what had happened to Jon, and the dentist agreed to see him.

Theodore had also talked to Martin Fender's father that morning but could not get the other two parents. Both were probably at the hospital, but Theodore planned to call them after getting to the office.

Penelope got Christine up and told her she was going with them on a round of errands that morning. When Christine saw Jon, she burst into tears. Penelope let her go back to her room and get the crying done. Jon went to the guest bedroom to tell Teresa they were leaving. She was sitting on the side of the bed nursing Jennifer, and she didn't turn around. "Just go," she had said.

At the police station, it went pretty quickly since Jon wasn't pressing charges. He asked for carbon paper so he could make a copy of his statement. After he was finished writing, an officer compared his statement to what the officers had written up earlier that morning, and then he said he could go. They were in the dentist's office at 1015. He examined Jon, took x-rays, and told him it would take a few days for the swelling to go down before anyone would be able to start working on a new tooth for him. Jon was lucky, the dentist had told him because his bottom teeth were okay, and there might be enough root left of the upper to attach a permanent replacement.

The last thing they did was to visit Nathan Runner in the hospital. Penelope had tried to call the Runners, but there was no answer at the house. It was 1145, and Nathan was having lunch, the nurse informed them. They could have ten minutes.

Nathan had a private room, and Penelope went in first and talked to Nathan a moment; then she beckoned, and Christine and Jon entered the room. He and Jon stared at each other for a moment. Jon looked at the bandage across the knuckles of his right hand.

"I'd just like to say three things," Jon said. "First, you hit hard. Second, I hope you can play football again." He looked at his bandaged knuckles again and said, "And last, I'm up to date on my rabies shots."

Suddenly, a hand grabbed his shoulder and spun Jon around. The hand grabbed the front of his shirt and dragged him out of the room and into the hallway.

"What the hell are you doing here?" The man was big, just an inch or two shorter than Peter Feldman.

He was almost the twin of the young man in the bed: a bit on the slender side of his beefy son, probably about six-three, just under 200 pounds maybe, and nothing but well-toned muscle. From behind Jon, Penelope reached up and slapped the man.

"George, we're in a hospital, and your son is in there, and he's injured. Get a hold of yourself."

George let Jon go.

"You're going to get sued to pauper-dom," he said with a finger in Jon's face.

"You moron," Penelope said. "You make sure you talk to Theodore before you try to sue anyone."

Penelope turned, her face abruptly turned soft, and said, "Nathan, I hope you are well soon." Then, "Go," she said to Christine.

Christine touched Nathan on the arm; then she walked out of his room, and she and Jon started down the hallway for the elevators. Jon punched the button and looked back at Penelope. She was a good seven inches shorter than George Runner, but she had him leaning back from the finger-wagging just under his nose. When the elevator came, Jon took another look at Penelope, but she wasn't done with George, so Christine and Jon went down and got the car to wait for her.

When he got to the dental clinic on base, Jon turned over his dental record to the second-class sailor behind the raised counter and told him his problem, as if it wasn't obvious. Then he sat, opened the inside cover of his book, and looked at the three envelopes from the XO, Cecil, and Admiral Ensign. The only one that could possibly have good news was the one from Cecil. He was ready for some good news.

Dear Jon,

I cannot begin to tell you how moved I was by your poem. "The Sea Road to Zamboangey." A lot more Kipling than Whitman, but it was marvelous.

I wanted to work in foreign affairs in our government since I was in high school and have been very fortunate to be able to do what I really love to do all my adult life. Since I have been here, I have developed a real fondness for the Filipinos that rivals my feelings for my own countrymen. I have tried, in my own limited way, to serve my country and to help the Filipinos, as well. Your poem said, in effect, that you see me to be the man I most want to be. A crusty old bastard I most assuredly am, but your poem choked me up. So thank you for the excessively kind thoughts and for stirring my cynical soul.

I will be retiring from government service next year. My wife, a Filipina, by the way, will probably get a job at Clark AFB. We have some property from her family in the hills to the west of the base.

I hope we will stay in touch, and if you make it to the Philippines again, I will be crushed if you do not visit.

Thank you, Sir Two Buckets. Very best wishes,

Cecil

Jon was learning how to smile small. Cecil, he thought, God bless you.

He hadn't noticed before, but the return address on the next envelope was from LT (jg) E. Chalmers.

Two Buckets

Heard some bad news today, and I thought you'd want to know. I know you remember Duke Savage, the marine A-4 pilot Cowboy made friends with. Just found out that just after *Manfred* left the PI, he was in a landing accident with his A-4 at Chu Lai. AAA hit his plane, and when he landed, the gear collapsed. He had injuries and was getting better, but then he got pneumonia, and that killed him. Anyway, thought you'd like to know. Bummer.

Me, I am in training here in Pensacola. So I'm a schoolboy again. I did solo this week. Cool stuff this aviating.

Edgar

Jon remembered Duke from the wetting down party and thought Duke had been lifted off a US Marine Corps recruiting poster and brought to life.

"Ensign Zachery," was called from the reception counter.

The dentist who saw Jon was probably thirty years old or so, skinny, bald on top, wearing glasses. He looked at the x-rays he had brought from Uncle Theodore's dentist and then had more taken. Jon got the feeling he was really pleased to have a mouth with those problems to work on.

While the x-rays were being developed, Jon opened the XO's letter.

Jon

You are probably surprised by what DD and I have done. But we both felt we had no other moral course open to us.

I know what you did with Tutu. You sent him into a burning compartment. And I think I know why.

DD and I have to leave the Navy. You don't and shouldn't. Do not get the hell out of here.

XO

When Tutu had gone into the CO's cabin to plant bug body parts, he'd discovered the CO's anti-depression meds. He and Jon discussed the situation, and they agreed that Tutu would replace the meds with aspirin, which looked like the CO's pills. Tutu also discovered a vodka bottle locked in the CO's desk. Tutu had had no problem jimmying the desk open.

Jon didn't know what Tutu had done on that last day when the CO tried to commit suicide, but he was sure there was a part of the story only Tutu knew.

Father God, Who art in heaven, forgive us, Tutu and me, our trespasses.

The dentist told Jon he could not do a thing until the swelling subsided. Then he would build a temporary false Bucky Beaver, which would have to serve for several months. Then they could consider permanent implants.

After the dentist, Jon spent forty-five minutes with a navy lawyer, giving him the story, and the phone number, he had for the police department in the San Fernando Valley.

Next, the Navy Credit Union, gave him the loan he needed, and he got back to the ship in time for lunch. The cooks gave him chicken noodle soup and ice cream for dessert. That night, he had the same thing for dinner. The acting CO offered to excuse him from standing duty with his section, but Jon told him he wanted to stand his mid-watch.

That evening in the Locker, Jon put on his Chopin *Nocturnes* cassette and said a rosary. Then, he wrote a note to Cecil and LT (jg) Chalmers. A few months ago, he could not imagine himself writing to Edgar. He also intended to write to Teresa, but after looking at a blank piece of paper for several minutes, it was clear, that words were not going to happen.

So, he sat and thought about Teresa at their apartment alone with Jennifer. She was still angry. Sunday night, after they got back to Chula Vista, so, Jon slept on the sofa.

They did get a new car out of the deal. On Saturday afternoon, after Theodore got home from work, he told Jon he was talking to the fathers of the three boys, and it was his intention that the four of them would buy the Zacherys a car. Jon told Theodore he didn't want those people's money, and he sure didn't want Uncle Theodore to have to pay for any part of a new car. Christine came to Jon that evening, though, and begged Jon to let her use her college money to help pay for the new car.

Theodore had taken Jon to a Chevrolet place a couple of miles from their house, and he steamrollered the manager into a deal that had him driving a new Impala off the lot that afternoon. Jon agreed to let Christine contribute five hundred dollars to the deal, and he borrowed the rest from Uncle Theodore with the promise he would let Jon pay it back.

When they drove back down to San Diego Sunday afternoon, Jon was on much better terms with Christine than he was with Teresa. The ride back to Chula Vista was forever, and it was silent. The worst of it was that he couldn't see how to begin to get out of whatever it was they were in. And, too, he hated having Jennifer in her infant seat between the two of them, absorbing the animosity flowing from Teresa to him.

After the nocturnes were done, he changed cassettes and just listened to Beethoven's Ninth. He never just listened to music. Always before, music was the background to writing a letter or reading. But that night, he just listened without knowing what he was looking for. The symphony was written as an *Ode to Joy*. Though it seemed to Jon as if he hadn't tasted much joy the whole blinking year, and it didn't seem possible just then, but he had been wallowing in joy the last two weeks. Until they drove up to visit the Prescotts.

The cassette ended, and the player clicked off.

Father in heaven, I could use a little help down here.

Jon undressed, climbed up onto his bunk, put his hand on the angle iron, and slept. He slept pretty well for an hour. Then the messenger woke him for the mid-watch.

49

The next morning, Jon was in the tiny crypto broom closet filling out a destruction report for the outdated keying material from the last month when there was a knock on the door. It was 1102 by the clock on the bulkhead.

Jon opened the door, and one of his seamen said, "Acting CO is on the phone for you, Mr. Z."

Working in crypto could be a pain. You had to lock everything up, even if you were leaving to take a short phone call; however, Jon wasn't about to take a shortcut with the protections of those highly sensitive materials.

Finally, he got to the phone. "Sorry, sir. It just takes a while to lock everything up."

"The important thing, Jon, is that there's a woman on the quarterdeck who says she wants to take you to lunch," the Gun Boss said. "I think you should let her. The way you look, you're not going to get too many offers."

Jon remembered to smile a little; then he went back into the crypto room and double-checked he locked everything properly.

Back on the quarterdeck, he found Rose Herbert standing behind the gun mount.

"That's not a lip," Rose said when she saw him. She kind of cocked her head to the side a bit. "God must have ripped one of your butt cheeks off last night when you were sleeping and stuck it under your nose."

"Rose! It hurts when I smile."

"Oh, you poor crippled, little dear."

She gave Jon a hug and kissed him on the cheek.

"Teresa is at my house. I am feeding you lunch. Then, you and Teresa are going to talk. And your acting CO said you don't have to come back this afternoon. So, come along, sailor boy."

Rose talked as they walked down the pier. Jon listened and returned salutes of the sailors coming at them. Teresa had called Rose around 1900 last night. Teresa had been in tears. Rose went over to their apartment and wound up spending the night. This morning Rose had called in sick, and she and Teresa talked some more.

Rose had parked in the Gun Boss's parking spot because he had parked in the XO's. Rose amazed Jon frequently with the things she pulled off. She drove Jon to his car behind the chapel; then she drove off, and Jon followed in their new, red Impala. When Uncle Theodore and Jon had gone to buy a car, he had picked the red one because it was Teresa's favorite color.

Fred and Rose had a townhouse apartment. The kitchen, dining area, and living room were on the bottom floor. Stairs led to two bedrooms on the second floor. Teresa and Jennifer were on the floor with the Herberts' "oof-oof," Henri, a light-grey poodle.

Henri raced over to Joon and was affectionate with his leg.

"Hank, you oversexed Frenchman, get down. Get down," Rose said.

Henri ran back to Jennifer and began slobbering over her face. Jon was always a bit taken aback by the dog's affection blitzkrieg when he walked into the Herberts' place. But, the energetic little beast did make him smile enough to cause him to wince. Teresa stood up and lifted Jennifer off the floor.

Looking at her made Jon's knees go weak. There was a bit of redness around her eyes, and under them were dark smudges. She hadn't slept any better than he had, it seemed. But she looked good, except that he couldn't read that fulfilled, I'm-so-satisfied-with-my-life face he was used to seeing.

"Okay, you two, seats," Rose said.

Jon took Jennifer and put her in her highchair, and then Rose pointed to where she wanted him and Teresa to sit. Jennifer was between Rose and Jon. There were chef's salads for Rose and Teresa. Jon was having soup, and there were wine glasses at each place. Rose got a bottle of Chablis from the refrigerator and poured a little in Teresa's glass and a full glass for her and Jon.

She sat and said, "To Jon and Teresa. If ever there was a marriage made in heaven, yours is it. But, you damn well better not let it go to hell. I do not want to have to train another bridge partner."

Rose's toasts tended to be like that, a bit of schmaltz and a lot of two-by-four counseling. They clinked glasses, and Jon watched Teresa as she took a sip, wrinkled her nose, and kind of glared at Rose. But Rose was looking at Jon, and as soon as his eyes met hers, her face asked him, "Yo, blockhead, do I have to do all the work here?"

Jon took a sip, brought the glass under his nose, sniffed, took another sip, and said, "Very nice, Rose. Tart, crisp, a pleasant little aftertaste of lemon. Very nice."

Rose smiled a teensy smile and picked up her fork.

"Uh, Rose, I know I'm a guest in your house, and I hope I'm not overly presumptuous, but would you permit me to say a prayer?"

Rose nodded and put her fork down.

Teresa bowed her head.

"Heavenly Father, we thank you for the blessings of this day: blessings of family, of friends, and of good food and drink, which are the product of human hands working on Your bounteous blessings. And we thank you for the hard days, as well as the good because we know they are all part of your divine plan."

Teresa's eyes were still down. Rose rolled her eyes and gave Jon a look that he thought said, "I knew I should have written a script for you."

"And, Father, please, watch over Fred on the other side of the world. Let him know we are thinking of him this afternoon. Please bring him back safely to us. Amen."

Lunch was civil. Rose kept Jennifer occupied with Gerber's products, and Teresa and Rose chatted. Teresa never looked at Jon, but once, Rose gave him a wink when Teresa was looking down at her salad.

When lunch was done, Jon offered to do the dishes.

"No," Rose almost shouted. "You two, get the hell out of here. I have Jennifer for the night. I will take care of the rest. And, Teresa, I'll drop her off in the morning on my way to work. Go. Shoo."

50

Jon drove them north on I-5, and they had just passed the last turnoff for National City when Jon reached across the top of Jennifer's car seat and put his hand on Teresa's shoulder. After a moment, she reached up, took the hand, and squeezed it. There was no joy, but there was hope.

As they drove, silence hung in the air. Jon knew it was up to him to get the conversation going, but words were tough to come by. Perspiration dotted his upper lip.

"Teresa, this is harder even than it was on cruise, after my letter from the PI about the wetting down. When things were good with us on cruise, I felt as if I could reach out a finger and touch you all the way from the other side of the world. Since Friday night, though, I have been this close to you a lot, and I've still felt farther away from you than if I'd been on the far side of the moon. Whatever I need to do to fix this, tell me."

Teresa let go of his hand, and he put it with its mate on the steering wheel. He glanced at her quickly, then back at the road. A frown was wrinkling her brow. She was having trouble getting the words to start, too. Jon took her hand again and kissed the tips of her fingers, but only his swollen upper lip touched her skin. It seemed to loosen things up a bit, though.

Teresa sighed. "Saturday morning, when you confronted those boys, you went out after three of them. They might have had guns or knives. Did you think of that? Did you think what would happen to Jennifer and me if something happened to you?"

"Teresa, I stood on the porch there for several moments, and I just watched them before I did anything. There were two guys around our car and a third by their car. I knew they were kids, and I knew they didn't have weapons. I don't know how I knew, but I knew."

"You left the front door open when you went out. I was in the foyer and watched you run after those three guys. You grabbed the one who fell and punched him. Then, that big guy came after you, and I couldn't even scream for you to watch out. But, I was sure no sane, sober person would have taken after three guys like you did."

"Teresa, we had just gotten the car paid off. It and a few pieces of furniture are all we own. I wasn't going to just let those guys ruin our car. As it turned out, I was too late to stop them."

Teresa was quiet for a moment, and then she was close to whispering. "I talked to Aunt Penelope yesterday morning. She told me you weren't drunk. Uncle Theodore told her he had seen you dump almost all of the Scotch in the flowerbed. Uncle Theodore didn't think you had more than two sips. And, you had one glass of wine. Aunt Penelope said she had seen drunks and that you weren't drunk at dinner. And, she knew you didn't drink anything after that, and so you couldn't have been drunk for the encounter with the boys outside."

After a moment, he said, "How did Rose get you to drink some wine?"

He glanced over at her, and she was blushing. She glanced up at him and then back to her hands in her lap.

"I called Rose last night. We talked till late. She stayed over, and we got up early, for me anyway, and talked some more. Around 9 a.m., Rose said something like, 'Well, Miss Prissy Pants, you probably think your own poop doesn't stink, don't you? You should have handled enough bedpans to know that all of it smells pretty much the same.'"

Then, Rose had come up with the idea to do lunch. She threatened Teresa to use the lunch opportunity, or else she, Rose, would knock the snot out of her, Teresa, with an unsanitary bedpan.

Jon pulled into the parking lot at the Point Loma lighthouse, and he shut off the motor, undid his seat belt, reached across the car seat, and took Teresa's hand. He couldn't talk for the lump in his throat, and his heart was smiling so big it was squeezing water out of his eyes. She smiled at him and made everything between his Adam's apple and belly button just melt.

"If Rose knew what I was thinking, she'd call for one of my buckets."

"You say the sweetest things, Jon Zachery."

Then, they walked up to the far side of the lighthouse holding hands. As they walked, Jon remembered Cecil's note that had come with *Leaves of Grass*. Cecil had written that Whitman had sort of calibrated his senses for him. Jon felt like he knew what Cecil was getting at.

Jon had seen blue skies and blue water before, but their sky, his and Teresa's, that day was a deep royal blue. Monet, or one of his compatriots, had painted swathes of wispy, swirly cirrus in a couple of spots in the sky, just to sort of show you how blue the blue was. The breeze was just short of a right smart wind, and it chilled exposed flesh. He and Teresa had their jackets zipped up. On the side exposed to the sun, it felt as if the sun drizzled warmth like melted butter onto that cheek. There was a flagpole with no flag, just a halyard running up to a pulley at the top, and the halyard rattled and clanged against the aluminum pole. From the channel into the harbor below them, a buoy horn wailed a dirge for a sailor who never returned from the sea. Jon thought of Cowboy and Hank Allman. Then he thought of Peter Peacock and almost resented his intrusion into the company, but then another thought occurred. There are all kinds of casualties, so he stopped trying to push the thought of the troubled man away from the others.

On the ocean side of the lighthouse, they stood and looked in a direction Jon said was a bit north of west. A thin dark sliver sat on the horizon, not quite able to hide in the hazy distance. Teresa's eyes weren't good at distances, so she couldn't see it. It was San Clemente Island. To the left of San Clemente and closer to them, a lone destroyer sat dead in the water in a patch of wind-crinkled sea. In closer than the destroyer, there was a swath of smooth, blue water just before a band of kelp on the surface. At the shore-side edge of the kelp, a seal and a pelican splashed occasionally. Inshore from the kelp, the water was wind crinkled again, and directly below them, the waves came ashore with a *swoosh*.

They started walking back around the lighthouse. "Teresa, if I had any sense, I'd just take today and be happy with it. But I don't want to get happy for a couple of days, and then tell you what I started on Friday night after we got in bed. So if I screw this up, I'll throw myself between you and Rose's bedpan, okay?"

"Jon, I'm not going to let Rose after you with a bedpan. You have enough healing to do the way it is."

Jon stopped walking, faced Teresa, took both her hands in his, looked into her eyes. He thought he knew her so well, but she, and he, were like icebergs. Most of both of them were under the water and not visible, not knowable until their big under-parts bumped together. When they bumped, they broke parts of each other away. There was a lot Jon needed to tell Teresa. One was that his Bronze Star had arrived. He was going to have to explain that.

The other was that, since the night of the dog poop, he decided he wanted to stay in the navy. That night, the anti-war protest became personal, much more so than it had been with Dormant. Jon disagreed with the protestors. They were more anti-America than anti-war, he was convinced. If he disagreed, it was his duty to do what he could do, which was to continue to serve. And not only to serve but to apply for aviation. He'd always told her he would never be an aviator.

According to him, they were suicidal maniacs. But from their aircraft carriers, the aviators served in a way he couldn't from a destroyer.

He didn't have a clue as to where to start. But he had to figure it out—these things he had to tell her. Staying in, flying, he couldn't do either if she didn't agree to it.

They had taken a step on a thousand-mile journey to healing, and any one of his items could blow their beginnings of progress to smithereens.

They started walking toward the car again, and he was on the verge of just blurting it all out there when he noticed, ahead of them, San Diego gleaming in the bright afternoon. Jon stopped and pointed.

"See it, Teresa? An alabaster city."

She looked. "Except this one is dimmed by tears."

"Yes," he said, "and the song doesn't say how many human tears have to be shed to turn concrete, steel, and glass into an alabaster city."

"I never saw an alabaster city before, Jon. Thanks for showing one to me."

"You have done such good to me, Teresa, and nothing on God's earth pleases me more, than to be able to do the same to you."

US NAVY ACRONYMS & Terms

A US Navy ship's general announcing system	1MC
Anti-submarine Warfare	ASW
Boatswain Mate	Enlisted men who maintain the hull, anchor, and boats. Called Bosun.
Chief Petty Officer	CPO
Commanding Officer	CO, also called Skipper, and captain (as in captain of a ship)
Command Post	CP
Crow	Insignia worn on the shoulder indicating petty officer rank
Drone ASW Helicopter	DASH
Executive Officer	XO
Explosive Ordnance Disposal	EOD
Forward Air Controller	FAC
Gunnery Liaison Officer	GLO
Harassment and Interdiction	H&I
High Explosive	HE
Huey Helicopter	UH-1
Identification Friend or Foe electronic equip.	IFF
Junior Officer of the Deck	JOOD
Observation Post	OP
Officer of the Deck	OOD
Operations Officer	Ops O

Patrol Boat, River	PBR
Vietcong	VC
Underway Replenishment	UNREP

US Navy officer ranks	Abbreviations	Pay Grade
Admiral	ADM	O-10
Vice Admiral	VADM	O-9
Rear Admiral	RADM	O-8
Rear Admiral (lower half)	RADM	O-7
Captain	CAPT	O-6
Commander	CDR	O-5
Lieutenant Commander	LCDR	O-4
Lieutenant	LT	O-3
Lieutenant (junior grade)	LT(JG) or JG	O-2
Ensign	ENS	O-1
Warrant Officer	WO	W-1, W-2, W-3, W-4

US Navy Enlisted	Abbreviations	Pay Grade
Senior Chief Petty Officer	SCPO	E-8
Chief Petty Officer	CPO	E-7
First Class Petty Officer	PO1	E-6
Second Class Petty Officer	PO2	E-5
Third Class Petty Officer	PO3	E-4
Seaman	SN	E-3
Seaman Apprentice	SA	E-2
Seaman Recruit	SR	E-1

PART I

No welcome in the wagon.

1

Not many hings, aside from the baby crying, rousted Teresa Zachery out of bed before 0700. That morning, List Almighty would determine their future, and her husband, Jon, could get a permanent bridge to replace his two upper-front false teeth.

She slid her feet into her bunny slippers and padded across the living room carpet to the kitchen. Jon stood at the sink, water running, and Teresa stopped to watch from the doorway. It wasn't spying; it was more like when she discovered two-year-old Jennifer deeply engrossed in her coloring book, one of those precious and rare motherhood moments. She frowned. Watching her husband felt like spying.

Jon turned off the faucet, shook the water from what he was fond of calling his falsies, put them in, and looked down at the front of his navy uniform shirt. She smiled as he ran through his get-ready-for-work routine: Teeth in. Edge of shirt, edge of belt buckle, and edge of fly in a line—gig line straight. Zipper up. Hat tucked under the belt on the left.

"Everything shipshape," Teresa said.

He spun around, an annoyed look on his face, but it didn't last.

"Sleeping Beauty up at," he checked his watch, "0554? The handsome prince was about to awaken you with a chaste, fairy-tale, industrial-strength lip-lock."

She shook her head but couldn't keep from smiling. He loved to do that, to package "fairy-tale," "chaste," and "industrial-strength lip-lock" in one sentence. She crossed the kitchen and kissed him, dislodging his teeth.

"Rats, now I have to start the routine all over again."

"You look squared away to me, sailor."

"I was about to come in and tell you I was leaving," he said.

She hugged him. "Call me after you leave the clinic. I'd like to know if they can do permanent Bucky Beavers for you."

He looked away. "I decided to skip the dentist."

"Jon Zachery, it took months to get that appointment. Heaven only knows how long to get another. I'm not ready to spend the rest of my life sleeping with a man who puts his teeth in a glass of water every night."

"It's only the two uppers."

"There's no *only* about it. You keep that appointment."

Teresa felt it happen like it always did. Jon's blue eyes softened the hard edges of her scolding.

"Jon, I know you're worried about List Almighty, but even if it is posted today, you aren't going to change what's written on it by going in early."

"I wasn't looking for help with the logic of the situation."

"You were looking for sympathy?"

"I know. Dictionary. End of the S section."

"I love you, Jon Joseph Zachery."

"And you are a hard woman, Teresa Ann née Velmer, but I couldn't love you more."

She returned his goodbye kiss carefully. Then, at the door to the carport, he stopped with his hand on the knob.

When he turned to face her, it surprised her, the way it always did, that she was married to this handsome man. He stood so straight and appeared to be taller than his actual five-seven frame.

Broad shoulders and without a shirt, he looked almost as muscled as those men on the covers of romance novels. Although, in profile, his nose did stick out a bit.

He gave her his mischievous little-boy grin that only used half his face. "Thanks, Teresa."

"For what?"

"For getting up."

The door closed before Teresa came up with an appropriate reply. He'd been irritated with her because she awoke early and didn't let him skip the dentist. Then he thanked her.

She poured a glass of orange juice, turned out the kitchen light, and sat in the gloom at the table, at her table. She caressed the tabletop. After four years of living in furnished apartments, she appreciated owning a few pieces of furniture.

She sipped and thought men were complicated creatures. They never outgrew some parts of their boyhood. Aviators seemed a lot more juvenile than the officers Jon associated with on his destroyer. In flight training, most of the student pilots were just out of college. Despite, or maybe because of, the danger in flying, pilots had to act fearless.

Boys. Schoolboys.

She recalled asking Jon why flight training took so long.

"Navy flight training is like going through school," Jon told her. "Primary at Saufley Field is kindergarten. Next is basic training. That's grade school. We then do advanced training— that's high school. After advanced, we pin on our wings. We're naval aviators then."

"That's a year and a half, right?" Teresa asked.

"About that, but there's still another six months of training in the specific jet I'll fly in the fleet. That's college."

Teresa finished her juice and thought about the night of the dog poop. Night of the dog poop. Encounter some life-altering experience, and navy men had to trivialize it with a juvenile and profane name.

It was November 1966. Jon had just returned from a deployment to Vietnam on a navy destroyer. At that point, they had planned for him to leave the service as soon as he completed his three remaining years of obligation. Then he would get a job as an electrical engineer, and they "would live happily ever after."

The plan changed a week after his ship returned to San Diego. They had driven to Los Angeles to visit the Prescotts, Teresa's Uncle Edgar, and Aunt Penelope. The Prescotts did not expect their daughter Christine to come home from Berkeley that weekend, but she caught an opportune ride. She entered the house while her parents and the Zacherys were still at the dinner table.

On previous visits, Christine liked Jon. She told Teresa, "He talks to my friends and me like we're adults, not kids." But in the three months she'd been away at college; she'd been caught up in the antiwar movement. "Baby killer!" she shouted at Jon and stormed back out.

Early the next morning, three of Christine's male friends trashed the Zachery car with dog poop and a garden hose. Jon heard the noise and fought with them, losing his top two front teeth. Two of the three boys were hospitalized, though.

After the police and ambulances left, Uncle Edgar sat Christine down. Teresa had always thought her uncle spoiled and indulged his only child, but that morning he was furious.

"Explain yourself, young lady."

The boys she'd ridden home with were local friends, a year ahead of Christine at Berkeley. Shortly after the fall semester began, they had taken her with them to meet a group of four men and three women, none of them Berkeley students. The group had no name, only strong views. They considered the Vietnam War immoral—soldiers, sailors, and airmen indiscriminately killed women and children. American servicemen were war criminals.

"You believe this crap?" Uncle Edgar leaned toward Christine, his hands on his knees.

Christine looked up. She looked defiant, determined, but her lips quivered, and she was close to tears.

Teresa felt uncomfortable being in the Prescott living room with the father-daughter confrontation, and she started to stand.

"Stay," Uncle Edgar commanded without taking his eyes away from his daughter. "Please."

"You called Jon a baby killer. Baby killers are cowards. What he did last night—charged into the middle of three guys, all bigger than him—whatever he is, is sure as hell, not a coward."

Christine looked back at her hands.

"What the hell were you kids thinking?" Uncle Edgar asked.

Christine didn't want to answer, but he pushed.

The group, she said, met once or twice a week. They went over news accounts of the war. They talked about doing something, picketing the Naval Air Station at Alameda, maybe. But that's all they did: talk. During the ride down to LA Friday, they discussed the "all talk, no action" bunch. It was time they did something. If the group wasn't going to act, then the three of them would. They came up with wording for signs each of them would carry outside the Alameda main gate. Next week they would act. They agreed on that, and then Christine got out of the car and entered her home.

"Look at Jon, Christine. Look at what you did to him."

Jon's upper lip was swollen and purple. Blood spots speckled the front of his T-shirt.

Christine sobbed.

A week after the fight, Jon sat next to Teresa on the sofa. "I've been thinking," he said.

Cold fingers squeezed Teresa's heart.

"Before the encounter with Christine's friends, I didn't pay that much attention to all the protests going on in the country. It's all over the papers and TV, but it didn't have anything to do with us. Now it does.

"Some of it I understand. Dr. King, for instance. The Emancipation Proclamation was 103 years ago. It's time it becomes real. I understand that protest. I think Dr. King is right about many things, but he would have us fight the domestic problem and forget about the foreign one. Our country has enemies, foreign and domestic. The foreign enemies aren't going to let us say, 'Hey, Foreign Enemies, we've got some domestic problems to solve. Don't attack us for a while, okay?' So I don't think he's right about us getting out of Vietnam and concentrating only on fixing race issues."

Teresa realized she'd been holding her breath.

"In the newspaper accounts and on TV, I don't think the protestors know what they are protesting," Jon said. "It's more anti-establishment than anything. These people scare me. They seem to want to tear the country apart, not fix it. And nobody seems to stand up to them and tell them they're wrong. It's like the country doesn't know what to do about these protestors."

Jon took both her hands. "I can't climb on a soapbox and try to shout these protestors down. What I think I need to do is to stay in the navy, but I can't do that unless you support the decision."

Teresa couldn't think of what to say for a moment.

"I'm not just knee-jerk reacting to what happened at the Prescotts if that's what you're thinking."

She'd been thinking just that. Then, finally, she said, "Jon, have you thought this through? You've never liked being in the navy. And you did enough, already, on the *Manfred*. You say it's not a knee-jerk reaction to the fight with Christine's friends, but it seems like it to me."

"I think I'm objective, Teresa. I have thought about it. And you're right. I never wanted to be in the navy in the first place. Pop pushed me in. Being a junior enlisted man was not fun, and I agonized over staying in to get the navy college scholarship. Being an ensign on the *Manfred* wasn't pleasant either, and I looked forward to getting out. I was going to be an electrical engineer, and we'd have four babies. But these protestors scare me. Christine went from a friend to an enemy in the seven months I was gone. The protest business seems to involve most of our generation. What's going to happen to our country when these yahoos take over? I need to do something. Staying in is what I can do. It's not much, maybe, but it's something."

Teresa sighed. "You have to do what you think is right."

Then he told her he wanted to apply for aviation, and she got angry, feeling as though he'd suckered her in with the "stay in" part. When she bought that, he hit her with aviation. Aviation was dangerous, even in peacetime. He wanted to drop bombs on North Vietnam, and the newspaper articles about the strikes into the north all reported US aircraft losses.

"You have to do what you think is right," she said again. Then she went into the bedroom and cried.

For weeks she prayed that he'd be found physically unfit for flying, but those prayers were not answered. Eventually, she found the bedrock on which Teresa Ann Velmer Zachery stood. God would not give them anything they couldn't handle. So, in the end, many times, you just had to trust in God and go forward.

Fourteen months and a second baby later, they were in Pensacola. Jon had completed kindergarten, and now they awaited List Almighty.

The list would tell them where they'd go for the next phase of Jon's training. Jon wanted jets. Helicopters or propeller planes would not do. It had to be jets. And jet training was in Meridian, Mississippi.

Wherever they were ordered, the move would happen fast. The navy organized the flight-training program as if all the students were bachelors with little or no household goods to move. If one was married, had two small children, and lived in a rented, partially furnished, three-bedroom house, as she and Jon did, the navy expected that person to be just as mobile as a guy who lived in Bachelor Officer Quarters with all his belongings in one seabag. The next couple of weeks were going to be interesting.

Jets were more dangerous to fly than helos or props. Flying onto and off the carriers at night posed the greatest risk—or challenge, as the pilots called it.

Part of her wanted to say a prayer that Jon got jets and Meridian. Part of her wanted to pray for anything but jets. Another part wanted to pray that he'd wash out of flight training.

A tear ran down her right cheek and hung on her chin.

In you, oh Lord, I place my trust. Please bless Jon with Meridian, but Thy will be done.

When he'd first told her about wanting to apply for aviation, he'd made her angry. But, now that jets were close, the fear of losing him left no room in her head or heart for anger.

And teeth, Lord. Permanent ones, please.

She didn't know whether to laugh or cry, and she did some of both. Then seven-week-old Edgar Jon sounded off, and there was no time for laughing or crying.

She looked at the framed eight-by-ten needlepoint hanging on the wall behind the table. Her best friend, Rose, had made it for her.

Toughest Job in the Navy:

Navy Wife.

The period after "wife" was oversized. Only Rose would say, "Go ahead, knock the chip off my shoulder," in needlepoint.

Teresa went to do her duty.